Rad[iation]

A Colt Kelley Thriller

by

James D. Kellogg

Radical Action
James D. Kellogg

Radical Action is a revision of
E-Force by James D. Kellogg

For more information, visit
www.jamesdkellogg.com

Published and printed in
The United States of America

future looked bleak.

"I'll find another way to eliminate Harris." Marchotti leveled a finger at Zharikov. "You're going to punish every fool that failed me."

Zharikov felt the walls closing in around him. "Maybe a change in tactics is warranted. We could--"

"Shut up!" All color drained from Marchotti's face when the tape from the EcoFriends office started playing.

"You remember Deb Olson's accident, don't you, Howard?" Price's words were clear. "She decided to be a whistle-blower."

"You scum killed Deb!" Howard Anderson's retort emanated from the recording. "Marchotti ordered you and Cain to murder her!"

"Murder is the wrong term. It was preventive maintenance. Only a fool would expect Mr. Marchotti had no insurance policy to protect his investments. Mr. Cain specializes in risk reduction."

Like Marchotti, Yuri Zharikov was transfixed on the television. His boss was doomed. That meant he was lost too.

"You've come here to kill me," the voice of Anderson echoed. "It's part of Marchotti's insurance plan, isn't it?"

"You've left us with no other option, Howard," Price replied. "You've been a privileged member of Mr. Marchotti's organization. When you betrayed his trust, you sealed your fate."

Shouts and the clamor of a scuffle emanated from the sound system. Reverberating gun blasts were followed by a distinct heavy thud. The murder of Howard Anderson had been presented to the world. In a profound twist of irony, the media empire of Darius Marchotti had been used to condemn him.

"What the hell happened?" Marchotti staggered backward. For an instant, Zharikov thought he would collapse. "Get the chopper started. I'm getting out of the country now."

Like a high-stakes gambler, Zharikov cast his lot. Instead of complying with the directive, the big bodyguard stepped between Marchotti and the door. The move effectively blocked the media mogul's path of escape.

"What are you doing? I gave you an order, damn it."

"And I choose to ignore it." Zharikov lunged sideways to counter Marchotti's effort to dart past.

"Do what I say, you bastard!" The tyrant's raving obscenities were cut short when the behemoth seized him.

* * * *

When Colt's recording finished playing, every cop's firearm was trained on Price.

"Drop your weapon and let her go," the sergeant commanded.

Instead of complying, Price twisted Carrie's arm behind her. His gun pressed against the back of the young woman's head. It hurt, but she remained silent.

"Let her go, Price," Colt said. "You can't help yourself by doing this."

"Stay out of my way. I'll kill her!"

The sergeant called out. "There's no way out. Let's end this without more bloodshed."

"Colt, stay back." Carrie pleaded when he bounded onto the stage. All her anger was gone. She felt an overwhelming desire to be in his arms.

Price rasped in Carrie's ear. "I'll take you all to hell with me. I'll start with you, bitch."

The muzzle of the Glock 23 pressed against her skull. The fear was paralyzing. *God, how could you let it come to this?* Her eyes swept across those surrounding her. Every cop's face was hardened by grim determination. Agonized terror contorted the face of her father.

Carrie's gaze locked with Colt. "I love you," she said in

a cracking voice. "Never forget that."

"I would die for you." Colt dropped to his knees.

"Wish granted." Price struck with the deadly quickness of a mantis. Colt barely flinched when the murderous cop turned his gun and squeezed the trigger. The semi-automatic weapon boomed a bar of staccato death. Three .40 caliber bullets slammed into the young man's chest in rapid succession. Colt's eyes rolled back and he toppled over.

"No!" Carrie screamed, tearing away from her captor. "Colt!"

The instant after Carrie bolted, the police opened fire on Price. He jerked as the bullets slashed into his body. When the barrage ended, Price slumped to the floor, dead as a stone. It was finally over.

People came running from all directions, while Chris Morgan rolled tape. Respectfully, he lowered his camera and watched as Carrie rushed to Colt's crumpled and motionless form. She knelt next to Colt and sobbed with grief. Harris stood behind his daughter and tenderly placed his hand on her shoulder.

Chapter Twenty
Thursday, November 3

The morning program was a blend of news, politics, and pop culture. It was the trend-setting show of the genre, largely because of the hosts. Kayla Jones was beautiful with smarts and a charming southern accent. Brian Rivers was endowed with intelligence and a sharp wit. The pair consistently landed the most intriguing guests. On this morning, Senator John Harris was patched into the New York studio via satellite link from Denver.

"Congratulations on your reelection to the Senate on Tuesday," Kayla said.

Harris smiled. "Thank you. It was a long tough campaign."

"And a resounding victory," Rivers said.

"In June, you were trailing in the polls." Kayla voiced her recollection. "That was before the assassination attempt. Do you think Darius Marchotti's effort to destroy you strengthened you from a political standpoint?"

The Senator's smile disappeared. "What happened at the Developers' Forum was a terrible tragedy. Honestly, I would secede from the Senate if it would bring back the innocent people who lost their lives that day."

"But it certainly seems that awful day led to a political shift in Colorado," Rivers said.

"I think Darius Marchotti simply revealed his true nature." Harris shook his head in mild disagreement. "When people learned about his dealings, they were shocked and revolted. It was clear that Marchotti was using leftwing social and political agendas to further his ambitions of power. Independent voters in Colorado cast their votes against the candidates who espoused to the philosophies Marchotti exploited. I was the beneficiary. Sometimes a person is best-defined by his adversaries."

"You don't believe voters made a statement of support for you?" Kayla was surprised.

Harris shrugged. "I think people just saw something that scared them and did what they could to stop it."

"You're very modest, Senator Harris," Kayla replied. "Do you still plan to push for a more strict interpretation of the United States Constitution in your upcoming term?"

Harris nodded, and the smile returned like the sun emerging from behind a cloud. "The rights of American citizens shouldn't be trumped by self-serving politicians. The campaign reform bill was a prime example of unconstitutional laws that infringe on the right to free speech. Our political system isn't perfect, but we have to work within the framework of the Constitution. More government isn't the answer."

Rivers appeared thoughtful. "I've heard you talk about the role of the courts. You're a stickler when it comes to federal separation of powers."

"It doesn't matter what happens in Congress if judges legislate from the bench. Politicians need to stand up against activist judges. It's imperative that we educate ourselves and our kids about our history and political system. Revisionist agendas will jeopardize the future of the country."

"I understand you're just as resolute about fighting eco-terrorism." Kayla probed for a hint.

"Darius Marchotti established a world-wide network of subversive terrorist cells before his demise." Harris furrowed his brow with concern. "Rooting them out is critical to ensure the future of America."

Rivers raised an eyebrow. "There's a rumor that you're working with Phillip Barrett to disrupt eco-terrorist networks."

"Let's just say that Phillip Barrett and I have some common interests." Harris flashed a sly grin. "For now, I'm concentrating on my job as a Senator for the great State of Colorado."

* * * *

John F. Kennedy airport was teeming with travelers. Luke Parson sat in a crowded waiting area, anxious to board a plane to Denver. His spirits were buoyed by anticipation of a rendezvous with Sarah Farmington. After dating her for a few months, Luke was infatuated and itching to see his sweetheart.

"Everything is wrapped up here in New York," Luke told Phillip Barrett over a cell phone connection. "I'll be at the meeting tomorrow afternoon."

"I'm glad you've decided to join the team. Your investigative reporting skills are an important asset."

At last, he was allowed to perform as a real journalist. "It's a chance to help rid the world of Marchotti's network," he said with an appreciative smile.

"We'll start the campaign at the AmeResort offices tomorrow," Barrett promised.

After the phone conversation, Luke turned his attention to the United Media Network's 24-hour news channel on the T.V. mounted near his seat. The UMN was in a tailspin. It seemed counter-productive for the network to document the trial of its founder. It was all in the pursuit of ratings.

From the television coverage, Luke could see the crowd gathered before the federal courthouse in New York. The verdict against Marchotti had just been announced. *Guilty as sin.* Luke nodded with satisfaction. During the trial, he was an important witness for the prosecution. His testimony about murders, assumed identities, and clandestine organizations were well publicized. The personnel file of Jonathan Forde provided irrefutable evidence against the media despot.

Of course, some harbored profound hatred for Luke as they witnessed the crumbling demise of conglomerates within the United Media Network. *Issue Insight Magazine* was among the bankrupt subsidiaries. But many people considered Luke a hero of sorts. Since the start of the trial, he had received dozens of propositions and offers of employment. The opportunity to join Phillip Barrett's newly-created organization stood out above the rest.

The television commentators chattered when Yuri Zharikov emerged from the courthouse. A contingent of cops maintained a corridor on the broad steps in front of the building. Marchotti's enforcer was wearing a bulletproof vest and surrounded by federal agents. Luke watched with disgust as Zharikov was escorted down to the street.

Luke grumbled. "I can't believe the feds might let a sadist ex-KGB agent walk free."

Disgusted, Luke turned and meandered toward the gate. His thoughts shifted to Sarah, and his ire dissipated like perfume in a summer breeze.

* * * *

A raucous throng pressed against the barricades as Zharikov was escorted toward a pair of black Chevy Suburbans at the curb. Reporters jockeyed for position in the volatile crowd. Passing through a gauntlet of insults and obscenities, the eyes of the former-KGB operative bored straight ahead. Regardless of the outrage, it was inarguable that Zharikov had been the master key to unlock many of Marchotti's dark secrets. And thus federal investigators had been willing to strike a deal.

During the trial, Zharikov revealed the sinister truths behind the E-Force conspiracy. It had begun with Jonathan Forde, embroiled in a hopeless predicament and willing to sell his soul for a reprieve. By Marchotti's directive, an unfortunate loner from California was eliminated. Forde was reincarnated as Howard Anderson. With the help of Common Cause for Humanity, the assets of his former self were funneled to Anderson along with the funding to found

EcoFriends. The organization became the source of capital for forging E-Force. Only at the end did Anderson realize that he and E-Force were nothing more than patsies.

The E-Force campaign of terror against AmeResort Corporation was a ploy to manipulate Phillip Barrett. Marchotti had gambled that if Barrett was backed against a wall, he could be coerced into seeking assistance from Senator Harris. Using Stephen Chandler, the Developers' Forum was conjured as a stage to choreograph the death of the politician who obstructed Marchotti's plans in America. The one underlying purpose of the entire complex E-Force conspiracy was shockingly simple...the assassination of John Harris.

To further Marchotti's diabolical pursuit of power, E-Force had depended on widespread notoriety, but also an enhanced image. Though she had been ignorant of the plot to kill Harris, the blind ambition of Marla Wells was harnessed to guide media coverage. While Marla worked to portray E-Force as a band of righteous vigilantes, Special Agent Price kept the reigns pulled back on investigators, ensuring they didn't move too quickly.

As the plan hurtled toward its terrible climax, anyone who posed a potential threat was eliminated with cold brutality. It was not until Colt Kelley recorded the murder of Anderson that a real crisis ensued for the conspiracy. When the tape was coupled with the incriminating evidence discovered by Luke, everything began to unravel. Resolute in his madness, Marchotti had been unwilling to relent.

In the end, it was mostly fate that thwarted the assassination of Senator Harris. But in a stinging stroke of injustice, Cain and Ruddock had both managed to escape. The blood on the mechanical room floor was the only testament to the bullet wound that Cain had survived. Ruddock had simply vanished. The heart of E-Force still lived and nobody knew what impact that would have in the future.

On the verge of a riot, the crowd threatened to overwhelm the police as Zharikov and his escorts neared the curb. Officers shoved back those who tried to breach the barricades. Zharikov was stuffed into one of the Suburbans. Both vehicles, packed with federal agents, sped off when the doors shut. The howling demonstrators were left behind.

* * * *

Gray clouds had descended upon Denver, choking out the last remnants of blue sky over the metro area. Gazing out the windows of his downtown office, Phillip Barrett watched the first snowflakes drift lazily toward the streets far below. For the first time in years, the expectation of a big snow elicited his excitement for purely personal reasons. He reflected on his days as a teenager with skis readied. Once again, Barrett felt invigorated and ready to take on the world and all the challenges it presented. A deep sense of satisfaction prevailed as he thought about Marchotti being led out of the federal courthouse in handcuffs.

"He's the worst kind of evil." Barrett shook his head with disgust. "Marchotti nearly destroyed everything I built over the course of a lifetime."

It was a metaphorical kick in the groin to discover that it was all just to draw Harris into Marchotti's crosshairs. *I thought I was too savvy to be conned by somebody like Stephen Chandler. He used me as a pawn.* Bitter chagrin steeled his resolve to prevent such errors in the future.

With Chandler in federal custody and awaiting his own day in court, Barrett initiated a campaign to root out other moles in his organization. Nobody at any level would escape scrutiny. It was an absolute necessity to confirm that everybody in AmeResort had the best interests of the corporation in mind. Breaches such as the compromised security staff at the Gateway to the Rockies Conference Center were inexcusable.

Barrett was embarrassed by how little he had understood about the conspiracy. Though Travis Price's behavior had warranted suspicion and concern, Barrett had not suspected that Price was part of the scheme. That hadn't stopped him from retaining Gordon Trovato and Joey Morris as a counter-measure. The two specialists had been retained by Barrett to hunt down Colt Kelley, extract first-hand information about E-Force, and turn him over to the authorities. The ploy had turned into a tragic mess.

But over the past few months, resurgence in tourism at AmeResort properties had boosted stock values and spurred hope for the future. That was important, given the threat that had materialized against one of AmeResort's international ventures. The first test of Barrett's new organization was at hand.

* * * *

"What a morning." Chris Morgan strode out of an elevator. The day was already a blur of hectic studio taping sessions. No longer spending time behind a television camera, Chris was the producer of an investigative reporting series. It was a challenging undertaking.

Forced into duty at the Developers' Forum, his footage on that fateful day had captivated the nation. Barrett learned that Chris Morgan had convinced police to deploy forces to the conference center, an important contribution to saving the life of John Harris. In gratitude, Barrett gave Chris the chance to produce his new television venture. It was an opportunity he couldn't refuse, especially since the show was based in Denver. He could go home to his family at the end of almost every day.

Morgan entered his office and settled behind his desk. The blinking light on the telephone signaled new voice mail messages. *Probably from people who need me to make decisions.* He still found it a little daunting to be the boss.

For a moment, Chris reflected on the changes of the past few months. Marla's career was in the toilet. Her credibility was gone, and she had been indicted for conspiring with E-Force. She was ratting out anyone she could in hopes of saving her own skin. UMN's Vice President of News, Ted Rogers, was the biggest name to fall so far. For Marla's sake, Morgan hoped the feds were providing her with some serious protection. She was going to need it if she kept fingering people.

The greatest disgrace fell on Drew Harmon. Everyone had witnessed the actor's cowardly narcissistic flight. When Luke punched his lights out, Harmon was overrun by the stampeding masses. The physical injuries he suffered paled in comparison to the irreparable damage to his public image. His Hollywood heyday was over.

A phone call snatched Morgan from the reverie. "How's work on the show's newest installment?" Phillip Barrett asked.

"We're making great strides," Morgan said. "The ratings climb every week."

"You and your staff are doing a good job. I knew you could make this thing a success."

"Thank you, Mr. Barrett. I appreciate your trust."

"A tenuous situation has developed south of the border," Barrett said after a short pause. "I've scheduled a briefing for tomorrow."

Morgan felt his breathing quicken. "I'm ready."

Barrett provided a few details about the meeting. After the call, Chris Morgan tingled with excitement. *Time to get down to business.*

* * * *

Snowflakes drifted softly to the ground while Carrie sat on a boulder next to Snowmass Lake. The crests of Snowmass Peak, Hagerman Peak, and Snowmass Mountain were veiled by a curtain of airborne snow. She savored the last few minutes of her visit to the special place where Colt had first brought her. That time seemed so long ago. Her life had been so deeply impacted by Colt and all that had happened back then. It was painful, but Carrie chose to keep the memories clear. She believed recollection of one's past was the best compass to plot a course for the future.

It's time to get moving. The snow was starting to intensify and accumulate in earnest. Carrie was properly dressed and equipped, but it was an eight-mile hike down to the trailhead. From there, it would take an hour to drive back to Glenwood Springs. With a heavy heart, Carrie stood and looked wistfully across the frigid lake that would soon be frozen over and covered with snow. Gazing at the stark beauty, she knew it was going to take time to fill the void in her life. It was harder than expected. She hoped the challenges of her new career would help.

The wind was absent at the lake elevation. It was so quiet that Carrie could hear the snowflakes landing on the rocks. She turned up the collar of her parka and pulled the zipper as high as it would go. Carrie barely started her descent when she heard a sound that was totally out of place.

A ring tone? She frowned. An instant later, Colt Kelley stepped from the spruce grove. Carrie shook her head with amazement.

"I hear you loud and clear," Colt declared.

Carrie approached the strapping young man as he stood listening to the caller speak. When he flashed a smile, she noticed the charming sparkle in his eye. It was one of the little things she loved about Colt.

"We'll be there." Colt snapped the phone closed. "These satellite phones are amazing."

"Yeah, there's no place left to hide," Carrie said wryly. "Was that Phillip Barrett?"

"You guessed it, Ms. Forde." Colt gave her a seductive smile.

Dedicated to Lauren Ryan Pascucci, an angel called back to
God after an eye-blink on this Earth.

Thank you to Nancy Crenshaw for the insight and guidance
that helped transform a dream into reality.

Chapter One

Wednesday, April 18

Zed Cain leaned his tall frame into the wind-driven deluge, traversing the upper slopes of Copper Mountain Resort. The onslaught above the tree line threatened to tear his backpack away. Scraping the crust from his goggles, Cain checked his compass. Based on his reckoning, the objective was only a few hundred yards farther.

The hood of Cain's parka buffeted his sharp cheekbones while he strained to see through the ice-laden darkness. In the tempest, every detail of the rugged terrain was erased. A disoriented trekker was no match for the deadly assault of exhaustion, dehydration, and hypothermia. But Cain had no intention of seeking solace from the savage storm. His navigation skills were superb and the topography of the mountain was hammered into his brain.

A relentless machine, Cain pressed toward the saddle between Copper Peak and Union Peak. Textured like the belly of a mythical mountain dragon, the skins attached to the bottom of his telemark skis enabled his ascent.

At last, Cain confronted the dark shape of a building. Releasing the bindings gripping his boots, he turned away from the structure and stripped off his goggles. His eyes bored into the horizontal waves of white particles. The other team members had fallen behind on the trek up the mountain. Cain figured they had fifteen minutes before the arctic fury obliterated his tracks.

* * * *

Chuck Schroeder studied the van from the warmth of his Explorer. The towering vehicle was equipped with four-wheel-drive and large off-road tires. It was parked in a space reserved for one of countless condominium residences at the

1

Copper Mountain base area.

A member of the resort security staff, Schroeder's duties included enforcing parking regulations. Many people who owned or leased the units tended to get unduly upset when their parking spaces were taken. Schroeder noted the Colorado license plate on the rear of the van before leaving the warmth of his vehicle to check for a parking pass. He shivered and hunched his shoulders as he stepped into the icy wind, wincing as a blast of snow whipped against his face.

Plodding to the window on the driver's side, he brushed away snow and pressed his face near the glass. A sudden movement inside made him jump back in surprise. A young woman sat behind the wheel. Embarrassed by his reaction, Schroeder pointed to the security emblem on his jacket and motioned for her to crank down the window.

"I didn't mean to startle you." Schroeder shouted over the wind.

"You didn't." She shivered at the icy invasion through the open window. "Is there a problem?"

Schroeder fibbed. "I wanted to make sure you were okay. It's awful cold out here tonight."

"I'm fine." The woman shrugged and avoided eye contact with the guard.

"Why are you sitting out here?" the security guard asked, bracing against the gale.

"I'm waiting for a friend. She rented a condo."

Schroeder was skeptical, noting that no parking pass hung from the rearview mirror. "Which unit?"

"It's in that building." She pointed to the nearest gargantuan condominium complex. "I don't know which unit."

Schroeder glanced at the impressive structure. "Your friend must have some money."

"She goes all-out." The woman fidgeted with the steering wheel.

2

"What's your name, miss?"

"Delilah." The response was terse.

Something didn't feel right. "How do you know she's not up there, Delilah?" Schroeder leaned closer to the van.

Delilah countered without missing a beat. "Everybody's got a cell phone."

Schroeder relaxed, hearing the reasonable explanation. He noticed Delilah's beautiful green eyes. They embodied the sensuality of a woman, but a sprinkle of freckles across her nose suggested girlish innocence. Schroeder snapped out of his brief enchantment. *You're old enough to be her grandfather.*

"This parking space is reserved," Schroeder explained with a softened tone. "You need to park in one of the guest spaces over there."

Delilah looked to where the guard indicated. "No problem."

"Have a pleasant evening." Schroeder retreated to his idling vehicle after a curt nod. As he drove away, his mirror revealed the van backing out of the parking space.

* * * *

A tall slender apparition appeared in front of Trigger Ruddock. It was one of the towers supporting the Rendezvous ski lift. The tracks he followed veered sharply up the mountain, on a course parallel to the massive suspended cable. Ruddock lowered his head and thrust his skis through the drifting snow.

Though Ruddock was wiry and well-conditioned, his breathing was heavy while he labored under the load strapped to his back. Cain's trail was fading fast. Every second was critical: the difference between success and failure.

When he crested the top of the slope, Powderbowl Station was masked by a veil of driving snow. For a moment, Ruddock leaned on his ski poles, breathing deeply to lower his heart rate. When he looked up, Cain was standing a yard away. *The man appears out of thin air.*

Cain asked over the ice-filled wind. "Where's Landin?"

"I don't know," Ruddock yelled back. "I thought he was right behind me."

Five minutes later, Billy Landin arrived, gasping for breath. His scruffy blonde goatee was coated with ice. His back was bent under the weight of his backpack.

Ruddock was impatient. "Where've you been? We're behind schedule!"

"My skins were icing up," Landin said.

"It's too cold for that."

Cain reprimanded the pair. "Cut the chatter. Let's move."

The three men advanced on Powderbowl Station. It was a large building with overhanging eaves, covered porches, and stone chimneys protruding from steep rooflines. Inside, there were several cavernous rooms supported by huge log posts and beams. The architecture and furnishings were that of an alpine ski lodge, tempered by the rugged American West. Large expanses of windows provided breathtaking views of snow-capped peaks. On any given winter day, the restaurant and bar in Powderbowl Station teemed with skiers while fires crackled in the stone hearths.

AmeResort Corporation, the owner of Copper Mountain, had plans to capitalize on the success of the facility. Construction of a gondola stretching from the base village to Powderbowl Station would allow year-round operation, transporting patrons to first class dining and entertainment in a magnificent setting. Local environmentalists were deadest against the plan to expand development.

The team members thrust the tail ends of their skis into the snow. Cain approached the main entrance, while Ruddock and Landin trudged along opposite sides of the building.

Radical Action

When Ruddock arrived at a small alcove with a service entrance, he found Landin shrugging off his backpack. The young man's hands were trembling.

"Get us inside," Ruddock said.

"Just give me a little space." Landin donned a small headlamp.

To improve dexterity, the computer guru stripped his heavy gloves from the thin nylon liners. In a race against the onset of numbing cold in his fingers, Landin used a screwdriver to remove the cover-plate from a keypad next to the door. The keypad was the interface to a security system that would be triggered if a door or window were breached. There were no motion detectors or surveillance cameras.

Ruddock turned and assessed the forbidding weather. The snow was ebbing; a circumstance that would facilitate the team's descent from the mountain, but also lift the cloak of invisibility. It was the tail end of the ski season, but the condominiums and hotel rooms in the base village were packed with potential witnesses.

Landin finished hot-wiring a laptop computer to the alarm system. After double-checking the connections, the shaggy-looking kid initiated the code-breaking sequence of a computer program he had developed. It didn't take long for the indicator light on the keypad to change from red to green.

The technical wizard's face lit with excitement. "The alarm's down!"

Without uttering a word, Ruddock pushed past Landin. He used an ice axe to smash the narrow window next to the service door. Careful not to gouge his arm, Ruddock reached through the jagged opening and unlocked the door.

Ruddock sneered at Landin and winked. "Don't keep us waiting, sport." He slipped into the dark building with night vision goggles on his head.

Like a ghost, Ruddock glided through a reconnaissance of the rear part of the building. The night vision equipment revealed features bathed in an eerie green light.

At the meeting place, Ruddock found Landin waiting and shivering. The scrawny programmer looked ready to collapse under the weight of the gear stowed in his pack.

"What's wrong?" Ruddock asked in derision. "Adrenaline rush wearing off?"

"Give me a break. I did my job."

A faint noise caused Landin to turn. The bulky equipment on his eyes made the move awkward. Landin jolted when he discovered Cain at his side.

"Crap, you scared me!" Landin said to the team leader.

Cain ignored Landin's comment. "The front of the building's clear," the team leader said to Ruddock.

"So is the rear," the wiry explosives expert replied. "It's a go."

"Let's get the devices set." Cain started toward the first location.

"It's freezing in here. How about starting the fire now?" Landin was clearly searching for some semblance of bravado.

Ruddock turned on the kid with annoyance. "Shut up, Landin. This isn't some game."

"Cut the bullshit." Cain's warning quieted his subordinates.

Landin and Ruddock followed Cain in silence. Arriving at a log post in a corner of the building, Ruddock removed his backpack and knelt down to extract a three-gallon gasoline container. Cain moved off into the darkness.

Ruddock shoved the container at Landin. "Put this next to the wood post and take the cap off."

"You don't want me to pour the gas out?"

"Hell no! Don't splash it around. We want to set the building on fire, not just burn the damned finish off the floor."

Landin looked confused. "Seems like spreading the gasoline around would make the whole place go up pretty quick."

"It's accelerant; equal parts gasoline and diesel fuel." Ruddock bent down and replaced the cap on the container with a homemade igniter unit. Two wires dangled from the assembly.

"Why the cocktail?"

"Diesel slows the burn rate." Ruddock couldn't resist talking about his passion. "We only hauled a little bit of accelerant up this frozen rock. I've got to increase the odds of success. The best way to do that is focus intense, prolonged heat on one spot. At the right locations, that'll set the building structure on fire."

"How does it ignite?"

"It just needs a little spark." Ruddock positioned a small Tupperware container on the floor next to the accelerant. It held a digital timer fitted with two firing wires. Bullet connectors made it easy to complete the wiring circuit between the timer and the igniter on the accelerant. Ruddock removed the Tupperware lid as if it were a trip wire on a booby trap. A gentle flip of a switch initiated the countdown sequence.

"Tick-tock." Ruddock stood up and turned his back on Landin.

When the timer reached zero, an electrical current to the igniter would generate a small flame, which in turn would initiate combustion of the accelerant mixture.

"It's all set," Ruddock said when Cain reappeared.

Cain eyed the timer. "Get to the next location."

During the course of several minutes, similar incendiary devices were prepared at two more positions in the building. The goal was to initiate combustion of key structural members. Ideally, the flames would climb from the posts to beams that supported the roof. Ultimately the fire would climb up the rafters to the apex of the roof, transforming the entire building into a blazing inferno.

After Ruddock finished the last device, he trudged

outside. Blinding waves of crystalline ice pummeled the mountainside. He pulled off the night vision goggles and felt the sting against his exposed face. Cain and Landin were locked into their skis. Ruddock signaled that preparations were complete. Cain shoved forward on his poles and dropped over the edge of slope. Landin followed the leader while Ruddock fastened his bindings.

The team members used the shadows of the ski lift towers as a navigation aid. With quick kneeling telemark turns, they negotiated a minefield of moguls. It was a daunting undertaking.

Visibility was better on the lower flank of the mountain where trees held the wind at bay. A long descent to the base of the mountain still lay ahead. It was worth a short pause to switch from goggles to night vision gear. While Ruddock and Landin adjusted their equipment, Cain pulled a cell phone from his pocket.

* * * *

A piercing electronic tone jolted Delilah. *It's the first signal.* She fumbled for phone and read the text message. "ETA 10 minutes."

Delilah shivered and adjusted the heater to the maximum setting. Lukewarm air belched from the defrost vents. Her foot tapped with nervous impatience. Bright lights from the convenience store suddenly seemed like searchlights as she waited on the edge of the parking lot.

Nearly ten minutes passed. The second text tone had the effect of a bucket of ice water. Delilah sucked in a breath of air and squeezed her hands on the steering wheel. She switched on the headlights and pressed her foot on the accelerator. Snow crunched under the tires as she rumbled toward State Highway 91.

The van rounded a huge pile of dirty snow, accumulated from a winter of plowing. Delilah slammed on the brakes. In front of her, a vehicle bumped into the lot from the highway. It was the security guard. The man's eyes met hers. Recognition registered in his gaze before his Explorer moved past.

"Son-of-a-bitch." Delilah didn't hesitate. She turned out onto the road and headed south. A sigh of relief escaped her lips when the mirrors revealed only darkness behind her. The rent-a-cop wasn't following.

After traveling about a mile on Highway 91, Delilah made a tight U-turn and slowed to a crawl.

A dark shape darted from the trees to the west. Two shadows chased after the first. An instant after the van stopped, the side door was yanked open. With a clatter of skis and poles, Ruddock and Landin clambered inside. Cain entered last, pulling the door closed.

"Move out." Cain pushed the hood of his parka back. Long black hair spilled onto his shoulders.

Goose bumps rose on Delilah's skin when Cain dialed a number on a pre-paid cell phone.

* * * *

Sleep was a casualty of Marla Wells' career ambitions. It was routine for her to work well past midnight and rise before six o'clock. Every so often, exhaustion overcame mind and body. Sometimes the deep slumber ushered in panicked dreams, like the terrible feeling of sitting in a crowded conference hall and hearing herself introduced for an important presentation that had slipped her mind.

Panting with fear, Marla bolted upright in bed in response to the ringing telephone. Feeling an uncharacteristic frantic urge to answer the incoming call, Marla lunged for the nightstand.

"Hello," Marla gasped.

"Are you Marla Wells?" an unfamiliar masculine voice asked.

"Yes," Marla said, extricating herself from a tangle of bedcovers.

"You need to listen carefully."

"Who are you?" Marla glanced at the clock near her bed. "Do you know what time it is? If this is some kind of prank." The caller ignored her outburst. "E-Force has chosen you to broadcast our statements to the nation."

Marla's anger mounted. "What's E-Force? What are you talking about?"

The voice continued. "Corporate developers are destroying this planet in their pursuit of obscene profits. These criminals are enabled by corrupt politicians and special interest groups. The earth is headed for a cataclysmic disaster. Radical action is the only remedy."

"I've heard all this before." Marla resented the intrusion of a tree-hugging nut.

"E-Force is launching a campaign of economic damage at Copper Mountain." The caller did not relent. "Tonight, we're punishing AmeResort Corporation, the most repugnant violator of our sacred planet."

"You're eco-terrorists?" Marla asked, her eyes narrowing.

"Terror is a matter of perspective. Educate the public about those who commit atrocities against the Earth. We'll be watching you, Ms. Wells. Your actions will determine whether we contact you again."

There was a click, followed by silence. Marla lowered the phone. *Could it truly be a warning from extremists?*

How the hell did that jerk get my cell phone number? A chill trickled down Marla's spine.

Marla's fingers trembled as she started to call the police. At the last instant, she hesitated, reflecting on the caller's assertions. If E-Force was real, something was about to happen at Copper Mountain.

Why pass up an opportunity? Marla rubbed her hands together. When her feet touched the floor, a burst of energy and vigor vanquished the last traces of fatigue.

* * * *

Caffeine tempered boredom for Chuck Schroeder. A mug of steaming coffee in hand, he ambled toward the front door of the convenience store. Movement outside on the highway caught his eye. The big Ford van sped by, heading north toward the interstate. *Where's she going now?*

"Did you notice that 4-wheel drive van outside earlier?" Schroeder turned back toward the clerk.

When the clerk glanced outside, the vehicle was out of sight. "I don't know. There was some kind of van parked out there earlier. I didn't pay much attention."

"I had an encounter with that vehicle earlier. There was a beautiful green-eyed girl inside."

The clerk chuckled. "You sound excited. I figured you'd given up on wild women."

"I guess you're never too old to fantasize." Schroeder laughed on his way out.

Schroeder sipped his coffee while driving back to the base area. Looking above the mountains to the south, he noticed a few stars. The cloud cover was breaking up, but arctic gusts still buffeted his vehicle. Cold-induced aching in his joints made Schroeder long for the warmth of a Florida retirement.

At that instant, a thunderous boom emanated from the direction of the ski slopes. In shock, Schroeder watched a red-orange glow erupt behind a ridge, high on the mountain.

"What the hell!" Schroeder slammed on the brakes and stared dumbfounded. "That's Powderbowl Station. It just blew up!"

Chapter Two
Thursday, April 19

Happy hour was just starting at the Alpenglow Brew Pub, just west of Aspen. With his muscular arms folded across his chest, Colt Kelley sat at a table with a good view of one of the establishment's televisions. The place would soon be full of thirsty patrons looking to unwind from a long day. That meant the news would be drowned out by a growing din at the bar. Before that happened, Colt wanted to learn more about the arson at Copper Mountain Resort.

"I guarantee it was a bunch of idiot eco-radicals," Colt muttered. *Every time we take a step forward, they drag us backward.*

As an employee of an environmental and conservationist organization called EcoFriends, Colt loathed such activism. From what he had seen, "Save the Earth" was a rallying cry for fringe groups with all types of unsavory agendas. Such bastardization was a detriment to the real conservationists.

Headquartered in Boulder, EcoFriends was a well-established entity in the western United States. Their mission was to use education to balance human progress with preservation of nature. It wasn't an easy task for an organization funded entirely by private donations. Colt was in charge of the Western Colorado chapter, which was based in Aspen. Perpetually short of staff and money, Colt wore many hats during the course of any given workday. While he was innovative and enjoyed filling a variety of roles, it was exhausting.

A server placed a frosty mug of beer in front of Colt. "You look like you could use this."

"Thanks. Maybe you can start an IV."

The server laughed. "I hate needles. But there's more where that came from."

Struck by the dancing brown eyes and charming smile,

Colt considered asking the waitress out to dinner. Instead, he watched her waltz away.

Colt lamented his ineptitude at the dating game. *Idiot, she probably has customers hitting on her all the time.*

It had been less than a year since Colt and his fiancée cancelled their wedding plans. "I don't want to be tied down by someone who's structured and regimented," the bride-to-be declared when the date grew near. "I need fun and spontaneity. You're too responsible."

Feeling worthless and depressed, Colt wanted to turn the page and move on with his life. Something in his life had to change. His interest in a consuming job was waning. Each day was wandering with no purpose. *The world is passing me by.* Colt scratched his head of thick blonde hair and sipped his beer.

"Now, let's go to Marla Wells, who's on the scene at Copper Mountain." The news anchor's statement swatted Colt's tumultuous thoughts away as if they were a pesky insect.

Marla's image appeared on the television screen. "The destruction of Powderbowl Station has grabbed the attention of everyone in Summit County. While investigators work to determine what happened, the entire resort is virtually shutting down."

"The queen bee is out in the snow," Colt murmured, surprised to see Marla filling the role of a reporter. For as long as he could remember, she had been a fixture in the climate-controlled studio. *What's gotten into her?*

Marla continued. "All day, we've observed an exodus of skiers and vacationers. Financial losses for AmeResort will total far more than the ruined lodge."

* * * *

The temperature plummeted with the onset of dusk. After the snowmobile ride down from Powderbowl Station,

Special Agent Travis Price was numb with cold. He hobbled into one of the base village buildings.

An African-American man stepped into the corridor. "You'll want to get a look at this, boss."

Price peeled off his stiff gloves and flexed his fingers. "I need to warm my freaking hands first."

"Marla Wells is broadcasting from outside."

"Alright, Hill. Let's see how she's going to spin this thing." Price followed Malcolm Hill into a room with a television. Several chairs were available, but he remained standing with his coat zipped.

"Turn the volume up." Price blew on his hands and rubbed his palms together.

Price was the Special Agent in Charge of the FBI field office in Denver. Ambition and hard work had factored into his ascendance to the position. More important, he knew how to make influential people notice him for the right reasons.

Earlier in the afternoon, Price and Hill had arrived in Summit County. Because the destruction of Powderbowl Station was deemed a possible act of domestic terrorism, the case was within the jurisdiction of the FBI. The crime involved a situation of concurrent jurisdiction, where a violation of local, state, and federal law had occurred at the same time. That meant an investigative task force of personnel from the FBI and other law enforcement agencies would be formed. Price was positioned as the task force leader.

"Think she'll try to manipulate the storyline?" Hill looked like he had taken a bite out of a bad apple.

"She'll turn this thing into a circus." Price muttered his response, thinking about counter measures to cover his rear.

* * * *

At the base of the mountain, Marla Wells was dressed in

a heavy coat with a scarf and gloves. She abhorred hats and hoods. They looked ridiculous on camera. Suffering in the bitter chill was preferable to looking foolish in front of the viewers. Her television image was everything. Artfully applied makeup hid the little lines adjacent to her eyes. Masterful tailoring helped compensate for a figure that was no longer slim and youthful. It wasn't easy for a middle-aged woman to compete in television news.

Marla's tone was serious. "We got a look at the remains of Powderbowl Station before authorities cordoned off the area. Our camera captured some sobering images."

Video showed Powderbowl Station had been reduced to little more than a smoldering heap of ashes. A few chimneys and posts still stood, leaning at precarious angles. Blackened debris was scattered in all directions.

"The fire resulted in total destruction of the facility. Authorities don't know who is responsible for this destruction."

Because she was the producer and anchor of her channel's nightly newscast, Marla had few limitations. E-Force was an opportunity to resurrect her career.

"AmeResort Corporation acquired Copper Mountain Resort several years ago." Marla was authoritative, like the narrator of a National Geographic documentary. "Headed by founder and CEO, Phillip Barrett, AmeResort controls an empire of ski and beach resorts, casinos, and amusement parks. Environmental and conservation groups have been highly critical of the negative impacts these facilities have on local communities and the environment. They fought a long legal battle to try to stop the campaign of expansion and development at Copper Mountain. This incident may be a last-ditch tactic in a desperate struggle."

* * * *

Carrie Forde quickened her pace as the computer

15

program increased the speed of the treadmill. Her toned, muscular body moved with feline grace. She knew every male member of the Natural High Rock Gym and Fitness Club was drawn to her athletic build and striking face. And most of the women were envious of the attention she garnered. But Carrie wasn't interested in picking up a date or joining social circles.

Several televisions were mounted in front of the cardio-training machines. The images of the charred and smoking remains of Powderbowl Station had captured Carrie's attention.

"That was the best lunch spot," Carrie said to the man on the next machine. "I can't believe it's destroyed."

"It's a shame," the man gasped between breaths.

Carrie was offended by Marla's flippant treatment of a blatant criminal act. "Marla Wells clearly doesn't share our sentiments."

"You think some kind of eco-terrorists did it?" The man clung to the handrails on his treadmill.

"Probably, but it doesn't matter. Marla Wells wants people to believe AmeResort had it coming. It's not the first time the media has twisted morality to fit a script."

Carrie increased the speed of the treadmill. The physical demand tempered her ire.

* * * *

Drew Harmon surveyed the group at the table in the Alpenglow Brew Pub like a monarch. Less than two years had passed since the handsome young actor had gotten his big break. He relished basking in the fame and fortune that came with Hollywood stardom.

"We'll head over to the house after dinner," Harmon said to his agent, Sam Spencer. "I gave my chef the night off."

"I can't wait to see your new place," Spencer's wife,

Penny said.

"It's really big." Katarina, the gorgeous brunette next to Harmon, gushed.

Spencer nodded in approval. "What better way to elevate your status than a trophy home in Aspen?"

"How about starring in the next big Hollywood hit?" Harmon leaned back and polished of his drink. "Sam, you did a hell of a job securing my contract for that new Adamo film. That damned director is a pain in the ass."

"Sid Adamo is a legend," Spencer said. "His movies are always blockbusters."

Katarina voiced her enthusiastic prediction. "You're going to be a huge star!"

"I'm already there, baby." Harmon flashed his trademark grin and eyed his companion. Her IQ wasn't much larger than her bust size, but that wasn't important. When the thrills were over, he would move on.

The dazzling young woman snuggled up against the actor and caressed his shoulder. Harmon toyed with his empty glass. The alcohol had flowed since his jet lifted off the runway in Los Angeles.

"I need another drink."

"Our waitress must be around here somewhere." Penny craned her neck. "I'm hungry."

Impatient, Harmon noticed a different girl trotting away from the adjacent table. She had just delivered a plate of food to a stout young blond guy. His eyes followed her as she rounded the bar. The images of a destroyed building on the television caught his attention.

"Hey, honey!" Harmon called out to the server. "Turn the volume up on that TV!"

The young woman hesitated to comply with Harmon's demand.

Spencer squirmed in his seat as Harmon shouted again. "What's gotten into you, Drew?"

The bartender reluctantly turned the sound up. Harmon

motioned to the T.V. "Take a look at this. The winds of change are blowing."

* * * *

Standing in the snow, Chris Morgan kept his television camera focused on Marla Wells. The cold didn't bother him. Happy to be out of the studio, he reveled in the fresh air. Field time was rare since Marla had commandeered him as her personal cameraman.

Someday I'll be out from under your thumb, Morgan vowed. Marla Wells was selfish and egotistical; the first to blame others for problems and quick to accept the accolades of success.

"As I mentioned, investigators don't know who is responsible for the explosion. But I've obtained exclusive information." Marla sounded pompous.

There was a discernible gleam in Marla's eye. A sixth sense triggered an internal alarm in Morgan. His body tingled with trepidation.

"I was contacted by a group called E-Force." Marla's revelation was accompanied by a smug expression. "They are disgusted by the huge profits reaped by corporate developers. Such wealth sways politicians and regulators at every level of government. E-Force proclaims that radical action is the only means to save the planet for future generations."

Where are you going with this? Morgan's thoughts were steeped in suspicion. He didn't trust Marla in the slightest. Something was seriously wrong. *Why didn't you call the cops about this before bragging on the air?*

"E-Force claimed responsibility for the destruction of Powderbowl Station," Marla said with authority. "They decreed environmental vigilantism as the only means available to save the Earth from invincible offenders like AmeResort Corporation. E-Force made that point last night

18

at Copper Mountain."

* * * *

"Can you believe the audacity? She's taking up for some unheard of wackos that destroyed millions of dollars of private property?" Carrie said before Marla's image disappeared from the television screen.

"It is a little hard to feel sorry for AmeResort," the guy next to Carrie said, breathing heavily and wiping the sweat from his brow with a towel.

"That's what Marla Wells wants you to think." The computer program brought her treadmill to a halt.

After a deep breath, Carrie stepped down to the floor. She was disturbed. It seemed the beneficiaries of media bias usually escaped the consequences of their actions. Carrie hoped that wouldn't be the case for E-Force. Stalking toward the exit, she met an aerobics instructor with whom she was acquainted.

The woman stood a bit straighter when she saw Carrie. "How's the workout?"

"Best part of the day." Carrie paused and shook her head with lament. "Have you heard about Copper Mountain?"

"There was a bomb up there or something, right?" The other woman asked.

"That awesome lodge at the top is gone. Some eco-terrorist nuts called E-Force did it." Carrie didn't hide her disgust.

"I heard they wanted to get back at the ski resort for destroying the environment," the aerobics instructor argued. "Plus they screw everybody over with ridiculous prices for lift tickets."

"You been to Copper lately?" Carrie shook her head with disbelief. "It's not exactly a wasteland. And AmeResort has provided jobs and prosperity to a whole lot of people over the years."

The instructor's face tightened with a frown. "That doesn't mean they give a damn about preserving wilderness."

"I worked part-time for AmeResort when I was a teenager. Everybody I worked with loved wild places just like I do."

The aerobic teacher shrugged. "That doesn't mean the company cares. Now somebody's finally taking a stand."

Carrie was taken aback. "You don't think it's right to destroy property, do you?"

"Developers will keep the bulldozers running if nobody stops them," the fitness instructor replied.

"My CrossFit class is about to start." Carrie ended the debate. She turned and rolled her eyes as the other woman huffed away.

Carrie knew change was inevitable. Some called it progress. Others viewed it as a travesty. In truth, it was both...a package deal. In Colorado alone, there were vast areas that deserved preservation as God had created them. But such an approach couldn't be taken everywhere. People and society had to be able to advance. That was reality. You couldn't blame all the world's problems on corporations and capitalist economies.

Her long lean figure glistening with perspiration, Carrie strode into the CrossFit box and grabbed a Styrofoam roller.

* * * *

Drew Harmon fancied himself an environmental activist. He had agreed to promote an insignificant group called StayGreen when they solicited his aid. Their platform was based more on socialism than environmentalism, but that didn't really matter. StayGreen was engaged in a major campaign to gain prominence. Harmon anticipated that by serving as their celebrity spokesperson, he would have easy access to more publicity. It was a career advancement tool.

"This thing at the ski resort was inevitable," Harmon said to his companions at the table. "The corporate owners are greedy bastards!"

Penny Spencer broke in. "There's our server, Drew. We should order dinner."

Harmon spoke louder, ignoring the ploy to distract him. "Those sons-of-bitches get a foothold and start expanding. It's all in pursuit of the almighty dollar!"

"There's not much we can do about it right now." Sam Spencer glanced around at the surrounding patrons.

"The damned developers only care about the bottom line. Well, now E-Force is taking the fight to those criminals. It's about time somebody stood up for what's right!"

"Get off your soap box," somebody said from a nearby table.

"Can't we discuss this later?" Sam Spencer pleaded with his client.

Harmon quoted the script from his recent StayGreen commercial. "The damaging effects of corporate industry reach far beyond the natural environment. The engines of capitalist economies condemn the unempowered to poverty and servitude."

"Put a lid on it, pal!" Another patron voiced a sentiment that appeared to be spreading among the diners.

Spencer looked sick. "You're right. Developers shouldn't be allowed to continue irresponsible practices."

"The whole capitalist system is the problem!" Harmon raised his voice another decibel. "E-Force is fighting back the only way they can."

Despite his condemnation of the free-market system, Harmon had no qualms about pursuing personal fame and fortune. The actor considered the Hollywood movie industry, and its vast money and influence, exempt from criticism.

"Let's have dinner and leave the public education campaign to StayGreen," Penny Spencer said.

Harmon was outraged by her attempt at placation.

"There are too many corrupt politicians and special interest groups! The corporations have to be destroyed, the same way they kill off native cultures, forests, and animals."

"They're killing animals at ski areas?" Katarina stammered with obvious horror. It seemed part of the conversation finally made sense to her. "Why are they doing that?"

"That's what it's all about. They go in and bulldoze huge areas!"

In the midst of a dramatic sweep of his arm, Harmon knocked over his drink. Scrambling out of his chair to escape the cascade onto his lap, he tripped and stumbled backward. With alcohol-dulled reflexes, Harmon crashed into the blond man at the neighboring table.

Everyone in the restaurant gaped at the spectacle. Colt Kelley was dumbfounded. Harmon was sprawled across his dinner plate. The spilled beverage soaked everything. Red-faced with anger, Colt stood up and yanked Harmon up by his shirt.

"Chill out, man!" The actor pushed away from Colt and straightened his shirt like a dissed gangster. "Don't touch me again."

Colt stabbed his finger at Harmon. "You're out of control."

"Are you going put me in my place, tough guy?" Harmon sneered and reached out to shove Colt.

In an instant, Colt snatched Harmon by the wrist and spun him around. The actor stood on his toes and cried out with pain as his arm was twisted behind his back. "I'll throw you out of here myself," Colt said.

A number of Alpenglow employees intervened. In total embarrassment, Sam Spencer pulled Harmon toward the door. It was time to leave. His wife was already escorting Katarina to the parking lot.

* * * *

"Well, that was a blockbuster report," Special Agent Travis Price said. "What the hell was this secret conversation? Instead of coming to us she's pushing propaganda."

To some degree, Marla's conduct didn't surprise Price. *She probably considers E-Force to be a source, instead of a perpetrator of a crime. She deems it her journalistic right to protect a source.*

Price turned to his subordinate. "Bring Marla Wells in for a little chat. I've got some questions about her little romance with E-Force."

"Sure, boss." Special Agent Hill nodded. "She's acting like a typical reporter."

"She's wants to be a trendsetter. I want to know how far she's willing to go."

* * * *

Colt Kelley watched Harmon's friends hustle him out of the Alpenglow Brewpub. *He's like the blustering bully's I encountered as a youth.* Usually the bark was worse than the bite.

"I'm sorry, sir." The Alpenglow manager was flustered. "Everything's on the house tonight."

"Thanks, but it's not your fault." Colt's wave was dismissive. "That guy's an idiot."

The manager persisted. "I insist. We want you to remain a customer."

"Okay, you win." Colt shrugged. "I appreciate it."

Like everybody else, Colt was satisfied that the loudmouth was dragged out the door. It was disappointing that the beautiful brunette had to go too. *Maybe she was an actress or a model. For all I know, the drunk was a big movie star.* Pop culture and celebrities were topics of which Colt had little interest.

Outdoor adventures were Colt's true passion. That enthusiasm had guided him to EcoFriends, a career that promised to be an extension of his personal life. He had been excited about working to preserve the outdoors he loved so much. But the hours required by the job put a damper on Colt's recreational pursuits, especially since he had been elevated to manager of the Western Colorado chapter.

After making such personal sacrifices, Colt found it discouraging that the expanding EcoFriends organization was adopting ideologies and political positions of the far leftwing. Colt believed such radical stances served the interests of very few people. It was an ineffective tact to build a coalition that would promote commonsense approaches to preservation of the natural environment. At EcoFriends, it seemed as if the days of positive progress were gone.

Finishing the new beer he'd been given, Colt reflected on the foolish assertions of the drunk. *Are radical environmentalists supposed to be given a pass because they claim to fight for the weak and powerless? What if the opponents of radicals took the same approach?* It was a slippery slope with a dark abyss at the bottom.

It only took a moment for Colt to decide he was too tired to think about it further. There was still a sixty-mile drive home to Silt to contend with. The nearest housing he could afford was in the little bedroom community. *It's ironic that an employee of an environmental organization has to spend so much money on gasoline to travel back and forth to work.* Shaking his head with disgust, Colt placed a tip on the table and headed for the door.

Chapter Three
Friday, May 11

"Go lock the door before somebody else comes in," Johnny Wong barked in Chinese. "It's past midnight!"

"Too much rain." Su Wong, Johnny's wife, scrambled to the front door. "Nobody wants to do anything except drink."

"Rain is good for business." Johnny didn't look up from the cash register where he worked to total the night's haul.

It had been a busy night at the little liquor store in Steamboat Springs. Su figured most of the customers were locals, drifting in the doldrums of mud season. The ski area was closed, but lingering snow and soggy conditions in the high country kept the summer tourists at bay.

Su turned the lock with her key. Switching off the neon signs in the windows, she peered outside. Rain continued to saturate the town, boosting the seasonal swelling of the Yampa River.

"There's a big van stopped outside," Su said as if on a police stakeout.

"I don't care about that. I'm interested in profit. It'll all be gone if we have to pay for electricity to leave the lights on all night!"

"You talk like a cheapskate." Su waved her hand with disgust. She watched the van lurch forward and drive away. With hunched shoulders, a disembarked passenger in a broad-brimmed hat trotted across the street and disappeared at an intersecting road.

Johnny brandished a stack of bills. "I'm a shrewd businessman."

"You wouldn't make it through a week without me." Su turned and shuffled to switch off the lights.

* * * *

Zed Cain looked down the west side of Thunderhead Peak. Sleet and mist drowned the lights of Steamboat Village below. Turning away from the mountain flank, Cain trudged toward the massive Thunderhead Lodge. Some of the icy precipitation infiltrated the defenses of his parka. Cain pulled the zipper up closer to his chin.

"This weather sucks." Billy Landin shifted about restlessly in the frigid deluge. Condensation from his breath hung in a cloud in front of his face.

"That means AmeResort isn't paying attention." Cain's response was devoid of emotion.

Since AmeResort Corporation had acquired Steamboat Resort, the Thunderhead Lodge had been renovated and expanded. With direct access from the base village via the Silver Bullet gondola, the facility was a popular skier and tourist destination. It was protected by an alarm system, but the security staff in the base village had no idea the E-Force team was present. Landin had utilized his extraordinary computer hacking skills to thwart AmeResort's defenses.

"I can't see a damned thing through these goggles." Landin fiddled with his night vision gear. "It seems like we've been standing in this freezing rain for hours."

Cain turned on Landin. "Quit bitching. When Ruddock's done, we leave."

Landin nodded humbly in compliance. "Okay, I got it."

Cain turned his back on the shivering computer hacker. He had no interest in providing moral support to anybody, especially a whining punk.

Finally, Trigger Ruddock emerged from the building. He swung a backpack over his shoulders and trotted toward the leader.

Ruddock patted the cell phone in the pocket of his jacket. "All five incendiaries are locked and loaded. I'll trigger the igniters after we get the hell out of Dodge."

"No explosion this time?" Cain's question was a warning.

The Powderbowl Station blast at Copper Mountain was unintended. The fire had ignited a huge propane tank. The resulting fireball had literally blown the roof off the building. By some act of fate, the flames survived the oxygen-consuming blast and burned the timber framing to the ground. Cain knew they wouldn't be so lucky at the Thunderhead Lodge. It was two stories and much of the framing was steel. The team was relying on Ruddock's careful study of the structure during the past weeks. The demolitions man had settled upon the weak points, locations where sustained high temperatures would cause the most damage.

Ruddock was quick to assure Cain. "The gas is shut off. We're good as long as Wonder Boy disabled the fire alarm and sprinklers."

"I took care of it," Landin countered.

"You'd better be right," Ruddock said. "The whole mission's on the line!"

"I understand, trust me."

Ruddock stepped toward the kid. "I don't trust anybody, especially you."

"Stand down," Cain said to his high-strung henchman. "We're moving out."

The wiry hothead backed off and spat on the ground with disgust.

"We're due at the top of the lift. Both of you stay on my heels like dogs on a leash." Cain turned and loped toward the descent point.

* * * *

It took a few seconds to lock the store and scurry to the car. Su Wong was half drenched by the time she darted inside the vehicle. Her husband was waiting with the engine running.

"Why didn't you move the car closer?" Su asked after

slamming the door.

"Why didn't you bring an umbrella?" Johnny quipped.

Driving west on Franklin Avenue, Johnny proceeded at a cautious pace. Su sat with her arms folded, steaming at her inconsiderate spouse. Peering through the windshield, Su noticed a van at the edge of the street. The guy with the hat and slicker sprinted from the saturated shadows and clambered into the side door.

Su grabbed her husband by the arm. "That's the van I saw before. The man that got out is back."

"Why would you even care?" Johnny glanced at the vehicle with disinterest.

"I think they're up to no good." Su squinted through her spectacles, trying to read the Wyoming license plate before the driver accelerated away from the curb.

Johnny yawned. "Don't be ridiculous. How would you know that?

"I just have a funny feeling." Su's quiet reply was accented by a shrug of her shoulders.

"You should be feeling one thing: tired. Forget about those fools outside."

"You're impossible," Su said, turning her back on Johnny.

* * * *

There're the freaking pliers. Barry Conley breathed a sigh of relief when he glimpsed the tool embedded in the mud.

With the lineman's pliers in hand, Conley trudged through the muck, retracing his steps across the saturated lower reach of the ski run. The bottom of the Thunderhead Express lift resembled an alien spacecraft in the weird green backlight of the night vision gear. He had already pried open the door to the mechanical space in the canopy above the loading area. It was the only protection for the massive

28

electric motor.

A stone's throw from completing his return trip to the lift, Conley heard an automobile engine and the swish of tires on wet pavement. A floodlight blazed to life from below, boring into the mountainside.

Oh, shit! Panic gripped Conley when the shaft of light cut off his path and swept toward him.

Conley was like a novice skater on a sloping rink as he fled toward the trees that bordered the ski run. While he struggled to keep his footing, the obelisk of light loomed closer.

Conley knew he wasn't going to make it. "Son-of-a-bitch!"

Suddenly his foot found nothing but air and he careened into a ditch. Mud broke his fall, but the impact still hurt. Crumpled in water and filth, the electrician craned his neck and turned his eyes upward. Just inches above his prone form, the ditch bank was bathed in illumination.

* * * *

The gray Ford van lumbered along while the wiper blades slapped back and forth in a frantic rhythm. Driving conditions were miserable.

"I just turned onto Mt. Werner Road," Delilah said to her passenger. "We're almost to the shopping center."

Grayson Miller grumbled in the rear cargo area. "We can get this over with. This rain is going to wash the new primer coat off this vehicle."

Miller had stripped off his Stetson and slicker. Drying his curly hair with a towel, he moved to the passenger seat.

Delilah turned into a parking lot occupied by a few scattered vehicles. All the stores were closed. On the outskirts of the pavement, she turned off the lights and engine. Rain drummed on the roof of the van.

"Are you sure that house will burn in this weather?"

Delilah's jittery nerves were getting the best of her. Her fingers tap-danced on the steering wheel.

"Hell yes, it'll burn. I know how to start a fire in a building."

"I thought maybe the can of gas hidden in the bushes got wet or--"

"It's called accelerant," Miller interrupted, staring out the windshield.

"I guess I'm not a pyromaniac like you. We're counting on your decoy to distract every cop and firefighter in this place."

Miller whipped around and stabbed his finger at Delilah. "You just keep the freaking van on the road tonight. That's your job."

"Excuse me for being a team player." Delilah shrunk back.

"Get real." Miller turned his back to Delilah. "You're acting like some high school chic."

Delilah recoiled. She had expected E-Force to be more of a family. Instead, it might as well have been some kind of military boot camp where nobody gave a shit about anyone else. She sulked in silence, feeling cheated and disrespected.

* * * *

The floodlight on Officer Westbrook's police cruiser probed the darkness near the bottom of the Thunderhead Express Lift.

I swear something moved up there. Westbrook could barely see the rain-soaked slope.

The obelisk of illumination revealed only tree trunks and undergrowth. For nearly a minute, Westbrook examined the fringe of the forest to no avail.

"Where did it go?" The cop rubbed his tired eyes.

As part of an agreement with AmeResort, the city police department had stepped up patrols at the ski area. The developer was worried about another incident like the one at Copper Mountain. *I should get out and investigate.*

"Tree-hugger nuts are going to make my life miserable," Westbrook said as he reached for his raincoat.

Suddenly, a call from dispatch crackled over the radio. There was a house fire in town. Westbrook radioed his response and shifted the car into gear.

"Beats chasing shadows in the rain." Westbrook smiled and switched off his light. With his flashers on, he sped toward Mt. Werner Road and the highway beyond.

* * * *

"Here comes a cop." Delilah pointed toward the road.

Grayson Miller looked up to see Westbrook's police car racing past. Red and blue flashers pierced the night.

"Dude took the bait." Miller was jealous that the cop would witness his creation. The thought of the flames roaring without him was tortuous.

"I guess he's headed for your fire," Delilah said, craning her neck as the vehicle sped out of sight toward Highway 40.

"Where the hell else would he be going in this town. It's time to go."

"Yeah, no shit." She turned the key in the ignition.

"What's wrong with you?" Miller's gaze settled on Delilah's hands gripping the steering wheel.

"I could ask you the same question." Delilah's glare was ice cold.

Miller refused to relent. "Your hands are shaking. Are you sick or something?"

"I'm just nervous, alright." Delilah took a deep breath. "There're a lot of things that can go wrong on these missions. I don't want to get caught."

"Don't panic. And keep your speed under control."

"Hey, driving is my job! Remember?" Delilah jammed the transmission into gear. "You're the pyrotechnics guy."

"Whatever, babe." Miller puckered his lips in a kiss as the van rumbled toward the ski area.

* * * *

With the cop gone, Conley extracted himself from the ditch and dashed for the ski lift. *That was way too close.* He shuddered at the thought of nearly blowing the mission.

At the loading station, Conley scampered into the overhead mechanical space. There was hardly any time left. Switching on a headlamp, he sweated over the electrical components of the motor. The phone in Conley's hip pocket vibrated. *The signal.* He held his breath and connected the last two wires.

When the motor jolted to life, Conley ripped off his headlamp and almost tumbled off the ladder in his haste to descend. The lift chairs mounted on the thick cable lurched forward when he punched the button on the control pad. An endless procession of suspended seats whisked in from the darkness, circled the giant wheel, and zipped out of sight to begin the ascent up the mountain. Conley donned his night vision goggles to survey the area below. If the cop showed up again, he would have to shut down in an instant.

The road at the bottom of the slope remained desolate. When Conley glanced back to the lift, a dark figure sprang from an approaching chair. He recoiled in surprise, nearly falling over backward.

"Shit, you startled me!" Conley knew his reaction looked foolish to Cain.

The sullen leader ignored the electrician. The next seat materialized out of the rain-sodden darkness. It held Billy Landin, who was hunched over. Soaked and shivering, the computer hacker unloaded and shuffled toward the lift shack.

"Are you okay, man?" Conley lifted his night vision gear for a better look at the scruffy kid.

"I'm freaking cold," Landin stammered.

"You need to get out of the rain," Conley said, frowning. "You look hypothermic."

"He'll be fine." Cain's curt reprimand was devoid of compassion.

Another empty lift chair passed before Trigger Ruddock joined the team. He smirked at Conley's mud-covered clothes. "Did you fall down?"

Without dignifying the comment with a response, Conley jammed the bottom of his fist against the button to stop the lift. He scuttled up the ladder to the mechanical area while the other team members retreated across the ski run. After a few seconds, the trapdoor was closed and secured. By the time anyone at the resort figured out that E-Force had pirated rides on the lift, the Thunderhead Lodge would be long gone.

Back on the ground, Conley scrambled to the trees. When he reached the rest of the team, he avoided eye contact with Ruddock. It was tough enough to control his fear of Cain without Ruddock's hostility.

"We've got two bikes at the rack over there." Conley directed Cain's attention to an area beyond the road. "There're two more in front of the far building."

"You and Conley take the closest rack," Cain ordered Ruddock. "Landin's going with me."

"Let's go." Ruddock winked at the electrician. "Time's ticking away."

"I'm waiting for you." Conley was indignant as he started down to the road. He hated the wiry man's animosity and arrogance. They were supposed to be part of a team, but Ruddock kept trying to pick a fight.

"It looks like you're running away!" Ruddock snapped in a flare of anger.

Conley bristled. "Try to keep up." Immediately, he was afraid his reaction was a mistake.

"Shut up and go." Cain cut the bickering short.

Several minutes later, the two pairs of men reached the

mountain bikes. They were designed for off-road riding, but the wide tires would provide some traction on the wet roads. Night vision gear was replaced with riding glasses that would arouse less suspicion from anyone in a passing vehicle.

Cain was the first to depart, flashing past Conley and Ruddock at the lower bike rack. About a minute later, Landin went by at a slower pace. The two adversaries waited while Landin disappeared. A group of riders would attract attention. It was important to have space between team members.

Ruddock taunted Conley with a crooked smile creasing his harsh face. "You're up, Sparky. You better keep making like a scared rabbit."

Conley ignored Ruddock. He was afraid a response would instigate a physical fight...something that was out of the question during the mission. Besides, he knew the smaller man would kill him. It was not a second too soon when Conley cranked on the pedals and left the volatile demolitions man alone to be swallowed by the night.

* * * *

A wailing siren sent Su Wong scurrying to one of the apartment windows. The cheap glass panes were laden with condensation. She used a sleeve of her blouse to wipe some of it away. "It's another fire truck."

"And it's full of firefighters." Johnny Wong was changing into pajamas. "Let them worry about where they're going."

Su tried to imagine what was unfolding in the dreary downpour. "I think they're responding to something the guy from that van did."

"That's not thinking. It's delusional."

Su shuffled across the bedroom floor, envisioning the shadowy Stetson-wearer tossing a lit match toward a spreading pool of gasoline. "What if that man started a fire somewhere?"

"Then the fire department will put it out."

"Arson is a crime." Su was reluctant to give up. "I should call the police."

"Get real!" Johnny's tone conveyed the depletion of his patience. "You don't have a clue about anything that's going on out there. Just go to bed."

Su seethed. "Good idea. You get the couch."

"That suits me just fine." Johnny snatched up a pillow and stormed out of the room.

* * * *

"I wish I had some weed," Delilah said. "That would take the edge off."

Grayson Miller didn't offer a response as he wiped the sweat from his brow. The blaze he had created drew him like scrap iron to a magnet. His foot tapped an erratic beat on the floorboard.

"A little late to be checking in," Delilah said when a car pulled into the lot and stopped under the porte cochere at the hotel. A couple kids piled out with their parents.

Frustrated, Miller's gaze settled on the family. Impatience ate at him while he watched the clan struggle to extract their luggage from the vehicle.

"I don't know why Cain is making us rendezvous here," Delilah whined as the little group disappeared inside the hotel. "It's stupid to be in plain view. We're asking to get busted."

"You tell Cain his plan is stupid." Miller's response was scathing. "Freaking women are always bitching."

"You're such an ass!"

Miller glared at Delilah, noting that she appeared on the verge of tears. *Fires are so much easier to predict.*

Miller glanced toward the road a moment later. "There's

somebody up there."

The phantom figure evaporated. Miller strained his eyes in a futile effort to locate the apparition. When the rear door was yanked open, he and Delilah whirled to see Zed Cain spring into the cargo area.

"Don't start the engine yet."

"Okay, I won't." Delilah stammered.

Landin careened into view on the road. Miller watched him drag his feet in an awkward effort to stop the bike. The computer hacker was struggling to drag the bicycle off the road when Conley emerged from the wet gloom. Without wasting time, the electrician pitched his fat-tired frame into the ditch next to Landin's. The team had no further need for the stolen machines.

When the two new arrivals climbed into the van, Miller was shocked by Landin's appearance. He was shaking and looked dazed.

"You look half dead, dude." Miller tossed his towel into the cargo area. "Dry off with this."

The towel hit Landin in the face and dropped to the floorboard. With a dull stare, the shivering young man reached down and fumbled for it.

Miller turned his head just in time to see the family man emerge from the hotel. While hurrying to his car, the guy peered in the direction of the van.

"We've got company," Miller said with concern.

Everyone in the E-Force van watched the car roll out from the shelter of the porte cochere. In the parking lot, the vehicle cornered and veered toward a parking space.

"Shit! The guy saw Trigger," Miller said when the headlights briefly exposed Ruddock discarding a bike in the ditch.

"What if he calls the cops?" Conley asked. "We've got to get out of here."

"Everybody shut up!" Cain commanded. "That guy's clueless."

Ruddock bolted into the van with a string of expletives. "Where the hell did that car come from? Now we've been compromised!"

"Cool it." Cain turned to Delilah. "Move out. Stick to the speed limit."

Delilah eased the accelerator down. The vehicle rumbled for an escape from the parking lot.

The side mirror provided Miller with a glimpse of the father standing next to his parked car. "Looks like we got the old man's attention."

"Everybody cut the bullshit." Cain's withering gaze subdued the van occupants. "In five minutes, it won't matter."

The team was silent as the van rattled down Mt. Werner Road.

Cain produced one of his pre-paid cell phones. "Our publicist needs an update."

* * * *

Flames devoured the innards of the Thunderhead Lodge. A simple call from Ruddock's cell phone had triggered the incendiary devices. While the fire spread like a voracious parasite inside its host, the alarm remained silent. No water sprayed from the sprinklers mounted in the ceilings. Unchecked, the flames burst from the confines of the building's outer shell.

Radiance emanating from the blaze was snuffed out by the canopy of rain and fog. By the time the E-Force strike-team crested Rabbit Ears Pass, the Thunderhead Lodge was a raging inferno.

Chapter Four
Sunday, May 13

The terminals of the Los Angeles Airport were teeming with people. Passenger holding areas at the gates were crowded, with few empty seats. Carrie Forde felt fortunate to have claimed one of the uncomfortable chairs. Travelers and their belongings took up nearly every square inch of space around her. The din emanating from all the voices and a nearby television resonated in Carrie's head.

Carrie realized the plane was going to be crammed full. *I should have skipped the beach and left this morning.* After a two-day professional seminar, the weekend was a mini vacation.

Hoping to counter the chaos, Carrie lifted her bag and extracted a copy of *Issue Insight Magazine*. Thumbing through the weekly publication, she came upon an article on political campaign reform. It was authored by a journalist named Luke Parson.

Let's see how objective you are, Mr. Parson. Carrie delved into the piece, knowing a bill was being debated in the U.S. Senate. The President couldn't wait to sign it into law.

From the first paragraphs of the article, Carrie was disappointed by the notes of a shrill theme; assertions that the United States government was run by corporations and special interest groups. Candidates backed by big contributors were able to spend obscene amounts of money on political advertising campaigns to cement public support. Once in office, the politicians were indebted to their benefactors. In this way, powerful unelected entities could advance their political agendas.

The same old garbage. Carrie shook her head with disappointment before reading about the key provisions of the proposed laws. All campaign funding would come from taxpayer dollars, allocated to qualifying candidates. A new government agency was going to hold the purse strings. And political advertising would be restricted to a fixed amount of low-cost airtime. This service was to be provided by a list of government-approved television networks and radio stations.

"You media people can't wait to eliminate everyone else's free speech," Carrie declared under her breath. None of this was going to stop corruption in politics. It would just be another government limitation on personal freedom.

Carrie stuffed the magazine back into her carry-on. "You're just another partisan journalist, Parson."

An announcement sounded above the noise in the seating area. The flight to Denver was delayed by thirty minutes. Carrie sighed with dismay. In search of a reprieve from boredom, she shuffled through the pamphlets from the seminar.

* * * *

The delivery van parked at the base village of Steamboat Resort looked ordinary from the outside. When Special Agent Travis Price entered the vehicle, it was clear that the vehicle was extraordinary. The interior was packed with computers, and high-tech surveillance and communications equipment. Price moved to a chair in front of a high-definition screen. Special Agent Malcolm Hill settled into a nearby seat.

"Her highness is working over time." Price issued the remark when the evening news broadcast started with Marla Wells at the desk. Weekend duty was usually delegated to less senior personnel. He had a craving for a cigarette. It was a vice he had given up for more than a year.

"Maybe she's got another stunt to pull." Hill tightened his grip on the chair armrests.

Investigators had scarcely arrived at the smoldering remains of the Thunderhead Lodge when Marla and her team showed up. While firefighters and engineers were assessing the stability of the blackened steel framing, Marla marched up to the destroyed building with television camera rolling. The crime scene had been thrown into turmoil until authorities hustled her away.

"Our top story tonight is the devastation at Steamboat Resort early Saturday morning." Marla's tone was somber, but there was a gleam in her eyes. "Yesterday, E-Force contacted me and claimed responsibility."

"Damn that arrogant bitch!"

"Her news updates are making us look like idiots." Hill looked ready to punch the television screen. "She's sure as hell not on our side."

"Just keep talking, sweetheart." Seething, Price rubbed his jaw. "I'm hanging on every word."

* * * *

Static filled the giant flat screen. Perched on the edge of the couch, Colt Kelley punched buttons on a remote control to no avail. The coffee table held a half-dozen more of the devices, ostensible links to the array of electronics stacked on shelves and crammed into the entertainment center cabinets.

"How do you work this stupid T.V.?" Colt repressed the urge to hurl the remote across the room.

Eric Lowery emerged from the kitchen. "Dude, it's not rocket science. Use the universal remote. I programmed it to work with all my components."

"Spare me the technical details, Edison," Colt said. "Just turn the T.V. on."

Lowery walked over, snatched a remote from the table, and punched a button. Sound blasted from stereo speakers mounted around the perimeter of the room.

"Turn that down!" Colt shouted over the din. "Are you deaf?"

"This is a high-performance system," Lowery said as he dampened the volume. "It's better than almost anything you could find in those Aspen mansions."

Colt held up his hand to express his lack of interest. "Congratulations. Now, if you don't mind, I'd like to watch the news and see what happened over the weekend."

Colt and Lowery had spent the weekend camping and fishing in the Flat Tops. A little downtime away from civilization and amongst beautiful scenery was refreshing for Colt. The trip had been marred only by Lowery's complaints. He didn't care for Colt's Toyota Land Cruiser. There was no radio in the vehicle, let alone a high-watt stereo system.

"The news?" Lowery rolled his eyes. "Are you kidding me, dude?"

In Colt's mind, the man's behavior marked him no more educated than a third grader. "Yeah, they talk about current events."

"Sounds as interesting as verb conjugation." Lowery made no attempt to hide his disdain.

"You can watch cartoons later." Colt folded his hands behind his head. When the doorbell rang, he nodded toward a twenty-dollar bill he had placed on the table. "That should cover the pizza."

While Lowery stalked away, Colt saw Sarah Farmington, the usual weekend anchor, sharing the news desk with Marla Wells. In seconds, it was clear why. Video of the ruined Thunderhead Lodge garnered his attention. When he heard the name E-Force, he couldn't draw away.

Lowery returned with a pizza box. A couple beers from the refrigerator were in his other hand. "That twenty barely covered it. Beer's getting just as--"

Colt scolded him with a snap of his fingers. "E-Force destroyed a building at Steamboat."

"Big deal. Ski resorts have been ripping people off for--"

A sharp reprimand silenced Lowery.

Resembling an angry child, Lowery stuffed a slice of pizza into his mouth. Colt ignored the dramatics and honed in on the news. *E-Force is waging war against AmeResort Corporation.* The realization triggered the sensation of snake venom spreading through his circulatory system.

"This is suicidal," Colt muttered, shaking his head in disbelief.

"It's important to understand the motivation behind E-Force's backlash against the resort industry," Marla professed with a raised eyebrow. "To gain some insight, I talked with Howard Anderson, the founder and president of EcoFriends."

"What the hell," Colt said as the taped interview began to play. "Now my boss is getting into the fray!"

Uninterested, Lowery snatched up his bottle of beer. He refused to look at the screen.

* * * *

In the television studio, Marla Wells rifled through papers while her interview with Howard Anderson was broadcast for the viewers. Excitement surged through her. Viewer ratings for Marla's newscasts had spiked dramatically since the E-Force strikes. *My fame and fortune are about to rocket skyward.* Marla was certain of it. Trembling inside, she glanced up at one of the video monitors near the news desk.

Marla addressed Anderson on the videotape. "You're the head of a prominent environmental organization. I imagine you've dealt with tremendous adversity."

Anderson's furrowed brow gave the impression of a concerned father. "EcoFriends is like David, facing a Goliath comprised of industries and corporations."

"Those entities have powerful special interests working for them." Marla rubbed her chin in thought.

"Corporate America has the politicians in their back

pockets." Anderson's eyes flashed behind his glasses. "That means permissive laws and a pittance of regulation. Of course, government funding for environmental programs has been slashed. It's an impossible situation."

"It sounds incredibly frustrating." Marla wore a pained expression. "Is that what prompts a group like E-Force to take radical actions?"

"Absolutely." Anderson nodded his head. "It's no different than a revolution against a corrupt dictator in some third world country. People reach the breaking point."

"Has EcoFriends reached that breaking point?" Marla asked her guest.

Anderson's eyes narrowed. "I don't condone violent or destructive tactics. But when backed into the proverbial corner, it's surprising that more groups don't lash out."

Marla feigned empathy for the radicals. "Maybe E-Force will help the American public understand the dangers they're really facing."

She was no different than the defense attorney of a repugnant criminal, portraying her client as the disadvantaged victim. At the end of the day, Marla didn't give a rip about E-Force or their causes. It was all about the career boost from the group's continued phone calls.

Since her audience size had exploded, Marla reasoned that scores of radical environmental groups were envious of the publicity and promotion E-Force was receiving. *They're all desperate for a powerful media voice capable of massaging public perception while conveying their messages.*

As extremist groups vied for her attention, Marla expected to have the inside scoop during their competition to outdo each other with outrageous acts. There would be no bounds to her influence as an important journalist.

"During the next few weeks, I'll present a series of special reports on environmental vigilantism," Marla said when the camera turned back to her in the studio. "I'll take a close look at E-Force and other groups that have been pushed to radical action. The first report will air on Wednesday. You won't want to miss it."

Sarah Farmington spoke up, her tone laden with uncertainty. "I have a question, Marla."

Turning, Marla was surprised at Sarah's inappropriate behavior. *She's supposed to be reporting on the next story, not asking unscripted questions.*

Marla forced a smile. "What would you like to know?"

"There's a rumor that witnesses at Copper Mountain and Steamboat Resort observed suspicious persons in a van, shortly before each of the fires," Sarah said. "Is it possible that those individuals were part of E-Force?"

"The police are handling the investigation." Marla's response was curt.

"Should people be on the lookout for vans in the vicinity of AmeResort properties?" Sarah asked.

"I don't think we should try to play detective." A wisp of Marla's anger escaped. "The public is best served when people understand the problems that cause groups like E-Force to take extreme actions."

Sarah continued after an awkward pause. "Well, on to our next story. An automobile accident on Interstate 25 claimed the lives of two people earlier today."

While Sarah rambled on with the details of the wreck, Marla's anger simmered. Facts had nothing to do with shaping public perception. *I'll make her pay for that insubordination.*

* * * *

Slouched in her chair Carrie Forde stopped thumbing through seminar pamphlets. Feeling lonely, her mind wandered to unsettling memories of the past. She remembered the time before she had built the wall. There had been family and friends to confide in. A fleeting glimpse of a happy romance flittered through her head. Sadness gathered and grew, ushering in the storm clouds of pending depression. Carrie didn't want to be reminded of the painful past. She tried to brush the tumultuous thoughts aside.

"AmeResort is destroying this planet," a heavyset woman next to her said.

"Are you talking to me?" Carrie turned, relieved by the distraction.

"Those jerks at AmeResort are ruining everything." The woman wagged her finger, conveying disgust.

"What makes you say that?" Carrie's guard went up. She knew about the E-Force strike against Steamboat Resort.

"They've got the money and political influence to get away with murder." The woman vented while stabbing her thick index finger at the television. "You should listen to this."

Carrie looked to the T.V., which was blaring the United Media Network's 24-hour news channel. Some media analyst was beginning a commentary on AmeResort.

"AmeResort Corporation was founded in Denver by Phillip Barrett," the UMN pundit stated. "Under Barrett's shrewd management, the company accumulated large property holdings in the 1980's when struggling businesses and individuals were forced to liquidate their assets.

"During the economic boom of the 1990's, AmeResort used its property holdings to acquire and develop dozens of ski areas and beach resorts." The haughty commentator continued. "The enormous profits were reinvested in continuous expansion. AmeResort grew into the largest developer in North America and Phillip Barrett made billions. Not bad for a guy who started out buying repossessed houses."

There was a tone of disapproval underlying the UMN critic's remarks. It irked Carrie that Phillip Barrett was cast as a greedy man, a person who had built an empire by wresting away the last assets of the downtrodden. She wondered if the guy had ever met Barrett.

"Phillip Barrett has manufactured quite a legacy. Associates call him a visionary with tremendous tenacity. Environmentalists and conservationists contend his ignorance is as colossal as his ego."

Carrie wanted to voice a rebuttal. Instead, she bit her lip and continued to listen.

"The tremendous wealth of AmeResort Corporation casts a shadow over the political process, dictating government policies and smothering environmental regulations," the UMN analyst said. "Meanwhile local communities see deforestation, degradation of aquifers, and agricultural lands carved into commercial money-making ventures. It's no surprise that so many people view corporate developers as the only beneficiaries of big development."

"Everything he said is true," the woman next to Carrie said. "I'm an arts and crafts dealer and I've been to places developed by AmeResort. They totally destroy historic mountain towns. The beaches they touch turn into strips of asphalt and concrete."

"I don't think that's true," Carrie replied. Balanced and well-planned development had brought prosperity to many communities that had endured stagnation for years. "AmeResort creates jobs and helps diversify the economy."

"You sound like the CEO," the woman said. "Everyone knows companies like AmeResort are driven by capitalist greed. They worship the almighty dollar!"

Carrie repressed a flood of other responses that came to mind. "That doesn't make sense from a business or economic standpoint."

"Of course it doesn't. They're not interested in the future. The only concern is the money they can scoop up now."

"I suppose you like the sound of, 'from each according to his abilities, to each according to his needs,'" Carrie quoted Karl Marx.

"That's a recipe for global fairness." The woman nodded with approval. "Corporate America will never let it happen."

A flight attendant's voice echoed from the overhead speakers. "It's time to board the plane. Have a good flight."

The woman leaned toward Carrie. "Just remember, honey, the world runs on money."

"Thanks for the tip." Carrie's sarcasm was unveiled. *I hate radical leftists.*

The flight attendant announced that first class passengers could begin boarding the plane. Carrie was surprised when the woman next to her got up and waddled towards the gate. She chuckled at the irony. "It figures that the old communist is flying first class."

* * * *

Waves pounded the rocks a hundred feet below the house, which was perched on the edge of a bluff. The view of the magnificent Pacific coastline stretching north and south was breathtaking. It was an ideal stage for exquisite sunsets on the ocean horizon.

Dramatic beauty didn't really matter to Drew Harmon as he leaned against the terrace wall with a cocktail in hand. The multi-million dollar, southern California home was a trophy. With designer furniture and high-priced artwork on the walls, the house was a prop for entertaining the influential people he sought as friends. And it was a platform to launch his campaign for sophistication.

Most people were mingling near the bar and buffet tables inside the house, but a dozen guests lounged on the terrace with Harmon. As usual, the conversation included a debate about who was the most influential person in Hollywood. It was unclear whether the criteria for consideration were actual accomplishments or burgeoning popularity. Harmon only knew that nobody had ever mentioned him as a candidate.

While the Hollywood elites argued, a beautiful redhead walked out into the open air. All heads turned as she sauntered over to Harmon. She wrapped her arms around him and planted a kiss on his lips.

"Where've you been, baby?" Harmon asked. *I wish my old man could see me know. That bastard said I'd never amount to anything.*

"I was watching the news," the girl said proudly. "Another ski resort in Colorado was vandalized."

"I would have expected you to be more interested in the party, Katie," a handsome man with steel-gray hair said.

"She's interested in that hunk who anchors the newscasts," a middle-aged woman wearing lots of makeup said. "I know how women are, darling."

"I don't need to window shop, honey." Katie pressed closer to Harmon.

"Enlighten us with your analysis of AmeResort Corporation, sweetheart," the woman said with a smug smile. "You know that's who owns that ski area, don't you?"

"Of course I do," Katie said, exasperation written on her face. "I keep up with the news. In fact, I'll be sitting behind a news desk someday soon. Drew can help get me there."

All eyes shifted to Harmon as Katie squeezed his arm in a silent plea for assistance. His guests were curious as to how he could influence the television news industry on behalf of his newest romantic fling.

"I've got connections in the media," Harmon said with a shrug. "That's what happens when you grant a lot of interviews."

"You're talking about interviews for pop-culture magazines and appearances on glamour-shows about Hollywood celebrities," one of the men retorted. "The news media isn't the paparazzi."

"That's right," the woman with the makeup said. "News people have backgrounds in journalism. I forgot to ask where you earned your college degree, sweetie."

Katie fought back. "I got an early start in show business. There wasn't time for college."

"Look, I've got connections with influential people in the news industry." Harmon maintained his winning smile. "Reporters want my opinion all the time."

There were a few chuckles. It was clear that nobody viewed Harmon as an intellectual type with something to offer a journalist. The actor felt his facial muscles tighten at the lack of respect.

The man with the gray hair raised an eyebrow. "And what do they want to know?"

"They ask me about the environment." Harmon tempered his response. "I understand how corporations like AmeResort are destroying the environment and pocketing the profits."

The gray-haired gentleman wasn't satisfied. "But why do they ask you when there are people whose careers revolve around those issues?"

"Because I'm the celebrity spokesperson for StayGreen."

"What's StayGreen?" several people asked in a chorus of bewilderment.

"Haven't you seen their ads on T.V.?" Harmon blurted out his disbelief.

"I've seen a couple of those television spots," one man said with a nod. "They were boring. I hit the mute button."

"Well, that reaction is about to change." Harmon stepped away from Katie. "Their new ads will feature me."

"So you've become their poster boy?" the bald man asked.

"StayGreen needs a celebrity to publicize their efforts. I'm surprised you sophisticated people aren't familiar with them."

"It sounds like you've got a lot of work to do." Steel-gray hair was cynical.

"My endorsement will get their message out," Harmon said.

"And what is that message, Drew?" the bald man asked with unabashed bluntness.

"Big corporations have taken capitalist principles to the extreme." Harmon regurgitated his script in an authoritative tone. "They have no regard for clean air and water, and a healthy environment. With each dollar they stuff into their coffers, they become more powerful and emboldened, using their wealth to buy protection in the political and legal systems."

The man with the gray hair finished his cocktail. "So what's the solution?"

"It sounds like the corporations are invincible," somebody else said.

"That's not true." Harmon felt an ember of anger ignite. "E-Force has shown that giants have weaknesses. They've wounded AmeResort. That should encourage everyone who's concerned about the natural environment."

"I'm sure there are better strategies than E-Force." The gray-haired man folded his arms.

"You haven't explained your relationship with the news media, Drew," the bald man said.

"The media types know about my work with StayGreen." Harmon elected to promote himself instead of E-Force. "They're always after my opinions and insight. The latest example is some news anchor in Denver. She wants to interview me about the radical environmental movement."

"I'll be watching," Katie gushed. "It'll be so cool!"

"Congratulations, Drew," the steel-gray haired man said with a touch of sarcasm. "You've parlayed stardom into the ability to shape public opinion."

"That's right. Well, I should mingle with the guests inside."

Striding into the house with Katie on his arm, Harmon felt good. He was sure the guests on the terrace were impressed. That meant his status had been elevated. *It's all part of the game.*

* * * *

"What the hell are you trying to pull?" Marla said to Sarah Farmington the instant the newscast was over.

Sarah blinked with surprise. "I don't know what you mean."

"Don't give me that crap! You broke format on the air."

"If you're talking about the question I--"

Marla leapt up from her chair. "You tried to show me up."

"I wasn't trying to be malicious," Sarah said with wide-eyed fear.

"Do you think I'm stupid?" Marla thrust her finger at the young woman. "You were trying to put me on the spot, to make me look ignorant."

"No! I just thought the viewers would--"

"You better start thinking about your job." Marla took a step toward Sarah. "I'm not going to put up with that kind of bullshit."

"Let's take a step back and calm down." The haggard looking producer attempted to defuse the fight. Nobody paid attention to him.

Sarah's demeanor hardened. "Now wait a minute. I didn't attack you or your credibility."

"The hell you didn't! Don't do it again or you're through here."

"You're threatening me." Sarah rose from her seat behind the desk.

"Consider it a promise, sweetheart."

Marla nearly ran the young anchor over as she stormed past. Muttering obscenities, she stalked off the set while everyone stood with mouths agape. Morgan wished his camera had been rolling so the public could see the real Marla Wells.

When Morgan looked back to Sarah, she appeared

51

dazed, perhaps on the verge of tears. Glancing around at the onlookers, she gathered up her papers and hurried from the room.

"Hang in there." Chris Morgan offered quiet support as the young woman fled past. He was afraid she would not survive at the television station much longer.

Morgan was angered and disgusted at the way Marla wielded her power like a tyrant. It was frustrating that she could prosper and advance her career at the expense of everybody else. There seemed to be no justice in the world.

"E-Force has pushed her over the edge," Morgan muttered to the producer.

"Yeah, no kidding," the overweight executive said.

With countless people in the media, why had E-Force chosen Marla? The question baffled Morgan. And he suspected she wasn't revealing everything she knew about E-Force. Instead, she was swimming in shark-infested waters. Eventually she would get bitten...or eaten. *If somebody ends up dead because of E-Force, there will be hell to pay.*

"You've got to rein Marla in," Morgan told his boss. "She'll drag us all down when her ship finally sinks."

* * * *

As soon as Marla Wells finished her commentary, Travis Price muted the sound. The announcement about her investigative reporting series on eco-terrorism had caught him off-guard. In effect, it was a call-to-arms to environmental extremist groups, complete with an enticing offer to represent their cases in the court of public opinion.

"Marla Wells is becoming a problem." Price leaned back in his chair and pulled a pack of cigarettes from his pocket. Stress had pushed him off the wagon.

"Want to charge her with withholding evidence in a federal investigation?" Special Agent Hill asked. "We can stop her right now."

Price lit a cigarette. "There's not enough evidence yet. If we bring her in, she'll cry foul. The media will make us look like fools."

"We can't let her meddle this way."

"I know that." He took a deep drag and exhaled a cloud of smoke. "She's turning this thing into a circus to advance her career."

"What are we going to do?" Hill's frustration was obvious.

"I'm going to make a phone call." Price got up from his seat. "There's got to be a way to dial that bitch back."

* * * *

Colt grumbled as he ambled to the front door of his dark and lonely house. "Home, Sweet Home." Since the breakup with his fiancée, the place had become the domain of self-loathing and deprecation. Such demons tormented Colt's soul.

Now E-Force was making everything worse. There was serious trouble on the horizon for EcoFriends and for Colt. His employer wasn't exactly as clean as the wind-driven snow. Colt had lacked the spine to stand up and protest. Those hard facts were eating at him with increasing voracity.

"Those E-Force idiots are going to screw us all." Colt kicked his shoes off on the way through the kitchen. "Anderson's going to make sure of that."

At one time, Colt had believed EcoFriends was part of an insurance policy to provide a sustainable future for generations to come. He and his colleagues had trusted the leadership of Howard Anderson. Now, Colt was certain that Anderson had led them all astray. He'd been as mindless as a lemming.

Maybe we're on the path to hell. Colt stripped off his shirt and hurled it at a laundry basket near the bedroom closet.

Colt switched off the light and collapsed on the bed. He hoped other EcoFriends managers were as worried about the prospects for the future. Trying to speculate how the manager's meeting in Boulder would play out tomorrow was a waste of time. The logic and actions of his colleagues often seemed as erratic as the flight paths of bats. Colt wished he could just walk away from EcoFriends. The days of clear choices and easy answers were long gone. For a moment Colt longed for someone with whom he could discuss his deepest thoughts and emotions. He felt a twinge of sadness.

I need to toughen up. Colt admonished himself and rolled onto his side. *Self-pity doesn't help anyone.*

* * * *

The house was a few blocks from the University of Colorado campus in Boulder. Inside the beautiful home was a study with a mahogany desk. The room was embellished by the gurgling of a miniature fountain and the soft, soothing refrain of new-age music.

Howard Anderson sat in the chair behind the desk with a glass of Merlot cradled in one hand. Without a strand of gray in his neatly-trimmed hair and beard, he appeared younger than his forty years.

"The chapter managers will follow my lead." Anderson did his best to push aside any nagging doubt.

"There may be some holdouts." An authoritative voice echoed from the speakerphone on the desk. "You're not a magician."

Anderson was offended by the shot across his bow. "My people are dedicated. I built this organization from the ground up."

Almost a decade earlier, Anderson had founded EcoFriends. Armed with intelligence, a good education, financial savvy, and a knack for public speaking, his skills rivaled top business executives. He had transformed his creation into one of the most publicized environmental organizations in the western United States.

"And I funded the damned thing!" the voice on the phone said. "Turn that music off and listen to me."

"Sorry, I was out of line," Anderson stammered as he fumbled with the stereo remote.

"You will do whatever it takes to ensure that your managers fall into line. E-Force has injured a giant that was invincible to EcoFriends. If we keep the wounds open, AmeResort Corporation will bleed to death."

"That will scare some of our personnel," Anderson said, setting down his glass and rubbing his temples. "They'll be afraid the authorities will come down hard on E-Force."

"The media has the power to shape the future for E-Force," the voice on the phone ranted. "That's why you did the interview with Marla Wells. Public opinion polls show that the majority of Americans believe corporations are guilty of myriad offenses."

Anderson fretted. "Eventually, opinion will shift."

"Until that time, you will capitalize on the current opportunity."

"I understand, Mr. Marchotti." Anderson called on every fiber of his being to mask his misgivings.

The call ended with a click and a dial tone. Anderson hated being treated like an incompetent fool. There was nothing he could do to change that now. He had only one option; to instill in the chapter managers an understanding of what was at stake. It was imperative that they adopt his policy regarding E-Force. Success for the radicals was critical.

Anderson lifted his hands and stared at them. They were trembling again. The condition was worsening. He was afraid he was losing control. Frustrated, he snatched up the wine glass. In one gulp, Anderson finished the Merlot.

Chapter Five
Monday, May 14

The conference room occupied a choice corner of an upper floor of the AmeResort high-rise. Beyond the expansive windows, the Front Range peaks loomed above the Denver metro area. Cresting the horizon of the eastern plains, the sun bathed the towering mountains in the light of a new day. Phillip Barrett took no notice of the stunning backdrop when he burst through the double doors. A cane in his left hand helped him maintain a brisk pace.

At the head of the long table, Barrett stopped and surveyed the men and women who comprised the operating board of his company. The faces before him were grim. A few papers shuffling marred silence.

"Forgive me for dispensing with pleasantries this morning." Barrett took his seat. The cane rested across his lap. "I trust you all understand the future of AmeResort is in jeopardy."

"We've all looked at the division reports," Stephen Chandler, a tall man with a lean face, said. "The outlook isn't good."

Others seated around the table concurred with Chandler's assessment. Barrett nodded, knowing the executives had been working double-time in an effort to diagnose the full extent of AmeResort's ailments and prescribe an effective treatment. It was what the chief executive officer expected from his people.

"Since the E-Force terrorists started targeting our facilities, cancellations have been rampant at our resorts," Barrett said. "Investors are backing away from our projects. Our property sales have declined. Nobody wants to get caught in the crossfire. AmeResort stock values are plummeting. How are we going to stop this disaster?"

"I think we'll have to implement layoffs and liquidate

assets." One woman asserted her opinion with a pained expression.

"That means E-Force wins," a male board member replied. "We've got to beef up security and stop those bastards from destroying the entire infrastructure of this company!"

"The attacks have just given us a bloody nose." Barrett's voice crackled with impatience. "It's the aftermath that's killing us. The media is making E-Force look like heroes. And we're the bad guys."

"A public relations campaign would help," somebody suggested. "We could educate the public about all the good things we do for the environment."

"It won't be effective when the mainstream media's hammering us twenty-four, seven." Barrett gripped his walking stick with both hands. He fought the urge to snap it over his knee. "If we spent every last dime on advertising, we'd still lose!"

Chandler said, "I agree that the media will beat us. But if we team up with others in the industry, we can change our public image."

"AmeResort is in business to develop real estate," Barrett said. "We're not a media outlet."

"That's true," Chandler said, "but we have experience shaping public opinion. We have to win public support for every project we initiate."

"I'm aware of that." Barrett's frustration with Chandler was growing. "That's different than challenging the mainstream media on a national stage. They can depict the situation any way they want. Look at what's happening! Instead of demanding justice, a huge segment of the population has started to believe that E-Force is fighting for the greater good of society. On the other hand, we've been characterized as an insidious giant, bent on destroying the planet in pursuit of market share and profits."

A heavyset man spoke up. "Polling indicates Americans

view corporations as corrupt and destructive. The pundits keep harping on that."

"Survey results depend on the phrasing and presentation of the questions," the second woman on the board professed. "Maybe reality isn't as bad as the media claims."

"That doesn't matter!" Barrett slammed his fist on the table. "Too many Americans don't see terrorist acts as a cancer on a free and civilized society. They don't perceive eco-terrorism as a threat to people's personal lives."

Barrett laid one forearm on the table and paused to allow his words to sink in. He was convinced that battling the media was an exercise in futility. Besides, AmeResort was in a financial crunch. There was no money for serious public relations efforts on a nationwide scale.

Barrett went on. "You all know about Marla Wells' plans for a reporting series on environmental vigilantism. She wants to promote understanding for criminality. Every wacko group on the planet is going to take potshots at AmeResort, hoping to get their free television publicity. E-Force is just the beginning."

"If that happens, there will be a massive public outcry for law enforcement to root out the terrorists." Chandler looked around the room for support.

"By the time that happens, it'll be too late to save AmeResort," Barrett said.

"Then what do we do?" someone asked. The question was echoed in the defeated countenances around the room.

"I founded this corporation with blood and sweat." The cadence of Barrett's voice slowed. "When my rivals failed in the bust times of the early 1980's, I didn't give up. I risked everything to buy properties from owners who needed to shed mortgages they couldn't afford to pay. Some people in the Denver media called me a parasite. But the people I saved from foreclosure and bankruptcy had a different perspective. They salvaged pride and the chance to start again.

"When the economy finally rebounded, some of those people even became my employees." Barrett placed both hands on the table and sat straight in his chair. "We redeveloped the real estate holdings I amassed during the turbulent times. AmeResort Corporation reaped profits and the media hated it. But that financial success gave this company the means to hire more people. Our compensation and incentives have always been generous for talented and motivated employees."

"I can't imagine that anyone in here would want to work anywhere else." Chandler's proclamation was that of an eager assistant.

Barrett noted that a few people in the room appeared embarrassed by Chandler's patronizing outburst. He let the remark pass without comment. "So now the media condemns us because we're the big kid on the block. Like never before, they want to see us fail and collapse. I'm not going to let that happen."

"Do you have a strategy in mind?" the first woman asked and pushed her glasses higher.

"I've arranged for a meeting with the FBI agent in charge of the investigation." Barrett glanced at a clock on the wall. "It's time to demand results."

* * * *

Managers from twenty-eight chapters, spread across eleven western states, had arrived at EcoFriends headquarters in Boulder, Colorado. The seven members of the board of directors were also present. It was a mandatory meeting for everyone in a leadership position. Most people milled about, engaged in conversation as the start time approached.

Colt had already chatted with a few colleagues. To his dismay, they reveled in the destruction that E-Force had wrought. They were glad AmeResort Corporation was on the defensive. Nobody shared his concern about the E-Force situation spinning out of control. Not one person supported his suggestion of a public statement by EcoFriends to denounce the sabotage and destruction.

Disappointed and disgusted, Colt disengaged himself from further discussion. There was still time to pour a cup of coffee before the meeting was called to order. As Colt turned toward the back of the room, he nearly ran into a young woman who was hurrying the other way. Her dark hair was done in a thick braid.

She raised her arms in defense. "Watch it there, pal."

"Well, if it isn't Deb Olson." Colt's spirits lifted. "Our lives collide again. One of us must be going the wrong direction on a one-way street."

"That would be me." Deb's reaction was reserved, but she embraced him. "It's good to see you, Colt. Are you trying to sneak out of the meeting?"

"Unfortunately, I'm only fleeing as far as the coffee pot." He sensed Deb wasn't at ease. "Are you okay?"

Deb glanced around the room and gripped Colt's arm. "This organization is on the path to hell." Her voice was hushed.

Colt looked into Deb's eyes. The dancing sparkle he remembered was gone. It was blotted out by fear.

"What do you mean?" Colt's gut churned as if he had been punched.

"We'll talk later, someplace away from here." Deb turned on her heel and hurried to claim one of the few empty chairs left in the room.

For a few seconds, Colt watched Deb walk away. Paranoia gripped his psyche. He felt that he'd just been summoned by a doctor to hear the results of medical tests regarding a potential illness. Colt wasn't sure he wanted to hear the diagnosis, but not knowing was torture. Trying to repress the disturbing thoughts that invaded his mind, Colt filled his Styrofoam coffee cup.

* * * *

Marla Wells shuffled through her notes, hunched over the table in the corner booth she had claimed. The little café in Denver was a good place to work outside the office. It had high-speed wireless access to the Internet and an unassertive staff. Marla knew they wouldn't object if she occupied the space all morning.

"You're Marla Wells from Channel 4 News, aren't you?" The waiter couldn't hide his excitement as he poured coffee in her cup. His aim was imperfect and some, splashed on the table.

"That's right." Marla's eyes fell upon several droplets of dark liquid that fell on her notes. She snatched them away. "Careful! I'm working here."

"I'm sorry. I'll clean that up right away." The young man seemed to deflate. He used a towel to wipe up the spill.

"Are you a fan?"

"Yes. I've been watching your reports on E-Force," the server said as he finished the clean up. "I had no idea the developers were so powerful in Colorado. Again, I sincerely apologize."

A slight smile spread across Marla's face. Her efforts were working. "Mistakes will happen. Be more careful when you refill it next time."

The waiter scurried away. Marla took a swig from her mug before furiously tapping away at the keys of her laptop computer. She was burning the candle at both ends to prepare for the first installment of her series. The Internet had a plethora of information about an endless array of extremist groups. Some of the website propaganda was shocking. But that meant it was a good bet that the more militant groups would go to great extremes to garner attention.

It'll be great television. She leaned back and snickered.

People love to watch a train wreck.

Taking a break, Marla used her cell phone to dial the office and check voicemail.

"Marla, this is Ted Rogers, Vice President of News for United Media Network." The message took Marla's breath away. "I've seen some of your recent newscasts. They're good. And the investigative series you're planning is intriguing. Let's talk. Give me a call when you get a chance."

Marla's fingers trembled as she scribbled down the phone number the network honcho provided. *I've got the network's attention.* She exhaled, clasping her hands together. "This is the big break!"

Buzzing with excitement, Marla skimmed over a page of her notebook. The questions she had jotted down were formulated for a phone interview she had arranged with Drew Harmon. A Hollywood star would draw viewers. The average tube-boob was enamored by celebrities. It didn't matter what incoherent drivel they spouted out.

Marla checked her watch, mindful that it was an hour earlier in Los Angeles. She decided to wait a little longer before calling the actor. The staccato clicking of her keyboard resumed.

* * * *

The receptionist offered a warm greeting. "Good morning. May I help you?"

"I'm FBI Special Agent Price." Light glinted off the shiny badge he flashed. "I have an appointment with Phillip Barrett."

The young woman's pleasant smile vanished. "I'll call his assistant and let her know you're here."

Price straightened his tie and brushed his thinning hair back into place

"Mr. Barrett and the Board of Directors are waiting on

the twenty-fifth floor," the receptionist said as she hung up the phone. "The elevators are out in the lobby. Ms. Vonn will meet you at the top and escort you to the conference room."

During his ascent, Price mulled over Barrett's request for an update on the E-Force case. Dealing with Phillip Barrett could prove difficult. The man was powerful. His political allies were numerous. The head of AmeResort Corporation undoubtedly had the kind of vast influence that could ruin careers.

Price took a deep breath when the elevator completed its climb. The doors opened to a striking Asian woman waiting in the lobby.

"Hello, Special Agent Price. I'm Ms. Vonn. Mr. Barrett and the Board are waiting for you."

The black-haired beauty wasted no time with small talk. Her stride was quick and purposeful. When his guide stopped at a set of double doors, Price swallowed hard. The inquisition was about to begin.

"Good luck, Mr. Price." Ms. Vonn's eyes narrowed. Her thin smile gave Price the impression that she perceived and enjoyed his discomfort.

She pushed one of the doors aside. All eyes focused on the FBI agent. He stepped into the conference room and the door closed behind him. Any chance of escape was cut off.

* * * *

The room quieted after Howard Anderson called the meeting to order. As President of the Board of Directors, he sat in the center of the long table facing the group of chapter managers. Three board members flanked him on either side. One was Zed Cain.

Anderson started the meeting. "Good morning, everyone. Many of you traveled long distances to get here. Your presence is exemplary of your hard work and dedication."

Assessing the expressions of those near him, Colt judged most of the managers wouldn't be satisfied unless Anderson started writing expense checks. *That's the way of the world.*

"EcoFriends effectively promotes responsible human stewardship of the earth." The leader continued. "More than any other organization, EcoFriends has demanded that corporations and government agencies take responsibility for reducing environmental destruction. Victories haven't come easily. They've only been won with your sacrifice and commitment."

Colt was skeptical. He was interested in the future, not lofty praise for past actions.

"Unfortunately, a serious problem has come to the attention of the Board." Anderson's expression was solemn. "It's threatening all we've worked for."

The hairs on the back of Colt's neck stood straight. When he glanced around the room, it was as if a serious illness had been diagnosed in a family member. The expressions on the managers' faces revealed anxiety.

"A large percentage of the money raised by each chapter isn't reported to the government. You skimmed it off and sent it here. Funding for environmental programs has been slashed from government budgets and grant money is tougher to secure. Our largest financial contributors are redirecting their money to international organizations, which they perceive as more capable to address the global environmental crisis. To survive, EcoFriends was forced to take certain liberties with fund raising. You all agreed to this practice and swore an oath of loyalty."

Colt's mouth was as dry as cotton. Like every other EcoFriends chapter manager, he had misrepresented income. Now it was evident that there were looming consequences.

"I've learned that an anonymous manager informed the authorities about our fundraising procedures." Anderson's face flashed anger. "One of you betrayed us."

* * * *

The telephone rang nearly a dozen times. Marla was about to give up when a gruff male voice answered.

"I'm calling for Drew Harmon."

"It's early," the voice said.

Marla retorted with an air of impatience. "Mr. Harmon should be expecting my call."

"Really?" The voice was condescending. "And who might you be?"

"Marla Wells from Channel 4 News in Denver. We have an interview scheduled."

"Ah, Marla Wells." The voice became friendlier and Marla recognized it as Harmon's. "I'd forgotten about our appointment."

Marla was careful not to express her annoyance. "I you still have the time to provide your insight about the environmental movement in this country."

"I'm willing to help educate the public," Harmon proclaimed.

What an arrogant ass. Marla's lip curled with distaste. "In that case, I'll get started. In your view, what is the driving force behind environmental-vigilantism?"

"I think there are a lot of reasons for it." Harmon was hesitant. "They're all melded together."

Marla hated wasting time. "But which do you see as being the most important?"

"Big corporations have taken capitalist principles to the extreme." Harmon seemed to be reading from a script. "They have no regard for clean air and water, and a healthy environment."

Marla interrupted him, the fingers of one hand drumming on the table. "You mentioned that the first time we talked, but why has the response been vigilantism?"

"Environmental groups get frustrated, I suppose."

Harmon was no different than a high school student who hadn't done his homework. "We'll have to go over this another time. I have an important appointment."

"I understand." Marla puckered her lips with contempt. It takes time to discuss such a complex topic."

"That's right." Harmon was quick to agree.

The man is an ignoramus, Marla concluded. "Why don't we set a date for the television interview? We could conduct it at our studios here in Denver."

Harmon stalled. "That may be difficult."

"Your work with StayGreen is important." Marla pressed a little harder. "My viewers will be interested in your commentary. As you know, celebrities have a lot of influence."

Harmon took the bait. "I'll be in the Denver area on June 14 and 15. A StayGreen contingent will be at the One World Festival at Red Rocks Amphitheater. I could work the interview into that trip."

Marla glanced at her calendar. "That's almost four weeks away. I was hoping to do this sooner."

"My schedule is tight," Harmon said without apology.

"Okay, you win. We need to agree upon the compensation for your time."

"There's no need to finance my participation." Harmon was magnanimous. "Your series will increase public exposure for StayGreen. That's enough compensation for me."

"That's very noble." Marla managed not to snicker. "My staff will make the necessary arrangements. I'll send you a transcript of the interview questions in advance."

"I look forward to it," Harmon said before hanging up the phone.

Marla wore a smug smile. One had to walk a fine line when dealing with the supremely arrogant. It was important to feed their egos in moderate doses. If you embellished such people too much, they wouldn't respect you. Marla was good at the game.

* * * *

Rage and panic swirled together, forming a volatile concoction in the EcoFriends meeting room. Howard Anderson's assertions of a traitor incited paranoia steeped in resentment. Demands and accusations flew in abundance.

"Who's the son-of-bitch that leaked?" somebody asked.

"It's got to be a California manager!" Another voice sounded above the fray. "They always resented not being in control!"

"Screw you, man!"

"Everybody swore loyalty. Who broke the oath?"

"You're all hypocrites," Deb Olson said as the meeting became a free-for-all. "There's no loyalty in here. You all want to persecute your brothers and sisters!"

"Order, order!" Anderson pounded the table. "Everybody calm down!"

Gradually, the uproar subsided. Emotions were running high and everybody was on edge. It didn't help that the room was hot and stuffy with no windows.

"I told you we don't know who leaked." Anderson spoke in a calmer tone. "We only know that someone who claimed to be an EcoFriends chapter manager tipped off the FBI with a phone call."

More bedlam erupted at the revelation that the leak had been to the FBI. The thought of the feds initiating an investigation into EcoFriends was terrifying. Anderson and the board members shouted and hammered on the table to regain control of the meeting. Among them, only Zed Cain remained emotionless and seated.

"This isn't a conviction," Anderson said when the group settled down. "The feds won't be able to trace anything. There aren't any records of the money that was skimmed off. Besides, we've already distributed the money in ways that can't be tracked."

One manager said with unbridled anger, "That means the board distributed hundreds of thousands of dollars without consulting us."

"We're charged with those decisions." Anderson's retort was sharp. "It's in the charter."

"You dispersed all that money, but you can't compensate us for travel expenses today?" an enraged person asked. "That's wrong."

"You're all missing the point!" Exasperated, Anderson clenched his fists in the air. "We covered for you. Each one of you is guilty of income tax fraud. Do you understand that?"

A sober air filled the room. The facts were undeniable. Illegal business practices had been rampant. If it could be proven in a court of law, every manager would pay the price.

"I'll put it to you straight." Anderson's tone was unwavering. "As long as we stick together, we'll be fine. But we have to find the source of our leak."

"Did any of our money go to E-Force?" Deb asked. "We all saw you talking about E-Force on the news, Howard."

"No money went to E-Force." Anderson's assertion was calm as every pair of eyes before him narrowed with suspicion.

"Nobody's going to believe that after your interview." Colt broke in with his thick-muscled arms folded across his chest. "The FBI is going to give us an anal exam."

"There's good reason for my actions." Anderson worked to subdue his flaring emotions. Cain got up and walked out of the room. "E-Force has done what we couldn't. They've wounded AmeResort. People are starting to understand that politicians and government policies are enabling crimes against our planet."

Colt refused to back off. "And E-Force is committing its own crimes. Why should we put our heads on the chopping block?"

"Because our funds are drying up." Anderson plopped back down in his chair and leaned back. "Our Judas just cost us a critical source of revenue. EcoFriends is wasting away like a marooned sailor on a desert island. Without groups like E-Force, we can't win."

Deb looked close to tears. "We shouldn't sell our souls."

"The public is fed up with corporate greed and its corrupting effect on the politics and the law. But most people don't believe meaningful changes can ever be implemented. E-Force can change all that. If we do our part to educate the masses, they'll see radical action as a justifiable way to initiate a revolution."

The room was quiet when Anderson paused. People glanced at each other to evaluate the consensus of the group.

"I'm not suggesting direct involvement with E-Force," Anderson proclaimed before a cynic could spark discontent. "Our goal is to promote public understanding and empathy. Make no mistake. All we've worked for is on the line. The longer E-Force remains virulent, the better the odds become for EcoFriends to survive and fight another day. Let's make sure our life's work hasn't been wasted!"

Like the first drops of rain falling in a dry cornfield, a few scattered people clapped their hands slowly. Soon, the applause swept across the entire meeting hall, the intensity growing as if it were a late summer downpour.

"Long live E-Force!"

"Give those corporate bastards hell, E-Force!" another manager said.

Anderson breathed a shallow sigh of relief. He had garnered the support of his organization. There would be no scathing reprimand from Marchotti to endure. Movement at the door caught his eye. It was Cain. The lanky Native American strode behind the table and stopped next to Anderson. Cain bent down and spoke only a few quiet words. The cadence of Anderson's heartbeat increased.

"We have a consensus," Anderson said as the applause

and cheers died down. "Each of you has been granted the trust of your colleagues and the entire EcoFriends organization. That brings us back to the topic of our leak. We have new information. It was a woman."

* * * *

The briefing from Special Agent Price failed to boost the confidence of Phillip Barrett and his executives. Price's assessment of the investigation provided no more insight than one could get by reading the paper or watching the evening news. AmeResort leadership pressed for more information. Like a wily politician in a press conference, Price dodged and parried, providing no real answers to the questions fired at him.

"That's about all the time I have ladies and gentlemen." Price prepared to rise from his seat at the conference table. "I can't provide all the answers you want at this time. Without a doubt, we are making progress in the investigation."

"This meeting hasn't led me to that conclusion." Barrett's dismay was unbridled. "We're getting the run around."

"There's only so much I can reveal." There was a subtle twitch below Price's eye as he glanced around the room. "Surely, none of you wants to compromise the investigation."

"I'm as frustrated as Mr. Barrett," Stephen Chandler said as if he were stepping between two men about to go to blows. "But you've probably been as informative as we can expect, Special Agent Price. At this point, I'm willing to trust that you have the best interests of AmeResort Corporation in mind."

"That's part of my job." Price wore the faintest semblance of a smile.

From the expressions on the board members' faces, it was evident that they shared Chandler's sentiments. Barrett couldn't deny that the FBI agent was professional, articulate, and intelligent. There was no concrete reason to suspect he was an incompetent detective. Still, something nagged at Barrett. As an experienced businessman, he knew one had to delve deeper than appearance and behavior to uncover an individual's true character and motives.

Regardless of instincts, Phillip Barrett was not willing to rely on anyone to look out for the best interests of AmeResort. He was the type of person who created his own destiny. At the Naval Academy, he had excelled and graduated near the top of his class. As a combat pilot in Vietnam, Barrett demonstrated extraordinary skill and bravery. With numerous decorations and promotions, he was on his way to an outstanding career as a naval officer. The real test started when he was shot down.

With a shattered leg from the parachute landing in the jungle, he had been easy prey for the enemy. During two years as a prisoner of war, he was starved and beaten. There had been no medical attention for his injuries. His body deteriorated with abuse, malnutrition, and disease. Somehow Barrett survived to be released as part of a prisoner exchange during the months after Saigon fell.

Slowly, Barrett had regained health and strength at the Navy Medical Center in Portsmouth, Virginia. Unfortunately, doctors told him his traumatized leg would never fully recover. His flying days were past. The naval career ended and Barrett descended into despair and self-pity. His entire life had plummeted downward.

If not for the influence of a young nurse, Barrett would have become a shell of a man. Caroline helped Barrett understand and accept that God's plans are often different from a person's own. With faith, strength, and courage Barrett embarked on a new direction in life. As their lives intertwined, the couple married and moved to Colorado. The foundation of AmeResort Corporation was cast soon afterward. Now the company provided a livelihood for thousands of people. All of them were dependent on sound leadership. Barrett was not about to delegate any part of his responsibilities to an outsider.

"Before you leave, I have one more question." Barrett gripped the head of his cane.

Price's wary eyes narrowed. "Okay, I'll give it a shot."

"Is the FBI looking into Marla Wells?" Barrett asked. "Surely, you're aware of her meddling with E-Force."

Price replied after a brief hesitation. "Ms. Wells is a person of interest. We have no reason to believe she's associated with E-Force."

"The media is doing its best to help E-Force destroy this company. Marla Wells is leading the charge. My intuition tells me you'll solve this case faster if you put heat on her."

"I'm a professional, Mr. Barrett." Price glowered. "I don't need instructions on how to lead my team. Our people have years of experience on countless cases."

There was uncomfortable silence in the conference room. The air of contention was thick and heavy. It seemed the board members hardly dared to breathe.

"Thank you for your time, Special Agent Price," Barrett finally said as he pushed a button on the table. "I know you understand the position of AmeResort."

Barrett realized he would get nowhere by pushing Price harder. Given the man's relative youth and position of seniority, Barrett assumed he possessed considerable ambition. Such a trait was often a detriment.

"It's my job to analyze such things." Price rose to his feet. "I don't doubt that your firm is in a difficult situation. You have my assurance that we're closing in on E-Force."

One of the conference room doors opened. The striking Asian assistant stood waiting.

"Ms. Vonn will show you to the elevator." Barrett didn't offer a handshake.

"People, our problem is more serious than I realized," Barrett said after the FBI agent was gone. "It's time to implement protective measures."

* * * *

Tempers were flaring at the manager's meeting. Colt was certain that the Salem Witch Trials couldn't have been more chilling. With the suddenness of an ocean squall, the forum had degenerated into a hostile volley of accusations and defenses. The handwriting on the wall was plain for Colt to see. The days of EcoFriends were numbered.

A female manager turned on the other five women. "Which one of you ratted on us! Everybody knows I've put my heart and soul into this organization."

"You probably sold us out!"One fiery vixen stepped forward to confront the haughty accuser. "How much is the FBI paying you?"

"Let's make them all take polygraph tests." One board member stepped between the two potential combatants.

"There're better ways to get a confession than that," another person said.

"Enough of this!" Howard Anderson finally took control. "We're tearing ourselves apart. If we're going to survive, we've got to stick together. The truth is going to come out. Whoever is guilty has one last chance for redemption. I'll give you until the end of the week to come to me and confess. Then we'll figure out how to make things right again."

Adjournment was an armistice in an escalating war. At the reprieve, people scattered. Colt looked for Deb, but she was gone. The air in the building seemed poisoned. He hurried outside where he could breathe.

"Damned horde of barbarians," Colt muttered on the sidewalk, shaking his head with disgust for the behavior his colleagues had exhibited. The organization was supposedly founded on trust and loyalty, yet every leader was bent on crucifying one of their own.

Anderson has lost his mind. Colt stormed toward the street. It was insane to prop up the terrorist group E-Force as a means to stabilize EcoFriends. *It's like skydiving without a parachute so you didn't risk getting tangled in the lines. Everybody's following him into the sea like a bunch of damned lemmings.*

Without a doubt, Colt regretted his involvement with EcoFriends. Foolishly, he'd been a complacent passenger in his life and work. It was time to move behind the wheel and take command. EcoFriends was going to be part of the past, not the future.

"Colt, wait for me!" a familiar voice said.

Colt turned to see Deb dart across the street. A car braked hard to avoid running her down. She drew alongside Colt, ignoring the blaring horn as the vehicle resumed course.

"You almost got killed!" Colt was alarmed by Deb's reckless action.

"What does it matter?"

"I don't understand why you would ask that." Colt evaluated his friend's pale sickly appearance. "What's going on? Where've you been?"

"Vomiting in the restroom." Deb's voice wavered. "We need to have that talk."

"Let's get away from the street." Colt grabbed her by the arm. "I'll walk you to your car."

The pair didn't speak during the brisk trip to a parking lot at the end of the block. When they reached Deb's vehicle, she couldn't contain herself any longer.

"Colt, can I trust you?" Deb asked in a hushed tone.

"Of course you can trust me," Colt said, frowning. "What's going on Deb?"

"I'm the one who went to the FBI. I told them about the money laundering."

"So it was you." Colt's pulse quickened. "Holy crap. The meeting must have been a nightmare for you."

"I can't believe what's happening." Tears welled up in Deb's eyes. "When I called the FBI agent, he promised my statements were confidential. I don't know how Anderson found out. Colt, I'm scared."

"It's going to be okay." Colt dabbed a tear from her cheek. "Nobody can pin the leak on you."

"There's more to the story." Deb's eyes were hollow. "All the dirty money went to E-Force."

Colt's heart skipped a beat at the assertion. Deb had uncovered the truth. Months ago, Colt had discovered that tens of thousands were going to E-Force. But he had done nothing. Like a fool, he continued to divert funds from his chapter, knowing the money was being laundered and funneled to E-Force.

"Is that what you told the Feds?" Colt sputtered. "How do you even know that?"

"I overheard a conversation between Anderson and Cain. And, yes, I told the FBI!"

"Deb, keep your voice down." Colt cast a nervous glance around. "Maybe we should talk inside your car."

"I haven't told you the worst part," Deb said after they were seated in the vehicle with the doors shut. "I'm not sure if I should."

"What could be worse?" Colt felt as if he was about to be sentenced by a judge.

"Zed Cain is part of E-Force." Deb was trembling. "If he finds out I know the truth, he'll do something terrible. Colt, I don't know what to do."

"Just calm down." A shiver rippled through Colt's body. "This is bad, but I won't let anyone hurt you. Did you tell the FBI about Cain?"

"Not yet." Deb bit he lip, struggling to retain her composure. "But I'm going to. It's the only way to stop these crimes."

"But you don't know who tipped off Anderson." A light bulb went off in Colt's head. "Maybe he's got somebody inside the FBI."

Deb shook her head with doubt. "We're talking about Howard Anderson, not some foreign government."

"Then how did he find out?" Colt's unease was growing. "That's a serious question, and we've got to find an answer."

"Once Cain and Anderson are behind bars, it won't matter. Then I'll be safe."

"It's not going to be that simple." Colt gripped Deb's shoulder and looked her in the eye. "Something's not right here."

"Then what am I supposed to do?" Deb thumped a fist against the steering wheel. Another tear rolled down her cheek.

Colt suddenly felt conspicuous. "I don't know yet, but we need to continue this conversation at a different time and place."

"Okay, you're right." Deb nodded and reached for a tissue. "I'll call you when I get back to Boise."

They hugged for a few seconds before Colt stepped out onto the pavement. Deb ventured a weak smile and waved goodbye. Feeling lost and lonely, Colt looked after her car until it was swallowed in the traffic.

With eyes cast downward, Colt turned and walked away. Before he traveled twenty paces, a shadow crossed his path. Colt looked up to find Zed Cain standing in front of him. The man's tall figure was imposing. With long black hair, he resembled a fierce Comanche warrior from days of old. Colt stopped dead in his tracks.

"Are you lost?" Cain asked without an ember of warmth.

A chill went down Colt's spine. *Does Cain suspect something? Maybe he overheard the conversation with Deb.*

Colt managed a dismissive air. "I forgot where I parked. My vehicle's over there. See you at the next meeting."

Colt moved past Cain and retreated toward his Land Cruiser. He maintained a casual stride and resisted the urge to cast a backward glance.

Chapter Six
Wednesday, May 16

Sitting at her kitchen table, Deb Olson's heels tapped up and down like pistons. Her jerky movements mimicked those of a nervous squirrel. A parrot sat on a perch in a gage in a sunlit corner. With tired eyes, casualties of another fitful night, Deb glanced at the telephone on the counter. It beckoned, but she resisted. Slurping more coffee, the mug felt heavy in her shaky grasp.

"Go away. We don't want any." At the outburst, Deb jumped as if she had been branded with a hot iron.

"Stop that, Rascal!" She admonished the parrot. "It's not the time."

Turning back to her coffee, a shiver racked Deb's body. Fear was taking its toll. Each tiny noise in the night and every shadow were catalysts of terror. She imagined Cain stalking her, bent on ending her existence. Paranoia was transforming her life into a parade of unbearable hours. It had to end. Standing up, Deb approached the phone with trepidation, as if it were an alien object that had just fallen to earth. But the pull was irresistible. Her breathing quickened as she picked it up and dialed the number written on a scrap of paper.

"FBI," a bored-sounding voice answered. "This is Special Agent Price."

"I'm the one who called you about EcoFriends. We talked a while back."

"Yes, I remember." Price perked up. "You never told me your name."

Deb was unapologetic. "You never told me people would find out I called."

"What happened? Who knows about our conversation?"

"My boss, Howard Anderson, found out. You lied to me! Now everyone in EcoFriends is on a witch hunt. I'm in big trouble!"

"I had nothing to do with this." Price was insistent. "But we've got to take counter-measures. Where are you?"

"I'm at home." Deb winced as if she was about to receive a shot. "I know you can trace the call anyway."

"That's right. Does anybody in EcoFriends know you're the leak?"

"Not yet." Deb decided not to mention Colt. "But Anderson is hell bent on rooting me out. The stakes have gotten higher. Remember that EcoFriends money I told you about? Anderson is using it to fund E-Force. And one of our board members is an E-Force operative. If they find out how much I know...they'll probably try to kill me."

"This is serious." Price sounded concerned. "How long have you known about this?"

"Awhile." Deb fidgeted with her coffee mug. "You've got to do something to help me."

"Have you talked to anybody else about this?"

"No, just you." Stress overwhelmed Deb. "Look, I don't want to keep talking on the phone. I'll give you any information you want, but I need protection."

Price concurred. "You're right. I'll send people out from our field office in Boise. That's close to where you are."

Deb shuddered that the federal agent had deduced her location. "When will they get here?"

"They'll be there this afternoon, Ms. Olson. That's your name, right?"

"That's me." Deb's response was barely audible.

"Our agents will keep you safe." Price's voice was reassuring. "Hang in there."

"I don't have a choice." Deb ended the call. She folded her arms and squeezed her eyes shut in hopes of chasing the nightmare away.

* * * *

Luke Parson took a deep breath and rapped on the door of the publisher's office. A gruff voice beckoned him inside. Saunders didn't smile when Luke ventured into the office.

"Have a seat." Saunders motioned to a chair in front of his desk. "Keyser was in here a little while ago. It sounds like we have a problem."

Keyser had edited Luke's political campaign reform article into an abomination. Luke considered the piece that ended up in *Issue Insight Magazine*, supposedly penned by him, to be a professional embarrassment. His subsequent confrontation with the editor had gotten ugly.

"I want to tell my side of the story." Luke dropped his stout frame into the seat.

"I don't need a recap. How long have you been at *Issue Insight*--about a year?"

"That's pretty close," Luke said, fuming at the thought of Keyser.

"And how many conflicts have you had with editors in that time?"

"I don't know." Luke threw his hands up in frustration. "These things get blown out of--"

"It's a weekly thing for you, Parson. It's going to stop now. This isn't some damned high school newsletter!"

"I know that, but my campaign finance piece was well-researched."

"You didn't follow the guidelines of your assignment."

Luke knew he was pushing his luck. "That doesn't justify Keyser destroying my article without any discussion."

"Keyser did his job. You broadened your scope without authorization."

"But Senator Cardin sits on only one side of the political fence." Luke squirmed.

"Keyser directed you to write a perspective piece about Edward Cardin and his push for campaign finance reform." Saunders' face was flush with anger. "John Harris should have been a footnote."

"But Cardin and Harris are in a huge Senate battle," Luke said. "Harris has rallied up so much opposition that the vote on Cardin's bill is postponed."

"I don't give a crap about any of that!" Saunders looked ready to leap from behind his desk. "*Issue Insight* is in business to sell subscriptions. I know what the readers want and I make sure they get it. If they're not interested in what we print, then we don't have a magazine. Does that make sense to you?"

"Of course." Luke held back his true opinion. He didn't want to lose his job at *Issue Insight*...yet.

Saunders went on. "Senior editors like Keyser are paid to keep this publication marketable. From now on, I expect you to stick to the assigned topic. There's no room for mavericks here."

"I understand." Luke's disappointment grew. He had expected employment at *Issue Insight* to provide opportunities to blossom as a professional. Instead, he was being instructed to compromise his journalistic principles.

"If we have another meeting like this, it'll be our last." Saunders glowered before Luke turned and hurried out the door.

* * * *

Marla Wells' hostile gaze was fixed on the computer screen in her office. For the third time, she tried to send her document to the printer. The process failed again. An error message informed her that there was a problem with the network.

"Those stupid idiots in IT." Marla shoved her chair back and grabbed the phone. "Get up here, Rajah," she said when the head of the station's information technology department answered. "You guys have got my computer system all screwed up again."

The phone rang seconds after Marla slammed it down. It

was another interruption. In her foul mood, Marla was ready to lay into somebody. Her tone was rude when she took the call.

"Marla, this is Ted Rogers from the network offices in New York. Did I call at a bad time?"

Marla was mortified. "Oh, Mr. Rogers. I wasn't expecting you on the phone."

"You sound upset," Rogers said.

"I was just working through a problem." Marla stammered. "Everything will be okay."

"From the quality of your work, I imagine you know how to overcome adversity. Your work is the reason I wanted to talk to you this week."

"That's quite a compliment." Marla's trepidation transformed into pride. "Thank you, Mr. Rogers."

"Please, call me Ted. Marla, I like the way you've handled this E-Force drama."

"I don't know what to say." She was careful to sound humble.

"I want you to come to New York." Rogers got to the point. "I'd like to discuss your career goals. Have you ever thought about working at the network level?"

"I've always just tried to do my job," Marla lied even as she subdued her excitement.

"We think you have a lot of potential. The UMN is expanding its array of news shows. There're opportunities for ambitious seasoned journalists like you."

"I'm very flattered. This is so unexpected."

"We can talk about the details when we meet," Rogers said. "It's short notice, but could you come up on Friday?"

"That's two days from now." Marla was surprised. "I could probably make it work though."

"The UMN will make the arrangements for your trip and cover the expenses. I'm looking forward to our meeting."

When the phone call was over, Marla tingled with excitement. Her career was about to rocket upward at breathtaking speed. It was fate when E-Force had first called. But her ingenuity had pulled the pinnacle of success within reach.

* * * *

John Harris, the senior Senator from Colorado, perused a menu at a restaurant near Capitol Hill in Washington, D.C. He sat alone at the table. He glanced at his watch. Edward Cardin was ten minutes late. It was the same with every meeting between the two adversaries. Harris knew it was a deliberate tactic to irritate him.

"Good afternoon, John." Cardin wheezed without apology as he arrived. "It's been a busy day."

Harris shrugged off the tardy arrival. "You just missed Arnie Tillman."

"What's he up to?" Cardin asked, unable to hide his dismay.

"He's got his finger on the pulse of the people. We just talked shop for awhile."

"I'm sure he had a take on campaign reform." Cardin fished for information.

"You could have asked him about his polling data if you'd been here on time." Harris smiled. "Lunch is on me."

Cardin's face turned red, but he contained his anger. Harris smiled inwardly. He had scored a point and nudged his rival off balance. The old man settled his portly frame into the chair across from Harris and picked up a menu.

"You're busy, so let's get started," Harris said after the waiter took their orders. "What's the agenda for this meeting?"

Harris studied the Senator from New York while waiting for an answer. It was obvious that the aging politician's health was declining. Cardin was in the twilight of his long Senate tenure. The campaign reform bill was probably his last chance to establish a legacy after a career scarred by scandal.

"I'll make a deal with you," Cardin said like he was making a gracious concession to his opponent. "We'll strike the private spending limits, and you call off the dogs. Let's get this bill up for a vote and onto the President's desk. The American people want these reforms."

"That's not a compromise." Harris leaned back and scratched his mostly-bald head. "Private political advertising would still be prohibited. What are you going to spend the money on?"

"It gives your big business interests a way to stay in the game," Cardin said, "but it keeps them on a leash."

"That's not the real issue. I disagree with the entire premise of your bill."

Cardin sputtered after nearly choking on his glass of water. "Your statement is outrageous. These reforms will open politics to the common man."

"You want to put limitations on free speech." Harris didn't waver. "That's unconstitutional."

Cardin's voice raised another decibel. "Regulating funding and advertising is the only way to keep the special interests from corrupting our political system."

"Dictate is a better word than regulate. And it won't stop corruption by dishonest people."

"There'll be an agency to manage all aspects of funding." Cardin's jowls shook. "You know the stipulations."

"And who's going to control this new agency?" Harris leaned forward and leveled a finger at his adversary. "Will it be your party or mine?"

"This is a waste of time!" Cardin was clearly flustered.

Harris knew he was prevailing in the battle. There were enough votes in the Senate to defeat Cardin's bill. If he could keep ratcheting up opposition, the outlook for the elderly Senator was grim.

"Ed, I'm not trying to insult you," Harris said as the

older man struggled to his feet. "This thing just goes against everything I stand for."

"You're blinded by partisan politics." Cardin couldn't contain his fury. "I won't forget this, John."

Harris said as the old man waddled away, "You already ordered lunch."

"Get a doggie bag." Cardin didn't look back.

* * * *

The suspension on the mountain bike reverberated from the relentless descent of the Scout Trail. With teeth rattling, Colt squeezed the brake levers and slid into a sharp switchback turn. At the right instant, he hopped his back tire to the outside, changing direction. A steep path studded with rocks and roots loomed ahead, ready to punish rider and bike alike.

Colt charged forward. With the skill of a trials rider, he negotiated the obstacle course constructed by nature. His movements were instinctive, refined with balance and timing. Reaching a smoother stretch of trail, he cranked hard and the bike shot down toward the next challenge that stood between him and the town.

Victorious, Colt finally entered Glenwood Springs and ground to a halt. After a refreshing shot of water, he pulled a cell phone from his CamelBack. His temporary escape from the consequences of his poor judgment with EcoFriends was over.

"I haven't heard from you, Deb. What's going on?"

"I'm getting the hell out of this mess." Deb's tone was that of a suffering mother, driven to her wits end by a colicky baby.

"You're going to go to the FBI?" Colt imagined himself being marched into a courtroom to face a federal judge.

"I've already talked to someone named Price. He's sending some of his people out."

"Then it's over for EcoFriends." Colt was somber. "We

all have to face the music."

"Colt, it's the only way." Deb's voice broke. "The cat's out of the bag, and I'm scared. I have these terrible premonitions about Cain. In the nightmares, he's coming for me. I can't go on like this."

Colt's mind flashed back to the parking lot encounter with Zed Cain. *Does Cain know about Deb's revelations to me?*

"I understand." Colt felt helpless. "You're doing the right thing. And you've got to protect yourself."

"Price said the FBI will keep me safe." Deb's voice steadied. "When they get here, I'll be fine."

Colt paced next to his bike. "Maybe I should come up there with you."

"You don't need to do that," Deb said in a gentle tone. "You've always been there for me, Colt. I'll make sure the FBI understands you're on my side in this."

"Thanks, Deb." Colt's confidence was bolstered a little. "Just stay safe."

When the call ended, Colt walked over and picked up his bike. As he mounted, he wondered if he could escape the morass of quicksand he found himself in before he sank too deep. He was filled with self-loathing and guilt.

Colt muttered a quiet reprimand to himself. "This is all your fault." He bent over the handlebars and pedaled toward his Land Cruiser, parked several blocks away.

* * * *

Carrie Forde was breathing hard as she leapt across a little stream. Her running shoes kicked up sand when she landed and charged after her loping shepherd-mix mutt. This was the farthest she and Bandit had ever advanced into the canyon that was carved into the ancient rock of the Uncompahgre Plateau. The rock walls contrasted with the green desert plants, adorned with spring flowers.

After a few hundred more yards of climbing, Carrie decided she had come far enough. There was nobody around to invade her space...to see her weakness.

Carrie sat down on a boulder worn smooth by water flowing eons ago. She placed her sweaty face in her hands and cried. The tears flowed silently. The evening wind ebbed. Bandit trotted back and sat near her feet. His gaze suggested that he shared her pain.

It was one of those rare days when Carrie felt hopeless. Tough and independent, she was used to dealing with problems. But sometimes she just felt alone. The self-built wall around her kept the painful past at bay, but it was also a prison that prevented striking out anew and forging fresh relationships. Shame goaded Carrie to continue paying penance, keeping the barricades erected. Some days they were close to crumbling.

For several minutes, Carrie let her emotions pour out. "You're so weak!" She boiled with self-deprecating anger. It was as if the tears inside had sublimed into pressurized steam. Leaping to her feet, Carrie picked up a rock and hurled it at a cliff. Crack! The impact echoed off the canyon walls.

When Carrie sat back down, her tumultuous feelings flowed as wild as a mountain stream. Likewise, they were slow to recede. The beauty of her surroundings helped ignite the embers of hope. It was a reminder that God's creation was full of wonderful things that transcended the darkest hours of personal crisis. In reality, problems were fleeting, and Carrie asserted that her faith would be the key to perseverance.

You've got to live day by day, minute by minute, she affirmed, standing up.

When Carrie glanced at Bandit, he was sniffing at a paw print. It was from a mountain lion...a large one. The big cats started hunting at dusk. With unease, she looked up and down the canyon. The waning light revealed nothing. She was glad she had the dog along.

"Let's go, Bandit." Carrie started the retreat toward the mouth of the canyon. "We've still got a lot to live for."

Her cadence was broken by frequent anxious glances over her shoulder.

* * * *

The vintage Dodge Charger's engine rumbled. Trigger Ruddock loved the sound of a predator. It was ominous, emanating power. The mechanical vibrations of the muscle car, racing along a rural road, transformed the passenger seat into a massage chair. The experience tempered Ruddock's impatience. Gravel crunched under the wide tires when the vehicle veered off the road onto a driveway. The name Olson was painted on the side of a metal mailbox.

A hundred yards from the pavement, Cain parked near a weather-beaten barn. The structure appeared on the verge of collapse. Ruddock lifted his dark glasses and studied the house. It was a sturdy looking place surrounded by a picket fence. A contingent of pinion and juniper trees occupied the rolling ground behind the building.

"It looks pretty quiet." Ruddock turned to Cain. The fresh haircut and professional attire made him snicker. "That suit is you. You look like the most tight-ass FBI agent ever."

Cain didn't bother with a response. "Go to the front door. I'll take the back."

Wearing sunglasses, the two men got out of the car and straightened their suit coats. Ruddock tugged at his tie. "We could be the freaking Beatles in '62."

As he neared the dwelling, a breeze carried the odor of cut grass and fresh-turned earth to Ruddock's nostrils. The flower beds were tilled and awaiting planting. A mower was on the front lawn. When he placed his hand near the machine, heat radiated from the engine.

"Little Debbie's home." A cruel smile creased

Ruddock's face.

Wood planks groaned and creaked when he ascended the steps and strode across the porch. Ruddock pushed the doorbell and listened. Reverberating chimes were followed by silence. When he rapped on the door, the result was the same. Eyeing the knob, Ruddock resisted the temptation to force his way inside.

With his footsteps echoing off the overhanging roof, Ruddock stalked to the end of the porch. Glancing in the windows, he saw no sign of Deb Olson. Peering around the corner of the house, he noted a shed tucked in the trees. It was about the size of a single-car garage. A window on the building was bronzed by the low-hanging sun. The door was open, swinging gently in the evening draft.

"Are you in there, Little Debbie?" Ruddock whispered. The pistol in his shoulder holster suddenly seemed to strain against the confines of the suit coat.

Sounds of movement escaped the little building as Ruddock advanced. Cain materialized off to his side. The leader's harsh expression demanded an explanation for the change in tactics. Without a verbal response, the lean subordinate motioned toward the open door. Cain nodded, giving notice to proceed.

Ruddock called out. "Is anybody in there? We're with the FBI."

"Go away! Nobody's home," a cracked voice said. The scratching in the shed didn't abate.

"Don't be alarmed." Ruddock's hand was on his weapon. He eased closer to the entrance. "We're here to help you."

"Go away. We don't want any." The doorway remained vacant.

Ruddock drew his gun and leapt into the shed. Deb Olson wasn't among the clutter of lawn furniture, garden tools, and flower pots. Frantic fluttering of wings pulled his eyes and aim to the birdcage on a workbench below the window. The incarcerated parrot settled back onto the perch and faced the muzzle of the pistol.

The bird cackled, "Nobody's home."

Ruddock resisted the urge to pull the trigger and darted back outside. "It's a freaking bird!"

An engine came to life with the squealing of a serpentine belt. Cain and Ruddock whipped around. It was in the old barn.

"Son-of-a bitch!" Ruddock cursed as the pair sprinted to prevent their quarry from escaping.

A loud crash was accented by splintering wood. By the time the would-be assassins reached the driveway, Deb Olson's Subaru was tearing away. Gravel sprayed until the tires screeched on the asphalt of the road. A piece of the wrecked barn door careened off the vehicle and cartwheeled into the weeds.

"Damn it!" Ruddock leapt into the Dodge Charger and slammed the door. "She's getting away."

Without a spoken word, Cain jammed the accelerator to the floorboard. The tires ripped across splintered boards, flinging one into the empty space of the barn.

* * * *

There were two sharp raps on Price's office door. Before he could bark an annoyed response, Malcolm Hill burst into the room.

"What is it?" Price asked from his desk.

"You wanted me to keep tabs on Marla Wells." Hill's breath came in sharp gasps. "She's taking a little trip to New York."

"Denver shopping doesn't cut it anymore?"

"She's got a meeting set at the UMN offices." Hill raised an eyebrow. "Her contact is Ted Rogers."

Price scoffed. "Let me guess. Rogers wants to make her part of his team."

"That's a pretty good bet." Hill nodded. "I expect Marla Wells will jump at a promotion to the network."

"How could she refuse?" Price had a vile taste in his mouth. "She's looking to make the big time. That means E-Force is going national."

"We're in for trouble. She could become a real problem."

"You let me worry about Marla Wells. I know how to deal with her. Besides, there's been a positive development."

"What are you talking about?" Hill lowered his voice and stepped closer to Price's desk.

"The EcoFriends informant called again." Price leaned back in his chair and pressed the palms of his hands together.

"Did she tell anything new?"

"EcoFriends is linked to E-Force." Price couldn't resist a smug smile. "She wouldn't say more over the phone, but we got her name and location."

Hill made a fist and drove it into his other hand. "That's the break we needed."

* * * *

Deb Olson didn't apply the brakes until she was streaking into the curve. The car threatened to launch off the road. It took all her strength to cling to the steering wheel. Beyond the windshield, the mangled hood vibrated and threatened to tear loose from the tenacious grip of the safety latch. The vehicle held together and Deb escaped from the bend unscathed.

When Deb hit the gas, the Subaru resumed the reckless pace. Her speed on the undulating ribbon of pavement was double the limit posted on the steel sign that flashed past. But fear pushed her to flee faster...screaming for abandonment of the last shreds of reason.

Deb moaned. "My God, this can't be happening. I don't even have my cell phone."

Only luck had placed Deb in the barn, car key in her jeans pocket, a moment before the black car arrived. Her dash for survival was spontaneous, fueled by primal fear. There were only a few more miles until the intersection with a busier road that led into the city. She had to get to a police station, a grocery store, a bowling alley...anyplace where there was a phone.

"I've got to call Price." A tear streaked across Deb's face. "If his men don't stop Cain, I'm dead."

A glance in the rearview mirror sent icy fingers down her spine. The black demon car was behind her. Deb's speedometer needle refused to rise. "Come on, come on," she begged.

A formula racer couldn't have negotiated the curves better than Cain. And through each straight stretch, the horsepower under the hood of the vintage car propelled it forward like a rocket. Deb was no different than a swimmer being chased by a shark. It was hopeless. The Dodge Charger drew closer to the Subaru.

Deb screamed when Cain and his cohort were only a few feet from the rear of her car. "Leave me alone!"

The Charger drifted left and shot forward. Deb reacted too slowly to block the opening. The roaring vehicle filled the gap and pulled alongside the fleeing wagon. She kept a two-handed death grip on the steering wheel, but tore her eyes from the road to chance a glance to her left. The smoked glass of the passenger window slid down as if it were a guillotine. Cain's henchman was brandishing a pistol. He leaned toward the opening, the hair on his head thrashing in the wind.

In a flush of panic, Deb stepped on the brake pedal. The bigger car instantly followed suit and stayed abreast of the Subaru. One side of the road dropped into a rocky ravine, terrain carved over eons by the creek far below. A mountainside adorned with trees and brush bordered the other edge of the pavement. There was nowhere to go. She was a gazelle, culled from the herd by a cheetah. In a desperate bid for life, she stomped on the accelerator again. The Charger was as inescapable as a shadow. Tears clouded Deb's vision. The paint of the dark car was nearly scraping against the metallic blue tint of her fleeing vehicle.

"Get away from me!"

Ruddock sneered and beckoned her to come closer. Cain turned his head. For a brief second, Deb's gaze locked with that of a killer. With the dark glasses, his expression revealed only indifference, an exterminator dealing with an insect.

The road veered left, and Cain's car pushed to the outside of the turn. The vehicle checked against the Subaru, slamming the smaller car. The wheels on the right side of the wagon lurched from the pavement. For a fraction of a second, the tires clawed at the small semblance of a gravel shoulder. Deb was helpless to prevent the little car from pitching sideways and careening onto a path to oblivion.

Deb's drawn out screech was hardly human when her Subaru twisted into the air. In mid-trajectory the launched vehicle turned upside down. At the first impact on the rocks, smashing steel and exploding glass silenced her horrified cries. The crumpled roof snapped her neck the way a camper would break a stick before tossing it in a campfire.

On the descent to the bottom of the ravine, the coffin on twisted axles bounced and tumbled. Momentum increased all the way to the last violent smash against a giant boulder next to the cascading creek.

A flame burst from the concoction of fuel and automotive fluids. In seconds, a raging blaze eagerly consumed the twisted wreckage. On the road, the Charger departed the scene of carnage at a leisurely pace.

Chapter Seven
Friday, May 18

The limousine pulled up to the curb at the Star Theater in New York. A crowd pressed against barricades that bordered the walkway to doors under the marquee. Uniformed police officers kept the energized throng from spilling into the pathway as people jostled for better vantage points. A rising crescendo of excited cries penetrated the smoked glass windows.

A barrage of camera flashes was triggered when Yuri Zharikov opened the front passenger door of the limo. On the sidewalk, he pulled his suit coat tighter over his broad chest. He kept an eye on the masses while striding to the rear door of the vehicle. The handle was far below his towering waistline. Bending down to grab it, his face came near the window. Zharikov allowed himself an instant to admire the reflection of his thick shock of red hair.

Behind Zharikov's image, raucous fans and chattering television commentators carried on. The atmosphere reminded him of a film premier rather than a humanitarian awards ceremony. It was still business as usual for the big bodyguard. He verified that the cops still maintained a secure corridor before swinging the car door open.

"It's all clear, Mr. Marchotti," Zharikov said in his thick Russian accent before moving aside.

Darius Marchotti, founder of the United Media Network, stepped out into the limelight. In his mid-sixties, Marchotti had robust white hair and a matching mustache. His dark eyes seemed to probe one's innermost thoughts. As always, the founder and CEO of the United Media Network projected a presence of power. He acknowledged the jubilant spectators with a regal nod of his head.

Marchotti turned to a beautiful blond who emerged from the limo. "Welcome to the big time, my dear."

Thirty-five years younger than he, the gorgeous young woman was a trophy of success. She beamed and clasped the media mogul's arm.

Zharikov closed the limo door, and Marchotti escorted his stunning companion up the strip of red carpet. Rapid-fire camera flashes were like strobe lights. Treading two steps behind the couple, Zharikov remained on alert, ready to provide lethal force in an instant. They passed a contingent of security guards at the entrance to the grand building. The big Russian was relieved when the doors shut behind them, muffling the noise from the crowd.

* * * *

Rain clouds had given way to the glorious Colorado sunshine. The sun sunk low on the horizon west of Grand Junction, setting the desert sky on fire with myriad shades of red, orange, and gold. The glow radiated off the spires and cliffs of the Colorado National Monument to the southwest. North of the Grand Valley, the Book Cliffs were bathed in the day's last rays of sunlight.

The astounding display barely registered with Colt Kelley. He stood at a pay phone, the receiver pressed against his ear. For several minutes he had been on hold.

A voice finally answered. "This is Special Agent Price."

"Are you the one who Deb Olson contacted?" Colt asked.

"Who are you?"

"I was her friend." Colt simmered with anger. "She told me she talked to someone with the FBI named Price."

"What else did she say?" Price sounded cold and suspicious.

"That doesn't matter. Deb's dead and I don't think it was an accident."

"Deb Olson's death was a terrible tragedy. But I'm not going to discuss the incident with an anonymous caller.

What's your name?"

Colt was unwilling to provide identification. "She told me about the criminal activity she'd uncovered at EcoFriends. Deb wanted to put a stop to it, but somebody in the group got wind of her revelation to you guys at the FBI."

"Ms. Olson wanted to provide information about illicit activities in EcoFriends. I assume you're wrapped up in the scandal too."

Colt's temper flared, but he ignored the accusation. "Did you take her seriously? Or did you just leave her out there to be slaughtered?"

"My agents were on their way to see her when the accident occurred." Price's reply was acidic.

"You know her death was no accident!" Colt wished he could grab Price by the collar and slam him against the wall.

"I don't know that." Price's tone was hard. "And I don't know your name. We're not going any further until I do."

Colt refused to take the bait. "Maybe later. I'll contact you another time."

Feeling tremendous frustration, Colt banged the grimy phone onto the hanger. Part of him wanted to cooperate with Price to help solve the mystery of Deb's death. But some sixth sense made him wary. It was too early to know whom to trust. Somehow, Anderson and Cain had learned about Deb's intentions. Without caution, Colt was afraid his fate would resemble Deb's.

Colt decided it wasn't a good idea to loiter near the gas station there he'd called. Hurrying to his Land Cruiser, he started the engine and roared away.

A few minutes later, Colt rolled into the parking lot at the Natural High Rock Gym and Fitness Club. He sat staring at the building for a while. Tears welled up in his eyes. His friend, Deb, a genuinely good person, was gone. It was another example of the inequities of the world.

With a shirtsleeve, Colt wiped the wet streak from his cheek. "Whoever killed her is going to taste justice." He uttered a declaration of war.

Colt's tumultuous emotions gradually ebbed. At the reprieve, the stubborn demands of his psyche resurfaced. Desperate for a brief escape from pain and confusion, it had pushed him toward the gym tonight. Colt didn't understand the impulse, but an unseen presence commanded him to stop resisting.

Colt's reluctance crumbled. Stewing in misery and hate wasn't going to bring Deb back. And it was not going to solve the crime of her death. He snatched his gym bag and strode toward the front entrance.

* * * *

Marla Wells swigged the last of the champagne in her glass and reveled in the comfort of the limousine. She imagined that such luxuries would soon be commonplace in her life.

"I have to thank you again for dinner, Ted." Marla smiled. "The food and company were exquisite."

"I'm glad you enjoyed it," Rogers said, running a hand through his gray-flecked hair. "My colleagues and I were glad to have the chance to visit with you."

"Everybody has made me feel like a rock star." Marla struggled to appear humble.

"I think your work is exemplary. The other executives share that sentiment."

Marla kept her breathing even. "That's very encouraging."

"There are lots of ambitious journalists out there, but most of them don't have the talent we're looking for. You stand out above your peers, Marla."

Pride bubbled in her breast. "I hardly know what to say."

"Maybe you'll find inspiration at the CCH awards." Rogers chuckled. "We've arrived at the theater."

The Common Cause for Humanity awards was a star-studded event dedicated to recognizing the humanitarian achievements of numerous celebrities. It was something Marla had only watched on television.

"It's amazing to be here and experience this!"

"Life at the top has its perks." Rogers winked as the chauffeur opened the door.

Marla and Rogers crossed the sidewalk from the car to the Star Theater. They heard the distant cries of the crowd conglomerated around the celebrity entrance. When they entered the lobby, Rogers handed Marla her ticket.

"I need to make a quick stop at the ladies room before the show starts."

"Understood." Rogers saluted. "We'll rendezvous here."

A row of well-dressed women adorned with sparkling jewelry lined the marble vanity. Makeup was dabbed on with the deft darting movements of an artist. Scents from a plethora of perfumes swirled in a concoction that was somewhere between obnoxious and intoxicating. There was flittering talk about high-profile people, fashionable parties, expensive homes, and exotic trips.

Marla was intrigued by the haughty conversations. The socialite women weren't all that impressive on their own merit, but Marla coveted their lifestyle, their membership in high-society circles. She was determined to do more than join the ranks of the chattering elitists. In a matter of months, maybe weeks, Marla expected to become one of the people the wealthy trend–setters boasted about knowing.

The crowd in front of the mirror waned as the starting time of the awards ceremony approached. Glancing at her reflection one last time, Marla was pleased. *Knock 'em dead, honey.* She whirled around and strutted out to the lobby.

* * * *

The Star Theater was a fabulous ultramodern facility.

The main performance hall was cavernous. Its curved walls were dramatic, yet graceful. Huge arches in the ceiling stepped upward and outward from the broad stage, producing profound acoustics. A sea of reclining seats filled the sloping main floor. Around the perimeter, three levels of fantastically contorted balconies provided sweeping views. It was a venue that formed lasting impressions on audiences.

Excitement crackled in the air when the lights dimmed. A round of thundering applause followed the introduction of the host for the evening. Music blared as Gregory Parker, a popular comedian and actor, ambled out onto the stage. His fast-paced style of comic entertainment was always a hit.

Luke Parson was trying to get to his seat when Parker's antics began. His frame was too stocky to slip unobtrusively through the narrow corridor between kneecaps and seatbacks. Struggling through semi-darkness, Luke stepped on feet and stumbled over legs. Cast into the role of inconsiderate bumbling fool, he lost count of his muttered apologies.

The theater reverberated with laughter when Luke finally settled into his chair. Parker wasted no time providing a raucous kickoff for the ceremony. The audience roared with approval.

The humor didn't strike a chord with Luke. Of course he hadn't shown up at the CCH awards for the entertainment value. His attendance strictly stemmed from the research needs of his new assignment for *Issue Insight Magazine*. It was to be a feature article on philanthropy and humanitarianism, with special highlights on movers and shakers like Darius Marchotti. The CCH awards show was a gala full of films and testimonials about the supposedly selfless deeds of a handful of celebrity honorees.

Luke scoffed in silence. The people who truly dedicate their lives to humanitarian causes would never be recognized. It wasn't fair, but it was reality.

On stage, Parker announced the name of the first award

recipient. Television cameras panned in on the woman as she rose to acknowledge the audience ovation. The applause died down as attention turned to the huge movie screen at the back of the stage. A short documentary film would chronicle her achievements. With limited interest, Luke watched the film begin. For now, it was business as usual...within the dictated boundaries.

* * * *

Friday evenings were always busy at the Natural High Rock Gym and Fitness Club. Climbers of all levels of ability attached themselves to ropes and tested their skills on a dizzying array of climbing routes. As a member of the Natural High, Carrie Forde spent a fair amount of time in the gym. She was acquainted with most of the employees.

A college-aged kid at the reception counter shouted, "Carrie, you've got a phone call!"

When Carrie trotted over and took the phone, she heard her climbing partner Jocelyn's voice.

"I've got to blow off climbing tonight." Jocelyn sounded harried.

"Is everything okay?" Carrie frowned.

Jocelyn fumed. "My boss is making me work tonight. Some new chick didn't show up, and I have to cover the shift."

While Jocelyn digressed into the details of her convenience store drama, a young man with blond hair entered the gym. He was handsome with broad shoulders and a trim waistline. *Looks like the actor, Sam Worthington.*

At last, Carrie ended the phone conversation with her talkative friend. She handed the phone back to the college kid at the counter. He'd barely started a brief orientation for the new guy when the phone rang again. On cue, several people trudged into the gym and laid siege to the counter.

"Carrie, can you do me a favor and give this gentleman

James D. Kellogg

the nickel tour?" The young employee looked ready to quit. "This place is crazy right now!"

"I can spare a few minutes." Carrie turned toward the newcomer.

The young man stepped forward with a hint of uncertainty. But when Carrie looked into his gray-blue eyes, she detected honesty and strength.

"I'm Carrie Forde." She thrust her right hand forward.

"Colt Kelley." The visitor accepted her handshake with a smile. "It's nice to meet you."

"Do you want the express tour or the extended version?" Carrie asked with a raised eyebrow.

Colt shrugged his shoulders. "I'm sure you'd rather be climbing with your friends instead of acting as my tour guide."

"You don't know anyone here, do you?"

"How'd you guess?" Colt's grin was disarming.

"I can read minds."

She could tell Colt was impressed as his gaze swept around the rock gym. The main part of the facility seemed large enough to serve as a commercial jet hangar. Most walls jutted at crazy angles that formed overhangs or slopes. A few sections were vertical. Wall panels were covered with simulated rock fascia, pierced by a grid of threaded holes. They provided the means to bolt on rock handholds and footholds.

"I was hoping to meet a climbing partner," Colt said. "It'd be nice to try a few lead routes tonight."

Climbers were always attached to the end of a safety rope. For the rope to arrest a fall, the climber needed a partner to provide a belay from the base of the wall. It was a critical component of climbing safety.

When a climber was top-roping, the rope extended from the climber's harness to an anchor point at the top of the route, and then down to the belayer. Equipped with a friction device, the belayer constantly pulled the rope through the

100

anchor point in order to take up slack as the climber moved upward.

Lead climbing was more complicated. In this case, the climber moved upward with the rope trailing behind. The belayer had to constantly feed out rope to allow the climber to advance. As the climber ascended the route, he would fasten the rope into periodic anchor points which could check a potential fall. With either type of climbing, the belayer had to be constantly on alert. But in a lead-climbing situation, the distance of the potential fall was much greater, thus requiring a more skilled belayer.

"Maybe it's your lucky day." Carrie raised an eyebrow. "My climbing partner bailed. Want to give it a whirl?"

"That sounds great," Colt said eagerly.

Colt loped off to the locker room to change clothes, leaving Carrie with swirling feelings. It was unfamiliar territory. The wall around her heart had been tall and sturdy for so long. Such a structure not only kept others at a distance, but blocked from view the sights of what she was missing. Suddenly that barricade resembled a windshield struck by a stone with a spreading spider web of cracks. After only a few moments, Colt drew her inexplicably. She had a premonition that something special could unfold with him. Was she ready to let her newly transparent barrier shatter?

* * * *

Gregory Parker adopted a more serious tone as he spoke from behind the podium on the huge stage of the Star Theater. After an evening with a plethora of awards, the time had arrived to announce the winner of the prestigious Global Giving Award. It was presented annually to the person who, in the view of Common Cause for Humanity, had done the most to improve the human condition around the globe. The CCH was a powerful conglomeration of environmental and humanitarian groups. The decrees it issued were accepted as truth.

"This year's recipient has worked tirelessly to improve the condition of disadvantaged people all over the world," Parker said. "While doing this, he has focused increasing attention on the state of the natural environment. His efforts are nothing less than inspiring. On behalf of the Common Cause for Humanity, I'm honored to present the Global Giving Award to Mr. Darius Marchotti!"

A crescendo of applause erupted as Darius Marchotti rose from his front row seat. He turned and bowed to acknowledge the ovation. The media mogul wore an appreciative smile during his ambling trek to the stage.

Parker hurried to meet Marchotti at the top of the stairs. After a hearty handshake, they approached the podium together. A woman in a long dress delivered an impressive plaque to the master of ceremonies. In turn, he presented the plaque to Marchotti. The crowd cheered and applauded with renewed fervor.

Marchotti spoke when he could be heard. "This award is a great honor. It's good to know people support the causes I've adopted."

Parker said, "His documentary film is longer than the others!"

A ripple of laughter rolled through the audience. Marchotti knew he was adored. Why not? He was a mega successful businessman who doubled as a benevolent celebrity. His opinions were treated as gospel. And soon everyone would hang on every word of his acceptance speech. It was all so easy.

Decades earlier, Marchotti had used little more than confidence to assemble the capital to purchase a small radio station. He integrated new technology, contracted with cutting-edge personalities, and implemented new programming formats. The station's advertising sales went through the roof, and the young entrepreneur invested the profits in television stations. The United Media Network was born. As the holdings of the company grew, Marchotti forged partnerships with fledgling cellular phone service providers, satellite television companies, and Internet businesses. The United Media Network financed construction of the high-tech infrastructure required by these new entities. As the owner of the information superhighway, the power and wealth of the UMN and Darius Marchotti were unsurpassed.

"For many years, I've worked to create humanitarian centers around the world." Marchotti stood like a fiery preacher behind the pulpit. "We pay entire villages to farm, make clothes, create traditional artwork, and protect the natural habitat. While they work to improve the world, we care for and educate their children. In effect, we eliminate the need for disadvantaged people to follow in the destructive footsteps of industrialized nations."

The tycoon had to pause while another round of cheers and applause went up. His congregation was elated, putty in his hands.

"There's no need for those who aren't empowered to fend for themselves " Marchotti uttered his decree with an arching wave of his hand. "We have the ability to provide for them. I won't rest until people in every part of the globe can rely on the sustainable practices of my centers. But my efforts alone won't make this dream a reality. To be successful, we need the moral and financial support of every person here tonight."

There was another ovation. Marchotti could tell his followers were in lockstep with his plan. The world waited for him, and soon it would be his.

"I'm deeply honored to be recognized by the Common Cause for Humanity. The Global Giving Award affirms that we are on the right path. Someday, the entire industrialized world will join our campaign to improve the lives of everyone in the human family. I accept this award in honor of my anonymous supporters, people who have sacrificed so much for the cause. Thank you very much."

People leapt from their seats in a passionate standing ovation. Tears of emotion streaked down the cheeks of many women. Some of the men cried too. Darius Marchotti beamed and basked in his glory.

* * * *

The next handhold looked uninvitingly small. Colt's fingers and forearms burned in protest. Using good sport climbing technique, he shifted his bodyweight to his feet and one hand. The strategy allowed him to release and relax his right arm. The brief reprieve was vital to preserve the stamina needed to grip the tiny hold. He would have to maintain a grasp long enough to make the next clip with his left hand. On the ground, Carrie played out just enough rope for Colt to reach the carabiner dangling from the overhanging wall.

Only a couple moves stood between Colt and the end of the climb. His gas gauge hovered on empty. After ascending a number of punishing routes throughout the evening, it was painfully clear that his muscles weren't conditioned to the rigors of climbing. The route was difficult, and he was facing the crux: the most difficult part of the climb. Success would hinge on precise movements and sheer determination.

With his left hand giving out, Colt knew there was not a second to waste. His feet were jammed against the holds as he twisted and reached with his right. When his fingers clamped onto the protrusion above, he discovered the hold was too small to provide salvation. There was no turning back. Adrenaline surged through Colt's body as his left hand started slipping. Colt struggled to reposition his feet. The carabiner was just inches above of him, but the holds were too small for his faltering fingers.

Desperate to make the clip, Colt released his left hand

and flailed for the rope. With the suddenness of a broken shoelace, his right hand was torn from the precarious pinchhold. He plunged downward until the rope tied to his climbing harness went taught. Instead of a jolting halt, his descent was curtailed progressively until there was a gentle rebound. When the experience was over, Colt dangled in mid-air. He looked down to see Carrie dangling from the rope by her belay device. She had provided a perfect dynamic belay, serving as a moving counterweight.

"Nice belay!" Colt was impressed.

"Thanks." Carrie grinned. "Good effort up there. You kept at it."

"Yeah. I climb like a turtle. You scampered up there like a monkey."

Carrie's graceful ascents of an assortment of difficult climbing routes were a testament to her skill and athleticism. During interludes of conversation, Colt had discovered that she was also smart and insightful. He was enraptured.

"You calling me a monkey?" Carrie feigned outrage.

"That's the way you climb. You look more like Catwoman." In a sport tank top and spandex shorts, her muscular feminine physique was impossible not to notice.

"Flattery will get you nowhere, tough guy." Carrie laughed as she rappelled down the rope. When her feet hit the mat, she lowered Colt with proficient skill.

Colt plopped down and gingerly removed his climbing shoes. "My feet feel like I've been playing soccer with a bowling ball." He winced with pain.

"Looks like you're done for the night."

"The odds of a rapid recovery are slim to none."

"I've had enough too." Carrie unclipped from the rope. "You want to go grab a late dinner?"

"You really are psychic. I've been thinking about food for the last half hour."

Colt tingled with excitement when he hurried to shower and change clothes. Life was full of unexpected changes.

Thank God that this time it's good.

* * * *

"Darius Marchotti is a man of such vision and purpose," Marla said during the mass exodus from the Star Theater. "He's building a Utopian network."

Rogers nodded in agreement. "Mr. Marchotti is passionate about using his wealth to better the world."

"As a journalist, I want to help spread his message," Marla said.

"I'm glad you mentioned your work," Rogers said as they moved into the crowded lobby. "The first segment of your environmental vigilantism series was interesting. But there's room for improvement."

"The pilot segment is always tough." Her cheeks pinkened with embarrassment. "Subsequent broadcasts will be better."

"It's not your work that needs enhancement." Rogers stopped and locked eyes with her. "The viewing audience needs to be much larger. You're in the unique position of knowing what pushes E-Force and others to act as vigilantes."

"Are you saying you want to syndicate my series for broadcast on other stations?" Marla asked cautiously.

"We want to make it a network series. You would be the host, working at our studios here in New York."

"This is all happening so fast," Marla said, exhilaration singing in her veins.

"Think about it overnight." Rogers' pitch softened a bit. "If you decide to accept our offer, I'll have a contract drafted by the end of your studio tour tomorrow."

* * * *

Fresh from a boring interview with one of the CCH

honorees, Luke Parson searched for another celebrity. A group of people with media credentials rushed past. Several of them mentioned Marchotti. Luke wanted a shot at asking the media mogul a question. He whirled around to follow his peers and collided with a woman who was headed in the opposite direction. The impact was not gentle.

Luke grabbed her by the arm to keep her from falling. "I'm terribly sorry." He was mortified. "Are you okay?"

The woman shoved him away and glared. "You need to watch where you're going!"

That press pass isn't a license for recklessness." Her male companion pushed past.

The woman looked familiar. Through the glass facade of the building, he watched the couple strut to a waiting limousine. When the chauffeur opened the door, Luke realized she was Marla Wells from Channel 4 in Denver.

"What are you doing here if you're not part of the media brigade?" Luke asked under his breath.

Dismissing the incident, Luke turned and chased down the media cluster hounding Marchotti's entourage. A cacophony of voices called out with questions. Luke jockeyed for a favorable position, hoping to ask Marchotti about the risk of fostering dependent cultures with his humanitarian centers.

Security personnel and Marchotti's bodyguards kept the media at bay. The beautiful young woman at Marchotti's side looked annoyed and impatient. Raising a hand, the founder of the UMN shook his head emphatically.

"I don't have time to field questions," Marchotti said to the gathering when the din ebbed. "Those with excess must provide for those who have little or nothing. Private donations and government grants will help our centers spread sustainability around the world. Thank you for your understanding."

Shouts and questions from the press resumed, but security cleared a path for Marchotti and his companion.

Yuri Zharikov shoved an encroaching reporter, sending him to the floor. The group escaped from the building, fleeing for the waiting car. Uniformed security guards blocked a potential pursuit from the band of reporters and photographers.

Luke's intuition whispered frantically to him as he trudged away. With a growing segment of the world dependent on Marchotti's organization, Luke wasn't convinced that the billionaire benefactor had their best interests in mind. *What if Marchotti was really after power?* The thought was scary…maybe even crazy.

* * * *

"I'll get that," Carrie protested when Colt snatched up the bill left by the waitress. "It was my idea to come here."

"The least I can do is pay for dinner," Colt said cheerfully. "It's compensation for your services as a climbing guide and conversationalist."

"At least let me pay for half."

Colt smiled. "I wouldn't dream of charging you to spend time with me."

"So I get a discount?" Carrie's eyes sparkled with the concession.

During dinner, the conversation had flowed warm and plentiful. A person who rarely shared his personal thoughts and desires, Colt felt willing to reveal them all to Carrie.

"I've had a great time tonight," Colt said. "I'm really glad we met."

Carrie concurred with a warm smile. "I've had fun too. With my schedule at the clinic and everything, I've just become so regimented. This was a welcome change."

"Maybe I'm a bad influence. Hopefully, your new lack of discipline doesn't torpedo your physical therapy practice."

Carrie's laugh highlighted every aspect of her beauty. Colt was incredulous that he wasn't a terrified bumbling fool. It seemed ridiculous, but something assured him that she was the one.

Colt blurted out his thoughts. "Carrie, I'd like to spend time with you again soon."

"I think that would be nice. I have to work at the clinic tomorrow, but we could do something on Sunday after church."

"That sounds great." Enthusiasm flowed through him.

The server returned to the table with Colt's change. While he separated part of it to leave a tip, Carrie glanced at a nearby television. The restaurant was a sports-oriented franchise, but a precursor to an eleven o'clock newscast invaded the screen.

"United Media Network founder, Darius Marchotti, wins the Global Giving Award at the Common Cause for Humanity Awards in New York," the anchor said. "Tune in at eleven for the full story along with sports and weather."

"Darius Marchotti is full of garbage," Carrie muttered.

"What did you say?" Colt stuffed his wallet back in a pocket.

"Darius Marchotti is promoting communes that make people dependent on him." Carrie pointed to the T.V. "His fan club just gave him an award for it. If Marchotti really wants to help the Third World, he should promote independence and personal accountability."

"I know who Darius Marchotti is, but not much more," Colt replied with a shrug. "I guess I should pay more attention."

"Don't expect to get the real story from the media. His company, the United Media Network, owns most of it. I don't want to think about that, though. It would be a shame to end the evening on a bad note."

Colt and Carrie rose from the booth and headed for the door. Out on the sidewalk, the couple stood facing each other for an awkward moment. Both hesitated, unsure of how to part for the night.

"I'll walk you to your vehicle," Colt suggested. "We can say goodnight there."

Carrie agreed with a mischievous grin. Together, they trotted across the parking lot.

Chapter Eight

Saturday, June 2

The house was a small one-story structure with a covered front porch and a garage. A trio of ash trees stood like sentries between the lawn and the dwelling. Leaves rustled in a gentle breeze, filtering the morning sunlight before it reached the big front window.

Colt Kelley sat in a chair at his kitchen table, enjoying the solar warmth radiating through the glass. A large backpack rested on the floor between his knees. He stuffed a couple bottles of Alaskan Amber into the main compartment of the pack. "Those will taste good after a long hike," he said while securing the zipper.

Outside on the street, the sound of an approaching vehicle grew louder. Colt looked up to see a Jeep Cherokee slow and turn into the driveway. Excitement surged through his veins. He hefted his backpack and loped out the front door.

"Good morning," Colt said when Carrie stepped out of her vehicle. Bandit leapt onto the concrete behind her. The dog careened across the yard, searching for the source of some scent that had captured his attention. "I hope you had a big breakfast so you can keep up with that fuzz ball."

"I'd have to eat a bowl of gunpowder." Carrie glanced at Bandit and chuckled. With her hands on her hips, she raised her eyebrows in amusement. "You on the other hand, will be eating my dust."

Colt dropped his backpack and snatched Carrie up in a hug. "Maybe we should expend some of that extra energy now."

Carrie retuned the hug and delivered a kiss to Colt's lips. "Tempting, but you're going to have to work harder than that."

"Nothing worthwhile in life is easy." Colt stepped back and grinned. "After hanging out with you for the past couple weeks, I'm in for the long haul. You're definitely worth it."

"Now you're scoring points." Carrie tossed her head back and laughed. Her eyes radiated beauty and energy. Colt was mesmerized. All the amazing hours he had spent with Carrie suddenly seemed to sum up to this one instant. It was almost intoxicating. His mind dared to drift amongst hopes and dreams of sharing his life with her. It had only been two weeks, yet he felt himself falling hard for this beautiful woman. *I've barely gotten to know her, but I love what I know.*

"Are you ready to go?" Carrie's question broke Colt's trance.

Colt noted Carrie's knowing smile. He felt a flush of warmth in his cheeks. Recovering his poise, Colt pointed to his pack. "Sure, everything's right there. I just need to grab the ice axes from the cabinet in the garage."

"I'll get those. You toss your backpack in the back of the Cherokee."

Colt ambled toward the vehicle, but his gaze followed Carrie as she sauntered across the driveway. In a pair of shorts, her lean muscular legs were eye-popping. Firm curvaceous buttocks were topped by a slender waist. Carrie's tight tank-top revealed a V-shaped back and strong shoulders. Her supple muscles moved like those of a lioness. She was athletic, feminine, and exquisitely sexy. *I must be dreaming.* Colt snapped to attention when he bumped into the side of the SUV. *Idiot!*

Colt pulled open the rear door and heaved his backpack inside. He stepped out from behind the Cherokee, just as Carrie exited the garage with an ice axe in each hand. The view from the front was just as rousing. *She's an eleven on a scale of ten!*

"Are you fired up to climb a mountain now?" Carrie asked, handing over the axes. The tone of her voice was playful with an undertone of sensuality. Her pursed lips conveyed her delight.

She knew I'd be watching. I love this girl! Colt felt his heartbeat accelerate. "I feel like I could climb all the fourteeners in Colorado today."

"Let's just start with Snowmass Mountain," Carrie said with a sly smile. "We'll find a way to occupy your time after that."

"I've got a few ideas." Colt put his empty hand around Carrie's waist and pulled her close. She pressed against Colt. For a moment they shared a kiss. Climbing plans seemed trivial.

Colt beamed when the couple finally stepped apart. "Sure you don't want to just stay here?"

"Nothing worthwhile is easy, right?" Carrie's eyes sparkled in the bright sun as she handed her keys to Colt. "Start driving."

* * * *

The reception area was plush at EcoFriends headquarters in Boulder, Colorado. Half a dozen comfortable chairs were arranged around a couple of small tables. Several exotic plants occupied one corner of the room. Large photographs of spectacular Western vistas adorned the walls. Luke Parson sat back and sipped the coffee the receptionist had provided. *None of this stuff is cheap.* Luke tossed an EcoFriends pamphlet back on the table. It didn't answer the question that interested him.

"Hi, Mr. Parson. Sorry to keep you waiting." A well-dressed, bearded man strode into the room and offered a handshake. Luke recognized Howard Anderson from his television appearance.

"No problem and call me Luke," the journalist replied, grasping his host's hand. "Thanks for agreeing to meet with me on a Saturday, Mr. Anderson."

"Please, it's Howard," Anderson said with a smile. "We depend on media coverage to educate the public. EcoFriends' outreach doesn't take weekends off."

"Maybe that's the secret to you success, Howard," Luke was thoughtful. "You never let up."

"It's part of the formula." Anderson motioned to the door, which led to the main part of the building. "Let's talk in my office."

Contrary to Luke's expectation, the EcoFriends founder's office was large and spacious. It was neat and organized. Everything seemed to have a place. Soft music emanated from an iHome speaker adjacent to a laptop computer. Anderson settled into his chair behind the desk. Luke sat across from him.

"I read your article in Issue Insight, Luke." Anderson was pleasant as he began the dialogue. "It provided a concise explanation of corporate America's influence on politics in this country. Big business runs the country at the expense of everyone else."

Luke shrugged his shoulders and feigned a smile. "Don't believe everything you read."

"I don't," Anderson countered with a slightly hardened countenance. "You wanted to talk about the vision EcoFriends has for this nation, I believe."

"I saw your interview with Marla Wells. Your comments indicated that the environmental movement is losing ground. It's hard to believe that with the spread of "green" talk everywhere. Recycling, water conservation, light bulbs, you name it."

"Success requires more than those things you've mentioned, Luke," Anderson said. "The corporations still have all the money.

Luke's gaze swept around the room. "From the looks of this building, I'd guess EcoFriends has a sizeable bank account."

"We've chosen to put our best foot forward. That doesn't mean we're flush with cash."

The conversation paused for a few awkward seconds. Luke suddenly found the music irritating. "Why are corporate profits a problem, Howard?"

"They use that wealth to control politicians. Government works for corporate America, not the people. Organizations like EcoFriends are outgunned."

"Is E-Force part of the solution?" Luke asked.

"E-Force is not EcoFriends." Anderson kept his tone measured. "Their actions are their own."

"Do you see them as a promotional tool for your efforts?" Luke watched Anderson's body language.

"How could that be? We have no control of E-Force." The EcoFriends leader's smile was void of warmth. "Though I understand what motivates E-Force, our organization does not condone their destructive radical action."

"But you're willing to accept those tactics if it helps EcoFriends." Luke was ready to push harder. "What if somebody gets hurt or killed? Shouldn't we all be working to stop E-Force before something like that happens?"

"That's the job of the police, Mr. Parson." Anderson's eyes narrowed as he cocked his head to one side. "None of your media colleagues are siding with AmeResort."

"I didn't say I was on their side."

"You're eager to cast E-Force as violent criminals attacking a developer who has a heart of gold." Anderson leaned forward and placed the palms of his hands together.

"Isn't that what E-Force is when you get down to it?" Luke asked. He sensed he was on the verge of a breakthrough.

"They're just ordinary people who have reached the breaking point." Anderson shot back with anger in his voice. "They're unwilling to allow this planet to be destroyed by corporate power and greed."

"It sounds like you know E-Force well." Luke kept his eyes locked with Anderson. "Do you know who they are?"

Howard Anderson rose from his chair. "How would I know that? EcoFriends has nothing to do with E-Force, Mr. Parson. But I do know it's time to conclude this interview. I have work to do."

Thank you for your time, Mr. Anderson." Luke's offer to shake hands was grudgingly accepted. A moment later he stepped onto the sidewalk. His senses were tingling. *You've got something to hide, Howard.*

* * * *

Snowmass Creek was swollen with runoff from the melting snowpack. Frigid water poured over logs and cascaded through rocks. Rays of sunlight danced on the undulating water. Greenery adorned with wildflowers waved in the light wind that slipped down from the high peaks. Remnants of snow drifts sent rivulets of shimmering water across the trail as contributions to the gushing stream.

Ahead of Carrie, the path curved to the right around a small ridge. When Carrie rounded the bend, she was treated to the sight of Snowmass Lake beyond a glade of big spruce trees. Like an overflow drain, Snowmass Creek spilled into the valley from the lake. A dramatic circ, soaring nearly 3,000 feet, flanked the body of water on three sides. It was crowned by Snowmass Peak, Hagerman Peak, and Snowmass Mountain. The 14,092 ft summit of the latter peak would be the destination in the morning. From the vantage point of the east end of the lake, the fourteener looked diminutive compared to its two shorter neighbors. That was just an illusion. It reminded Carrie that the same could be true of people. First impressions were not always windows into reality. She prayed her attraction to Colt was not founded on delusion.

"It's so beautiful," Carrie said as she paused to unclip Bandit's leash. Upon freedom, the dog dashed toward the lake.

"And we have it all to ourselves." Colt moved to Carrie's side. "It'll be different in a couple weeks when more of the snow is gone."

"I hope we can find a dry place to camp."

"I noticed a good spot back down the trail," Colt replied as they trudged through the trees for another 100 yards. "Let's chill out for little while before we get set up. That was a long hike."

Near the water's edge, the pair unstrapped their backpacks and dropped them on the rocks. With a water bottle in hand, Colt stretched out on the ground and rested his back against his pack. "I'm glad you came up here with me. You add a whole new dimension of fun."

"You have something special in mind?" Carrie asked in a playful tone while raising an eyebrow.

"Let's just say you make my adrenaline flow more than any mountain." Colt smiled like a mischievous kid and tossed a stick along the lakeshore. Bandit chased it like a cheetah pursuing a gazelle.

"That's quite a revelation Mr. Mountain Man." Carrie felt a surge of energy. Her attraction to Colt was hard to suppress. For the past two weeks they had spent time together nearly every day. The 80 miles between their respective homes was as insignificant an obstacle as a crack in a sidewalk. Carrie's wall was in ruins. Her defenses were nearly breached.

"The truth is out," Colt said with a chuckle. Carrie was mesmerized by the sparkle in his blue eyes. "Before long, I won't have any secrets."

"I don't know if that's good or bad." Carrie laughed while pulling a digital camera from her pocket. "I want to get a picture."

Bandit trotted back to Colt while Carrie extracted a small flexible tripod from her backpack. It was perfect for setting up on a boulder. She took a moment to line up the shot. "Okay, hold onto Bandit and get ready."

"I look terrible without my makeup," Colt quipped.

Carrie scurried over and plopped down next to Colt. She pressed close to Colt as the breeze blew in from across the water and tousled her hair. Colt put his arm around Carrie and pulled her tight. The warmth she felt pervaded her entire being. The camera snapped a photograph.

"I hope it's a good one." Carrie started to rise.

Colt resisted. "Check it later. Sit with me."

Together, Colt and Carrie gazed at the mountain majesty surrounding them. The whoosh of the breeze blended with the churning turmoil in the creek. Shadows of clouds raced across the towering, rocky slopes. Beams of sunlight against Carrie's face felt like they were straight from heaven. She smiled as Bandit waded in the shallows of the frigid lake. From time to time, Colt cast another stick and sent the dog charging after it. Carrie felt a deep contentment that she had not known for a long time. *Be careful. Don't be a fool.*

Carrie's eyes were drawn to the distant summit of Snowmass Mountain. It seemed to beckon to her. *Cast aside your fear.* She turned toward Colt and discovered he was watching her. His expression conveyed complete honesty.

"You are more beautiful than all this creation around us," Colt said.

He's perfect. This is perfect. Carrie pulled close to Colt and their lips met.

* * * *

A massive door was the portal into the coveted life of wealth and power. Inside was a spacious foyer, accented with Italian marble and master carpentry. Cavernous rooms stretched beyond arched openings on three sides. A glance confirmed the furnishings as exquisite and expensive. The paintings by prominent artists were worthy of a museum. From the entrance hall, a broad sweeping staircase rose to a mezzanine. More than one female visitor had imagined herself as Scarlet O'Hara, carried up those stairs by Rhett Butler. The bedroom suites were perfect for seclusion and romance. It was a fairy tale backdrop for a girl's dreams.

The slam of a door was followed by the staccato click of heels on marble. Marla Wells was on the verge of a runner's pace as she charged toward the staircase. Her emotions threatened to erupt like a Yellowstone geyser. *I won't let him see me cry. Never again!*

"Get back here!" A stocky man dressed in an expensive suit chased after Marla. "This conversation is not over."

"Everything is over!" Marla shouted on the way to the upper level. "I'm going to New York and starting over."

Glen Wells gained ground on his wife as he bounded up the stairs. "Damn right you'll be starting over. You won't get one dime out of me!"

Marla stumbled and broke a heel as she crested the last stair and bolted across the hallway. Her gait changed to an awkward limp. It only took a few seconds to strip the shoes from her feet. It was enough for Wells to catch Marla before she could slam the door of her bedroom suite. The stout attorney pushed into the room and grabbed Marla by one arm.

"Let go of me!" Marla shouted as she turned to face her spouse. In her bare feet, she was no longer eye-to-eye with the man. Unwilling to be intimidated, she twisted out of his grasp and took a backward step. "Don't ever touch me again."

Wells pointed his finger at Marla. "If you leave Denver, I'll file for divorce. You'll get nothing."

"I know the terms of the prenuptial agreement. You've repeated them to me incessantly for years."

"Do you think a network job is going to provide you with all this?" Broad sweeping movements of Wells' arms directed attention to the magnificent luxury of his home. "You'll be at the bottom of the totem pole. You won't succeed."

"You bastard, I will succeed!" The pain wrought by two decades of insult and neglect overtopped Marla's emotional check dam. The price for wealth and prominence had been steep. It was the dark secret, which drove Marla to hate the world. Tears poured forth as she shouted. "I'm a talented broadcaster. The network can see that. I'm not just a trophy of your success!"

"You think you're still a trophy." Wells snorted with contempt. "Your looks have faded. People want to see a hot young newsbabe, not an old woman. It won't matter how many god-forsaken fringe groups line up at your door."

"God, I hate you! You've taken everything from me. Happiness. Respect. Love. Children. I've had to live without all that."

"The last thing you could have handled was a child." Wells' face was flushed red and his hands balled up into fists. "You're the most selfish bitch I've ever met. I gave you everything that mattered to you. What have I gotten for my generosity? You don't even put out!"

"Get the hell out of here. Get out now!" Marla shoved her loathed husband. He staggered a step backward toward the door. His eyes flashed like those of an enraged beast when he raised his right arm. Marla flinched, but held her ground. For a few seconds, the pair appeared frozen in time.

Glen Wells' index finger suddenly protruded from his fist. "You'll receive divorce papers as soon as they can be drafted. There's nothing you can do to change that now. Pack your damned bags. I want you gone in the morning."

Marla slammed the door after Wells stormed out. She fled to the bed and collapsed. A deluge of tears were concocted in a stinging swirl of emotions. All the familiar ingredients of pain, humiliation, and resentment boiled in the depths of Marla's soul. But as the sobs eventually began to ebb and recede, she sensed something new. It was the resolve born of pending freedom and opportunity. Fame and fortune were within reach. She would finally have both on her own terms.

"You can have it all, Glen." Marla rasped, pushing disheveled hair from her face. "You can keep screwing that little bitch intern of yours too. I'm going to be a star."

* * * *

Colt's tent stood a dozen feet from the crackling campfire. It was a compact backcountry model, supposedly built for two. From Colt's perspective, double occupancy usually resulted in conditions that were a little too close for comfort. But the restricted interior space was perfect for sharing with Carrie.

Pulling his jacket tight around his neck, Colt zipped up and turned his gaze to the west. The last evidence of the sun was receding behind Snowmass Mountain. The cloud cover was still light. Countless stars spread across the heavens suggested the night would be frigid at 11,000 feet. *A good night to get close to a hot body.*

Colt stepped to the fire. Carrie was stretched out in a Crazy Creek chair. To ward off the chill, the collar of her jacket was zipped up to her chin. Sandy colored hair, spilled from below a snug fleece ski cap. The cold weather defenses retained body heat, but not her beauty. Carrie looked up and smiled at Colt when he approached. Flickering firelight accented her striking face. The flames danced in her mesmerizing eyes. Colt felt his heart race with excitement.

"Feel better now that you finally put a coat on, tough guy?" Carrie took a sip of her Alaskan Amber.

"Guess I needed a little more than your smoking hot looks," Colt said as he took a seat next to her. "Now, in the tent that may be a different story."

Carrie laughed and nudged him. "Mr. Kelley, I'm shocked at your suggestion."

"I admit it. I'm like any other guy. Just happen to be lucky enough to end up alone with you in the wilderness."

Colt wrapped an arm around Carrie. She nuzzled close. For a few minutes they stared into the fire. Colt savored the last drops of his beer. The sound of cascading water drifted in on the breeze. Bandit was curled up within petting reach of Carrie.

What do you want more than anything else in life?" Carrie asked.

"Just the usual stuff. You know, a platinum record, rabid fans... the ability to travel through time."

Carrie rolled her eyes and delivered a light punch to Colt's shoulder. "I'm serious. What do you really want out of life?"

"I want a soul mate. Then nothing else will matter." Colt was surprised at the readiness of his unabashed answer. "Does that sound silly?"

"No, of course not." Carrie stared into the flames. "I used to want the same thing. Seems like a long time ago."

Carrie's comment took Colt by surprise. Sadness saturated her voice. "You don't want that anymore?"

"I built a wall around my heart. I told myself I could live without loving and being loved. It seemed easier than going through more pain."

Colt took a moment to ponder Carrie's words. It dawned on him that she was extending the gift of her trust. She was taking a leap of faith. A lump formed in Colt's throat. Only moments ago, he had slipped into thinking about Carrie in purely sexual terms. He promised not to make that mistake again. "But that means you've prevented yourself from getting what you really want. What happened to push you to that point? Did you get hurt by someone?"

"It's more complicated than that," Carrie said after a moment of silence. "I'm not proud of my past. I guess I just stopped feeling like I was worthy of love. The only way to survive that way is to keep telling yourself love doesn't matter. After enough time, it just becomes reality."

"You're a religious person." Colt rubbed Carrie's shoulders. "Don't you feel like God loves you?"

"I have faith, but most of the time I'm not sure why God would love me." Carrie hugged her arms around her chest and shivered. "I've been cold and mean to people who've tried to get close to me. Who could care about a person like that?"

"I care about you. I care a lot. You're an amazing person."

"That's what worries me." Carrie craned her neck and looked into Colt's eyes. "I know you care. My ice-cold heart is thawing. You make me feel special, Colt. But what if I screw this up? I don't want to go through more pain if that happens."

"I think I understand. My desire to be close to you is almost overwhelming, Carrie. But if you have to go slow, that's fine. I'll be here to provide whatever you need. You're worth it."

"You're worth it too, Colt," Carrie replied, reaching out and squeezing his hand. "That's why I've got such a strong desire to change."

For a long time, the couple was silent and reflective. The flames were dying down, but red-hot coals radiated warmth. Colt imagined them melting the barriers that existed between Carrie and him. *What was it that made her shut herself off to the world? She'll talk about it when she's ready.* Colt subdued his hormones and sexual desires. He resolved to provide unwavering support to the extraordinary woman next to him. Something told him the reward would be bountiful.

With reluctance, Colt finally broke the silence. "It's probably about time for us to turn in for the night. We need to get an early start if we're going to bag Snowmass before noon tomorrow."

"Whatever you say. You're the leader of this expedition." Carrie chuckled.

The pair rose to their feet. Across the fire, Bandit took his cue and stood. Colt was reminded of a cat as the dog stretched and yawned. "I think he wore himself out."

"Yeah, it usually takes energy just to watch him." Carrie turned and wrapped her arms around Colt. Her cheek rested on his shoulder. "Thank you, Colt."

"Thank you for what?"

"Thank you for believing in me." Carrie's voice was soft like the call of a dove. "I believe things happen for a reason. Maybe I was behind my wall all those years because I was waiting for you."

The lump was back in Colt's throat again. This time it felt like a good thing. He found it difficult to speak. "That's the most meaningful thing anyone has ever said to me. I don't know what to say."

"How about, good night?" Carrie planted a kiss on his lips.

Chapter Nine
Saturday, June 9 (early morning)

A searchlight beam swept across a metal-skinned building, exposing a series of maintenance bay doors. At the end of the structure, a parked snowcat materialized from the saturated gloom. The obelisk of illumination moved past more of the machines, casting eerie shadows across mud and gravel.

Dressed in black paramilitary gear, Zed Cain hunkered behind one of the tracked vehicles with a large wrench in hand. His team had scarcely initiated the sabotage of the Crested Butte Mountain Resort facilities when a vehicle arrived outside the perimeter fence of the maintenance yard. It had to be a security guard.

Stay out there, and nobody gets hurt. Cain strained to see the unidentified person manning the light.

Rain found paths to penetrate Cain's parka as he lowered night vision goggles over his eyes. Peering down the row of snowcats, he honed in on Barry Conley. The electrician was crouched behind the track of the farthest machine.

With caution, Cain changed his stance and surveyed the front of the maintenance building. A pair of parked dump trucks shielded Billy Landin's electronic hardware from the probing searchlight. It dangled from the alarm keypad next to a door. Landin and Trigger Ruddock huddled in a pond-sized puddle that seemed on the verge of engulfing one of the ten-wheeled behemoths.

Cain checked his watch again. *We're pissing time away.*

Finally, the floodlight blacked out. Cain whipped his night vision gear toward the car and identified the markings of the Crested Butte police department.

Why the hell is a cop from the neighboring town up here? The team leader was itching to continue his operation, but the patrol vehicle stayed just beyond the chain-link fence, engine idling and headlights blazing into a glade of trees.

* * * *

A Ford van with a new coat of brown primer ambled along a narrow street in Crested Butte. A jumble of houses and cabins lined the strip of pavement; many dating back to the early 1900's when the mountain hamlet had subsisted on mining. Some were dilapidated and on the verge of collapse. Others had been restored into charming residences with brightly colored exteriors.

The windshield wipers slapped back and forth at a frantic pace in a losing battle to counter the downpour. Visibility was worsened by the fogging windshield. Delilah chomped on a wad of bubble gum and fiddled with the vent control to coax more air from the dashboard. She pulled over to the edge of the street and switched off the lights. The nearby houses were dark so she figured it was okay to let the engine run. A push of a button lit up her phone. There were about five minutes left until departure time for the first rendezvous.

The rain conjured up memories of the two years Delilah had spent in college. On rainy nights, she and her friends had lounged around, smoking dope and philosophizing. She and her peers had stumbled through a few political science courses. The professors had stressed one simple principle: imperialist western nations were a detriment to the world. In their view, western culture had prospered through the subjugation and exploitation of other cultures. Selfishness and greed were prevalent attitudes in the quest for power and those ugly traits were on prominent display in corporate America.

Delilah remembered her first meeting with Howard Anderson. Enlisting with E-Force had seemed like the perfect way to fight the power and join the battle against capitalist injustice. The romantic shine had worn off the idea since that time.

"Why did I get mixed up in this bullshit?" She pulled an envelope from the pocket of her jacket. It contained a letter that she had written to her ex-boyfriend. Delilah planned to mail it in the morning. It just needed a stamp. *I never should have left you. I hope you'll take me back.*

When the alarm chime on her phone went off, Delilah snapped back to reality. It was time to go. She turned the key in the ignition, and the starter motor ground in protest.

"Freaking moron!" Delilah chided herself. *The stupid engine's already running.*

With care, Delilah shifted the transmission into gear. She eased the van onto the street and headed for the rendezvous as quickly as she dared.

* * * *

Willard Filmore sat in a cramped office and leaned toward a bank of video monitors. They displayed looping images from surveillance cameras located throughout the AmeResort facilities at Crested Butte Mountain Resort. Filmore ignored them. He was glued to a small television and the highlights from a baseball game between the Colorado Rockies and the San Francisco Giants.

The security guard grumbled with disgust. "That's sorry pitching, Rockies. Giving up a walk-off homerun in the bottom of the ninth!"

The door to the security office burst open, and two young men squeezed into the room. They wore the uniforms of AmeResort security personnel. Despite the depressing weather, the newcomers were jovial. Their boisterous energy contrasted Filmore's sulking mood.

The taller of the two young guards had short hair that was bleached blond. The name, Schumacher, was stitched on his jacket.

"Hey, Willard!" Schumacher exclaimed. "A gang of thugs was cleaning out all the base village shops while you were watching SportsCenter."

Filmore snorted when Eddie Mendoza laughed at Schumacher's teasing. "Boys, I don't miss anything. When I was in the Navy, I was an air-traffic controller on an aircraft carrier. That's the most complicated job in the world."

"It's a good thing Eddie and I showed up. When those crooks got a look at us with our big guns, they surrendered on the spot."

Mendoza said with glee, "That's right. Those banditos weren't loco."

"Y'all would shoot your toes off if you had to draw your weapons and face a criminal." Filmore's prediction was delivered with arrogance.

Mendoza appeared stung by the assertion, but Schumacher burst out laughing. "Is that why you wear steel-toed boots, Willard?"

Filmore was tired of the banter. There were more sports highlights to watch. "It's time for you jokers to check the ski lifts. You've been briefed on the new procedures."

The young men grimaced. New AmeResort security protocol dictated that security personnel were no longer to rely on alarm systems and surveillance cameras. To thwart further sabotage, guards were to physically patrol all corporate facilities. Tonight that meant rambling all over the mountain in the cold driving rain.

"Seems like a lot of unnecessary misery," Schumacher said. "Why would eco-terrorists want to burn stuff up here? Everything that happens in this place is already dictated by tree-huggers."

"It's not your job to philosophize," Willard Filmore said, disdain dripping from his tone. "You just need to get the ATVs from the maintenance shop and make your rounds."

The young men reluctantly turned and trudged out the door. It was going to be an unpleasant night.

"Don't look so glum, boys." Filmore smirked. "We'll have hot cocoa with marshmallows when you get back."

"You're all heart, Willard." Schumacher trudged out the door.

* * * *

Cold rain poured off the brim of Grayson Miller's Stetson as he approached a contractor's trailer. It was up Washington Gulch, a narrow valley that sloped down from the flanks of Gothic Mountain. During the day, the surrounding majestic peaks, including Crested Butte Mountain, made it a spectacular place.

With mounting excitement, Miller scampered up the side of a roll-off dumpster that was near an unfinished house. Leaning over the edge, he tossed aside scrap lumber and construction waste. Two five-gallon buckets were nestled where he had left them. Straining as if pulling up a battleship anchor, Miller dragged the first container out of the dented steel refuse box. The accelerant mixture sloshed under the lid.

Miller gasped after both buckets sat in the muck near his feet. "Damn, those are heavy!" The fog of his labored breathing hung in the air.

With a handle in each hand, Miller struggled toward the house. Mud sucked at his boots. He gasped for oxygen as every muscle in his body burned with pain. He labored up a wood gangplank and through the front door. Dropping his cargo, he winced and massaged his aching arms.

Miller pulled his hated night vision goggles from beneath his rain slicker. Cain had forbidden the use of a light. Though he considered himself a rebel, Miller wasn't ready to defy the man who gave the orders. The thought of Cain sent a shiver down Miller's spine. He snatched off his hat and tugged the night vision gear down over his head.

"You've got to love that new house smell." Miller gazed

around at what would soon be the home of an AmeResort board member. The design and construction were typical of high-class mountain homes. Wood and stone were integrated with the precision of a jigsaw puzzle.

Several moments later, the incendiary devices were in place. The firing wires from both igniter units extended to a common location to facilitate use of a single timer. Miller flipped a switch and the countdown began. Arousing images of a timber-fueled conflagration flashed through his mind. *The flames will be so beautiful.*

With a heavy heart, Miller trotted outside and retreated into the dark countryside. It wouldn't be long until every cop and firefighter in the region arrived to confront his creation. He beat down his jealousy and kept moving.

* * * *

For three generations, the community of Crested Butte had subsisted on mining and ranching. When the last mine closed in 1960, the outlook had looked grim for most folks. Around that time, a few ski runs were built on the slopes of nearby Crested Butte Mountain. The town of Mt. Crested Butte sprang up on the ranchland at the bottom of the mountain. Slowly, the flow of tourist dollars increased each winter as people came to ski at Crested Butte Mountain Resort. As the years passed, the phenomena of mountain biking took root in the community. With an almost year-round influx of tourists, Crested Butte experienced new prosperity, but the soul of the town changed.

Almost everything Bernice Waldron loved about Crested Butte was relegated to fading memories. The house was the last thing she had to cling to. And the drafty old bedroom hadn't provided a decent night of sleep in the ten years since her husband died.

While lying awake in bed, Bernice heard the deep rumble of an engine in front of her house. According to the clock radio on the nightstand, it was almost two hours past midnight. Suspicious and apprehensive, she shuffled to the window. Moving the curtain aside, she spotted a van, a detested vehicle that provided a rolling haven for decadence. Bernice seethed with intolerance. "Probably a bunch of Trustafarians drinking or getting high." That was the local term for the young people in town who dressed like hippie-Rastafarians, while living off trust funds established by wealthy parents. Such people had sometimes been rude and disrespectful to Bernice.

Appalled at what she assumed was going on in front of her house, Bernice moved to call the police. The screeching grating sound of a grinding starter motor emanated from outside. For Bernice, it was proof-positive of substance abuse.

Turning back to the window, Bernice saw the brief flash of a yellow New Mexico plate when the van passed below a streetlight. She struggled to the phone to report her observations to the police.

"They need to get those deranged fools off the road before somebody gets killed." Bernice fumed.

* * * *

The night had been uneventful for Officer Carter Perkins. It was a pretty dull job most of the time, but it still annoyed him when people joked that the Crested Butte police had nothing to do at night besides arresting drunks. The role of law enforcement was important, and Perkins took his job seriously.

There was no sign of anything unusual in the Crested Butte Mountain Resort maintenance yard. Satisfied, Perkins switched on the interior light to do some paperwork. There was no sense in rushing back down to Crested Butte.

Patrolling at Crested Butte Mountain Resort was a new routine. AmcResort Corporation had just negotiated an agreement with the towns of Crested Butte and Mt. Crested Butte. In return for financial contributions, the police departments were patrolling the accessible parts of the ski resort at night. That would allow AmeResort security personnel to focus on the outlying components.

The voice of the dispatcher crackled across the radio. "A resident on Third Street reported a vehicle with a potentially impaired driver."

"I'm heading down to investigate." Perkins couldn't hide his lack of enthusiasm. *Another exhilarating night.*

Shifting the transmission into gear, he sped away from the AmeResort maintenance facility.

* * * *

Delilah ground to a halt along Slate River Road near the trailhead to the Smith Hill Mine. Her headlights winked off. In the darkness, it was impossible to discern the trail rising up the hillside. She was forced to wait in silent solitude.

Abruptly, the sliding door on the side of the van was yanked open. Delilah heard Grayson Miller's heavy breathing.

"Let's go!" Miller wrestled his body into the vehicle and slammed the door. "The igniters have already fired."

She was annoyed by Miller's tone of voice. "We're on our way."

Delilah stepped on the accelerator and cranked the steering wheel hard to make a sharp U-turn. Trying to strip off his backpack and rain gear, Miller flailed for something solid to cling to.

Miller lashed out. "Take it easy! Try keeping all four tires on the ground."

"You're late. Now I've got to make up time."

"Quit bitching. I've been soaked to the bone all night."

"My nerves are on edge." Delilah backed down from the confrontation. "Dude, if I had a joint, I'd smoke it right now.

I've had bad vibes all night. It feels like something's really wrong. We're taking lots of risks. I mean, what if...."

"Chill out!" Miller said with exasperation. "Quit overanalyzing the situation and do your job."

"Don't worry about my job." Stung by the reprimand, she sulked until they neared the intersection with Gothic Road. The lights of a vehicle flashed past as it headed down toward Crested Butte. On the way out of town, the team would travel the same exposed route.

Delilah fretted. "Cain should have picked a house farther from the escape route. We'll be going right past cops and firefighters."

Miller refrained from response. Delilah's fears mounted. *This scheme is crazy.* If they got busted, there might be jail time. The thought of being locked up made her tremble. *This is my last mission.*

* * * *

After passing Slate River Road, Officer Perkins slowed to search for a van with a New Mexico license plate. If the driver was under the influence of drugs or alcohol, he or she would spend the rest of the night in jail.

Perkins had barely entered the Crested Butte town limits when the dispatcher's voice sounded over the radio. It was an all points bulletin to all police and fire personnel in the area. There was a fire in Washington Gulch.

"I'm on my way to assist," Perkins said to the dispatcher before whipping his car around and switching on the flashers.

As Perkins sped up the hill, he contemplated the address of the burning house. *That place is being built for an executive with AmeResort Corporation.*

"That fire is no accident." He grimaced. "It's got to be E-Force."

Racing up Gothic Road, Perkins rounded a curve and

spied taillights. In seconds, the police cruiser overtook the vehicle. It was the van he had gone down to find. The fire took priority. He blasted past and veered left onto Washington Gulch Road. When Perkins looked in his rear view mirror, he saw the headlights of the van continue up toward Mt. Crested Butte.

* * * *

"Let's go, Wonder Boy." Ruddock shoved Landin toward the building an instant after Perkins' cop car sped away. "Get your ass in gear and deactivate that alarm."

The computer hacker stumbled to the door and finished connecting his laptop computer to the alarm keypad. In a matter of minutes, he was pecking away at the keyboard. Ruddock held a fire extinguisher-sized bottle of compressed air. A small piston was attached to the regulator. When the alarm was down, he planned to use the device to blast the door locks into the shop interior.

"What the hell's taking so long?" Ruddock thumped his forehead against the door and clenched a fist. "We're going to run out of time to set the incendiaries."

Landin activated his code-breaking program. "I'm almost there."

An engine roared out of the soggy night. The entrance suddenly was awash in blazing illumination. Vehicle doors burst open. "Freeze! Put your hands in the air!"

Ruddock tensed. The blinding headlights robbed him of the chance to determine what he was up against. He couldn't tell if it was armed cops or some fat maintenance guy. A chain-link gate clanked open and footsteps rushed forward.

Landin's computer emitted an electronic beep, signaling that the alarm was down. Buckets of accelerant rested on the gravel. The compressed air contraption was still in Ruddock's hand. E-Force logos on their clothing wouldn't have made their identities and intentions more obvious.

A startled voice shouted. "They're part of E-Force!"

Ruddock shifted his grip on the tank.

"Don't do something stupid! We're armed and authorized to shoot."

"Are you cops or something?" Ruddock squinted at the silhouettes before him. He glanced at Landin. The kid looked ready to wet himself.

"We're AmeResort security, and you're under arrest. Eddie, get Willard on the radio."

One of the guard's lights jerked around at the soft scuff of a footstep. Zed Cain and Barry Conley were caught in the beam.

"Stop where you are!" Mendoza's Spanish-accented cry was panicked. "Put your hands up!"

Ruddock cursed silently. *The whole team is exposed.* He watched Cain raise his hands to shoulder height, the big wrench still in his grasp. A few steps behind the leader, Conley stood quaking with fear.

"Drop the tool." The pitch of Eddie Mendoza's voice rose. "Drop it, or I'll shoot!"

"Make them lay face-down." Chris Schumacher's anxiety was audible.

"Get down on the ground. Keep your hands out front."

Conley dropped to his knees and prepared to stretch prone. In a movement like a striking snake, Cain hurled the wrench into the night. Succumbing to reflex, the guard's light flashed after the flying object. Utilizing the diversion, Cain bolted into the night. The jumpy electrician tore off in the other direction.

"Stop, or I'll shoot!" Mendoza failed to pull the trigger.

Alarmed by his partner's hysterics, Schumacher exercised poor judgment and turned his head. Without hesitation, Ruddock sprang. Slamming into the guard, he grabbed for the pistol. Both men crashed down, locked in a desperate struggle for the weapon.

Grappling on the ground, Ruddock jammed a thumb

against a pressure point in the guard's neck. Schumacher twisted in agony. Granting no reprieve, Ruddock kneed him in the groin. He wrenched the pistol in toward the guard's body. With wild-eyed desperation, Schumacher chomped down on Ruddock's forearm. The demolitions man cried out in pain and ripped the bleeding wound from his adversary's teeth. Transformed into a savage beast, Schumacher thrashed and kicked in an effort to break free of his foe. During the melee, the gun fired several times in rapid succession.

* * * *

The second Ruddock launched his attack, Landin regained his motor reflexes. The computer hacker sprinted for the open gate to the road. He stumbled in a water-filled pothole and fell. Intense pain shot through one knee when it hit the ground. Landin struggled to his feet and staggered onward.

The car with the burning headlights was blocking his path. Wincing in agony, Landin hobbled around to slip past the vehicle.

One of the slugs from Schumacher's Colt semi-automatic pistol slammed into his spine, just above the shoulder blades. His body crumpled across the hood before sliding down next to one tire. Blood mixed with water as he lay motionless. The life quickly poured out of him.

* * * *

The barking pistol initiated a counter-attack from Cain. At the fringe of the maintenance yard, he extracted a Colt Delta Elite from beneath his parka. He squeezed off several thundering rounds and scrambled for cover. The 10mm bullets punched through the metal sides of the maintenance shop.

Return fire spurted forth from the night. Behind the

refuge of a snowcat track, Cain took a second to enable his night vision gear. He spied the Hispanic guard shooting blindly into the darkness.

Barry Conley was clawing his way up the perimeter fence when one of Mendoza's 10mm slugs slammed into his back. Cain saw his fingers contort on the chain-links. The electrician's tortured cry was silenced when a second bullet struck behind his ear.

Unwilling to allow the guard to continue to blast away, Cain drew a bead on Mendoza. A cry of pain and surprise sounded when his gun retorted. With the threat eliminated, Cain heaved the Delta Elite at the AmeResort car and sprinted for the fence. In seconds, he scaled the barrier and disappeared into the darkness.

* * * *

Next to the building, Schumacher and Ruddock were still locked in combat. The guard fought as fiercely as a wounded bear, but Ruddock managed to wedge Schumacher's Colt between their grappling bodies. The pistol retorted only once. Schumacher went limp after the bullet sliced through his torso. Panting for oxygen, Ruddock shoved his vanquished opponent aside and scrambled to his feet. There was nobody left to prevent his escape.

* * * *

Eddie Mendoza writhed on the ground and moaned. Covered in filth and blood, he fought to a sitting position. The chest pain was intense, hindering breathing. He felt for his radio. It was gone.

A few yards away, rain splattered off his motionless partner. Mendoza clawed his way along the ground, praying that he would find Schumacher's radio intact and functional.

* * * *

Officer Perkins watched crewmembers from two fire departments attack the fire with their hoses. The roaring flames resisted being driven back down below the blackened skeleton of the house. There wasn't much Perkins could do to help. He trudged to his police cruiser with the mysterious van on his mind. With his computer, he ran a check on the New Mexico license plate he had observed.

"A stolen plate. Something's very wrong here."

Perkins' gut told him the van was linked to the fire. Maybe it was E-Force. The blaze was another assault against AmeResort. The eco-terrorists had beaten law enforcement again.

A call came across the radio. "Report of gunshots at the CBMR maintenance facility. All available police and medical personnel are requested to respond."

Perkins was stunned. The maintenance yard had appeared deserted. With his jaw clenched in anger, he jammed his car into gear and tore off toward Mt. Crested Butte.

That fire was a diversion. E-Force had played him like an incompetent imbecile. He was determined to have his retribution.

* * * *

Parked in the Gold Link neighborhood, which bordered the ski area, Delilah and Miller fidgeted in their seats. It was past the rendezvous time. There was no sign of the other team members.

Miller cocked his head to the side. "I hear a siren."

"It's a cop." Delilah was alarmed. "Something bad must have happened. What are we going to do?"

"Just shut up and don't panic. I can't think with you babbling."

The flashing strobe lights of a police car sped past on the road below the development. A moment later, an AmeResort security vehicle raced past followed by an ambulance.

"They're headed for the maintenance shop," Delilah cried out, twisting the key in the ignition. "We've got to get out of here!"

"Are you crazy? Shut the lights off!"

Delilah ignored Miller's orders and shifted the van into gear. He tried to snatch the keys away. She exploded with screams and a barrage of crazed punches. One shot caught Miller square in the face.

"Get out of there, you bitch!" After ripping Delilah from behind the wheel, he hurled her into the rear cargo area.

"Stay there and shut up or I'll kill you." Miller held his bleeding nose.

Delilah cowered as the E-Force arsonist scrambled behind the steering wheel. He switched off the lights. An instant later, bright light streamed through the windows.

"You freaking idiot! Now one of the cops spotted us."

"I'm sorry." She sobbed and pulled the letter from her pocket. "I'm scared. I just want to go back to my boyfriend and the life I used to have."

Delilah clawed for something to hang onto when Miller floored the accelerator. Mud from the road shoulder plastered the underside of the van until the spinning tires grabbed hold of the pavement. She slid backwards and smashed against the rear doors. "You're going to kill us!"

* * * *

Officer Perkins slammed the transmission of his car into reverse and roared backward. At the entrance to the Gold Link neighborhood, he spun the car around in a violent doughnut. The car fishtailed as it tore up the road in pursuit of the van.

"I'm in pursuit of that brown Ford van." Perkins recited

the license plate number over the radio.

"What about the CBMR shop," the dispatcher asked. "We've got gunshot victims."

"The shots, the fire, the van…it's all E-Force," Perkins said without hesitation. "I'm not letting them get away. The paramedics will take care of the wounded."

Barreling along the contorted roads, Perkins made up ground on the fleeing taillights. The van cornered poorly at high speeds, and the off-road tires provided limited traction on wet pavement. Still the driver showed no sign of giving up, hurtling along with reckless abandon.

The van shot into the intersection with Gothic Road and slid crazily toward the far shoulder. Perkins winced when the wheels on one side lifted off the road. Defying the laws of physics, the vehicle didn't roll over. The tires thudded back down, and the fugitives rocketed toward Crested Butte.

"They're insane," Perkins said under his breath.

Perkins knew Gothic Road well. His quarry was nearly upon the sharp curves at Washington Gulch. In anticipation of the treacherous turns, Perkins slowed his patrol car.

The fugitives refused to decelerate. Crossing into the realm of impossibility, the van stayed on the pavement and slid around the first bend. The feat could not prevent the inevitable. Perkins watched with dread as the vehicle weaved out of control. The van was sideways when it careened into the next curve. It sounded like the vehicle was dropped from a cliff when it flipped onto its side. The ruined shell of metal tumbled into the black abyss of a gulch.

* * * *

The E-Force members experienced every detail of their impending disaster in slow motion. It was a nightmare descent into oblivion. Without a seatbelt, Miller was hurled headfirst through the glass of the side window. His broken and bloodied body was crushed as the van rolled over him.

Delilah was thrown around inside the van. It was impossible to suck in a breath to scream. The repeated bludgeoning of metal against flesh ravaged her body. At the bottom of the gulch, the van suffered a final impact as violent as a bomb blast.

In the twisted wreckage, Delilah lay bleeding. Her field of vision was narrowing into a tunnel. *I'm going to die.* A tear diluted the blood on her cheek. A parade of memories marched through Delilah's head. The letter was clenched in one hand.

Suddenly, Perkins appeared and tugged at the mangled doors. She whimpered. "Please help me."

Chapter Ten
Saturday, June 9 (afternoon and evening)

The paper cut stung like crazy. Sitting in her home office, Marla Wells paled at the sight of blood seeping from the tiny wound. Her stomach turned and sent her stumbling to the bathroom. She almost tripped over one of the half-dozen, open boxes scattered about the floor.

After summoning the courage to cover the bleeding cut with a bandage, Marla returned and surveyed the disaster. Every part of the office was in disarray. It was as if a tornado had touched down in the room.

"I should throw all this crap away. I'm not postponing the move to New York."

Marla resumed rifling through the mountain of paper on the desk with a vengeance. A muffled cell phone ring sounded. She tossed debris aside. When she finally turned up the phone, the caller's information was blocked.

"It's got to be that damned divorce attorney again." Marla tossed the phone aside and continued with her work. "I've got no time for that bitch."

Seconds later, Marla was dismayed to hear the ring tone resume. Unable to restrain her temper, she snatched up the phone.

"Who's calling?!" Marla's demand was followed by silence. "I'm not going to let Glen ruin my life. This is harassment and I'll have you--"

A voice interrupted. "The murder of our brothers has strengthened our resolve against AmeResort. Our war for justice has only begun."

Marla was taken aback by the E-Force caller. *Where the hell has he been?*

"You were supposed to keep me informed. I ended up looking like a fool. I got scooped by one of my rivals!"

"Circumstances dictated a change of procedure." The

caller responded without remorse. "Your pride is irrelevant."

Marla ignored the reprimand. "What happened in Mt. Crested Butte?"

"Can you handle the truth, Ms. Wells?"

* * * *

Gray storm clouds cast a dark pall over downtown Denver. A melancholy mist cloaked the city and seemed to pervade the AmeResort conference room. An emergency meeting was in progress. Stress and fatigue were evident on the faces of the board members. Phillip Barrett was a rumbling volcano on the verge of eruption.

Barrett expected the worst. The media would use the Mt. Crested Butte incident to manufacture a scandal of epic proportions. Television reporters were already announcing that AmeResort Corporation had killed environmental activists. More business partnerships and investment deals were in danger of withering away. Tourism at AmeResort properties was already in decline. A media feeding frenzy would cause the stock price to slide off the precipice and plunge into oblivion.

"I'm not going to let the media destroy my life's work." Barrett glowered while the rest of the group slumped around the conference table.

Everyone looked up when the double doors opened. Ms. Vonn, the Asian goddess, ushered two men into the conference room. Each of the newcomers wore a dark-colored suit and displayed a serious countenance.

"Colonel Webber and Mr. Quinn have arrived," Ms. Vonn said.

Barrett rose and shook hands with the square-jawed former-Marine. "We're interested to hear your report, Colonel Webber."

The board had recently hired Webber as the head of security for AmeResort Corporation. He was responsible for new changes in protocol at the company's mountain property holdings. These procedures had resulted in the encounter at Crested Butte Mountain Resort.

Barrett turned to the chief in-house investigator, a man big enough to play offensive line in the National Football League. "Mr. Quinn, I hope your investigation into E-Force has given us something to work with."

Barrett spoke after the new arrivals were seated. "AmeResort Corporation is teetering on the brink of disaster. We're succumbing to a plague called E-Force. Our only hope is to wipe out the disease. Gentleman, can prescribe a cure?"

"We're still piecing the facts together." Quinn's soft voice contrasted his enormous size. "A local law enforcement officer has provided my team with valuable assistance. The FBI task force isn't aware of this relationship."

Stephen Chandler interrupted. "Are you sure you can trust him? We should have the opportunity to evaluate his credibility."

"This man is trustworthy." Quinn refused to reveal the name of his ally in Mt. Crested Butte. "And it's critical that he remain anonymous."

"You're the man in charge of the investigation." Barrett figured it was reasonable for AmeResort to defer from showing its hand.

Quinn nodded in appreciation. "As you know, two of our security guards encountered intruders at the CBMR maintenance facility. Everything went to hell, but we're sure our men were defending themselves. Before he lapsed into a coma, Mendoza claimed the trespassers were responsible for initiating the violence."

"Does that mean they fired the first shot?" someone asked.

"Mendoza said Schumacher's firearm discharged during his struggle with one of the criminals." Quinn looked uncomfortable. "Schumacher's dead so we can't confirm that. After those initial shots, the lead flying through the dark was as thick as mosquitoes on the Grand Mesa. Two of the intruders were killed."

"What do you know about them?" Barrett wanted more details.

Quinn shrugged. "The deceased were white males. Neither man carried identification, but we suspect they were part of E-Force."

"We don't expect the investigative task force to release much pertinent information," Webber said. "They don't seem to be getting anywhere."

"That's right." Quinn nodded in agreement. "For example, we believe the fire at Ms. Jacob's new house was meant to divert attention from the maintenance facility. So far, the investigators won't help us confirm that."

"Sorry, to hear about your house." Chandler extended his sympathies. "I'm sure it's very upsetting."

The woman swallowed hard. "I just want to stop these criminals before they completely destroy this company."

Barrett slammed his fist on the table. "I'm certain E-Force did this. The question is: are we any closer to stopping them?"

Webber and Quinn glanced at each other. Everybody at the conference table leaned forward in anticipation. The Marine colonel turned to Phillip Barrett. "Sir, this is where the plot thickens."

* * * *

The aroma of steaks floated on the breeze across Carrie's patio. She and Colt had just returned from a day of mountain biking in Moab. Less than two hours southwest of Grand Junction, the Utah town was in a valley surrounded by a desert wonderland that encompassed Arches and Canyonlands National Parks. Snowcapped mountain peaks protruded from the high aspen groves of the Manti-National Forest to the southeast. Public lands, engraved by sheer-walled canyons and studded with fantastic rock formations, stretched to the horizon in every direction.

Carrie tiptoed out of the house and crept up behind Colt. His gaze was fixed on Bandit. The shepherd-mix mutt charged across the yard after a tossed ball. Before the dog reached the bouncing orb, she wrapped Colt in a bear hug.

"I'm holding you hostage until those steaks are done." Carrie delivered her playful ransom notice in a husky voice.

"I need more time." Colt feigned panic. "You can't rush a masterpiece."

Bandit trotted back and sat down before the couple. The ball dropped from his mouth. He perked his ears and cocked his head, seeming to ask why the game was delayed.

Carrie changed her voice to a humorously higher-pitched tone. "Okay, whatever you need. I'll just settle for a sip of your beer." She planted a kiss on Colt's lips and confiscated the bottle from his grip.

"You've been abusing me all day." Colt pretended to whine as Carrie savored a sip of his Colorado microbrew. "First, it was the mountain biking and now this."

She laughed. "I seem to remember chasing you on the trails all day."

He grinned. "Are you sure it was me you were after?"

Carrie and Colt pulled together in a tight embrace. For a second, they kissed, lost in the moment. Bandit gave up on play and retreated to a shady spot under the picnic table to cool his black coat.

The couple moved apart. "Turn the grill up and finish those steaks." Carrie surveyed the lengthening shadows of the trees. "The ambiance is perfect for dinner outside."

"I'd eat them raw if it meant a romantic dinner with you." Colt bobbed his eyebrows.

Chuckling, Carrie bounded back inside the kitchen and pulled the baked potatoes out of the oven. She was energized by happiness. After less than a month with Colt, the problems of the past were distant memories. It was as if God had lighted a path for her to follow. She enjoyed every moment she spent with Colt. When they were apart, her thoughts constantly drifted to him. The sheer thrill of being alive coursed through her veins.

The local newscast was playing out on the television mounted in the corner. Carrie reached for the remote to switch it off.

"Our top story tonight involves the fatal shootings at Crested Butte Mountain Resort," the news anchor said. "The victims were shot by AmeResort security guards."

A wave of dismay swept through her. "Colt, you need to come in and see what's on the television!"

"Steaks take precedence over T.V." Colt walked through the sliding door with the sizzling cuts of meat.

Carrie didn't smile when she glanced at him. Colt's grin faded. He shifted his attention to the television and stopped dead in his tracks.

* * * *

The marked silence of Howard Anderson's study was broken only by the sound of his pacing footsteps. The EcoFriends president had yanked the plug on the miniature fountain and switched off the sound system. He needed an escape from the grating noise of gurgling water and new-age melodies. Marching around the study, Anderson eyed the empty Vodka bottle on the desk. He slapped it onto the floor. "I should have kept this place stocked better."

Forced to rely on the television news for information, Anderson could only speculate about the disaster in Mt. Crested Butte. Investigators had not released any pertinent information about the victims or the events leading to their deaths. That hadn't stopped a gathering storm of media accusations; AmeResort Corporation was guilty of abhorrent brutality. Anderson's intuition suggested the media was mounting a final assault on the enemy too quickly. They were risking a massive public backlash if all the speculation turned out to be wrong. AmeResort wouldn't look like the bad guys anymore. And a blowtorch would be applied to the E-Force investigation.

As he moved about the study, Anderson was shocked by his reflection on the glass covering a huge wall photo. The self-assured leader who had professed public support for E-Force was gone. Instead, he stared at the image of a bewildered beatnik whose lofty philosophizing had been exposed as fraudulent self-indulgence.

"Where are you, Cain?" Anderson collapsed into his leather chair. He clenched his hands into fists to counter the shaking. The tendrils of anxiety were taking root within his psyche. Feeling helpless, he sat contemplating the potential disaster he was facing.

Since the creation of E-Force, Zed Cain had been responsible for ensuring mission success. While Anderson selected targets and obtained financing, Cain was in charge of planning the operations...and preventing disasters. *You screwed up, you stupid psychopath!*

If Cain had been identified, captured or killed, it wouldn't be difficult for investigators to follow the trail back to EcoFriends. Deflecting charges of money laundering was hard enough. If EcoFriends was directly linked to E-Force, doom would be imminent. *What a damned fool I was to trust Marchotti, to get dragged into this debacle. I took the easy path. Now, everything is spiraling out of control.*

When the phone rang, Anderson jolted from his seat.

"Cain, where the hell have you been? I've been trying to contact you all day!"

Cain responded without emotion. "I've been preoccupied."

"Who's with you?" Anderson continued his inquisition.

"Trigger's with me. Landin and Conley are dead."

"What happened to Miller and Delilah?" Anderson's paranoia hardened.

"They wrecked the van," Cain answered without further explanation.

"Damn it! How'd this thing get screwed up so badly?"

Cain said, "There've never been guarantees on mission success."

"Explain how your team ended up in a gun battle." Anderson tugged at his hair.

"AmeResort security guards shot Conley and Landin in the back," Cain said. "I returned fire."

Anderson's temper exploded. "Why were you carrying a gun? The team wasn't supposed to be armed!"

"It kept me alive," Cain said without remorse.

"You were supposed to prevent something like this." Anderson could hardly think straight.

"AmeResort changed tactics." Cain sounded displeased by the accusations.

"That doesn't change the fact that the FBI has two dead bodies to identify. You understand that will lead them to EcoFriends, don't you? That means the FBI is coming for you and me!"

"The guards drew first blood," Cain said. "When that gets out to the public, AmeResort is finished."

"Maybe so," Anderson admitted, feeling a cold chill, "but AmeResort will take us down with them. They'll use every last resource to bring the hammer down on us."

"You're starting to balk, Howard," Cain said quietly. "This isn't just about you. Have you forgotten what we're doing?"

Anderson snapped, "Of course not. But sticking my head into a hornets' nest was never the plan."

Cain uttered a prediction. "With help from the media, this will end quickly."

Anderson didn't share Cain's certainty. With nothing left to lose, AmeResort would fight like a wounded grizzly. Fear welled up from the depths of his being.

"Have you contacted Marla Wells?"

"Yes," Cain answered.

"What did you tell her?" Anderson asked.

"I told her the truth."

That meant Marla Wells was primed to lead the media onslaught against AmeResort. The assault would be brutal, but Anderson didn't have the confidence to predict how the public would react.

"Get back to Boulder." Anderson issued his order as he paced the room. "We have to keep this situation under control."

Anderson resisted the urge to throw the phone when the call ended. Everything was hanging in the balance. If the plan didn't go right, Anderson knew no amount of media spin would save him.

* * * *

"The shooting victims at Crested Butte Mountain Resort haven't been identified," Channel 4 news anchor, Tom Roberts, reported. "And there's no word on whether a fatal vehicle crash is related to the incident. AmeResort hasn't made a public statement to shed light on the incident. We'll keep you updated with breaking news."

Chris Morgan's television camera panned back to reveal the entire news set. Marla was amused by Sarah Farmington's icy smile.

"Marla Wells has commentary from the environmental perspective." Roberts' attempt at affability was unconvincing.

Marla managed not to laugh at Roberts. The thrill of victory encouraged her. "As most of our viewers know, I've accepted a network position in New York. This is my last special report from Denver to provide some insight with regard to this tragedy."

Marla beamed at Roberts. "I got an ID on a young woman that was taken into custody after that crash you mentioned. Police ran her vehicle off the road. Her name is Delilah Francelli, and her residence is Boulder, Colorado." A photograph of Delilah was shown for the viewers. Roberts turned red with embarrassment. "I'll keep you posted with any other facts I turn up."

Marla continued with a haughty air. "A short time ago, I received a phone call from E-Force. I have confirmation that the two men gunned down by AmeResort personnel were unarmed E-Force members."

Roberts appeared not to be listening.

"Two AmeResort guards were killed by gunfire, but E-Force insists they never fired a shot," Marla said. "My informant claims the whole incident was a setup. He predicted that ballistic tests will prove every bullet at the crime scene was fired from AmeResort-owned weapons.

"Clearly AmeResort Corporation is taking a much more aggressive stance against opposition groups. AmeResort leadership refused to respond to my inquiries as to whether lethal force is part of a new corporate policy to deal with activists. It's a good bet that the public won't support draconian measures like shooting first and asking questions later."

"We don't know if E-Force is telling the whole story," Roberts said.

Marla remained unfazed. "The authorities and AmeResort aren't contradicting the caller's claims. These killings may be nothing short of murder."

Roberts coughed nervously and said, "Murder is a strong word to use until all the facts are known."

"AmeResort's silence is telling," Marla replied.

"E-Force can't be absolved from responsibility," Sarah said, looking into the camera instead of at Marla.

"I've never exonerated E-Force." Marla's forced smile barely contained her seething anger. "But their radical action is a symptom of a larger crisis. Corporate industry and development is likely reaping a harvest sown by callous greed. And with these killings, AmeResort may have signed its own death warrant."

* * * *

"This is unbelievable," Carrie said after listening to Marla. E-Force was engaged in outright domestic terrorism against a prominent component of the American economy. *The media is behaving like a kangaroo court, helping a corrupt dictator to convict and eliminate a political rival on trumped-up charges of subversion.*

"E-Force people get killed trying to vandalize a ski resort, and the reporters blame the resort owner! That's like condemning a homeowner who shoots a burglar that breaks into his house. And where does she get off with that death warrant stuff?"

When Colt didn't respond, Carrie turned around. Standing next to the counter, Colt's eyes were cast down at the floor.

"Colt, what's wrong?" Carrie asked with concern.

"We need to sit down and talk," Colt said quietly. "Dinner can wait."

"Let's go to the living room." Carrie was worried by Colt's sudden somber transformation.

"Carrie, I know the woman who was arrested in Mt. Crested Butte," Colt said after an awkward moment on the couch. "Delilah Francelli is my ex-fiancée."

"You were engaged?" Carrie felt a lump in her throat. "That's a surprise. And how could a woman you were going to marry be part of E-Force?"

Denial and disbelief combined in an unpalatable cocktail in her stomach. Everything seemed so wonderful. Now something was terribly wrong.

"I don't know all the details, but there's a chance I knew

the dead guys too."

"I don't understand." Carrie stammered. "This doesn't make sense."

"Carrie, I've made some mistakes. You deserve to know the truth."

* * * *

"Marla Wells has gone off the deep end." Luke rose from the couch and trudged to the kitchen of his Lakewood apartment. Far beyond the windows, the setting sun transformed the high-rises in downtown Denver to pillars of glittering gold.

I can't believe she's condemning AmeResort without an attempt to uncover the truth. Luke shook his head and retrieved a Coke from the refrigerator. An E-Force tragedy was bound to happen. They were playing with fire and got burned.

Luke plopped back down in front of the television. Marla was gone. Roberts and Sarah Farmington were engaged in small talk with the meteorologist. "She's so beautiful." He dreamed about meeting Sarah.

When the camera turned to the rambling weather guy, Luke's thoughts shifted to Darius Marchotti and his humanitarian centers. The suspicions germinated at the Common Cause for Humanity awards had pushed him into an investigation of the UMN patriarch. Luke discovered many prominent environmental groups had made large financial contributions to Marchotti's cause. One of those benefactors was EcoFriends.

Luke remembered Howard Anderson's claim that environmental groups were losing ground and failing in fundraising efforts. *If that's true, how did EcoFriends have revenue to donate to Marchotti's centers?*

His curiosity was piqued. Succumbing to his compulsive nature, Luke delved into the background of Howard

Anderson and EcoFriends. The man's past remained largely a mystery. Anderson had simply arrived in Boulder, Colorado, eight years earlier and founded EcoFriends. His group hit the ground running with a sizable staff, a newsletter, and lobbyists. It wasn't cheap to start off with such a big bang.

EcoFriends had quickly risen to prominence in the western United States. Luke found little evidence that the organization was losing ground as Anderson had claimed. Regardless, his refusal to condemn E-Force was baffling.

"Why are you tolerating E-Force?" Luke was thinking aloud. "Radical eco-terrorists could set the entire environmental movement back by decades."

Sipping on his Coke, Luke thought about the possibility of an E-Force conspiracy. That implied there was a coordinated clandestine effort to accomplish a particular covert task. There had to be a leader too. Luke considered the role Marla Wells had taken in spinning the E-Force business. *Could she be part of this thing?*

A light went off in Luke's head. Marla had been promoted to a network job with the United Media Network after taking up for E-Force. Maybe the UMN was the head of the conspiracy. If that were the case, what was the particular end they were after? And how was EcoFriends connected?

"This could be a scandal of monumental proportions." Luke's trembling hand could barely hold his drink steady.

* * * *

Special Agent Travis Price switched off the television in his Crested Butte hotel room. The E-Force deaths had turned the investigation into a media circus.

"Marla Wells crossed the line," Price said. "Her accusations against AmeResort are going to screw everything up."

"What do you think Barrett will do?" Special Agent Marvin Hill asked.

"He'll take matters into his own hands." Price stood up and paced across the room.

"We can't let that happen." Hill scratched his head and fidgeted.

"Her narcissism is going to destroy all we've worked for. I refuse to let that happen."

"What's the next move?"

"I'm going to call the head honcho." Price bolted for the door. He was resolute, convinced that the situation warranted such a measure.

* * * *

At the head of the conference table, Phillip Barrett looked over the faces of his board members. They maintained a stunned silence. Weber and Quinn waited for the AmeResort leaders to digest the implications of their allegations.

"The investigators could be keeping a lid on sensitive information." Phillip Barrett folded his arms across his chest. "How do you know there's a cover-up?"

"We can't be absolutely positive," Quinn admitted, "but we uncovered testimonials from witnesses: a security guard at Copper Mountain, a liquor store owner in Steamboat, and some guy who was checking into a hotel. They provided descriptions of E-Force members and their vehicle. There's no legitimate reason to withhold that type of information from the public. It could have helped stop E-Force before this fiasco."

"That's outrageous." Ms. Jacob trembled with anger. "It's criminal!"

Another board member said, "We need to take this to the head of the FBI. Whoever's responsible should be arrested and indicted."

"We don't have proof of illegal activity yet," Quinn said. "Besides, an FBI probe into the task force would further impede the E-Force case."

"Time is something we don't have." Barrett shook his head firmly. "How are we going to remedy this situation?"

"Our options are limited, and our predicament may worsen," Colonel Webber said. "Mr. Quinn's source claimed a Colt Delta Elite semi-automatic pistol was found in the maintenance yard at Crested Butte Mountain Resort. The weapon is identical to those carried by AmeResort security personnel, and it had been fired."

"Is there a chance that gun belongs to us?" Barrett asked.

"We've checked our entire weapons inventory." Webber was somber. "The one weapon we can't account for is a Colt Delta Elite. It's possible that all the bullets flying in Mt. Crested Butte were from AmeResort firearms."

It seemed the air had been sucked from the conference room. A gun from the AmeResort armory had mysteriously appeared at a crime scene.

"This is a disaster." Barrett shoved his chair away from the table. "How could this happen?"

"E-Force may have somebody inside AmeResort Corporation." Quinn's reply was hushed, as if he were telling a secret.

"A defector has got to be rooted out." Barrett seethed with anger.

"We're working to do just that," Quinn said.

Stephen Chandler nodded in approval. "That's good. You need to keep us updated."

Barrett struggled to maintain his composure. "With a potential traitor, we're forced to take matters into our hands. We've got to counter the media's scandalous reporting and take the fight to E-Force. We can't just sit around and wait for them to attack us again."

"The Developers' Forum is coming up on Friday," Chandler reminded everybody. "We can use it to develop a strategy with our colleagues in the industry."

"I haven't forgotten about your forum, Mr. Chandler," Barrett said, "but I'm not going to rely on an external committee to save this company. We have to be more proactive. I want to know how we can eradicate E-Force."

All eyes moved back to Webber and Quinn. It was apparent that the AmeResort executives agreed with Barrett. They wanted a plan to act upon.

"We do have a lead." Quinn's voice was hushed. "You know about the van that crashed in Mt. Crested Butte just after the shootings. My contact pulled Delilah Francelli from the wreckage. She regained consciousness for a moment. Before other law enforcement officers arrived at the scene, she begged him to deliver a letter."

"Did he take it?" Chandler asked tentatively.

"I have it right here." Quinn produced the small envelope that Delilah had given to Officer Perkins. "The letter discusses E-Force's activities."

There was a tense silence as Quinn walked over and placed the envelope on the table in front of Phillip Barrett. With no writing on the outside, it belied the significance of the contents.

"Who knows about this?" Barrett asked.

"Besides my source, only the people in this room," Quinn answered.

Everyone watched as Barrett opened the flap and removed two folded sheets of paper. The name of the intended recipient was written at the top of the first page. It was Colt Kelley.

* * * *

"You helped launder money that financed E-Force." Carrie slumped on her living room couch. She was afraid her desires had shaped her impression of Colt. "That's like making a deal with the devil!"

"I didn't know it was helping E-Force at first." Colt hung his head. "Nobody had even heard of them."

Anger mounted in her that Colt and the other supposed leaders at EcoFriends had acted with such arrogance and egocentricity. None of them had stopped to consider the consequences of breaking federal laws. They obviously hadn't bothered to think about the effects their actions would have on the other people in their lives either.

In exasperation, Carrie said, "It was still stupid. And you found out E-Force was the beneficiary later. How could you provide any kind of support for an evil like E-Force?"

"Everything spun out of control." Colt put his elbows on his knees and buried his forehead in his hands. "When we started misreporting the amount of funds we raised, it was to ensure the survival of EcoFriends. I used to believe in the ideals our organization stood for. After a few years, there was enough cash being diverted that it had to be laundered. I wasn't involved with that part, but I knew it was happening. It was only a few months ago when I discovered our dirty money was going to E-Force. I overheard part of a telephone conversation between Howard Anderson and somebody who seemed to be making demands."

"Why didn't you go to the police or something?" Carrie asked. "Those E-Force nuts could have been stopped before they gained momentum."

"I would have had to make a confession," Colt said. "I wasn't ready to accept responsibility for my actions. And I'd sworn an oath of loyalty to EcoFriends. It wasn't easy to toss that aside."

"That's not a very good excuse, Colt. It sounds like denial."

"There's not a day that goes by that I don't wish I could go back and do things differently." Colt's expression was pained. "But that's not going to happen. I have to live with guilt and regret. It's too late to make things right again."

"Colt, you've got to tell the FBI what you know," Carrie

said with as much certainty as she could muster. "Your window of opportunity will slam shut once the FBI figures out you helped fund E-Force. If you help the feds bring down E-Force before more people die, they might grant you clemency."

"It's not that simple," Colt proclaimed, shaking his head. "My friend Deb went to the FBI, and she ended up dead. It's my fault."

"What are you talking about?" Carrie's blood curdled. "You think somebody killed her?"

"Deb died in a car wreck the day before I met you. I think she was eliminated to cover up the truth about EcoFriends and E-Force."

"You're talking about cold-blooded murder." Carrie gripped his arm. "Somebody at the FBI has to look into that."

"I think there are dirty cops tied to E-Force." Colt shook his head. "If I go to the police, I'll become the next target for elimination."

"Are you sure you're not being paranoid?" Carrie's concerns continued to escalate.

"Somehow, I know I'm right," Colt said, "It's like I've fallen into a dark cave full of rattlesnakes. Ruthless people are waiting with their senses honed to detect any threats. I can't flee or call for help because they'll strike. So I've been huddling in fear, while the legitimate authorities approach like a horde of villagers with torches and kerosene. My choices are the serpents' fangs or incineration with them."

The gravity of the situation was staggering. The little hairs on her body stood on end as if a bolt of lightning was about to strike.

"We've got to come up with a plan of action." She kept her voice steady.

"There's no 'we,' Carrie." Colt looked away. "You don't need to do anything. This isn't your problem."

Embers of faith ignited fiery determination within

Carrie. "You're wrong, Colt. I love you and I don't want to lose you."

When Colt turned back to her, a flood of emotions spilled from his striking eyes. It was an epiphany that strengthened her unabashed gaze.

"I love you too." Colt pulled Carrie close, and he pressed his lips to hers.

Eyes closed, she put her hands behind Colt's head and caressed him as they kissed. Time seemed to stop as they focused only on each other. E-Force was forgotten for the time. On the kitchen counter, the steaks and potatoes had long since grown cold.

Chapter Eleven
Monday, June 11

"It's going to be a hectic day." Senator John Harris sat reviewing an agenda in his Washington, D.C. office. *Election years are brutal.*

Harris was immersed in a campaign for a third term in office and lagging behind his opponent in the polls. Battling Cardin's campaign finance legislation was taking a political toll. The media had stepped up efforts to portray Harris as a lapdog to big corporations. But his resolve was unwavering.

Harris knew the new laws would increase the media's influence on the outcome of elections. If severe limits on funding and advertising went into effect, candidates would be unable to fend for themselves. Only those who gained the favor of the media would succeed. That was the dirty little secret. The issue came down to power.

The basis of Harris' counter-offensive was a relentless campaign to educate American citizens about the fallacies of the proposed campaign reforms. As a guest on syndicated talk radio programs, Harris was reaching widespread audiences. He explained the basis for his opposition to the proposed political reforms and catalyzed growing public disapproval of the campaign bill. These rumblings had served as a wakeup call to Senators. Most of them were unwilling to risk their political futures by ignoring the demands of constituents.

An incoming phone call served as the starting gun for another Monday. "Phillip Barrett is on the line," his secretary said when he picked up the receiver.

"Phillip Barrett wants to speak with me? I suppose I'll take the call."

"I'll put him through."

Harris greeted the billionaire developer. "Good morning, Mr. Barrett. What can I do for you, sir?"

"Don't you 'sir' me, you beltway politician." The response from Barrett was terse.

"My apologies. You're not deserving of the title anyway."

Barrett chuckled at the banter. "It's been a while since we last spoke, John. How've you been?"

"Despite spending all my time in Washington, I'm doing pretty well," Harris answered. "How's everything with you and your family, Phillip?"

"The family's fine but I've seen better times." Barrett's jovial tone evaporated as if he had just been diagnosed with cancer. "I'm sure you've seen the news."

"I imagine the stress from dealing with that terrorist group is taking its toll," Harris said. "The media is really hammering on the latest incident."

"The E-Force situation has escalated into a fiasco that's threatening the future of AmeResort Corporation," Barrett admitted.

"E-Force is a despicable group of criminals." Harris shook his head sadly. "The media coverage has been outrageous. They're defending the violator instead of the victim."

"It's a big problem." Barrett's anger ricocheted through the phone line. "Frankly, we're running out of options."

"Is there anything I can do to help?" Harris furrowed his brow. "I still owe you more than I can ever repay."

The two men had become close friends while serving in the Navy during the Vietnam War. When Harris' plane was hit by heavy ground fire, Barrett provided covering fire while a rescue helicopter extracted Harris from enemy-held jungle. Without Barrett, the operation would not have succeeded. Six months later, when Barrett's plane was hit during a night bombing mission, there was no one there to help.

"That's nonsense, John," Barrett retorted.

Harris countered. "You helped pull me out of a jam. I

wasn't able to do the same for you."

"All bets are off in war. You weren't flying the night I got hit. It's just the way things happened. We've been over this before."

"Just remember, I'm always willing to lend a hand." Harris couldn't erase his guilt.

"That's the reason for my call," Barrett said. "I have a favor to ask."

* * * *

The airliner reached cruising altitude. In the first class section of the cabin, Marla Wells unfastened her seat belt and reclined the seat. She felt more powerful than ever.

Everyone wanted to probe into the mysteries of E-Force as the radical group's notoriety spread across the country. Since E-Force wasn't granting interviews, Marla was the sole path to enlightenment. Her calendar was full of interviews and television appearances, each a chance to shine.

Marla enjoyed a glass of champagne and contemplated what lay ahead. Upon arrival in New York, a corporate limousine was to transport her to the UMN offices. An orientation was scheduled for the afternoon. At the end of the day, Marla would be free to pursue the rewards of success without the shackles of a miserable marriage. Denver was already a distant memory.

The world is mine. Marla brimmed with self-assurance. The tiny bursting bubbles in the glass tickled her lips.

* * * *

Luke Parson burned his tongue and spilled coffee on the papers strewn about his computer. "Ouch! Damn it, that's hot!"

A sweatshirt hanging on the back of the chair served as a

towel to dab dry the disorganized results of his Internet research. For most of the past twenty-four hours, Luke had been compiling a list of media companies that were subsidiaries to the United Media Network. For all practical purposes, Darius Marchotti had a monopoly on information conveyed to the consuming public. The tycoon was the commanding general of an army of reporters and journalists who were pushing tolerance for E-Force.

There's got to be some link between Marchotti and radical environmentalists. Luke struggled against the mind-numbing symptoms of exhaustion. *I can feel it.*

Ready to beat a retreat to the shower, Luke conducted one last Google search using the keywords, 'United Media Network' and 'activist'.

"Environmental Activist Disappears at Sea." He read the resulting headline from a Boston newspaper.

Luke forced himself to delve into the brief piece. Eight years earlier, the U.S. Coastguard discovered a capsized sailboat several miles off the coast of Cape Cod. The body of a drowned college student was in the flooded cabin of the craft. She was identified as a romantic interest of Jonathan Forde, the wealthy young man who had chartered the boat. It turned out that Forde's body wasn't recovered. He was presumed drowned. The Coastguard blamed the tragedy on rough seas and the inexperience of the couple.

"It seems you were quite a rabble rouser at Harvard, Mr. Forde," Luke said after reading about Forde's campus activism. The anti-corporate protests he organized and led were disorderly and violent. According to the article, several students enrolled in the ROTC program were critically burned at the hands of his mob. Forde was arrested and indicted on numerous criminal charges.

Luke was startled by the last few lines of the brief article. "At the time of his run-in with the law, Forde was working part-time for *Issue Insight Magazine*." It was a breakthrough, a potential connection between a subsidiary of the United Media Network and radical activism. *It says Forde was free on bond at the time of the sailboat tragedy.* Luke was baffled. *That's crazy. How'd the cops know he didn't stage his death to avoid prison?* Certain there was more to the mystery, Luke searched for more information about Jonathan Forde.

Luke mouthed the words of another newspaper headline. "Memorial for Activist Passes Quietly." It was followed by a summary of a memorial organized by Forde's followers. Luke nearly fell out of his chair at the last paragraph. Forde's entire fortune was donated to Marchotti's humanitarian organization.

"This is big." Luke buzzed with tingling adrenaline.

* * * *

"We were a couple cocky sons-of-guns."

John Harris gazed at a photograph of two grinning young naval officers in flight gear. Harris and Barrett were standing next to a jet on an aircraft carrier deck. The fire in Barrett's eyes still leapt from the faded image.

Harris knew the terrible abuses of the Viet Cong hadn't conquered Barrett's indomitable spirit. Never willing to admit defeat, he possessed a stalwart strength that was the key to his remarkable successes in life. Today marked the first time Barrett had approached him with a significant request. Only a desperate predicament would warrant such behavior.

The meetings and committee work can be rescheduled or skipped. Harris thought about the coming week. *And I can take work with me.*

The Senator was prioritizing tasks when his conscience spurred an itch like poison ivy. It had been a long time since he had really tended to the roles of husband, father, and grandfather. A politician always had a full quiver of excuses for such personal failures. The best encompassed some reference to the commitment required of public servants to ensure a sustainable future for America. If that rang hollow, a leader might resort to pointing out the importance and magnitude of his duties. And so the people closest to Harris had often been relegated to the ranks of the neglected. For the better part of a year, his regret had been growing. The time had finally arrived to cast off into the currents of change. Harris decided the work could wait.

Harris pressed the intercom button on his phone. "Betty, let's look at the calendar. I need to take a trip to Denver."

His trusted secretary entered the office a moment later, toting a handheld computer. "This is unexpected. Is something wrong?"

"An old friend needs a hand. And I need a couple days with my family."

Betty nodded, understanding. "I'll make the travel arrangements."

"Lori and I just need a car to get to Reagan National," Harris said to his secretary. "There's no need for flight reservations."

"You already took care of that?" Betty was surprised.

"Phillip Barrett is furnishing his private jet."

* * * *

Darius Marchotti burst onto the top floor of the United Media Network building the instant the elevator doors parted. His rapid-fire footsteps echoed off the marble tiled floor. Yuri Zharikov maintained the brisk pace. The staff sprang to action when the pair passed through the portal to the executive office suite.

"Good morning, Mr. Marchotti." A shapely assistant greeted him with a cup of coffee. "The newspapers are on your desk."

"Very good." Marchotti barely broke his stride.

The woman called after him. "Mr. Feinstein requested a

meeting with you this morning."

"Tell him to be here in fifteen minutes," Marchotti said before charging into his office.

Zharikov shoved the heavy wood doors closed and turned toward the impressive views of Manhattan spread beyond two walls of glass. The vista was the backdrop for an expansive desk. Modern art pieces accented the décor of stainless steel and black leather. An incredible entertainment system with myriad television screens comprised one side of the immense room. The place was a fitting abode for the monarch of a media empire.

When Marchotti was seated, he turned his attention to the newspapers. The United Media Network owned all of them.

"AmeResort Murders Environmental Activists," Marchotti quoted a front-page headline. "The last nail is being driven into the AmeResort coffin."

"Did the cops find what you call a smoking gun?" Zharikov's inquiry was steeped in his thick accent.

"Literally." Marchotti rubbed his hands together with glee. "Ballistics tests proved that every bullet found at that backwater Colorado resort was fired from pistols recovered at the scene. All those guns are registered to AmeResort."

Zharikov frowned. "So AmeResort shot their own guards?"

"That's what Marla Wells thinks." Marchotti couldn't repress a smile as he tapped the paper with his finger. "According to her theory, AmeResort cronies staged a gun battle in Mt. Crested Butte. Knocking off a few of their own unsuspecting personnel was acceptable collateral damage. They figured it would warrant killing E-Force members."

Zharikov scoffed. "That would be a sloppy, stupid plan."

"I'd call it desperation." Marchotti chuckled. "But it doesn't matter. Marla Wells has ignited a firestorm. Every media pundit in the country is convinced AmeResort conjured up a criminal conspiracy to deal with the E-Force thorn in its side. They're bombarding the public with theories, and AmeResort is caught in a whirlwind they can't escape."

"So it's over for AmeResort?" Zharikov asked, scratching his head.

"Their sales and profits are in the toilet. People are cancelling reservations at AmeResort properties across the nation. It's a financial disaster. A fire-sale to liquidate corporate assets will only convince the last diehard investors that the game is over."

Marchotti rifled through the financial section of the newspaper. He wanted to see how low AmeResort stocks had fallen on the NASDAQ index. Before he could partake in his entertainment, the electronic tone of the intercom sounded.

"What is it?" Marchotti was annoyed by the disturbance.

"I'm sorry to interrupt you, Mr. Marchotti." The assistant's voice emanated from the speaker. "Mr. Feinstein is here as you requested."

"Send him in." Marchotti signaled to Zharikov.

The big bodyguard left the couch and moved to the entrance. He pulled the door open to a slender man in a business suit. The bespectacled attorney was dwarfed by Zharikov when he squeezed past and hurried toward Marchotti's desk. It was a path he had traveled many times.

"Have a seat, Feinstein." Marchotti directed his legal counsel to one of the leather chairs before his desk. "What brings you here this morning?"

"I'll get right to the point." Feinstein never wasted time with meaningless talk. "AmeResort Corporation has filed a lawsuit against the United Media Network. They're accusing us of defamation, specifically libel. They're claiming a monetary loss of more than half a billion dollars."

Marchotti glared at the lawyer. "When were you notified of this lawsuit?"

"It was filed this morning," Feinstein answered. "Our

legal staff has begun to analyze the case in order to--"

"I'm not interested in the methodology of your attorneys. What's your plan to stop this nonsense."

"Phillip Barrett doesn't normally resort to litigation," Feinstein said and swallowed hard. "Unfortunately, I don't have all the details yet."

"Then why are you here? Meetings occur only when you're ready to provide me with facts and details."

"This is a unique situation." Feinstein managed to stand firm. "AmeResort Corporation is coming after you this time. Phillip Barrett is holding you personally liable for his financial losses."

* * * *

The western bureau of *Issue Insight Magazine* was headquartered in downtown Denver. The magazine occupied several levels of an office tower, with human resources on the tenth floor. Luke was pleased to find Joanna Spencer at her desk when he ambled into the HR office.

A broad smile appeared on her face. "Hi, Luke. I was going to track you down."

"I hope you have good intentions." Luke's reply was cautious.

"I owe you big time for setting me up on that blind date." Joanna bubbled with enthusiasm. "The two of us have so much in common."

"It sounds like romance is blossoming," Luke said with a raised eyebrow.

"It just feels right to both of us," Joanna said with glee. "It's too amazing to describe."

"Well, I'm happy for both of you." Luke's gaze swept around the department. "Are you the only person here right now?"

"Everyone else is at lunch. Why do you ask?"

Luke tested the waters. "Maybe you could do something

for me."

"Just ask and you'll receive." Joanna seemed eager to help.

"Your department keeps a personnel record for each employee of this bureau of *Issue Insight*. Is there a comprehensive database for all the magazine's bureaus?"

"There's a central computer database for the entire United Media Network," Joanna answered without hesitation.

"So you maintain our bureau's files in the UMN system?" Luke felt a burst of excitement.

"We update it all the time. Do you want to check your file or something?"

"I'd like you to search for a record for a man named Jonathan Forde." Luke's voice was hushed.

"Luke, the files in the database are confidential. I'd get fired, maybe prosecuted, if anyone found out I was messing around in there."

"I understand the risk. You don't have to do it. I'm just asking."

Joanna cast her eyes downward as she considered the request. Luke hoped the blind date thing would bring home the bacon. "Okay, I'll do it. We have a few minutes before my supervisor gets back."

"Thank you." Luke placed his hand on her shoulder. "I have a good reason for looking into this guy."

"I really don't want to know the details."

Luke watched while Joanna clicked with her mouse. A security message appeared on the monitor. It included a prompt for a username and password.

"This stuff is off-limits," Joanna said bluntly. "Keep watch and warn me if someone is coming."

"No problem." Luke stepped closer to the windows that separated the office from the hallway.

The clicking of keyboard and mouse ceased. "I found the file."

"That's great." Luke rushed to Joanna. "What's in it?"

"I'm not authorized to open files from other bureaus," Joanna retorted. "You said you just wanted to know if there was a file for this guy."

"Jonathan Forde is deceased," Luke explained, leaning toward the computer screen. "I'm just trying to find--"

"You're supposed to be keeping watch, Luke!"

Luke and Joanna snapped their heads toward the window at the same time. A heavyset woman was lumbering in the hallway. She was almost to the office door.

"It's my boss!" Joanna scrambled to exit the UMN database and terminate her connection to the server.

Luke swore at his inattentiveness and whirled toward the door. The big woman barged into the room. "What brings you in here?" Her scowl was fit for a Halloween mask.

"I had questions about my health insurance benefits and Joanna was--"

"Those questions should be directed to me." The large gal brushed past and stalked toward Joanna's desk. "What are you doing?"

"I'm working on that memo." Joanna pointed to her screen at an open Microsoft Word document. There hadn't been a second to spare.

"I'll stop by when I have more time." Luke suppressed a sigh of relief. Joanna shot him a hard look that warned him not to ask any more favors.

Loping to the elevator, Luke was remorseful. He had no intention of asking his friend to stick her neck out again. A different approach was required.

Stepping out of the elevator on a lower floor, Luke trotted down a corridor. There was a door with a sign that said Information Technology. He navigated through the maze of office cubicles that comprised the IT department. The place was as quiet as a library.

Luke poked his head around one of the partitions. Inside the cubical, a young Asian man with long hair was typing computer code at a rapid-fire pace. His nose was only inches from the monitor. Engrossed in his work, Justin Yeung nearly leapt from his chair when Luke rapped on the partition wall.

"Man, you startled me," Justin said, adjusting his glasses.

"Sorry, Braveheart. We need to talk."

* * * *

"Cut! This scene isn't working!" Renowned film director, Sid Adamo threw his hat on the ground. A collective groan went up amongst the cast and crew.

"You've got to be kidding!" Drew Harmon exploded. "Now what's wrong?"

"You're ignoring my instructions." Adamo pressed his hands against his temples. "This film is a portrait of the harsh realities of war. Your role is that of a man struggling to remain human amidst a backdrop of death, carnage, and destruction. That has nothing to do with bravado!"

"You keep moving the bar higher." Harmon wished the fake rifle in his hands was real and loaded.

"I won't be satisfied until you convey the inner turmoil of your character."

"What the hell do you think I'm doing?"

"Pretending you're Rambo." Adamo spat out his accusation.

"Oh, now you want to make this personal?" Harmon stomped toward the director. "I'll tell you what--"

An assistant blocked Harmon's path to Adamo. "I think you both need to step back and cool off."

"This is pointless." Adamo threw his hands in the air. "Everybody take fifteen minutes, and we'll try it again."

The cast and crew dispersed, and Harmon stormed towards his trailer. He uttered a string of curses as his anger continued to boil. *Nobody cares about that jackass Adamo's opinions.* "The fans want to see me…they want to be me."

As soon as he set foot in his trailer, Harmon poured a shot of scotch. After downing it, he readied another drink. Harmon settled into a chair with the glass in one hand and the bottle in the other. It was the only way he knew to soothe the sting from Adamo's insults. An image of his drunken father appeared in his mind. Harmon pushed it aside. *Screw you old man. I made something of myself!*

"Maybe I've never been a marine, but I've been through hell. I'm a bad ass. That's what everybody wants to see on the freaking silver screen."

As far as Harmon was concerned, Adamo's incompetence had trashed the filming schedule. It wasn't his problem.

Harmon imagined his hands around Adamo's neck. *I'm flying to Denver on Thursday, come hell or high water.*

* * * *

The nightmare culminated in the same inevitable terror. Plunging into a black abyss, Delilah's tumbling body accelerated at an exponential rate. It became impossible to draw the breath to scream as her body spun ever more violently. The centrifugal force tore at her limbs and her innards threatened to explode from within. At the last possible second, she jolted awake, gasping for breath.

Delilah's frightened eyes darted around as she panted under sweat-soaked sheets. Grappling with disorientation, dull memories of the hospital room filtered through the haze of pain medication. A shaft of light spilled into the darkened room. The chair across the hall where the cop always sat was empty. For a moment, Delilah considered fleeing. It hurt just to push her back up to the point where she could lean against the headboard. A cast on her left arm made it as awkward as a seal's flipper on a ladder. The fractured long bones ached, but the broken ribs delivered agony. Sutures on her abdomen strained with each grimacing breath.

"I don't want to go to jail." Delilah moaned. Fading hope left a cold void that sent chills shooting through her body. *Oh God, I never believed in you, but if you're there, please use some of your magic and deliver me from this hell. I promise I'll change.*

A tidal surge of tears breached Delilah's eyelids. She slumped over and cried. When the sobs finally ebbed, her hollow gaze was drawn to a silhouette in the doorway.

"How are you feeling?" A male voice floated into the room. "You're lucky to have survived that terrible wreck."

Delusion blended with reality for Delilah. "All I remember is falling and tumbling."

"Ms. Francelli, I'm going to turn on the light." The man stepped into the room and flipped the wall switch. Bathed in radiance, his dark coat and tie suggested he was no doctor.

"Who are you?" Delilah demanded.

"I've forgotten my manners." His tone was apologetic. "I'm Special Agent Price from the FBI."

"You're a cop." Delilah made the accusation when Price displayed his badge.

"I'm a detective," Price admitted with a dismissive shrug. "Ms. Francelli, we need to have an important conversation."

Delilah bristled. "I'm not talking to any cops without an attorney."

"My goal isn't to incriminate you." Price advanced toward the bed. "I just need information about the events that led to your accident."

"Do you think I'm an idiot? You'll use anything I say to implicate me in--" Delilah stopped in mid-sentence, realizing she was already digging herself a hole. Everything was a blur...so confusing.

"The doctors expect you to make a complete recovery." Price settled into the chair next to the bed. "You still have your whole life ahead of you. Don't throw it away."

Delilah kept her mouth shut. She wasn't sure where Price's comments were leading.

"You're part of E-Force, Ms. Francelli," Price said. "The members of your group are wanted in connection with federal crimes. You're in a lot of trouble. You'll go to prison if you're convicted of the charges against you. There's plenty of strong evidence for a conviction. You understand that, don't you?"

Tears filled Delilah's eyes again. A lump formed in her throat, and she struggled to breathe. With her lip quivering, she clenched her fists and fought to control her emotions.

"There's a way you can save yourself," Price said in a quiet voice. "I can help you, if you help me."

Delilah could not dismiss Price. His words provided her with a glimpse of salvation. The man's countenance was soft and inviting.

"I want you to tell me everything you know about E-Force. Don't hold anything back. In return for your cooperation, you'll be granted immunity."

"I can't do that." Delilah burst out. "They'll come after me!"

"We'll protect you. Nobody will be able to hurt you. You have my word."

Delilah surrendered hoarsely after a long silence. "I don't want any part of that bullshit anymore. You better keep your promise."

Price reinforced his pledge to guarantee Delilah's safety. In return, a torrent of words gushed forth. Without prodding or coaxing, she betrayed the names of E-Force comrades and provided details of their operations.

Price provided an affirmation at the end of the rambling confession and revelations. "Your future looks much brighter."

"Now you have to get me off the hook."

"There's more to it than that." Price's gaze intensified. "Your fate depends on your willingness to provide testimony against E-Force in a court of law."

Fear descended upon Delilah. Images of Cain and Ruddock flashed in her mind. Price and a few cops wouldn't thwart their revenge.

"I can't testify in court. They'll come after me. I'd never be safe again!"

"If you help, everyone associated with E-Force can be arrested in short order." Price placed a hand on her shoulder. "No one is going to be free to hurt you. Every attorney on our side is going to want you to testify against E-Force. Would you do it if you knew you were safe?"

"Well, I guess so." Delilah wrung her hands. "I'd do it for the right deal."

"That's what I thought," Price replied in a near-whisper. "But before we go further, I need you to tell me what you know about E-Force's plans for the future."

Delilah's last threads of resistance snapped. "They're going to hit an event in Boulder on Friday. It'll be big and different from all the other strikes. I wasn't part of the team, but I know what's planned."

"What are the specifics?" Price leaned forward, and his eyes narrowed.

Without warning, a doctor in surgical scrubs burst into the room. A nurse followed close behind as he charged toward the FBI special agent.

"What are you doing in here?" the doctor demanded. "This patient is recovering from surgery."

Price displayed his badge. "I'm Special Agent Price with the FBI."

"Then you should know better." The doctor's anger filled the room. "Access to this patient is restricted."

"All visitors need to obtain clearance." The nurse wagged her finger. "FBI agents don't get to break the rules."

"You people can question this woman when her condition is stable," the doctor said. "Until then, you need to stay away."

176

Price issued a warning. "Ms. Francelli, our discussion is confidential. We'll continue at another time."

Without another word, Price turned on his heel and headed for the door. The nurse stepped out of the way as he strode past.

* * * *

Colt Kelley's staff at the Western Colorado Chapter of EcoFriends totaled a half dozen people. All of them were convinced that AmeResort Corporation had purposely killed unarmed activists and attempted to cover up the murders. Hatred spewed from their mouths during rants filled with the allegations of media mouthpieces like Marla Wells. It wasn't enough to see AmeResort go up in flames. His personnel were rooting for everybody with a stake in AmeResort to burn.

Colt was dismayed at the deaf ears his staff turned to his dissenting arguments. Not long ago, he had believed they were a team, working to ensure a sustainable future for generations to come. *I'm drowning in a sea of blind radical ideology.* He retreated to his office.

Carrie's assertions swirled in his head. The vast majority of American citizens would have no sympathy for E-Force if presented with the truth. People had been swayed by the deluge of misinformation on television and in the newspapers. *It's a media hoax.*

An epidemic of attacks by eco-terrorists was sure to backfire. The extremists would become a scourge to be eradicated with the public applying intense pressure on law enforcement agencies. Colt knew the dominos had begun to topple, and E-Force was at the end of the line. That meant the days were numbered for EcoFriends too.

Colt paced across his office, his mind awash in turbid thoughts. Deb had died trying to chop off one head of the Hydra. The only chance for survival was to destroy the entire

E-Force monster with one Herculean effort.

"Anderson claimed cash is the only link between us and E-Force. I don't buy it."

The bulk of the iceberg always lurked treacherously below the surface. Colt was sure Anderson and Cain were intimately involved with E-Force. If he could expose their criminal activity, there was a chance the cloak of deceit would be ripped from the entire conspiracy.

Colt shut his office door and sat down behind his desk. A deep breath helped steel his resolve. He picked up the phone and rang the main EcoFriends office in Boulder.

"How's everything in Aspen, Colt?" Howard Anderson didn't sound like he really wanted to know.

"Aspen is fine. I can't say the same thing about EcoFriends. We need to talk."

"What's the problem?"

Colt leveled his charge. "Cain is part of E-Force and maybe a lot worse."

"How do you know that?" Anderson asked after a pause.

Colt lied. "An FBI agent was poking around here. The FBI is closing in on Cain. That means EcoFriends is about to be implicated in serious crimes."

"What did they tell you?" The distress in Anderson's voice filtered through the phone.

"We can't discuss it over the phone. We should meet while I'm in Boulder tomorrow."

"That won't work," Anderson said. "I'll come to Aspen on Thursday. We'll talk about it then."

"You're going to wait three days to discuss this?" Colt was incredulous.

"I've got constraints," Anderson said with obvious irritation. "The meeting will have to wait."

"Don't you understand what's at stake, Howard? This should be our highest priority."

"I'll be dealing with this issue long before we meet," the EcoFriends president said. "We'll talk Thursday when I get up there."

"I hope the shit doesn't hit the fan between now and then."

"Likewise," Anderson agreed. "You shouldn't speak to anyone about this."

"Absolutely not," Colt said. "I expect you'll use the same discretion."

At the end of the call, Colt's nerves tingled with trepidation. The plan for redemption was initiated.

Chapter Twelve
Tuesday, June 12 (very early morning)

There has to be an easier way to do this. Luke Parson teetered on the brink of a disastrous fall. A headlamp lighted the route of his slow crawl along the tops of walls that separated offices and hallways.

A supply room in the vicinity of his desk provided a stealthy access point to the space above the ceiling. Luke had remained on a hidden perch in the dark for nearly an hour. He listened to the sounds of everyone trickling out of the building for the night.

Sweat dampened his clothes while he inched toward his destination. The taste of dust floated on the stale air. A cobweb stretched across Luke's face. He clawed at the sticky fibers and struggled to beat back pangs of arachnophobia. *This scheme seems crazier by the minute!*

Traversing above the ceiling was Luke's ploy to avoid detection by security. There were surveillance cameras in the main corridors of the building. And of course he did not have a key to the Human Resources office. Dropping in from above was a rudimentary ploy to circumvent those difficulties. After obtaining his information, he would simply reverse course along his hidden highway. A clean shirt and pair of slacks waited in the supply room. Luke would be able to step out into his office suite with clean clothes and saunter out of the building.

I'll just wave goodbye to the security guard on my way out and everything will be fine. It won't be the first time I've left this place late.

Luke deduced he had reached a position above the HR department. Stretching out on his belly, he pried up a ceiling panel. When his headlamp was off, it took a few seconds for his eyes to adjust.

Light from the hallway projected shadows of Venetian

blind slats on the floor and walls of the office below. Luke decided to make sure the coast was clear. Clinging to a cast iron pipe that comprised part of the fire sprinkler system, he thrust his head below the ceiling.

Blood rushing to his head ushered in dizziness. A silhouette suddenly dampened the light filtering into the room. Luke froze in fear. Someone was looking in through the window.

* * * *

The Colorado Rockies game was long over, and the hands on Justin Yeung's watch registered past midnight. He sat fidgeting on a bar stool in one of the establishments near Coors field. The crowd of patrons was waning. Justin discarded another empty cocktail glass next to the menagerie on the table.

A young woman cried out nearby. "Bull's-eye!"

"Nice toss, Patty," Justin said half-heartedly. He eyed the dart lodged in the red center circle with skepticism. "You're a natural."

Patty's smile faded. "That sounds a bit sarcastic."

Justin rolled his eyes. Though he had invited Patty out for the evening, he had little interest in her. She was a plain looking granola type; he fancied pretty city girls who had a flair for style and fashion. Unfortunately, he didn't know any women who fit such a profile. That meant Patty was his alibi for the night.

For the tenth time in ten minutes, Justin checked his watch. If everything was going as planned, Luke was accessing the UMN database. Against his better judgment, Justin had supplied a password and security code. Luke wasn't exactly a computer wizard. If he got busted, nobody would believe he had hacked into the database on his own. The drinks failed to quell Justin's worries.

"It's getting late," Justin said, standing up. "I'm done

with darts."

"You don't like to lose." Patty chided him with hands on her hips.

"You can see right through me." Justin shifted his feet.

"I'll pick up the tab for the drinks," Patty said with a flippant shrug.

Justin staged a weak protest. "I invited you out."

"Save your money for the therapist." She turned on her heel and marched toward the bar.

Justin picked up his jacket and stumbled after his scorned date. *I hope she'll still give me a ride home.*

* * * *

Charlie Watstull stood before the dark windows of the *Issue Insight* HR office. The image of his imposing six-foot-three-inch frame reflected off the glass. He pushed up his shirtsleeves and flexed his biceps. *Welcome to the gun show.* Watstull grinned and nodded his clean-shaven head.

The big man turned and strutted toward the break room at the end of the hall. He was craving a Diet Pepsi, and the vending machine downstairs was sold out. It was the start of a long dull shift, and Bobby Burns, the guard sitting down at the desk, itched to punch out on the time clock.

A distinct thud stopped him in his tracks. "What the hell was that?" Watstull trudged back to the windows. With his hand shielding the light from his eyes, he put his face up to the glass. "I can't see a damned thing in there."

The plethora of keys on his belt jingled as he searched for the one that would unlock the door before him. A moment later, he pushed the door open and flipped the light switch. The fluorescent bulbs flickered while his eyes played across the office.

Before Watstull could step inside the room, there was a racket down the hallway. Immediately, he turned off the lights, locked the office door, and hurried toward the elevators. When Watstull rounded the corner, he nearly collided with a young black man pushing a custodial cart in the opposite direction.

"Man, you scared me!" The custodian clutched the handle of his cart. "I almost had a heart attack."

"Sorry, Ernie." Watstull apologized. "I didn't know it was you. What are doing here so late?"

"My granny fell and broke her hip this afternoon." Ernie Jones straightened his cleaning utensils. "She had to have surgery."

"That's too bad. Is she going to be okay?"

"I don't know. Old people don't heal too well."

"I hope it works out for her." Watstull moved past the janitor. "I need a caffeine fix. And nature's calling."

"I guess I scared the shit out of you too." Jones chuckled and resumed pushing his cart down the hallway.

* * * *

Carrie was sprawled on her bed while Bandit slept on the floor nearby. Despite the late hour, she was reluctant to end the phone conversation with Colt. It might be like letting go of a string on a helium balloon. She had never been so comfortable with someone so quickly. It seemed so natural.

But Carrie had to face a cold hard fact. The man who had thawed her heart had done things that were inexcusable. Could he really be trusted? In moments of absolute honesty, Carrie worried that as painful as it would be, it would be safest to cut her losses and walk away. But she remained steadfast, praying that love hadn't blinded her to reality.

"I wish there was a way out of this mess," Carrie said. "We have to have faith that God has a plan."

"You keep saying that," Colt sounded unconvinced. "I believe in God, but it seems like the bad guys keep catching the breaks in this world."

"I can't deny that." She sighed. "But you have to believe

in something greater than yourself."

"I believe in you. I don't know what I'd do without you."

Carrie couldn't suppress a smile. "I'm disappointed that I won't get to see you tomorrow."

"I feel the same way," Colt said glumly, "but I can't skip out on my part of the presentation at the state assembly session."

"EcoFriends deserves to be abandoned," Carrie said.

"It's not quite that easy." Colt insisted.

"So you're committed to talking about water?"

"The state legislature is contemplating statutory changes that would alter the way water rights are administered in Colorado." Colt provided his explanation. "That might allow the Front Range metropolitan areas to divert more water from the Western Slope. EcoFriends has been trying to prevent that for a long time."

"Just don't get dragged in deeper. You're future's more important than water rights."

"Don't worry, Carrie. I'm just going to present some data on watersheds that my chapter compiled."

"So, why aren't you coming home tomorrow night?"

"We've got a wrap-up meeting after the state assembly session. It'll be pretty late by the time it's over."

"Colt, are you telling me everything?"

"Of course I am." Colt sounded frustrated. "Don't you trust me?"

Carrie tried to quell her suspicion. *It's not fair to doubt Colt about everything.* There were important things she hadn't revealed to him...details about her family and past. It was complicated and difficult to explain. Frankly, she was still trying to figure it all out.

"I trust you." Carrie relented. "But be careful. If what you suspect about--"

"Everything's going to be okay. I'll see you in a couple days," Colt said gently.

* * * *

You freaking idiot, Luke scolded himself. *You're going to get caught or killed!* The journalist-turned-cat-burglar wriggled and twisted his leg. Each scuff, rustle, and bump elicited winces of apprehension. Finally, his limb was free of the entrapment. A jagged hole gaped in the ceiling panel. When the behemoth in the uniform finished his antics outside the window, Luke had recoiled and nearly crashed down into the office. It was a miracle that the guard hadn't noticed the leg dangling in the room when the lights came on. *What the hell was that guard doing up here? They never come upstairs.*

"I didn't come this far for nothing." Luke grabbed the cast iron water pipe and lowered himself through the void of the ceiling panel he had removed. His fearful gaze was fixed on the windows. Panic soared for a few seconds as his dangling feet floundered for a chair below. Finally, he was down and scrambling behind Joanna's desk. *Damn, it's going to be hard to get back up there.* Luke's heart pounded in his throat.

Drawing in a deep breath, Luke lifted his head and surveyed the hallway. It was vacant. There was no way to know if it would stay that way. He nudged Joanna's chair aside and activated the computer. The machine whirred to life, and Luke fished a folded sheet of paper from his pocket. The steps to access the United Media Network database were scribbled on the creased page.

Under Luke's fingers, the keys clattered like the shoes of a troupe of tap dancers. In seconds the database interface program was running. Justin's password and security code worked without a hitch. *I'm in!* Luke's body buzzed with nervous energy.

A moment later, Luke was looking at Jonathan Forde's personnel file. There was an array of scanned documents. He scrolled through them, excitement zinging through him. Something that flashed across the screen stopped him cold. *Why is Forde's Last Will and Testament in there?* Pinpricks of suspicion erupted under Luke's skin. "I've got to print this thing."

The printer near the front of the office hummed through a warm up cycle. Luke's sweaty fingers snatched a flashdrive from his pocket and stuck it in a USB port on the computer. Soon the entire Forde file was copied to the flashdrive. *I need insurance.* He made a spontaneous decision and opened Microsoft Outlook. It took only a few seconds to type his email address in the heading of a new message. He attached a copy of the database file and hit the send icon. Jonathan Forde's personnel file blasted off through cyberspace.

The printer was spitting out pages while Luke exited the UMN database. His heart nearly stopped when a key slid into the lock on the office door. In alarm, he ducked under the desk and jerked the computer's power cord from the surge protector. The machine went dead. The copier was still churning when the lights blazed on for the second time during Luke's caper.

* * * *

It was almost 11:30 pm in Los Angeles. The last group of patrons in the restaurant consisted of Drew Harmon and a half-dozen of his fellow cast-members. Everybody at the table wore their fatigue. In an attempt to salvage the filming schedule, Sid Adamo had dictated that work on the set extend late into the evening. When the long day finally ended, Harmon had been quick to offer his co-stars dinner and drinks. It was a solicitation for support in his battle with the director. Throughout the evening, the leading man had engaged in ruthless disparagement of Adamo.

One of the actors knocked Harmon from the bully pulpit.

"When are you going to have us over to your beach house, Cody?"

"I sold it," Cody Bennett said. "The taxes on the place were killing me."

A dark-haired actress snorted. "You're young and rich. Why worry about taxes?"

"People shouldn't blindly accept high taxes," Bennett said. "Government isn't entitled to our money. It's blatant redistribution of wealth."

"What do you suggest, Cody?" Intoxication fueled Harmon's temper. "I suppose you want to increase tax rates on the poor so wealthy people like you can keep all their money."

"Taxes ought to be cut. Then government spending should be reigned in."

"You want to shortchange the government and scrap social programs?" Harmon asked.

"I think people should get to keep more of what they earn." Bennett was clearly annoyed by Harmon's belligerence. "It stimulates economic growth. That means there's less need for government giveaways."

A fourth actor laughed. "Good luck. If the government doesn't have any money, the economy will be a disaster."

"Most people wouldn't have a chance in life without government assistance," someone said.

Bennett said, "The politicians need to quit making things worse. We're human beings, not sheep!"

"You'd probably support dissolving the government." Harmon's courage inflated when he saw that Bennett was outnumbered.

Bennett replied hotly, "I'm not an anarchist. That group, E-Force you're always harping about...that's what they are."

"E-Force is leveling the playing field!"

"E-Force is a group of cowards and criminals." Bennett leaned forward. It appeared he might jerk Harmon from his seat and pummel him.

Harmon made a vociferous proclamation. "It doesn't matter what you think of E-Force. The storm has come ashore, man!"

"I'm going to bed." Bennett shoved his chair back and rose. "You better sober up before you show up on the set tomorrow."

As Bennett stalked away from the table, the other cast members made good on their escapes. Almost in unison, they said good night and fled from the restaurant. The captive audience was gone.

"You're a jackass, Bennett." Harmon steamed with drunken anger as he sat alone. "Everybody's on my side, you pretentious ass."

* * * *

The custodian pulled his cart into the human resources office. With a broom in hand, the man stared at the churning machine as if it was an alien spacecraft. After a few seconds, it stopped, and the office was quiet. Luke held his breath and kept his eyes fixed on the shiny metal of a waste basket. A distorted funhouse image of the janitor stepped to the printer. The sound of rustling paper betrayed that the man was examining the top sheets deposited on the tray.

Luke swore silently when the warped reflection of the custodian advanced his way. His body language conveyed the caution and concern of a man searching for a snake in tall grass. There was no place to run or hide. It was time for a new plan. Luke bolted to his feet.

The janitor leapt back and nearly fell in his startled retreat. "What the hell are you doing in here?" Ernie Jones gripped his broom like a baseball bat.

"You scared the crap out of me," Luke stammered, eyeing Forde's Will on the copier. "I was working late."

"You always work in the dark with the door locked?" Jones lowered his makeshift weapon.

"I'm just going to take the stuff I printed and go home."
Luke snatched the papers from the janitor's hand. "It's past
my bedtime."

The custodian backed toward the door and bumped into
his cart. "That stuff's got the word 'confidential' stamped on
it."

"That means you shouldn't have been looking at it."

The janitor's eyes fell on the chalky debris on the floor.
"Why the hell were you hiding?" His gaze rose to the void in
the ceiling. The jagged hole was punched in the adjacent
panel. The change in the man's countenance wouldn't have
been more profound if Luke had peeled off a mask to reveal
himself as an extraterrestrial.

"Stay where you are!" Jones brandished his broom
handle.

"Now, just a minute." Luke protested as he ventured
closer to the copier. "You're being paranoid."

"I'll bust your head!" Jones issued a warning with fear in
his voice.

"I'm just a guy trying to meet a deadline." Luke lifted
his hands in exasperation.

"Shut up! You can tell your story to security."

Luke was helpless as Jones grabbed the phone from the
desk. The custodian kept his threatening grasp on the broom
handle while he punched a direct dial button.

"This is ridiculous. I'm an employee here!"

"Security, there's an intruder up here," the young black
man said. "I need help now."

"You're making a big mistake." Luke clenched his fists
and started forward.

"Don't try anything stupid!"

While the two men faced off, the sound of an elevator
drifted in from far down the hall. Jones glanced away for a
moment. Luke's instincts took control, and he pounced at the
custodian. Though knocked off balance, Jones swung his
broom handle. It struck Luke on the shoulder and sent him

staggering into the copier. The deposit tray was ripped from the machine. Jonathan Forde's last will and testament fluttered and scattered across the floor.

The janitor continued the assault. Luke deflected a savage strike at his head. It felt like every bone in his hand shattered upon the impact. Crying out in agony, Luke doubled over. The wood handle landed across his back with the force of a falling tree. When Luke fell to his hands and knees, a whack across the temple splattered his blood across the carpet.

His vision blurred by pain, Luke witnessed the janitor's shoulders and torso twist in preparation for a mighty double-handed blow. The marauding stick tore through the air. Luke threw himself below its path. Jones nearly toppled at the end of his futile whiff.

With all the strength he could muster, Luke lunged forward and rammed his shoulder into Jones' ribs. The janitor grunted and doubled over. Luke's legs pumped with the power of a football fullback. Jones was driven backward across the office until his back thudded against his cart. It crashed to the floor with the two combatants. The janitor's head struck the edge of a filing cabinet with a thud similar to a smashing pumpkin.

Luke scrambled to his feet. His adversary remained sprawled and motionless. "Oh shit. He's dead!" Luke's burning rage was doused with a wave of panic. The custodian groaned and stirred. Luke was relieved to see the man's chest rise and fall with steady breathing.

In frantic haste, Luke scurried around, grabbing his printed pages. He collected a half-dozen before pounding footfalls reverberated in the hallway. Jingling keys and a voice crackling across a radio confirmed a security guard was bearing down on the HR office. There was no time to retrieve the flashdrive from the computer.

The big bald guard bellowed when Luke darted out the door. "Freeze! Stop where you are!"

Adrenaline fueled Luke's flight from the lumbering security man. At the end of the hallway, he skidded to a stop and slammed open a fire door to a stairwell. He bounded down multiple steps with each stride. The bang of steel against concrete echoed from below. It was followed by pounding footsteps. Someone was charging up the stairs. Security was boxing him in. A heavy flashlight clattered on the stairs and plunged down through the open stairwell. It bounced off a railing and careened against a wall, just missing Luke as he fled into a hallway.

* * * *

"He's on the fourth floor!" the guard from downstairs called out to Watstull.

"Get back downstairs, Bobby! Track the son-of-a-bitch with the cameras."

Bobby Burns turned and rushed to comply. Watstull barreled onto the fourth floor. His feet ached, and the muscles in his legs burned. A cramp knotted one side of his torso. Luke wasn't in sight. The security guard doubled over and gasped for oxygen. Anger and humiliation intensified the sting of sweat in his eyes.

"He entered the south stairwell," Burns said over the radio.

"Turn the lights off in there." Watstull labored toward the elevators. "Flush him out, and I'll nail him."

"It's done," Burns declared a moment later. "The bastard just exited to the third floor."

"We'll get this shithead." Watstull stumbled onto the elevator.

The doors slid apart at the third floor. He staggered out into the lobby and stopped. Only the sound of his labored breathing met his ears.

"Talk to me, Bobby. Where'd he go?"

"He's entering suite 350. You can trap him in there."

With renewed resolve, Watstull lurched forward. Nearing the office suite, he heard a sound like glass shattering. His hand found the grip of his pistol and pulled the weapon from its holster.

"You need backup, Charlie. I'll get a black and white over here."

Watstull huffed. "We're not calling the cops yet. I can handle this jackass."

With both hands gripping his firearm, Watstull crept to the office door. It was the only way in and out of the suite. After a deep breath, he turned the knob and flung the door open. Jumping aside, Watstull pressed his back against the hallway wall and listened. A rustling sound escaped the dark space. Gathering his resolve, Watstull darted through the door. A cool draft of air greeted him. With his flashlight gone, he had to feel for the light switch.

The office erupted in florescent light. Papers were strewn about, many taking flight from the desks. Across the room, one of the huge windows was shattered. *What the hell did he do that for?*

Watstull kept a tight grip on his pistol and checked every potential hiding place in the suite. A disturbing realization crept into his head as he eyed the broken window. It was more than thirty feet to the sidewalk. *You'd have to be out of your mind to jump.* The hairs on the back of his neck stood upright.

Stepping next to the void, Watstull peered down to a poorly-lighted area. Something was on the concrete. Straining his eyes, he discerned arms and legs splayed out from a human torso.

"Bobby, the guy took a dive from the window." Watstull turned away from the terrible sight. "Call 911 and get out there on the double."

* * * *

192

Burns leapt from his chair and abandoned the bank of surveillance monitors. He used his cell phone to dial the police while he hurried outside.

When he rounded the corner of the building, a crumpled heap on the sidewalk confronted him. Slowing his pace, Burns forced himself to proceed, not wanting to see blood and guts. "If it wasn't for Charlie's damned caffeine addiction, my shift would be over."

Getting closer, his aversion was replaced by confusion. In the beam of his flashlight, it became clear that the object on the concrete was no body. Burns rushed forward and kicked a coat tree wrapped with a heavy coat and other articles of clothing.

"Charlie, it was a trick," Burns said into the radio. "The guy's still loose in the building!"

* * * *

Watstull was exiting the office with his weapon holstered when his comrade's warning sounded. At the same instant, there was a thump inside a large cabinet he was passing. Before he could react, the door exploded outward.

The bald behemoth scrambled backward and tried to draw his gun. A power cord snaking across the floor snagged the guard's foot, and he pitched sideways. The ankle folded and snapped under his bulk. The large man crashed to the floor. The battery from his radio bounced across the floor after the device smashed against a desk. Writhing and howling with agony and fury, Watstull was helpless as his quarry fled.

* * * *

Perched on the fourth floor landing with bated breath, Luke listened to Burns pounding up the stairs. Only a freak accident had saved him from the big guard. He breathed a sigh of relief when he heard the subordinate guard wrench open the door to the third floor hallway. The stairwell was quiet after the door slammed shut.

Luke descended, silent as a puma. In seconds, he was at the street level. He scurried across the vacant lobby toward the front doors. Glancing at a surveillance camera near the ceiling, Luke knew it was one of many which had captured his fleeing image during this debacle. *Every cop in the city is going to be looking for me.*

Feeling like he had just emerged from a mine full of toxic fumes, Luke breathed deep in the air outside the building. Sirens betrayed the approach of police vehicles. He dodged a few cars and sprinted across the street. When the cops rounded the block, Luke was concealed in the shadows. He slipped away as the officers hurried to the building with weapons drawn.

* * * *

Where Eagles Dare starring Clint Eastwood and Richard Burton, was playing out on the huge high-definition screen. The World War II thriller had reached the cable-car scene, where Eastwood and Burton stop the Nazi villains from escaping a mountaintop fortress. Burton's character leapt from the top of one cable car to another as they dangled a thousand feet in the air.

"That's a gutsy move," Trovato muttered, shaking his head.

With thick gray hair and a mustache, Trovato looked like a heavyweight boxer, twenty years past his prime. His frame carried thirty pounds of excess weight that belied his extraordinary strength.

Trovato threw his head back and emptied a glass of scotch. While he debated whether to refill it, the telephone rang. His business required service around the clock. It didn't matter that it was well past 2:00 am on the east coast.

"Trovato here." His thick Brooklyn accent was gruff.

For a few seconds, Trovato was silent as he listened to the caller, a former client. He had worked for the man several times in the past.

Trovato shrugged. "What kind of job you have in mind?"

The prospective client was reluctant to provide details over the phone. It assured Trovato that the man was no fool.

"My fees are the same. I'll be at the drop-point at the designated time."

Without another word, Trovato ended the call. Immediately, he dialed another number. After many rings, a groggy-sounding voice answered with unveiled ire.

"Joey, get your stuff together," Trovato said. "We've got a new job."

Chapter Thirteen
Tuesday, June 12 (morning to evening)

"This freaking place looks like an office store, turned upside down." Valdez seethed when he entered the spare bedroom in Luke Parson's apartment. Every horizontal surface was buried in papers, magazines, and newspapers.

"How can anyone work in this?" Sale wrung his hands and followed his muscular boss through the debris.

Valdez admonished the technical guru. "Deal with the computer."

Wearing a pair of latex gloves, Valdez sat down and rifled through the mess on the desk. He found a printout of an archived newspaper article about Jonathan Forde lying amongst the clutter. Skimming through the piece, Valdez understood why Luke Parson had developed such a strong interest in Forde.

"Parson wants to be a maverick," Valdez said under his breath.

Sitting at Luke's computer, Sale's fingers flittered across the keyboard. He needed only a few moments to access the file management system on the machine.

"Okay, I'm in." Sweat glistened below Sale's thinning hair.

"What've you got?" Valdez' brow was furrowed below his clean-shaven scalp.

"He emailed the file to himself." Sale's face paled. "The message has been opened."

"That means it's been copied," Valdez said.

Sale rooted through the heaps of litter on the desk. "Maybe there's a flashdrive or a CD around here."

"He would have taken that with him. Just pull the hard drive."

When Sale was done, Valdez locked the door and hurried down the steps. The two men scrambled into a

Cadillac Escalade with tinted windows. Sale looked sick as Valdez stepped on the gas pedal. Several cars, some with police markings, screeched into the parking lot as the Escalade roared onto the street.

"That was close." Sale exhaled and slumped in his seat. Valdez shot a hostile glance at the computer expert. "You're not out of the woods yet."

* * * *

The man held his breath and winced with pain. With his arm stretched to the side, he was walking his fingers up the wall. "I can't go any higher," he gasped. "The shoulder's too sore and stiff."

"I see improvement since your last session." Carrie Forde provided encouragement. "Full recovery takes time. Keep working on your exercises, and I'll see you next session."

Carrie straightened out the exercise equipment in the little gymnasium after her physical therapy patient was gone. On the way back to her office, nagging concern about Colt's dilemma had the effect of a sharp stone in her shoe. It was driving her crazy.

Bandit greeted her at the door. After an obligatory pet, Carrie sat down to complete a report. The phone halted her progress.

"Hello, Carrie. It's Mom."

Carrie stiffened with surprise. "We haven't talked in a while."

"How are you doing?"

"The clinic keeps me busy," Carrie answered.

"You've always been passionate about your pursuits," her mother said. "Your father's the same way."

"You can't escape genetics," Carrie said.

"I hope you understand that he made sacrifices to do what he thought was right."

"Let's not get into that." Carrie felt herself slipping back into the mindset of a rebellious teenager.

"Carrie, I'm calling with an invitation. We'd like you to come to Denver for the weekend."

"Who is 'we'?" Carrie tapped her foot with impatience.

"Your father and I want to see you."

"It's short notice." Carrie hesitated. "I'm not sure if I can make it."

"Do you have a commitment?"

"Well, Colt and I were--" Carrie stopped, annoyed at her slip.

"Is Colt someone you're dating?" her mother asked with obvious interest.

She bumbled for a response. "Well, yes…we're dating."

"Where did you meet him? Is this something serious?"

"We met here in Grand Junction." Carrie sighed, not ready to let down her defenses. "Maybe we can talk about Colt another time."

"You could bring Colt with you. It'd be nice to meet him."

"I don't know." Carrie rubbed her temple and grimaced. "We'd have to talk first."

"I'm not trying to pressure you," her mother said. "If you can't make it, we'll accept it."

"Well, I want to come." The assertion betrayed Carrie's loneliness. "It's just that…"

"Your father and I just want to patch things up. We never got that chance with your brother."

For a moment, Carrie was at a loss for words. She knew it was foolish to let wounds from the past continue to fester, eradicating any chance of relationships with the rest of her family.

Carrie relented, struggling to repress a flood of emotions. "I'll ask Colt to come with me."

"Thank you for that, Carrie. It means a lot to us."

"I've got to meet with the next patient." Carrie closed

her eyes and firmed her jaw. "I'll let you know the plan in the next few days."

When the phone call was over, Carrie knew the moment of truth was at hand. The future of her relationship with Colt would depend on honesty and trust. That had to start by pulling a few things out of the closet.

* * * *

Three of the four men lined up before Darius Marchotti's desk flinched when their volatile boss hefted a sculpture and heaved it across the office. Valdez, wearing a black turtleneck under his sport coat, was unfazed when the artwork shattered into a hundred fragments against the wall.

"This is bullshit!" Marchotti said. "What the hell is going on here? You're a bunch of incompetents!"

Nobody answered, and Marchotti thudded into his chair. In utter disgust, he contemplated clubbing the heads of his minions with another piece of office décor.

"That damned Forde file should have been destroyed." Marchotti's rage boiled. "Now we have a crisis. Who the hell is Luke Parson?"

"Parson's a loose cannon at *Issue Insight*," a heavy-set man said. He looked on the verge of spontaneous combustion. "He's been working on an article focused on you and your humanitarian organization."

"Why's he interested in Forde?"

"We're looking into all of Parson's work," another subordinate said. "Our people are talking to--"

Marchotti nearly catapulted his body out of his chair. "I don't care about your methodology! What was he after?"

"We don't know for sure, sir," the second man admitted meekly.

"What have you figured out? How did that bastard access a restricted corporate database?"

"Somebody must have provided him with instructions, a

password, and security codes." Sale gulped. "It had to have been someone with specific knowledge of our system. We've got Parson's hard drive so we can--"

"I don't give a damn about that. You better find a way to contain this."

"That will be difficult," the muscular brute, Valdez, said. "Parson may have copied everything."

"The files were encrypted. Parson can't access them." Sale blanched when Yuri Zharikov stepped behind him.

"It'll just take a person with the right expertise," Valdez retorted

"This is a disaster." Marchotti slammed his fists down on the desk. "You three get the hell out of here."

"All our work is in jeopardy," Marchotti said to Valdez and Zharikov after the other men disappeared. "Parson has got to be neutralized now."

"We need to get him before he's in the cops' hands," Valdez said coldly.

Marchotti fumed. "Parson might decide to turn himself in. We can't allow that to happen."

"I have a plan to keep him on the run." Valdez' revelation was accompanied by a glint in his eye. "It'll only cost us the life of a janitor. Then we can take him out before somebody else gets him."

"I don't want any amateurs involved in this."

"I have access to skilled professionals," Valdez assured him.

"Your future is directly dependent on Luke Parson," Marchotti said.

"What about Sale?" Zharikov's eyes narrowed.

"Get rid of him. Make it look like a random act of violence."

* * * *

EcoFriends headquarters bustled like a beaver pond at

dusk. Staff members rushed about making final preparations for presenting study results to a joint assembly of the State Senate and House of Representatives. Water was increasingly the subject of debate and controversy in the American West and the upper Colorado River basin was ground zero. Huge quantities of water from the region were diverted through trans-mountain tunnels to quench the thirst of sprawling urban areas east of the Rocky Mountain spine.

At the same time, a federal compact stipulated a minimum flow for the Colorado River at the Colorado-Utah border. With western slope residents and entities demanding more water as well, the administrative pressures were immense. EcoFriends was one of a plethora of groups engaged in political lobbying efforts to influence potential changes in water administration.

It was ironic that at the most important time in the history of EcoFriends, Howard Anderson was bent on shirking the group he had founded. Since the disaster at Mt. Crested Butte, he had heard the clock ticking, denoting the last days of life for E-Force and EcoFriends alike. The media was a dam holding back a surge of public rage against E-Force. With cracks spreading rapidly throughout, the dam was about to burst. Anderson knew he would drown in a raging torrent.

A skinny young man with thick, bushy hair popped into Anderson's office. "The entire presentation team is here, except Colt Kelley. He called and said he's running late."

Anderson glanced at the clock on the wall. "We'll have a lunch meeting to go over the last minute details. Then it'll be the real thing."

"We're ready for prime time!" The kid pumped his fist and hurried away.

Anderson dismissed the display of enthusiasm. The EcoFriends staffers were blindly willing to be pushed along in a phony quest to change the world. They were clueless pawns in a game that exploited their ignorant ideology. But

201

with E-Force slipping out of his control, Anderson feared that he was no different. Perhaps he was nothing more than an insensible tool of Darius Marchotti.

Anxiety was pushing Anderson to abandon the monster he had helped create. It wasn't going to be easy. Zed Cain was a dangerous fanatic who would never permit desertion or betrayal. The man was nearly impossible to read, but Anderson was sure Cain suspected something. Like a dark shadow in the waning daylight, Cain seemed inescapable.

"None of this crap matters anymore," Anderson said to the presentation packet on his desk. In frustration, he shoved his chair away from the desk. With his elbows on his knees, he rubbed his tired eyes. The distinct ringtone of Cain's cell phone sounded above the office buzz.

Silent as a cat, Anderson crept to his office door. Peering past the edge of the opening, he spied Cain seated in an office across the hall. The E-Force commander declined to answer the call, silencing the device instead. With mounting suspicion, Anderson ducked back out of sight. *What the hell is he up to?*

There was a sudden crescendo of shouting in the front reception area. Unfamiliar voices screamed accusations of unethical behavior and corruption. EcoFriends staffers yelled, "Get the hell out of here! We're calling the police! Every damned one of you is going to jail!"

Insults and curses were lobbed back and forth in the intensifying fray. Some heavy object crashed to the floor. A handful of reinforcements stormed past Anderson's office. Like a frustrated school principle, Cain marched toward the commotion. The cell phone was left behind on the desk.

Anderson had no inclination to help restore order in the building. Instead, he rushed into Cain's office. His nerves were tingling with trepidation when he snatched Cain's phone and accessed the list of recent calls. After a few silent recitations, the phone number of the last incoming call was committed to memory.

Without wasting another second, Anderson replaced the phone and hurried to the rear of the building.

He burst out into an alleyway that bordered a parking lot. Scuttling across the deteriorating pavement, he slipped between two parked vehicles. Apprehension coerced his eyes to dart about. It was as if he were a teenager smoking pot outside the school. Anderson's heart hammered while he keyed the mystery number into his own phone.

"AmeResort Corporation," a woman's voice said. "How may I direct your call?"

A terrible cramping pain shot through Anderson's chest. For a few seconds, he thought it was cardiac arrest.

"You've reached AmeResort. Is anyone there?"

In panic, Anderson terminated the connection. Cain was communicating with the enemy. It could only mean an E-Force setup. Unable to resist the drive to flee, Anderson turned and staggered toward his Lexus LX 570. It pulled him like a powerful magnet.

A vehicle rumbled into the parking lot. Flinching with fear, Anderson retreated a few steps when it ground to a halt. A man leapt out and approached. The EcoFriends leader dully recognized him as Colt Kelly.

"What are you doing out here, Howard?" Colt strode across the blacktop.

"I needed some fresh air," Anderson muttered, scurrying for the building.

"I hope you've thought more about our phone conversation." Colt drew alongside his boss. "Have you looked into the Cain issue?"

Anderson stopped in mid-stride and stiffened as if gripping a high-voltage power line. His blood ran cold. Zed Cain was standing in the open doorway to the EcoFriends office.

* * * *

There were few working streetlights to chase the darkness from the vacant streets. Slinking through the ominous gloom, Luke Parson felt intense unease. He was in a rough neighborhood. It was a place where he would not normally venture on foot, especially at night.

From a saturated shadow, Luke peered at a car approaching a street intersection. It halted at the stop sign, and he charged forward. After sprinting to the vehicle, Luke yanked open the passenger side door. Without hesitation, he leapt inside.

The driver, a thin man with a cap covering a shock of white hair, didn't flinch at the intrusion. He glanced at Luke without surprise or fear.

"You're soaked." The driver pressed down the accelerator.

"Yeah, no kidding. You're late."

"Blame it on the rain." The driver eyed the mud and water Luke had brought into the car. "Don't worry. The car's a rental."

Luke dismissed the man's comment. "What do you have for me?"

"The envelope's under your seat."

Luke retrieved the small sealed package. "How about a summary?"

"I looked into every part of Howard Anderson's history," the older man said. "Everything checks out. A birth certificate and hospital records confirm he was born in Los Angeles. He's got a valid social security number. I found public school records and a transcript on file with the University of Southern California. It doesn't look like he has any family; spent his childhood in foster homes. There's no evidence of the guy being married or having kids. None of his employers remembered much about him."

"How did the invisible man become the founder and leader of a major environmental organization?" Luke slowly shook his head.

"The guy went off the deep end about eight years ago. Abandoned his job, apartment, car...everything. Anderson vanished from California."

"Did he get into some sort of trouble?" Luke frowned and scratched his head.

"I didn't turn up anything like that," the man said with a shrug.

"Didn't the authorities ever look into it?" Luke stared, unsatisfied with the answer.

"Who knows," the older man retorted.

"Well, Anderson obviously reappeared."

"That's right. The guy landed in Boulder and founded EcoFriends. Most of the seed money came from an organization called Common Cause for Humanity."

"That's important information." Luke turned in his seat. "It could explain his transformation."

The older man glanced over and raised one eyebrow. "I'm not convinced the California Anderson and the Colorado Anderson are the same guy."

"What evidence do you have?"

"Just records from social services. The kid that grew up in the orphanages was right-handed. Your buddy in Boulder is left-handed."

"Are you saying Anderson assumed the identity of some poor loner from Los Angeles?" Luke asked. "If that's true, what happened to that guy?"

"I don't know. It's just an opinion...mostly a gut feeling."

"You could be onto something." Luke leaned back and folded his hands. "I need you to track down some of the foster families in California. I've got to have more evidence."

"I can't do that." The white-haired man shook his head. "I'm an accessory to murder by meeting with you. Our contact ends tonight."

"I didn't kill that janitor at *Issue Insight*," Luke said

angrily. "I'm being set up."

"Can you prove that?"

"That's what I'm trying to do!" Luke pounded a fist on the dashboard. "And I need your help. You're a private investigator."

"There's too much risk for me to continue."

"You're making a mistake," Luke insisted.

"Is that why you're skulking around in the rain tonight?" the investigator asked with irritation.

"Forget it." Luke surrendered bitterly. "Is everything in the envelope?"

"Yes." The man stopped the car on a dark street. "This is your stop."

Angry, Luke jerked open the door and stepped out of the car. The car drove away the instant he slammed the door. Alone and discouraged, Luke tucked the envelope under his jacket.

* * * *

The cloak of nightfall had turned the house as dark as a subterranean labyrinth. A few dim lights cast macabre shadows on the floor and walls. It was a realm that nurtured spreading tendrils of irrational fear. Taking a moment to massage his aching temples, Howard Anderson tried to subdue the migraine that had gathered strength throughout the evening.

A hastily packed bag stuffed with clothing, some outdoor gear, and a few emergency rations rested near the door. Critical financial documents and a list of contacts were in an open briefcase on the desk. Most important were the bundles of cash. They totaled more than fifty-thousand dollars...a fraction of his holdings.

Though his EcoFriends salary was modest, Anderson had been well-compensated by a secret benefactor. Since the conception of EcoFriends, he had followed directives from

Darius Marchotti and kept the organization on a predetermined path. And for the better part of a decade, Anderson had transferred his payoffs to foreign bank accounts and investments. He had done the same with money skimmed from EcoFriends fundraising. These illicit practices had grown his total worth to nearly twenty million U.S. dollars.

Just calm down and make sure you don't forget anything. There's still plenty of time to make the flight.

In just a few hours, a chartered jet would depart Jefferson County Airport and carry him to Miami. From there, a boat would spirit him away to the Bahamas. At that point, Howard Anderson would morph into Evan Hartley, a Canadian citizen. The next stop would be Europe and a new life.

Hurrying out of the study with his duffel bag, briefcase, and laptop computer, Anderson froze in his tracks with an awful realization.

"Shit! The passport's in Aspen! Damn it."

Helpless paranoia swept over Anderson. He recalled taking possession of the Hartley passport and placing it in his safe at the Aspen chapter of EcoFriends.

"You freaking idiot!" Anderson heaved his bag. *That passport's the key to everything.* He rushed for the phone and punched in his pilot's number.

* * * *

Passengers spilled from one of the gates at Denver International Airport. Some people hesitated, taking a moment to get oriented or make cell phone calls. Gordon Trovato didn't slow his pace as he weaved through the gaggle. A man with the build of an NFL linebacker kept pace. Like Trovato, Joey Morris carried a briefcase.

"This place makes Newark look like a dump," Morris said.

"Baggage claim is that way," Trovato said with a gruff gesture. "We've got to take the train."

Fifteen minutes later, Trovato and Morris were on their way to the ground transportation area with luggage in hand. In addition to clothing and personal articles, the suitcases contained the tools of their trade.

Morris glanced at his watch. "What about dinner?"

"You can order room service at the hotel," Trovato retorted.

"I can't work on an empty stomach."

Trovato cast a sour glance. "You're gonna live."

The formidable pair reached a sidewalk. Shuttles and taxis sped past, some making brief stops at the curb. Trovato hailed a cab, which screeched to a halt. When their suitcases were stowed in the trunk, the two men slid into the back seat with briefcases in hand. The car bolted out and melted into the traffic.

* * * *

"I'll pay you the extra money. Just get me to Aspen before we make the run to Miami." Anderson slammed down the phone and scrambled to the garage. With luck, he would be out of the country as planned. His insurance was a Smith & Wesson M&P 9mm pistol tucked behind his belt.

Tossing his luggage on the passenger seat of his vehicle, Anderson activated the remote control clipped on the sun visor. The garage door rose, and blinding light flooded the garage.

What the hell's going on? Anderson realized a vehicle was in the driveway, blocking his escape. The glare from headlights and an array of off-road lights seemed as bright as the sun. Fear gripped him.

Anderson darted from his Lexus and raised a hand to shield his eyes. A silhouette approached from each side of the mystery vehicle. The cold steel of the pistol prodded his lower back. His hand itched to grab the weapon, but Anderson stood motionless. An icy claw scraped down his spine when Zed Cain and Trigger Ruddock stepped into the garage.

"Going somewhere, Howard?" Cain's inquiry was devoid of curiosity.

"What are you doing here?" Anderson struggled to control his bodily functions.

Cain hardly seemed human, and Ruddock was a ticking time bomb. Having such repugnant men as associates was like keeping tigers as pets. Foolishly, Anderson had belicved he could maintain control. It was a deadly misconception that he had discovered too late.

"We came to check on you, Howard." Ruddock's voice was brimming with sarcasm and condescension. "You look pale. Are you sick or something?"

Cain and Ruddock circled as if sensing blood. They had detected his malcontent in the afternoon and had arrived for the kill. Anderson beat back his terror.

"The lights on your damned Tonka truck are splitting my head," Anderson said with as much force as he could muster. "For all I knew, you were thugs from that opposition group that invaded the office this afternoon."

Ruddock sneered. "That sounds paranoid. You need to relax."

"Cut the bullshit, Ruddock. You're out of line."

"You haven't answered my question." Cain stepped closer. "Where are you going?"

Anderson lied. "I was going back to the office."

"Planning on working late?" Ruddock asked.

"I'm buried in paperwork."

"You haven't been interested in any of that lately," Cain said with skepticism.

"I'm under a lot of pressure. You know that as well as anyone."

"It seems like our relationship has deteriorated."

James D. Kellogg

Ruddock shook his head with mock disappointment. "You're not abandoning the cause are you, Howard?"

Anderson erupted. "Of course not. Without me, E-Force wouldn't have a dime of funding!"

"That doesn't mean you've got our best interests in mind," Ruddock said. "I think you're running out on us."

"You're delusional."

"How strong is your commitment to E-Force?" Cain's stare was unwavering.

"It hasn't changed. I've taken as much risk as anyone. Without me, E-Force would be an obscure gang of vandals."

"How in the hell do we know we can count on you?" Ruddock twitched with agitation.

"Can we depend on you, Howard?" Cain asked in an eerily quiet tone.

Anderson's knees weakened. "Absolutely. I'm in for the long haul."

For several seconds, nobody moved or spoke. The men faced Anderson, poised to strike. Despite his fear, he knew he had to act. The meeting time at the airport was rapidly approaching.

"You need to move your truck. I've got work to do."

"Why don't we give you a ride?" Ruddock's suggestion was laden with cold sarcasm. "You might get lost tonight."

"I've had enough of your inquisition," Anderson said. "I still run this show. I don't need a chauffeur or a babysitter. Move the freaking truck."

Time stood still. Anderson was shaken by Cain's indifference. The E-Force enforcer regarded him as having no further value to the cause: someone who could be dispatched at any time.

"Use your time wisely." Cain turned and trod away.

"Don't work all night, Howard. The future's as close as tomorrow." Ruddock stalked out of the garage.

Seconds later, the driveway was dark and empty. Anderson was trembling as he backed his vehicle into the rain. Driving across town, he sensed that Cain and Ruddock were following him. His escape plans ruined, Anderson cursed in bitter frustration.

* * * *

Max Reichner was a high roller with expensive European clothes and an apparently endless supply of cash. The Las Vegas casinos had creative ways to keep his wallet open. When Reichner was losing, gorgeous young ladies were deployed to help keep the money flowing. If he was winning, they were charged with breaking his streak, enticing him with a different sort of pleasure.

Tonight, the house was behind, and the siren song had begun. The establishment thought they were playing him, but Reichner wasn't interested in winning money. He had ample opportunities to finance his decadence. He was addicted to the power he felt when a beautiful temptress enticed him to keep playing on a losing night. It was the same when he was ahead and a femme fatale offered herself as a recreational alternative. Either way, Reichner considered himself the victor. Flaunting it up the ante, he decided it would take more than one seductress to lure him from the table.

Five minutes later, Reichner stepped from the elevator on the top floor of the hotel. The two dazzling beauties clinging to him revved their motors as they arrived at his suite. Buzzing with excitement, Reichner unlocked the door. The ring of his phone elicited a shudder.

Reichner sighed. "I must take this call, ladies." His explanation was delivered with a faint German accent. "Please make yourselves comfortable inside."

The women pretended to pout about the delay. After they sauntered into the room, Reichner closed the door behind them.

"Max here. What do you require?"

The voice on the phone spoke for just a few seconds. Reichner ran a hand through his blond hair. Each word was consumed and digested.

"Make the deposit. Then we will finalize the arrangements."

When the call ended, Reichner was charged with energy. *It is a good night indeed.* There was a new job to begin...an endeavor that provided a thrill no woman could match. Nevertheless, such escapades were not to be thrown aside for the night. With a thin smile on his face, Reichner opened the door to the adventure waiting inside his suite.

Chapter Fourteen

Wednesday, June 13 (morning to evening)

With an eye toward the sky, Colt stepped from his Land Cruiser at a gas station. The heavy pall of gray clouds hung like tethers on a balloon, keeping his somber mood grounded.

"This rain is crazy, especially in a year with a huge snowpack," he muttered. It was ironic that state government was pushing to enact drastic and far-reaching water policy measures at a time when streams and rivers were at flood stage. Most of the front-range reservoirs were on the verge of spilling.

As the gas tank filled, Colt opened the hood to get a look at the old engine. There was no telling what pending mechanical problem might be lurking. This time, it was just a dipstick that revealed a low oil level.

Colt straightened and brandished his cell phone. The battery was low, but he dialed Carrie's clinic anyway. It wasn't easy to get in touch with her. She was the only person he knew who didn't have a cell phone. Moreover, she didn't have an answering machine or voicemail at home. It seemed Carrie didn't want to be accessible to anyone. *Women are a mystery*, Colt griped.

A few seconds later, the clinic receptionist informed Colt that Carrie was between patients. *Perfect timing!* While Colt waited to hear the sound of her voice, the gas pump clunked to a stop. The tank was full, and his wallet would soon be empty.

"Hi, Colt." Carrie sounded cheerful. "Are you back in Aspen?"

"I'm not even close. We had another meeting in Boulder this morning. It was a waste of time, and I haven't even headed up into the hills yet."

"So much for getting back before lunch." Her

disappointment was obvious.

"The best-laid plans fall apart," Colt said dryly.

"We're probably better off flying by the seat of our pants," Carrie replied.

"Unfortunately, it's going to be a late night at the office. Everything piles up when I'm out."

"You sound stressed," Carrie said, concern in her voice.

"Anderson seems to be cracking up." Colt put a hand on his hip and shook his head. "I'm not sure what's going on with him."

Carrie pressed a bit harder. "What about that guy Cain? Was he there?"

Colt was convinced that Cain was watching him, though it was impossible to confirm. "His demeanor varies as much as a wooden totem pole, but it's not a good time to talk about that."

"I understand," Carrie said. "I'm just worried about you."

"You've got to keep your distance from this."

"That's not easy to do," she said. "I want us to keep growing closer. That means supporting each other during tough situations. You know, we haven't talked much about the past or where we want to go. I think it's important to--"

Colt interrupted with annoyance. "My stupid phone battery is dying."

Carrie sighed. "That's okay. My next patient is probably here. When you--"

The phone blinked off. "Piece of junk!" Colt managed not to hurl the device in the direction of a dumpster.

Frustrated, Colt tightened the gas cap on his Land Cruiser and walked into the convenience store. Several minutes later, he returned with a coffee, a newspaper, and a quart of oil. He set the dead phone on the front bumper and poured the lubricant into the engine.

After closing the hood, Colt settled into the driver's seat and turned the key in the ignition. The vehicle lurched into a gap in the heavy traffic on the street. His cell phone bounced from the bumper and clattered to the pavement. It was smashed by dozens of tires. Oblivious to the loss, Colt sped away. Drops of rain pelted the windshield.

* * * *

"Can't you feel that vibration?" Anderson asked.

The salesman shook his head. "This baby's smooth."

"I'm pulling over," Anderson retorted. "You need to check the front tire."

The Audi R8 sports car rolled to a stop alongside Interstate 70. After a reluctant sigh, the salesman got out and trudged to the front of the vehicle. "Everything looks fine. Are you sure--"

Anderson jammed his foot on the accelerator. The sales guy leapt to the side to avoid being run down. "Sorry, pal, no sale." He left the man sputtering in a swirl of exhaust fumes.

Since the encounter in the garage, Cain and Ruddock had kept him trapped. The presentation to the legislature, a sleepless night, and the morning meeting at EcoFriends headquarters...it was all tortuous. It was as if he were under a magnifying glass, subject to solar radiation concentrated into a burning ray of annihilation. His captor's gazes never seemed to waver. But a moment of distraction finally came. Anderson had fled to the Audi dealership with his briefcase. All else was abandoned to the wolves.

For thirty minutes, Howard Anderson kept his foot on the gas pedal, weaving through a tangle of traffic, climbing toward the tunnels below Loveland pass. The precipitation intensified. Sheets of rain made the highway resemble the Gulf Coast in a hurricane. He was more reckless with each passing mile.

Without that passport, I'm finished. Marchotti's people will monitor commercial flights and border crossings; every conceivable way out of the country. Time had run out for the man known as Howard Anderson.

The R8 chewed up a stretch of open road, sprinting toward the next cluster of vehicles. Anderson wrenched his arm around and snagged the handle of the briefcase behind his seat. The car swerved outside the confines of the lane. Finally, he completed the retrieval and tossed the case on the passenger seat. *I should chain the damned thing to my wrist.*

When Anderson looked back to the highway, he was overtaking a huge RV. He dodged left without easing off the gas. In a surprise maneuver, the camper veered left too. The driver was on the verge of rear-ending a slow-moving truck with a cargo of 55-gallon drums.

There was no time to brake. Anderson's right foot nearly punched through the floorboard. His diminutive vehicle shot past the rear of the massive RV. The steering wheel strained against his panicked grip. Terror choked off his breath. The camper was still drifting left. Space between the median and the behemoth was closing.

"Come on you son-of-a-bitch!"

Vibrations shook the Audi in concert with the sickening crunch of metal and fiberglass. The sports car scraped along the side of the encroaching giant. The front wheel loomed. A glancing blow from the thundering rubber hurled Anderson's car away. It smashed through a flimsy barrier and spun into the median, sending a plume of mud, rocks, and grass into the air. The momentum was insane. He plunged into the path of vehicles barreling down the mountain in the eastbound lanes. Anderson closed his eyes and screamed.

The impact to the front tire sent the RV veering to the right. The camper clipped the front of the two-axle truck it was passing and slid sideways on the wet pavement. Almost perpendicular to the highway, the top-heavy giant lurched and rolled like a breaching whale. It slammed over and slid in a shower of sparks and debris.

The hapless driver of the truck couldn't avoid the crumpled camper. Simulating a battering ram, the truck hit with the force of an artillery shell exploding. The rear end of the hauler swung around. Steel drums ripped through the side rails of the bed. They were hurled as easily as a handful of gravel.

Most of the drums burst against the pavement. Ominous-looking liquid spilled from the ruined containers, spreading across the rain-soaked highway.

Vehicles on both sides of the interstate median dodged and braked. Dozens smashed into the wreckage, turning the horrific wreck into something resembling the aftermath of a tornado. A deafening cacophony of destruction accompanied the escalating disaster.

* * * *

Huddled in an abandoned building, Luke's predicament surpassed that of the homeless. At least the downtrodden might seek solace at a shelter or a soup kitchen. He expected the police to be waiting for him at such places. With only a few dollars left in his wallet, the situation was grim.

Luke knew he couldn't stay hidden for long. If he avoided hypothermia, starvation, and demise at the hands of hoodlums, the authorities would still find him. His picture was all over the news. He cringed at the recollection of an experience outside an electronics store. Every television inside the windows had flittered with the damning video images from the surveillance cameras in the *Issue Insight* building.

I made it easy for those bastards to set me up. Luke lamented, shivering. *There's no way I can prove I didn't kill that janitor.*

Delving into the secrets of Jonathan Forde had aroused a savage response. The murder of the custodian was testament to how far somebody was willing to go to make sure Forde's past stayed forgotten. It was proof that people beyond the fringe of the law were hunting him down. The cops would

217

charge him with murder, but the clandestine operatives from the United Media Network were sure to attempt far worse.

With trembling hands, Luke pulled a few folded and crumpled sheets of paper from his pocket. A divine calling seemed to push him to ply deeper into the Forde mystery. Sitting on the dirty floor, he spread the salvaged pages in front of him.

The first few passages from Jonathan Forde's will were standard legalese. Undeterred, he sifted through subsequent rambling until a provision challenged his comprehension. The document stipulated that Forde's entire estate was to have been liquidated upon his death. From his research, Luke had learned Forde was from a very wealthy family. His personal estate had been worth millions of dollars.

Luke gasped when he continued reading. "All that money was donated to Marchotti's humanitarian organization. Why did Darius Marchotti get everything?"

Luke's suspicion soared when he studied Forde's signature. The ratification date was only a few weeks before his disappearance at sea. A shiver reverberated through his body. Jonathan Forde had perished eight years ago. It matched the timeframe of Howard Anderson's disappearance from Los Angeles and reincarnation in Boulder.

"Howard Anderson is really Jonathan Forde." Luke's breathing grew shallow and rapid. "And Darius Marchotti is behind it."

Thoughts of sinister forces, bent on protecting that dark secret triggered claxons of fear. Luke held his head in his hands, unsure how he could escape a gruesome fate long enough to prove his theory and refute the murder charge. An epiphany manifested inside his congested mind. There was one person who might shed more light on Jonathan Forde.

* * * *

The Blue Ridge Café in downtown Denver was packed

with patrons, many who toiled each day in the surrounding office towers. Like many people in the restaurant, it was Chris Morgan's favorite place for lunch.

Morgan's colleague complained while they waited for their food. "I can't believe we've got to deal with Marla again. I thought we got rid of her when she got that network gig."

"You get off easy, man," Morgan retorted. "I've been designated as her cameraman for Friday."

"Why are you being punished?"

Morgan grimaced. "I don't know. I thought I paid penance for my past sins."

"Maybe Marla just likes you." The coworker's suggestion was accented by a wink.

"Or maybe she just wants to keep the black man down."

"Fight the power." Morgan and his fellow African-American laughed as the they reached out and touched fists. "So, why's that bitch coming back to Denver? I thought she was too big a fish for our little pond."

"She's got something up her sleeve." Chris Morgan frowned. "It's part of that crap with those environmental nuts."

"I figured that was a gimmick to get the network's attention."

"Marla's never promoted anyone but herself." Morgan nodded. "Now that she's made the big time, it doesn't make sense to keep pushing the environmental extremist mantra."

"She's probably addicted to the publicity."

"Maybe that's it," Morgan said. "I'll keep my eye on her though."

"Don't look too hard. Remember the Medusa from that ancient Greek mythology and shit."

Morgan chuckled at his friend's joke. The two men looked up to see the waitress arrive at the table with their meals. When the plates were on the table, the conversation shifted to football. It complimented lunch better than Marla

Wells.

* * * *

The office walls kept squeezing inward, stealing space and transforming the room into a phone booth...or maybe a coffin. Travis Price was under immense pressure, akin to that on the hull of a sinking submarine nearing the point of implosion. The FBI agent thumped a fist against his forehead. *It's just a crazy illusion.*

A single rap on the doorframe preceded Special Agent Hill's entry. "What about Parson's computer?" Price asked when his subordinate closed the door.

"There's nothing of value there," Hill answered flatly. "What's the status on Parson?"

"His freaking location is still unknown." Price kicked the trash can in frustration.

"We'll get him."

"We'd better. Our problems are compounding."

"What do you mean?" Hill asked lowering his voice.

"A major wreck closed Interstate 70 in both directions this morning. Witnesses reported the whole thing was caused by some jackass driving an Audi like a bat out of hell."

Hill's eyes narrowed. "Do we know that jackass?"

"It was Howard Anderson. He's on the run."

* * * *

"My knee is so much better," Carrie Forde's patient exclaimed while lounging on the leg extension machine. "The doctor did a fabulous job. He's so skilled and his bedside manner is just amazing."

"Your range of motion is increasing," Carrie said when the woman paused for a breath.

"The physical therapy has been great." The patient released another torrent of words. "I'll be able to do anything

220

soon. Maybe I'll even try rock climbing at one of those gyms. Everybody says it's safer than the real thing. You're a climber, aren't you? Where do you go?"

"The Natural High Rock Gym and Fitness Club." Carrie refused to be distracted. "Let's finish your last set of exercises."

"Is it a good place to meet single men?" The woman initiated the movements.

"Don't extend your leg too far," Carrie said. "I go to the Natural High to work out."

"So there's no social scene there?" Carrie's patient looked dejected.

"It's where I met the guy I'm dating."

"That settles it," the woman announced when she completed the exercise. "I'm joining the Natural High!"

"Good for you." Carrie resisted the temptation to roll her eyes. "We're done for today. I'll see you next week."

After the talkative woman was gone, Carrie retreated to her office. Bandit trotted out to greet her. "You're such a good puppy." Carrie scratched behind his ear. "Always quiet."

The dog acted short-changed when Carrie straightened and stepped to her desk. She lifted the phone and dialed Colt's cell phone number. "The customer you are calling is not answering at this time." It was an automated message from the cell service provider.

I hope he didn't get caught behind that massive wreck on the interstate. Carrie sighed and delved into some paperwork.

* * * *

"Thanks for the ride." Delilah bolted from a pickup truck and streaked across the Wal-Mart parking lot in Rifle.

A few minutes later she stood in the store, shivering and staring at hordes of shoppers. The chill induced by wet cloths amplified the misery ushered in by waning hospital medications. She moaned with a hand over her fractured ribs. "My God, it hurts to breathe." Only hours had passed since her escape from the hospital, but it already seemed like days.

The rain-soaked refugee shuffled to the pharmaceutical section. The few soggy dollars and handful of change in the pocket of her jeans, wasn't enough to pay for the smallest bottle of ibuprofen. Picking up a bottle of the pain reliever, Delilah's eyes darted up and down the aisle. The time was right. She stuffed the loot in a pocket and beat a retreat.

In the restroom, the cast complicated the task of opening the container and popping a few pills. Water from the sink helped her swallow. Standing before the mirror, Delilah gingerly lifted her shirt to expose blood-soaked bandages. The stitches were still keeping her guts from spilling out of the surgical incision. Feeling faint, she let the garment fall back around her waist.

With a tight grip on the white porcelain, Delilah stared at her reflection. Injuries masked her beauty. *Damn, I look crappy.* One eye was ringed by bruising. Gnawing hunger pains were manifested in her gaunt expression. With no money and no place to go, the situation seemed hopeless.

"I never should have talked to Price."

Revelations about E-Force were supposed to garner salvation. It sounded so enticing: an escape from the repercussions of poor choices and inadvisable actions. With Price's coaxing, her flood of emotional testimony had poured over the levy of common sense.

It hadn't taken long for tendrils of reality to strangle Delilah's hopes. Visions of Cain and Ruddock invaded fitful bouts of sleep. Nothing would counter their murderous intents. Such men were ruthless and relentless. The protection promised by Price would be of no consequence. To Delilah, remaining in the hospital had been as foolish as sitting in the lions' den, waiting for the beasts to appear.

Looking at the pathetic image in the mirror, Delilah realized how slim her chances were. Nowhere near recuperated from her injuries, she had no place to hide from the cops or E-Force. A tear slid down her face and her lip quivered. Fearing that someone would walk into the restroom, she stifled a sob and dabbed her eyes with a sleeve.

Delilah had always run from adversity. Now, survival was dependent on logic, bravery, and stamina. Not possessing such traits, she needed a savior. *Colt can help me. He's always been my rock.*

Since Delilah had known Colt Kelley, he had been there to pick up the pieces when she crashed. Delilah longed for a return to his embrace.

* * * *

The Land Cruiser rumbled into a crowded gas station in Silverthorne. Colt had avoided the hassle and embarrassment of running out of gas on the side of the highway. It was little consolation. The entire afternoon had been wasted amongst thousands of other motorists parked on the Interstate.

I can't believe I lost my stupid cell phone. Colt filled his gas tank in the waning light. "What a freaking day."

He gathered the dismembered sections of the newspaper from the passenger seat. During his imprisonment on the highway, he had pored over almost every page to fend off boredom and frustration.

An article about the upcoming One World Festival at Red Rocks Amphitheater had caught Colt's attention. Sponsored by Common Cause for Humanity, it would be three days of concerts interspersed with speeches by environmentalists. The author of the article used pseudo-religious terms, preaching that the only hope of salvation for Mother Earth was an environmentalist movement with a worldview. With leadership from the festival organizers and attendees, Americans would finally accept a new world order. It would be dictated by ecological harmony instead of selfish nationalistic pride.

"What a bunch of crap," Colt said with disgust and stuffed the newspaper into a trashcan. *Those festival clowns claim to be open-minded and benevolent. I guarantee they're happy to watch E-Force philosophy crammed down people's throats.*

When Colt was finished fueling, he moved his vehicle and trotted to a payphone at the front of the convenience store. The phone at Carrie's house rang with no answer. Perturbed, Colt decided it was easier to contact somebody in the federal witness protection program.

Dejected, Colt was about to walk away when he realized Carrie might have left a message for him. He inserted the coins into the payphone again and dialed his home phone number. It took only a few seconds to access the answering machine.

"Colt, it's me." Delilah's voice was unmistakable.

Colt was shocked. Delilah was supposed to be in the custody of the authorities. *Did they let her go?* It didn't matter. Her phone call could link him with E-Force.

"It's been a while since we talked, and I'm sorry." Her speech wavered with emotional strain. "I was so stupid to have left. You were always there for me. Please forgive me. Colt, I really need to see you. I'm not far away. I'll call again soon. I love you."

She's messing with your head again. Colt tried to fend off an assault of turbid feelings. *Don't get sucked in.*

By the time Colt settled in behind the steering wheel, he couldn't resist the temptation to contact Delilah. With renewed energy, he headed for the highway.

Chapter Fifteen
Wednesday, June 13 (evening and night)

Burdened with groceries and a duffel bag, Carrie shoved the door open and stepped inside. The storm door slapped her backside, nearly jarring the wine bottle from the crook of her arm. When Carrie flipped the light switch, she was taken aback by the dirty dishes, cookware, and utensils strewn about Colt's kitchen.

"What a pigsty." She grumbled and cleared a spot for her cargo.

Throughout the evening, Carrie had been unable to get in touch with her beau. According to the news, the interstate had been open for several hours. But there was no word from Colt. To curb her concern, she had acted on impulse, purchasing a nice wine and ingredients for dessert. It would be a surprise for Colt.

Why is this place such a mess? Carrie's disquiet was growing.

At the refrigerator her eyes fell upon a photograph stuck to the metal door with a magnet. It was the shot of Colt, Carrie, and Bandit sitting on the rocks near Snowmass Lake. On that trek, Carrie had decided to topple the wall around her heart and soul. Now standing in a strange mist of doubt, Carrie contemplated whether she had opened Pandora's Box.

Unable to ignore her misgivings, Carrie ventured from the kitchen. Turning on the lights in the master bedroom, she saw that Colt's bed was a disheveled mess. The sheets and comforter were pulled out and twisted as if there had been a wrestling match. Carrie had a terrible sinking feeling.

An irresistible force pulled Carrie toward the adjoining bathroom. Her pounding heart reverberated on the lump in her throat. The instant the bathroom was illuminated, Carrie's soul deflated. A pair of woman's panties and a bra lay on the floor.

225

* * * *

The flickering light of televisions emanated from almost every house that lined the street of the Littleton neighborhood. It was a glimpse into the lives of typical Americans, held captive each night by myriad programming accessible via remote control. While he slinked along a sidewalk, Luke Parson contemplated the power wielded by the television networks.

Soaked and chilled, hunger and exhaustion compounded Luke's misery. When he came upon a house that was completely dark, his pulse quickened. Luke crept across the front yard. Thick clouds masked the light of the full moon. Slipping around the side of the building, he passed through a gate.

Through the shadows, Luke spied a door that led into the house from a patio. Pressing his face to the glass, there was no sign of anybody inside. The doorknob was locked. He felt a mat beneath his feet. Lifting it by a corner, Luke ran his hand across cold concrete. His fingertips encountered a lone key.

Seconds later, Luke clutched his shoes and crept through the house in his socks. Without turning on any lights, he navigated to the kitchen. A ravenous appetite served as his compass. Luke yanked open the refrigerator and accosted a pizza box. He seized the slices of pizza and shoved the empty box back in the clutter.

After devouring his booty, exhaustion descended. Luke fumbled his way up a staircase. A queen size bed in one of the bedrooms was irresistibly inviting. In a state of delirium, Luke stripped his wet clothes and dumped them in a pile. Sleep overcame him as soon as he burrowed into the covers.

* * * *

The magnificent full moon cast a ghostly glow over Aspen. A big Victorian-style house loomed ahead. The broad front porch was lined with darkened windows. Steep rooflines were crested with ornate ironwork and fringed by beautiful handcrafted eaves. A pair of giant spruce trees stood sentry in the front yard. Colt pressed next to one of the massive trunks while a lone car passed on the street. The coast was clear. He darted behind the house and bounded up a few steps to the back door. Several seconds had to be spent to disarm the security system. Colt slipped inside and locked the door behind him.

Probing the interior of the EcoFriends office with a small flashlight, Colt crossed the kitchen to a hallway. A computer monitor cast a faint glow in one of the rooms he passed. He glanced into a dining room that held a conference table and chairs. At the front of the house, Colt gripped a handcrafted railing at the bottom of a gorgeous wood staircase. The creaking boards broadcast his steady ascent.

Moonlight streamed through a window above the stairs and lighted the hallway. Colt padded softly past two front bedrooms that were converted to offices, one his own. A bedroom in the rear served as Howard Anderson's office. As the owner of the house, the EcoFriends president had sequestered the rest of the second floor for a private apartment. The living quarters could also be accessed from a staircase at the back of the house. Without a key to Anderson's apartment, Colt stood outside the door and listened. As expected, there was no sound from within. It was a green light to implement his plan.

Confidential conversations between Colt and his boss always took place in Anderson's office. He intended to record the next meeting. Convinced that Cain and Anderson were immersed in E-Force, Colt had conjured up the story about a snooping FBI agent. It was a scare tactic. By pretending not to suspect Anderson, Colt hoped to lure his boss into throwing Cain overboard. With luck, the leader might even stumble into the realm of self-incrimination while betraying his brutal henchman.

The scheme was a huge gamble. It was impossible to fathom the loyalty between Anderson and Cain. Colt was pretty sure there was no love lost between them. But it didn't matter. Memories of Deb steeled his resolve. *I'll make both of you pay,* he promised on the way to his office near the top of the stairs.

Colt's flashlight beam fell upon a portable stereo on a shelf. He turned and rummaged through a desk drawer and found a small microphone that plugged into the device. One hand fished a spool of wire and a pair of wire cutters from a jacket pocket. Both items were confiscated from the toolbox in his vehicle. A snip of the cutters separated the microphone from the plug-in jack. He stripped the insulation from the ends of the cut wire and twisted them onto opposite ends of the wire on the spool. A roll of electrical tape from his pocket helped complete the splicing. Colt had a microphone that could be extended almost thirty feet from his portable stereo.

With his handiwork, Colt trotted to Anderson's office. A pair of chairs in front of the desk provided seating for meetings. Shining his light upward, the head of a fire sprinkler glinted on the ceiling. It had been added during renovation of the old house. Colt bounded onto one of the chairs and pulled a screwdriver from the back pocket of his jeans. He jammed the tool between the plaster and the metal sprinkler head. Poking and prodding chiseled a hole just wide enough to insert the microphone plug.

Access to the attic was in a closet. It only took a moment to find the plug-in jack protruding above the insulation stuffed between the attic floor joists. Colt tugged it with the finesse of a fly fisherman landing a trout. A sudden resistance told him that the microphone was pulled snug against the ceiling below. Laying the wire like detonation cord, he stepped from joist to joist until he was above his office. Colt knelt down and pushed the plug-in jack down through a tiny opening. When he rushed down to his office, it was easy to hide most of the dangling wire behind a window curtain. The last step was plugging the jack into the stereo on the bookshelf.

I can't remember the last time I used the cassette deck on this thing. Better make sure this cobbled-together thing works.

Retrieving a blank tape that had been in the desk for years, Colt inserted it into the deck and pressed the record button. The little wheels on the tape churned. It was time to run to Anderson's office and test the crude bugging system.

Just as Colt turned toward the hall, he heard the pained protest of door hinges. *Somebody is in the house!* Instantly, Colt clicked off his flashlight. The hallway remained dark, but the sound of soft slow footsteps was unmistakable.

Like a guerrilla fighter, Colt retreated in silence. His progress was frightfully slow while the footfalls grew near. When he ducked behind his desk, the house was silent. His pulse thundered in his ears. Feeling like a rodent peering from under the desk, Colt spied a shadow cast by the lunar glow in the hall. Somebody was standing in the doorway.

* * * *

The burn of betrayal sent Carrie fleeing from Colt's bathroom. In the kitchen, she stopped and gripped the counter for support. It was as if a chucked brick had shattered all the delicate hopes and dreams recently created. Her reward for trust and an open heart was rejection and humiliation.

Carrie squeezed her eyes shut, but couldn't erase the image of the bra and panties discarded next to damp towels. Just as indelible was the disheveled bed where some of Colt's cloths lay upon the tangle of covers. *Maybe it's not what it seems. It can't be.*

When Carrie's eyelids fluttered open, her gaze fell upon the outdated answering machine. The movement was almost involuntary, when her arm stretched toward the device. Carrie inhaled an instant before her finger pushed the 'play' button.

"Colt, it's me. It's been a while since we talked, and I'm sorry. I was so stupid to have left. You were always there for me. Please forgive me. Colt, I really need to see you. I'm not far away. I'll call again soon. I love you."

For a few minutes, the dagger piercing Carrie's heart elicited an upwelling of tears. Unwilling to permit a deluge, she wiped a sleeve across her face. A residual salty drop sizzled away in the seething anger that filled her eyes.

Supported by trembling legs, Carrie picked up the phone. There was one number she hadn't tried.

"Come on, you gigolo!" Carrie listened to the phone ring at the EcoFriends office. "Where are you?"

There was no answer. Carrie slammed the phone down. In a monumental effort, she sucked in a deep breath and unclenched her fists. With as much composure as she could muster, she marched across the kitchen and snatched up her duffel bag. She stormed from the house, leaving the lights on. When the door slammed, Carrie didn't bother to lock it.

* * * *

Strolling down the sidewalk, Joey Morris approached the rear of a vehicle on a dark Aspen street. It was an old Land Cruiser. The numbers and letters on the license plate matched those he had memorized.

When Morris drew alongside the four-wheel-drive, the jingle of a chain put him on guard. The scuff of shoes on concrete accompanied rapid clicking. A man with a dog appeared from around a corner. Without breaking his stride, Morris kept moving past the Land Cruiser.

Seconds later, the hulking Morris met the diminutive

man on the sidewalk. His shaggy little terrier growled and snarled. Morris eyed the animal with disdain while the man grappled with the leash.

"Beautiful night for a walk," Morris said with a casual nod.

The dog owner brushed past without a word. The rude arrogance didn't bother a calloused New Yorker like Morris. At the end of the block, he glanced over his shoulder. The unfriendly fellow and his stupid dog were gone.

Morris trotted back to the Land Cruiser. Placing a hand on the hood, he felt warmth. The engine had been running recently. The door was locked when he gently tried the handle.

A growl startled Morris. The dog-walker had reappeared and the canine strained at the tether. Hurriedly, the man crossed to the other side of the street, dragging the vicious beast along. Morris decided it was time to move out, before he attracted more attention. A vehicle turned onto the street, and he faded into the dark.

* * * *

Howard Anderson scurried back toward the open door of his apartment in the EcoFriends house. The sudden ringing of the phone in Colt Kelley's office had triggered an overdose of adrenaline. His nerves were frayed to the verge of snapping.

A cool draft traveled up the back staircase and wafted into the hall. Anderson decided against further reconnaissance, limping around in the dark with a loaded pistol in hand. The place was certainly empty and his battered body was faltering after the torturous trek from the scene of the horrendous highway pileup. It was a miracle that he had emerged with only minor injuries. But Anderson was certain that divine intervention wouldn't save him from those he had betrayed.

There was no doubt that Cain and Ruddock had figured out what had happened. Anderson knew their hunt would be relentless. Currents of paranoia swirled below the surface of his psyche.

On the trip across his unlit office, Anderson tucked the Smith & Wesson M&P into his belt. At his desk, he switched on a lamp and turned to the safe built into the wall behind the chair. The ambient glow helped him dial the combination. He yanked open the heavy door and faced a jumble of items. Anderson grabbed an envelope, flush with bundles of crisp one-hundred dollar bills, and stuffed it into his jacket. Rifling through the contents of the safe, he extracted another package. It held the keys to his future; a fabricated passport and driver's license.

Sitting down at the desk, Anderson produced his wallet and emptied it of identification and credit cards. They went into a churning shredder near his feet. The pistol in his waistband jabbed and prodded. *I'm going to shoot my ass off.* He set the gun on top of the shredder.

Going back to the safe, Anderson rummaged for other critical items. Without warning, the room exploded in a blinding glare. Cornered, Anderson whirled and saw Zed Cain. His lean frame stretched across the doorway from top to bottom. A Ruger SR40, equipped with a suppressor, was in his grip. The gun didn't waver when the emotionless thug moved into the office. Another man appeared behind Cain, displaying a Glock 23 pistol and a smug smile.

"Don't do anything stupid, Howard," the stranger said. "I know you're a desperate man."

With fluid movements, Cain covered the distance to his boss and shoved him face-first against the wall. Anderson didn't resist the quick skillful frisking. Immediately, Cain discovered the two envelopes. He tossed the confiscated packages onto the desk.

"No weapons." Cain backed away.

"You left quite a mess out there on the interstate,

Howard." The stranger shook his head with staged lament when Anderson turned to face him.

"Who are you? You can't just break into my building and hold me at gunpoint. I'll have you both arrested!"

"You're the one who's wanted by the law."

"I want your name." Anderson insisted.

"I'm Special Agent Travis Price with the FBI. We've been watching you. After today, every cop in the country is looking for you. It's a good thing I found you first. Of course, I had an advantage."

"You're a damned FBI plant." Anderson felt a flush of rage when he looked at Cain. "Did you and this cop come to arrest me?"

Cain's stare pierced Anderson's soul while Price recited the Miranda rights.

"Have a seat," Price said after the formality. "You've got some explaining to do."

"I'm not saying anything without consulting with my attorney."

"Sit down!" Price lifted his Glock. His finger looked like it twitched on the trigger.

Detecting the flash of violence in Price's eyes, Anderson obeyed. Price wasn't bluffing.

"Keep your hands on the desk," Price commanded.

Anderson complied. The M&P was still on the shredder, just under the desk. He forced himself not to look down.

Holstering his weapon, Price settled into one of the chairs in front of the desk. Cain stayed near the door and held on to his firearm. Anderson watched Price open one of his envelopes. The FBI agent's eyebrows rose a bit when he peered inside. Turning it upside down, he dumped the bundles of cash onto the desktop.

"How much is this?"

"Fifty-thousand dollars." Anderson figured it was pointless to lie about the amount.

"It's not wise to carry that much cash around." Price

smirked.

Anderson declined to respond. His wistful stare was locked on the pile of currency as Price emptied the second envelope. The passport dropped onto the desk.

"The picture looks just like you, Howard." Price spoke with mock surprise. "But the name is Evan Hartley and the citizenship is Canadian. Isn't that odd?"

It's hopeless, Anderson thought. *I'm going to prison.*

"Obviously, you were planning a trip abroad." Price's tone dripped with disdain. "I doubt you were headed for a vacation."

There was still silence from Anderson. His mind was whirring with a frantic flock of thoughts. A bluff wouldn't work, but he wasn't prepared to spill his guts.

"Tell me what you were up to. I'm losing patience."

"I'm not saying anything without my attorney present." Anderson repeated his assertion. "If you're going to arrest me, then do it."

"I already did that. You want the handcuffs on?"

"I want to know what the charge is!"

"You're involved with E-Force." Price glanced at Cain. "That's a fact."

"You son-of-a-bitch." Anderson glowered at his former subordinate. "Are you FBI or just a freaking turncoat?"

Price's open hand came down hard on the desktop. "I'm asking the questions, and I expect answers."

"You have no grounds to arrest me." Anderson argued, shaking his head. "You're guilty of breaking and entering."

Price interrupted. "Get off your soap box, Howard. Do you think Mr. Cain is deaf and blind? I could write a book on your illicit activities."

"Cain can go to hell! He's got no proof. It's his word against mine."

"I know all about your past." Price sneered. "Jonathan Forde had a rap sheet as long as my arm. Murder was at the top of the list."

Anderson jerked at Price's assertions. It was information Cain couldn't have known. He felt he had stepped off a cliff, plummeting toward certain destruction.

"Did you expect nobody would notice when that poor slob from L.A. disappeared? You thought assuming his identity would erase all your crimes? I've got enough to lock you up and throw away the key."

"You can't pin everything on me. I had no choice. I've been blackmailed!"

"Is that so?" Price's eyes narrowed. "And who's been pulling your strings?"

"Darius Marchotti." Anderson divulged his forbidden secret. "Marchotti's people eliminated that man. He transformed me into Howard Anderson. E-Force was his idea. It was to promote his agenda!"

"You're telling me Darius Marchotti, media mogul and humanitarian, is a corrupt gangster of epic proportions?"

"That's right." The man formerly known as Jonathan Forde sensed an opening. "Marchotti controls a huge clandestine empire. I can help you bring him down."

Nobody in the room spoke for a few seconds. Anderson tried to catch his breath while his heart fluttered.

"You're making a serious charge against Darius Marchotti." Price raised an eyebrow. "He's a very powerful man. His demise would be earth-shattering."

"I have plenty of evidence against him." Anderson flailed for a chance at self-preservation. "He destroyed my life. I'll do whatever it takes to get it back."

"That's disappointing." Price pursed his lips.

"What are you talking about?" Anderson blinked in confusion.

"So many people are indebted to Mr. Marchotti." Price's tone was condescending. "Surely, you didn't suspect my first loyalty was to the FBI?"

Anderson gasped at his folly. "You bastard."

"Mr. Marchotti will be disheartened." Price taunted

Anderson. "He gave you a chance to escape the consequences of your past crimes. We had such big plans for you, Howard. Now, E-Force will make history without you."

"I knew it!" Anderson erupted. "E-Force was just a tool. That son-of-a-bitch was using us all along. I should have turned myself in to the police. I could have stopped him."

Price interrupted with a dismissive wave. "Stop with the illusions of grandeur. You've never been concerned with anything but your own interests. Who were you going to run to anyway? Mr. Marchotti's associates are embedded in every law enforcement agency. You have no idea who's with him."

"I still could have taken Cain down with me."

"You remember Deb Olson's accident, don't you?" Price asked. "She decided to be a whistle-blower."

"You scum killed Deb!" Anderson leapt from his seat. "Marchotti ordered you and Cain to murder her!"

"Sit down." Price warned Anderson as Cain moved to intervene. "Murder is the wrong term. It was preventive maintenance. Only a fool would expect Mr. Marchotti had no insurance policy to protect his investments. Mr. Cain specializes in risk reduction."

"How many others have you slaughtered in your quest for power?" Anderson was trembling with dread and disgust.

"Don't try to separate yourself from this. You set E-Force in motion. You're as involved as anyone."

Anger and hate simmered in Anderson. *The devil is incarnate in Darius Marchotti and his minions.*

"You've come here to kill me." The EcoFriends founder cast his eyes downward for an instant. His pistol was so close, just inches from his thigh. "It's part of Marchotti's insurance plan, isn't it?"

"You've left us with no other option, Howard. You've been a privileged member of Mr. Marchotti's organization. When you betrayed his trust, you sealed your fate."

Cain advanced with a hint of a smile on his face. A crack

like calving glacier ice sounded from somewhere outside the room. Cain and Price stiffened. It was the break Anderson needed.

In a lightening move, he snatched the Smith & Wesson from the shredder. Spring-loaded legs launched him from the chair. Possessed by insane desperation, Anderson disengaged the safety while swinging the muzzle toward Price.

The rogue FBI agent was caught off-guard. There was no time to draw his weapon. Price screamed a warning during an emergency ejection from his seat. Anderson was focused only on his terrified target. Even as Price crashed to the floor, it was a point blank shot. His finger tightened on the trigger.

A slug from Cain's SR40 plowed into Anderson's torso a fraction of a second before his M&P thundered. Knocked backward, the bullet from his gun splintered wood an inch from where Price was sprawled. Struggling to regain his balance, the E-Force moneyman heard two more thumps from Cain's weapon. A pair of bullets ravaged his chest, sending him spinning to the floor. When darkness enveloped Anderson, his finger clenched and the M&P boomed once more. A pool of blood expanded from his motionless body.

* * * *

The opening to the garage appeared too narrow for a vehicle to pass through unscathed. Justin Yeung opted to abandon his car in the driveway and venture into the rain. He teetered toward the front door of his house, tripped on the steps, and tumbled onto the porch. Unleashing a string of four-letter words, he struggled to his feet. Alcohol was a demon Justin had faced since adolescence. Once again, it had taken possession of his existence, delivering self-loathing and sorrow.

Not a minute passed without wallowing in regret.

Helping Luke hack into the UMN corporate database was stupid. Justin was scared, understanding that he would go to jail if the authorities discovered his role in the fiasco. Earlier in the day, a UMN investigator had questioned him. Before being sequestered, he resolved to deny any knowledge of Luke's caper. But during the interrogation, Justin felt the walls closing in. Valdez had uncanny intuition, as if he could read thoughts.

All seemed lost until Valdez abruptly ended the inquisition. When dismissed, Justin had hurried from the building. He was mired in quicksand and sinking fast. Inevitably, he found himself pounding drinks at a bar.

Justin managed to unlock the door and stumble into the house. He forced down a glass of water. *Maybe that'll prevent a hangover.* A hiccup followed his prediction. After reeling upstairs, Justin collapsed onto his bed. Within minutes, he was snoring.

* * * *

Hiding in his office, Colt recognized the voice of Howard Anderson, demanding an explanation for his arrest. His boss's loud outbursts about Darius Marchotti and E-Force were audible and clear. Colt's blood went cold when he heard shouted assertions about Deb's death.

All of Colt's worst fears were confirmed. He was caught up in a vast conspiracy...one comprised of killers. A shiver of dread passed through him when he realized the people in Anderson's office, apparently law enforcement agents, were part of Marchotti's corrupt network. *What if they search the building...my office?* Colt knew they would kill him, just like Deb. He slithered from below the desk and stood up. A flexing floorboard cracked under his foot. An instant later, yelling and gunfire erupted in Anderson's office. One of the bullets ripped through the wall, tearing past Colt in the darkness. The thud of a body was unmistakable.

With the thunder of gunplay reverberating in his head, Colt's thoughts flashed to the cassette tape. It was an unbelievable coincidence, a miracle. He had recorded the entire drama...culminating in a murder.

Footsteps pounded in the hallway when Colt darted to the bookshelf and ejected his precious tape from the recorder. He whirled, searching for an escape. *The window!* A twelve-foot drop was beyond the glass panes.

Colt tore at the window latch. Wood groaned in protest when he heaved the sash up. Somebody was at the door. In alarm, Colt spun and snatched the telephone from the desktop. He heaved it the instant the room was flooded with light. The missile struck Zed Cain in the nose as he charged with a pistol. Blood splattered, and the assassin staggered backward and fell.

Without wasting another second, Colt swung his legs over the windowsill and plunged toward the ground. Rain-soaked lawn cushioned the landing. He tumbled and rolled back to his feet. As soon as he was up, Colt sprinted for the sidewalk.

In the moonlight, Colt expected to be gunned down at any second. The sirens of police cars wailing in the distance only fueled his fears. He careened toward a corner where high hedges encroached on the sidewalk. Casting a backward glance, he spied a shadowy figure several hundred feet behind him. It had to be Cain. When Colt accelerated around the bend, someone blocked his path. Evasive action was impossible.

A violent impact pitched him into the hedge. The other man was launched backward onto the street. Clawing out of the shrubbery, Colt prepared to fight off the assailant. Intense pain burned in his ribs. Blood from a cut invaded one eye.

The man sprawled in the gutter was hysterical, screaming obscenities. One of his shoulders was contorted in a grotesque position. A rabid little dog tugged at a leash.

239

Lowering his fists, Colt realized the man was just a guy who happened to be at the wrong place at the wrong time.

"I'm sorry," Colt declared with regret before turning to flee. "Really, I am."

The man released his grip on the dog's tether, commanding the mutt to attack. Colt cried out in pain when the dog sunk its teeth into his ankle. Frantic, he shook the animal loose. In an instant, it lunged, snarling and salivating. Colt caught the canine with a solid kick that sent it airborne. Yelping, the dog scurried away in retreat.

"You bastard! I'll sue you for every penny you've got!"

* * * *

The injured dog owner's torrent of agonized expletives continued as Colt vanished. When the dog suddenly tucked its tail and fled, the man turned and looked up. He fell into a deathly silence at the sight of a phantom with a gun fitted with a suppressor. It was pointed straight at him.

* * * *

The glass in Marla's hand was a moving target. Ted Rogers tilted a bottle, sloshing most of the champagne into the hot tub. Attempting to alter his impaired aim, the bottle slipped from his clumsy grip and plopped into the churning water. Marla burst out in an inebriated giggle.

"Don't worry, Ted. We can drink from the hot tub."

"I suppose this gives new meaning to bubbly water," the UMN executive replied.

Marla cackled at the ridiculous remark. Rogers was seized by side-splitting laughter. The foolish drunken behavior was an ineffective cover for their true intents.

Dinner had been at an upscale Italian restaurant, purportedly to talk business. But after the first bottle of wine, the conversation diverged into the realm of personal interests. Lingering at the table long after dinner, their wine glasses were refilled many times.

The growing lust in Rogers' eyes was obvious. Marla was enthralled. The man hoping to seduce her was wealthy and powerful. His home was a penthouse suite in an exclusive building. The place was filled with fascinating artifacts and pieces of artwork, ranging from ancient Egypt to the American West. *The paintings and spectacular photographs on the walls put Glen's collection to shame.* Marla was impressed, sure that Rogers could provide her with everything she would require. But everything, including passion, had a price. Marla wanted assurance that he would keep promoting her career.

"New York is so exciting." Marla pressed against Rogers. "There are so many talented people."

"I know you'll separate yourself from the crowd. You were born for stardom."

"That's very flattering." Once again, Marla feigned humility. "You've worked with the best in the business for years."

"That's why I brought you here," Rogers said, moving closer.

"Are you offering to make a commitment, Ted?" Marla asked, caressing his fingers.

"I'd like to become your...partner."

"Are you sure that's not just the alcohol, Ted?" Marla asked warily.

"You've got a special intangible quality that I find incredibly desirable."

Rogers was holding nothing back, willing to advance her career in return for a sexual relationship. He could expedite her journey toward the summit of success. Marla understood there were no guarantees in life, but this was pretty close. *Rot in hell, Glen.*

"We're at the beginning of something very special." Marla set her champagne glass on the side of the tub.

"Perhaps we should consummate the partnership."

Marla didn't resist as Rogers swept her up in his arms. They pressed their lips together with unbridled passion.

* * * *

Grave concern spread through Special Agent Travis Price. Anderson was dead as a stone, but there was a new problem. He could only guess how much the person hiding in the adjacent office had seen or heard. It really didn't matter. *Any threat to Darius Marchotti must be eliminated.*

Price cursed again as he contemplated the catastrophe. A gun battle with Anderson had not been part of the plan. Now there were cops on the way. He stalked away from the corpse. The body and the safe had been purged of anything that might implicate Marchotti. Price felt a glimmer of consolation, knowing that his part in the charade would last only a couple more days.

Shuddering, Price eyed the jagged hole in the floor. Smugness had almost killed him. Cain's quick reaction was the slim margin between life and death. Looking closer, he noticed grains of a white powdery substance near the bullet hole. With suspicion, his gaze rose to the ceiling. A small object nestled against the fire sprinkler beckoned for investigation. Leaping onto a chair, Price grabbed it and pulled. "A freaking microphone!"

Price dashed to Colt Kelley's office as the first police car arrived on the street. His eyes fell on the stereo on the bookshelf. The cassette tape deck was open and empty. The FBI agent rushed across the room and found the wire leading to the ceiling.

In an awful instant, he knew. *Everything in Anderson's office was recorded.* A cop pounded on the front door.

Chapter Sixteen
Thursday, June 14 (early morning)

Colt Kelley crouched in the pseudo-safety of the shadows and pressed the sleeve of his jacket to the gash above his brow. The crimson stain on the fabric continued to expand. His eyes probed the moonlit street. For a few seconds, he halted his labored breathing and cocked an ear to the night air. Cain was out there somewhere...and others too. Colt was afraid the odds of escape were shrinking with each passing minute.

The Land Cruiser beckoned. Colt ventured onto the street, his head swiveling about. Halfway across the pavement, his senses crackled with trepidation. Quickening his pace, he reached the vehicle. Pulsating adrenaline filled his veins. The vibrations hampered the insertion of the key into the door. In the eerie gloom, it seemed like threading a needle. Finally, the lock disengaged with a click. Colt cast a backward glance as he yanked the Land Cruiser door open. The source of his fearful premonition remained invisible.

Before he could turn and scramble into the seat, something slammed against Colt's head with tremendous force. The impact sent him reeling backward. His feet tangled, and he dropped to the pavement. Sluggish reflexes hindered his attempt to rise. A dark figure sprang from inside the vehicle. Headlights blazed. A van roared abreast of victim and ambushing assailant. Dazed by the vicious blow, Colt was dragged inside. The side door slammed shut.

Sprawled on the floor of the accelerating vehicle, Colt's head pounded with pain. His attacker lunged forward, brandishing handcuffs. Exploding with primal rage, Colt launched a savage kick at the man's head. A grunt of pain and surprise announced his shoe striking the target. Joey Morris was bowled over. Colt scrambled up, but the big man grabbed his ankle. Unable to twist away, he crashed down as the van swerved and lurched. Agony flared in his injured torso.

Gordon Trovato swore from behind the wheel. "What the hell are you doing? Get him under control!"

Colt fought and grappled with Morris, an adversary who outweighed him by at least fifty pounds. His ferocity matched that of a wounded bear. The larger man was unable to gain the upper hand. Trovato slammed on the brakes. Both combatants were catapulted forward as if they had been thrown from a horse. Upon the impact of flesh against metal, the behemoth unclamped his viselike grip. Pushing his pain aside, Colt lunged for the side door and fumbled with the latch handle. The hard steel of a gun barrel jammed against his kidney.

"Move and I'll blow your guts out." Trovato's Brooklyn-accented voice delivered the threat.

For an instant, Colt contemplated whether he was willing to die fighting. He didn't want to give in, only to be slaughtered. As the gun pressed harder, it was clear he had no choice.

"You're no action hero, pal," Trovato said when Colt relented. "This is real life. People die."

Morris twisted Colt's arms behind his back. He refused to betray the discomfort while the handcuffs were clamped onto his wrists. Subdued by the steel bracelets, he was shoved against the metal ribbed wall of the van.

As the frisking for weapons started, Colt felt like a smuggler carrying contraband. *When they find the tape, it's all over*. E-Force will destroy me and all evidence of the truth. A hand moved over the jacket pocket that held the tape. When the probing fingers didn't pause, Colt's relief was overridden by dismay. *The cassette is gone!*

* * * *

Special Agent Malcolm Hill advanced on Colt Kelly's

house. Light spilled from the windows. His finger tightened on the trigger of his firearm. Moving onto the front porch, the corrupt FBI agent found the door ajar. Hill's weapon was poised and ready when he crept into the dwelling. A quick search of the place revealed that nobody was home.

Somebody left in a hurry. He surveyed the mess in the kitchen.

In one of the bathrooms, he stopped and eyed the women's underwear. It was an unexpected twist. Hill felt uneasy as he rooted through drawers and cabinets, looking for a cassette tape. The search was fruitless and time was short.

"This is bullshit." The FBI man fumed on his way out the front door. The phone rang. Hill stopped when the answering machine in the kitchen activated.

A distressed female voice whined. "Colt, it's Delilah. Where are you?"

Hill gasped at the shocking connection between Delilah Francelli and Colt Kelley. *What the hell is going on?*

"I'm freaking out at this motel," she continued. "Please come by as soon as you can. I'm really scared. I can't say more over the phone."

Hill dialed a number on his cell phone. "We've got a problem," he declared when Price answered. "Kelley's got himself a girlfriend. It's Delilah Francelli."

* * * *

Restrained in the windowless cargo area, Colt awaited his captors' next move with dread. Alone and helpless, it took all of his willpower to stay composed. There was no reason to be optimistic. Deb Olson and Howard Anderson were murdered. *I'm next.* Fighting fear and depression, memories of the past and hopes for the future flashed through Colt's mind.

Whining brakes slowed the van to a stop. The engine

went silent and Colt's pulse surged. Maybe they were on some remote back road. He dreaded being killed and dumped in some secluded area where he might never be found. Seconds later, his back was pinned against the interior of the vehicle. A bright light seared his eyes.

"Late night at the office, Kelley?" Gordon Trovato pressed close. Colt recoiled at the residual stench of cigarette smoke.

Joey Morris shoved Colt when he remained silent. "The man asked you a question."

These guys sound like New York mafia. Maybe Marchotti was the head of an organized crime family. It was impossible to know the breadth of the conspiracy. Colt only knew he had fallen into dark roiling water.

"It's in your best interest to answer my questions," Trovato said. "You know what I'm saying?"

Colt still didn't reply, not wanting to sound weak and scared.

Trovato's tone indicated he was about to snap. "You want to play the silent game? That's pretty stupid."

"This'll get very unpleasant for you," Morris pressed Colt tighter against the metal wall. "You got that?"

"I don't know what this is about," Colt burst out.

"Don't give me that bullshit," Trovato retorted. "You've got some special feelings for E-Force."

"I don't know what you're talking about, but I can tell you kidnapping is illegal."

"You want to talk about illegal activities?" Trovato asked. "There's plenty of evidence that links you to E-Force. The FBI's putting the pieces of the puzzle together. So where does that leave you? Maybe you would sell out your kin to save your skin."

The blood in Colt's veins ran cold. The brutes holding him suspected he was looking for a way to cut a deal with the FBI. "You're full of shit."

"And you're an accomplice to E-Force." Trovato

continued. "If they go down, so do you."

"So does every other EcoFriends manager."

"Maybe all your pals are in as deep as you," Morris said. "Has Howard Anderson been giving the marching orders?"

Colt's mind churned, and he considered using the murder recording as a bargaining chip. E-Force would be reluctant to kill him without having the tape in their possession. *But I don't have it either.*

"Anderson is just my boss at EcoFriends. I've got no knowledge of E-Force. There's no way I could compromise them."

"Acting stupid won't help you," Trovato said. "You've got a little thing going on with Delilah Francelli, an admitted E-Force operative."

"That doesn't mean anything." Colt hoped Delilah was still safe. It was clear that she had gotten herself in big trouble.

Trovato's bluster intensified. "Ms. Francelli slipped away from confinement at the hospital. She made phone calls to you. She came to you for help. Maybe you want to change you story about E-Force now."

"You're delusional," Colt retorted.

Morris smacked him on the head. "We heard the messages she left. She was at your house."

"Delilah's an old girlfriend. I don't know what she's gotten into."

"You're a lying sack of shit." Morris delivered another rough shove.

"I don't know anything about E-Force!" Colt's anger flared at the abuse. "I don't care about E-Force. None of it matters to me."

"Is that what you told the Senator's daughter?" Trovato asked.

"I don't know what you're talking about."

"We know about your relationship with Carrie Forde. She left messages on your answering machine too."

"Carrie and I have a casual friendship." Colt floundered in confusion and dread. "I don't know anything about her family. I had no idea her old man was a Senator."

"You're digging a deeper hole," Morris said. "We don't like lies."

"That young lady is going to get hurt because of you," Trovato stated coldly.

Colt tried to mask his frantic fear. *Why had Carrie not revealed the truth?* It didn't matter. She was in grave danger from the two animals behind the blinding light.

"We got a schedule to keep," Trovato muttered with disgust. "You better think about the other people in your life, jackass."

When the van started moving, Colt was awash in guilt and helpless frustration. Ruthless brutality was the essence of E-Force. He had thrust the woman he loved into a meat grinder. *Dear God, please protect Carrie...and Delilah.*

* * * *

Roaring water triggered an alarm in Boyd Pruitt's brain. The resulting rush of adrenaline was addictive...like a needle full of heroin to a junkie.

The torrent of water blasting past in the Eagle River was the culmination of melting snowpack and excessive spring rain. Churning currents, huge waves, looming rocks, and swirling eddies were part of an awesome spectacle of raw natural power. Most paddlers wouldn't consider paddling the Dowd Chutes at such a level. Pruitt was determined to hurtle though the rapids under the light of a full moon. He lived for the thrill.

"Surf's up, dude," Mad Cow exclaimed. His kayak thumped down next to Pruitt's.

"Is everybody ready?" Pruitt asked the stocky paddling guru. "This clear sky won't last long."

"As ready as they'll ever be." Mad Cow grinned while a

life vest strained to contain his barrel chest.

The two expert paddlers watched two other men approach with their boats. One seemed unsteady on his feet.

Pruitt was skeptical. "Are you sure Corey's ready for this? This is no beginner's run."

"No doubt, dude. We've paddled almost every day this season. He's definitely gung-ho."

"He threw-up part of his gut a little while ago," Pruitt said, frowning.

"So now he's ready." Mad Cow laughed. "Don't worry. Rhett will help babysit."

A moment later, the four paddlers stood together on the riverbank. Rhett discussed the best route to take on the wild ride. Corey stood silent and pale as a ghost.

Pruitt placed a hand on the kid's shoulder. "Don't feel pressured to go."

"This is a big goal for me." Corey stood firm. "I'm not going to back out."

"Let's do it then," Pruitt said. "Corey, you follow Mad Cow and me. Rhett will take up the rear. If you miss a move, hang on and we'll come after you. If you swim, don't panic. We'll get you to an eddy."

Corey nodded his head as the others whooped with excitement. Each man squeezed into his boat.

* * * *

Powered by a diesel engine, the Ford Excursion barreled along the interstate. It threatened to flatten a car before veering into the left lane and roaring past. The massive vehicle represented everything environmentalists loathed. But Zed Cain didn't give a damn about the environment or activist agendas. He was a mercenary, hired by the highest bidder.

Cain touched his swollen nose. *You'll pay, Kelley.* The desire to exact revenge was strong. But Marchotti would not permit a personal vendetta. Colt Kelley was an irritation to be eradicated by others. Cain's responsibilities lay elsewhere.

Howard Anderson had nearly destroyed a complex operation. The other E-Force fools would be stunned by the death of their leader. Some would want to disband in panic, aborting the Friday operation. That was not an option. Cain was to ensure that Marchotti's plans were carried out. *Those E-Force cowards are going to meet their destiny,* Cain vowed.

While contemplating his enforcer's task, Cain overtook a sedan that was putting along in the passing lane. Traveling in the right lane, Cain's Excursion was abreast of the car when he detected a van accelerating down an entrance ramp to the highway. It showed no sign of slowing and yielding. A collision seemed inevitable.

"Get out of the way." Cain laid on the horn and jammed the accelerator to the floor. The Excursion blasted forward. At the last second, the top-heavy van swerved and careened away. In his rearview mirror, he watched the thrashing headlights fade in the distance.

* * * *

"It sounds like a freight train," Marla grumbled, unable to escape the rumbling snoring of her new promoter.

Marla sat up in the bed and shoved Rogers. The racket subsided a decibel when the executive grunted and rolled over. To subdue her annoyance, she mulled over the plans that would soon secure her future. In less than eight hours, Marla would be on a plane headed to Denver and Channel 4 headquarters. The station had agreed to provide a remote broadcast team. She had insisted on Chris Morgan as the cameraman. He was good at his job and he didn't ask stupid questions. That was important because E-Force had something big planned at the new AmeResort conference center on Friday. Marla didn't know the details, but her contact promised it would be earthshaking. In no uncertain terms, Cain had threatened dire consequences if any leaks occurred. Such a warning was unnecessary. Marla wasn't about to jeopardize her golden goose before the moment of glory.

E-Force is going to make me media royalty. Marla clasped her hands together. *I'll be on every television talk-show. Maybe I'll even write a book.*

Marla was certain that E-Force would eventually be brought to justice, but she didn't care. By that time, some other radical group would arise and assume a position of prominence. *A never-ending succession of wackos will be dialing my phone. I'll have to establish a hotline.*

Of course, a relationship with E-Force was similar to walking a tightrope. It was best to have a safety net. Marla knew it was essential to have a bulletproof reason for showing up at a conference center an hour before an E-Force strike. Drew Harmon filled part of the bill. She was in town to interview the actor and listen to his empty insight about social issues.

But the real kicker was AmcResort executive, Stephen Chandler. He had been pestering Marla, demanding fair and balanced coverage of his company's plight. Chandler jumped at Marla's suggestion that she attend his Developers' Forum. It was the perfect alibi to be front and center with camera rolling during an E-Force assault.

It's so easy to manipulate men. Marla was certain that she alone controlled her destiny.

* * * *

With a barrage of swearing, Gordon Trovato struggled to control his van. Joey Morris clung to the framing and braced for a crash. Helpless in the handcuffs, Colt's head slammed against metal. Finally, the violent writhing subsided, and the vehicle came to rest without pitching over.

"That son-of-a-bitch almost killed us!" Trovato bellowed as the taillights on Zed Cain's Excursion disappeared in the darkness.

"We ought to run that jackass down." Morris pried his fingers from their holds. "Too bad we've still got you to deal with."

Reeling with nausea, Colt ignored the threat. The punishment dealt by hunger, exhaustion, and pain was too much. Worry about Carrie magnified the intensity of his misery.

Colt groaned a few miles after the mobile prison resumed its journey. "I'm sick. I'm going to throw up."

"You better not puke," Morris said.

There was no reprieve for Colt. Involuntary contortions racked his abdomen. With the abruptness of a geyser, vomiting erupted.

"Stop the van!" Morris scrambled for safety. "The son-of-a-bitch's puking!"

When the van finally ground to a halt, Morris fled out the side door. Colt was dragged out by Trovato and flung to the ground. His body heaved with convulsions. It was a supreme struggle to sit up with his hands restrained behind his back. Morris yanked Colt to his feet and forced him to face the gray-haired driver.

Trovato snarled. "Listen to me you piece of shit. You're going to clean out that van with your shirt. Let's move."

Trovato had pulled off the interstate and parked along a two-lane road. Morris remained behind while Colt was shoved across the asphalt. A spark of recognition flared in his mind. *We're on U.S. Highway 24, just north of Minturn. That's the Eagle River ripping past the embankment below the east side of the road.*

With Trovato behind him, Colt negotiated the pavement edge, searching for a place to descend the steep slope. It was a daunting prospect without the benefit of free hands.

Somehow, he managed to get down to the edge of the roaring water without injury

"I can't do this with handcuffs," Colt said over the din.

Trovato hesitated, glaring for a few seconds. He stepped forward, jerked his captive around, and unclamped the bonds. Colt shook his arms to return some feeling to them.

"Think about the hole a .45 caliber slug would put through you." Trovato brandished his Sig Sauer P220. "Don't try something stupid."

Colt stripped the shirt from his athletic torso and stepped onto a boulder that extended into the river. Heaving, silvery waves glistened in the light of the full moon. He knew it was the upper part of the Dowd Chutes. Colt had paddled the stretch. A nightmare image of being swept away in the torrent flashed through his mind. Taking care not to slip, he squatted and dunked his soiled shirt in the frigid water.

A whooping cry floated across the tumultuous surface of the river. Colt jerked his head up and saw the shadow of a paddler carving his kayak into an eddy along the shore. The boat was turned upriver as the man looked back toward the rapids. He was oblivious to Colt crouched on the boulder fifty feet downstream. Colt glanced toward his captor and saw Trovato move the pistol under his jacket.

"Ferry left, Corey!" a man yelled. "Catch this eddy. Work left!"

Colt witnessed Corey's kayak materialize on the water. It was farther from shore than the first boat had been. The paddle strokes were unassertive and the rogue current swept the craft past the safety of the eddy.

A boulder loomed like a prehistoric beast. It was too late when, the paddler changed tactics and tried to shoot past the rock. The boat slammed sideways against the huge hunk of granite. The terrific power of the water pummeled the upstream side, shoving it down. Corey didn't have a chance when the kayak capsized, its bottom squashed against the side of the boulder. The crushing force of the river was inescapable. Rolling the boat upright or ejecting from the cockpit was impossible.

"Corey's broached!" Boyd Pruitt screamed with frantic arm waving. "Get below the rock!"

A second kayak bounced through the boiling rapids. Exhibiting extreme skill, the other kayaker dodged the granite deathtrap and peeled into the swirling eddy below the massive rock. He clung to the rough surface to avoid being thrown back into the savage currents.

"Rhett, get over here!" the first man said, tearing off his spray skirt. "Corey's pinned!"

The last plastic craft rocketed through the churning gauntlet and sliced into the shoreline haven. Clambering from their boats, the men hugged the jagged riverbank. The kayaker called Rhett heaved a rope bag, keeping the free end of the line firmly in his grasp. Nylon rope played out like a streamer as the bag soared toward the middle of the raging river. Falling short of the rescuer behind the rock, the bag was ripped away by the deluge. The men above Colt hauled in the line like sailors pulling up an anchor in a squall.

The third kayaker managed to snag the evasive rope bag the second time. Gripping the carabiner attached to the bag, Mad Cow strained to reach the pinned craft. It required a heroic effort to clip the carabiner to a rescue handle on the bow. At once, the two remaining kayakers yanked the rescue line taut.

While the river drama unfolded, Trovato waved Colt toward the road. Feeling the urge to assist the rescuers, Colt was reluctant to comply with the directive. He watched the kayakers digging in their heels and leaning back on the rope. The last kayaker pounded on the hull of the boat. Finally, it budged enough to upset the deadly equilibrium. With the suddenness of a broken shoestring, the boat snapped around and broke free from the watery grave.

In the shoreline eddy, the other two men tugged with every ounce of strength, and the inverted kayak swung toward shore, plowing through the waves. The one still in the middle of the river ventured from behind the boulder and into the punishing whitewater. With gritty determination, he ferried and helped guide the capsized boat to the riverbank. The two boats clunked against the shore downstream of Colt and Trovato.

"Get your ass up to the road," Trovato said.

Trying to scramble across the rocks, Colt faltered and fell. He clutched his ankle and winced. There was no sympathy from Trovato. The ruffian tried to drag Colt to his feet and force him up the slope.

The kayaker still in the water struggled to drag his unfortunate comrade from the flooded cockpit. The first two scuttled down the riverbank. When they spotted Colt and Trovato, one of them didn't waste time wondering what they were doing alongside the river. "A paddler just drowned! We need an ambulance with paramedics."

Trovato didn't respond to the man's pleas. The hand gripping the Sig was stuffed into his jacket pocket. His eyes flashed between Colt and the traumatized whitewater thrill-seekers.

Colt felt worthless, sitting on the ground and massaging his injury. There was nothing he could do to help.

"Come on, man!" Pruitt grabbed Trovato's arm. "Look what's happening over there!"

Pulling from his grasp, Trovato looked toward the limp body draped across the rocks. The men were starting to perform CPR.

"What's wrong with you two? Time is running out!"

"I've got a phone at the vehicle," Trovato finally said. "I'll call 911."

"Tell them we're on the west bank of the Eagle River, about a mile north of Minturn." The man scurried downstream.

"Stay there," Trovato warned Colt. "I'll make your pain a lot worse."

Trovato was struggling up to the road when Colt sprang from the ground. He was nimble as a mountain goat, leaping across the boulders en route to the kayaks resting upstream.

"That son-of-a-bitch!" Trovato whirled.

Brandishing his pistol, Trovato turned to give chase, but it was too late. Colt plunged into the chill water, clinging to one of the boats. Within seconds, he was swept away by the torrent.

* * * *

The auditory intrusion of an alarm clock dragged Luke Parson from the bliss of sleep. Groggy and confused, he heard footsteps. Recollections from the past few days flashed in his mind. He bolted upright, eyes darting around the strange bedroom.

For a moment, Luke listened to the slow cadence of footfalls beyond the bedroom door. Running water announced that someone had stumbled into the shower. Luke bounded from the bed, gathered his soaked garments, and retreated downstairs.

A short time later, Justin Yeung shuffled into the kitchen holding his head and wincing. Dressed in a bathrobe, his hair fell loosely on his shoulders. He stopped dead in his tracks at the sight of Luke sitting at the table with only a towel around his waist.

"Sorry to drop in unannounced." Luke apologized with a mouthful of cereal.

"What are you doing here?" Justin's eyes shifted briefly to the humming dryer. "I want you out."

"I'm in a tough spot," Luke said. "My clothes aren't even dry."

"You dragged me into a mess. My life is ruined. If the FBI knew you were here, they'd lock me up for good."

"Settle down. The situation is complicated."

"Is that what you call killing a janitor?" Justin asked.

"You made me an accessory to that."

"Shut up and listen!" Luke jumped up. "I didn't kill anyone. I'm being framed."

Brushing his wet hair aside, Justin glanced into the adjoining living room. Luke had turned the television on. The sound volume was low, but the muffled voices on a morning news program were audible.

"You've been on T.V." Justin stabbed his index finger at Luke. "There's a video of you running through our office building."

Luke shook his head in dispute. "It's all a coverup operation. I stumbled onto a conspiracy that may go all the way to the top of the UMN. Somebody killed an innocent custodian to keep that secret. I'm next on the hit list."

"Why should I believe that? Nothing else you said was true."

"You've known me for years, Justin." The onset of desperation descended on Luke. "Do you really think I'd kill somebody?"

Justin removed his glasses and massaged his temples. Luke could sense that his friend was close to an emotional breaking point.

"I'm sorry you're involved with this." Luke stepped forward. "Everything's out of control. But no matter what happens, I won't tell anyone you helped me. You have my word."

"I don't know what to do anymore." Justin collapsed onto one of the kitchen chairs. "My life is crumbling down."

"You've got to hang tough, Justin. I'll find a way to blow the lid off this thing. Then we'll both be absolved of everything. We can be heroes."

"I don't want to be a hero." Justin trembled. "You shouldn't have come here."

"I had no other alternative. I need to borrow some cash and your old car. Without your help, it's over for me."

Justin sat with his elbows on the table, his face buried in

his hands. For a moment, the quiet voices on the television were the only sounds. Luke stiffened when someone on the UMN program spoke the name, Howard Anderson. *The man was killed!*

"I need to listen to this." Luke hitched up his towel and hurried closer to the television.

"Anderson arranged a meeting with FBI Special Agent Travis Price at the EcoFriends office in Aspen," the news anchor reported. "When Price arrived, the EcoFriends founder asserted that a subordinate named Colt Kelley is an integral part of E-Force. While Anderson proceeded to relate the details of the illicit activities, Kelley burst into the room, gunning his boss down in cold blood. We understand the quick reactions of Special Agent Price were all that saved him from the same fate. During his flight from the scene, Kelley's second victim was a pedestrian who got in his way."

A picture of Colt Kelley was displayed. The clean-cut young man didn't look like a killer, but Luke was painfully aware that appearances could be deceiving. His brain churned, trying to comprehend the links between Anderson, the UMN, and E-Force. It was a tangled web of deceit and murder.

"If you don't help me, I'm a dead man," Luke said in a weak, frightened voice. "The murder of that guy, Howard Anderson, is somehow tied to the things I discovered."

Justin scoffed, apparently immersed in self-pity. "That sounds far-fetched."

"There's a connection between the United Media Network and that eco-terrorist group, E-Force." Luke was insistent. "Howard Anderson may have been the link."

"What makes you say that?"

"Jonathan Forde's personnel file from the UMN database." Luke walked over to the kitchen counter and lifted his flashdrive. The device held a copy of the emailed Forde file. "It's encrypted, but you could crack the code."

"You weren't supposed to copy anything!" Justin jumped up from his seat, looking on the verge of combustion. "You lied to me."

"That file could be the key to getting out of this mess," Luke said, advancing toward his friend.

"I'm not helping you with this. You need to get the hell out of here."

"Okay, I'll go." Luke's arms fell limp. "But please loan me some cash and your car."

"Are you crazy? I should call the cops right now."

"My life is on the line. There's nobody else I can turn to," Luke pleaded. "But if I find a way to clear myself, it will absolve you too."

"Tell me where you're going," Justin said after quiet consideration.

"That would only put you more at risk." Luke shook his head and held up his hand. "I've already gotten you in enough trouble."

"Don't try to be magnanimous. Tell me or you're on your own."

"Okay, fine." Luke threw his hands up in frustration. "I'm going to Grand Junction. Are you going to help me or not?"

"Take the car." Justin opened a drawer and tossed a set of keys. "I'll see if I have any cash."

"I really appreciate this. You're giving me a fighting chance."

"Spare me the gratitude." Justin turned to go upstairs and retrieve his wallet. "If anybody asks, I'll tell them you stole the car and money."

* * * *

Luke was gone. Justin's thoughts and emotions were in chaotic turmoil. He was desperate enough to have given Luke the chance to find the path to reprieve. What other choice was there?

"You dragged me into this bullshit." Justin paced about the kitchen. "You better pull me out and clean up the mess."

Plodding out of the room, Justin stopped cold at the mention of Luke's name on the television. Panic surged through him when a police spokesman asserted that the fugitive journalist would soon be caught in a tightening dragnet. With utter dismay, Justin realized he was being dragged toward perdition.

Fueled by terror, Justin rushed to the table and snatched his wallet. His fingers felt cold and stiff as he dug out a business card. Pushing aside his feelings of fear and dread, Justin went to the phone. With a trembling hand he dialed the number seared on the card. A shiver traveled down his spine while he waited for Valdez to answer.

* * * *

The morning show host adopted a bright smile and a perky demeanor an instant before the broadcast went back on the air. Her co-host's imitation of happiness was less convincing.

"Welcome back to *A New Day in America*. I'm Janie Lake, and we're broadcasting live from our studio in New York."

"And I'm Gary Green," the co-host said.

"It's been a whirlwind morning." Janie continued. "The issue of campaign reform has created a sharp political divide in Washington."

"The rhetoric is heating up." Green raised an eyebrow. "The fate of Senator Edward Cardin's bill now appears uncertain. Senator John Harris of Colorado is pulling out all the stops in his opposition effort."

"We have Senator Cardin with us via satellite," Janie said. "Good morning, Senator. We're happy you could make time to join us."

Cardin appeared on the television. "It's my pleasure to speak with you."

"Senator Harris has also agreed to be with us." Janie introduced her other guest. The image of Harris filled the right half of the spilt-screen.

"I'm glad to have the opportunity to spread the word." Harris smiled.

Janie initiated the discussion by asking Cardin about his support for the bill currently before the Senate.

"Big money has taken over American politics," Cardin said, looking down his nose through spectacles. "Elected politicians are indebted to special interest groups and corporations. Ordinary citizens have no say in the political process."

"How will your bill improve the situation?" Janie leaned forward.

"My goal is to eliminate corrupting money sources from political campaigns," Cardin answered with a lofty air. "All financing will come from public funds. My bill also stipulates an equal amount of free advertising for each candidate. With a level playing field, politicians will be able to focus on the issues instead of money."

Gary Green said with a hint of condescension, "Obviously you don't agree with this approach, Senator Harris."

"Money is not the real problem with our political system. A gun doesn't kill without somebody pulling the trigger. Corrupt people taint politics, and no system of government is immune to impropriety. Turning campaigns into affairs strictly financed by public funds would be misguided. How can we expect to solve our problems by creating another government agency, one that's supposed to dole out money to qualifying political hopefuls?"

"Don't you think removing the big money would reduce the potential for unsavory practices?" Janie couldn't suppress her opposition.

"We shouldn't attack the problem by limiting the free political speech that's guaranteed by the Constitution." Harris remained calm. "After trampling on the First Amendment, the Cardin Bill would put candidates at the mercy of the government."

Senator Cardin interrupted. "This bill doesn't deny anyone's free speech. It'll give all candidates equal access to the media."

"All media advertising would be prohibited six weeks prior to the election." Harris raised a hand in protest. "That's when most people start to pay attention to political races. Of course, commentators and analysts would be unregulated, free to portray any candidate in whatever manner they choose. The media can build a person up or tear him down. A political candidate who is out of favor will have no way to set the record straight, let alone promote a campaign."

"You're demonizing the media." Cardin's jowls shook with ire. "Big donors are the problem. The media will act as an arbitrator."

"Your bill would strip Americans of the right to free speech. Candidates favored by the pundits will have a decided advantage. The mainstream media would run America."

"You're misleading the public!" Cardin sputtered from the left side of the screen. "Campaign reform is a necessity to save this country."

"We're talking about a very small loss of freedom." Green took up for Cardin. "It could be for the greater good."

"That attitude of acceptance enables government tyranny," Harris said sharply. "If the media reported the truth about this issue, it would never fly with rational citizens."

Cardin was red-faced with anger. "Now you've gone too far, John!"

* * * *

Radical Action

The televised debate between Harris and Cardin descended into a full-blown squabble. It seemed the hosts were powerless to regain control of their program. The Senator from Colorado kept his emotions in check and retained a semblance of logic and reason. In stark contrast, the older man floundered with fury and frustration.

Darius Marchotti snapped an ink pen in his hands. Sitting at the desk in the study of his mansion, he pressed his palms against his temples. "Cardin is a moron! He's destroying the push for campaign finance reform."

Zharikov contemplated what might be in store for Cardin. He could think of many methods to punish incompetence and satisfy his dark sadistic cravings.

"My influence made him powerful," Marchotti ranted. "Now he's a useless worn-out fool."

Zharikov nodded. "He's not worthy of your favors."

An all-out media assault, tying Harris to corporate developers and special interest groups, had failed to defeat the Coloradan legislator. His campaign for re-election was faltering, but he remained as dogged as a pit-bull in his battle with Cardin. He was like the Phoenix, continually rising from the ashes.

"I can't take any more of this." Marchotti switched off the television and hurled the remote control across the room. The device broke and clattered across the hard floor.

Zharikov looked to Marchotti, expecting instructions. A demonic presence emanated from his boss's eyes. A crocodile disguised in a man's body lurked below the surface of a stagnant muddy pool.

"Harris is going to pay for this." Marchotti's low voice rumbled. "And so will Cardin."

* * * *

The phone rang once, and Max Reichner was awake and cognizant. He pushed a beautiful brunette aside. Her silky skin was only partly covered by the bed linens.

"Who's calling?" Reichner rasped.

"I want to modify the contract," Marchotti's henchman, Valdez said.

The brunette in the bed moaned, lifting her head. "Who's the jerk calling at this hour?"

Reichner lowered the phone and covered the receiver. "This is confidential business. Leave the room."

She sat up, blinking with disbelief. "You can't just send me away."

"You will go now." The threat of violence wafted off of Reichner.

The young woman scrambled from the sheets. With a robe wrapped around her, she scurried out the bedroom door.

"What change are you requesting?" Reichner put the phone back to his ear.

"There's an additional target. An interrogation is required."

"It'll double my fee."

Valdez accepted the terms. "The critical information and fifty percent of the money will be provided as before."

"We will speak again in one hour," Reichner said to his client.

When the call ended, Reichner felt he was in a vibrating massage chair. He lifted a pillow and extracted a Walther PPQ pistol. Fifteen 9 x 19mm Parabellum cartridges awaited duty inside the magazine. Reichner caressed the weapon with more passion than he had shown his bedmate during the night.

Chapter Seventeen
Thursday, June 14 (morning to night)

A frothing wave crashed over Colt's head as he shot between a jumble of rocks. He surfaced with enough time to gasp a single breath of air before the next crest smashed against him. Clinging to the overturned kayak, Colt struggled to remain supine with his legs extended downstream, a defense against the onslaught of boulders. The torrid currents of the Eagle River tore at his body. He sputtered and coughed up water. Pain seared his shoulder as the angry river tried to rip away the boat, his last grip on life.

Granite and basalt pummeled Colt's flesh without mercy. During brief reprieves from the battering rapids, he turned over on his belly and floundered toward shore. The flooded kayak was a sea anchor that hindered swimming. With each passing moment the frigid water chipped away at the forces of life. Colt held on with cramping muscles, weakening and nearly powerless to navigate the surging flows. Finally, the boat careened off a boulder and spun into an eddy. Gravel and cobbles scraped Colt's knees. He abandoned his unwieldy life preserver and flailed onto the riverbank. *Thank you, God!*

It took a supreme effort for Colt to drag himself from the icy claws of the water. In the clutches of hypothermia, his body was shutting down. Visions of Carrie fortified the will to survive. He rose and staggered toward a beacon of light. With each agonized step, the tendrils of darkness closed in. The orb of light he stumbled toward transformed into a park. Colt's brain was fogging up when he lurched into the restroom facility. Salvation was mounted on one wall. He activated the hand dryer and soaked in its warming breath.

* * * *

Trepidation gripped Justin Yeung when he heard the knock at the door. The computer specialist shuffled to the front of the house. A series of sharp raps signaled impatience from the person on the porch. Justin opened the door and faced Valdez. Max Reichner was standing next to him.

"You have information for us, Mr. Yeung?" Valdez asked.

"Who's that?" Justin was nervous that Valdez had company.

Valdez nodded toward Reichner. "This is Detective Smith. He's one of our associates."

"I thought you would come alone." Justin didn't step out of the doorway.

A slight facial twitch betrayed Valdez' irritation. "You're not in a position to dictate procedure. Tell us what you know about Luke Parson."

"Let's get it over with." Justin allowed the pair to enter the house. "I want to get out of this mess."

For some time, Justin sat at the kitchen table and spilled his guts about helping Luke breach security to access confidential information. A cup trembled in his hands as he sipped coffee. While Valdez penciled notes on a pad of paper, Justin abandoned all lingering loyalty to his friend.

"So you don't know what Parson plans to do next?" Valdez leaned back in his chair.

Justin shrugged nervously. "It's like I said. He took my car and said he was going to Grand Junction. I need a smoke."

"What do you know about Jonathan Forde?" Valdez asked while the young man fumbled through the clutter on a kitchen counter, looking for his pack of cigarettes.

"Nothing." Justin lifted a lighter to the cigarette in his mouth. "Luke wanted to know about that guy. I don't care."

"He must have told you why he was interested in Forde." Valdez' tone became that of an enemy interrogator. "Did you help him access the encrypted files he stole?"

"I didn't access anything." Justin felt the onset of fear as Reichner rose from his chair, staring with cold unwavering eyes. "Look, I don't know anything about Forde. I just helped Luke beat the security protocols on the network."

"I can't accept that assertion." Valdez stood up, cocked his head, and scratched his bald scalp.

"Now wait a minute," Justin stammered when Reichner advanced. "We both wanted to keep the FBI out of this. I told you UMN people everything!"

"I'll be the judge of that." Reichner's voice hissed.

It was too late when Justin tried to run. Reichner was upon him, pressing a razor-sharp knife to his throat. The smoldering cigarette fell to the floor. Justin was hyperventilating when Valdez used a strip of cloth to bind his hands behind his back. The knife blade slid away from his throat.

"Somebody help me!" A rag was stuffed in Justin's mouth.

Reichner marched his prisoner into the living room. "Put the coffee table under the fan," he said to Valdez.

Terror ripped through Justin. Reichner forced the young man to step up onto the table.

"There's a noose on both ends." Reichner tossed a length of nylon rope to Valdez. "Wrap one end around the shaft of the fan and feed it through the loop."

The opposite end of the noose went around Justin's neck. With the rope stretched tight, he was forced to stand on his toes to avoid strangling.

"Now we're going to see what you know about your friend's plans." Valdez sneered and nodded to Reichner.

Reichner flipped the switch on the wall and the ceiling fan rotated. One of the blades caught the rope. Justin was dragged in a slow circle. His sock-covered feet pawed at the table. Blood rushed to his face as his oxygen supply dwindled.

"What did Parson tell you about Forde?" Marchotti's

henchman demanded after the fan slowed to a stop.

Justin cried out when Valdez ripped the rag from his mouth. "I don't know anything! I swear to God. Luke wouldn't tell me anything about Forde!"

"That's bullshit." Valdez' eyes burned with anger. "Hit it again."

"No, please--!" Justin's scream was cut off when the fan came to life again.

Tears of agony and hopeless terror streamed down his contorted face as the brutal inquisition continued. Each time Reichner allowed the fan to run longer. Justin floundered like a fish on a line, dangling above the water. Finally, Valdez had to keep Justin on his feet when the rotating gallows stopped.

"He knows nothing more than he's told you," Reichner said to Valdez.

Justin's eyes bulged, and he retched.

"You'll get the rest when the job is done." Valdez tossed an envelope of cash on the kitchen table and stormed from the house.

Reichner retrieved the cigarette from the kitchen floor. There was a cruel gleam in his eye when he walked over and stuck it in Justin's mouth. The computer programmer shook uncontrollably.

"Please let me go. I won't tell anybody about this," Justin pleaded as Reichner freed his hands.

"Desperation warps the mind." The assassin backed away from his victim. "Desperate people make rash decisions...like suicide."

"No!" Justin screamed as Reichner activated the fan.

With an evil smile, Reichner turned the fan to the high setting. Justin didn't have a chance. His feet flew outward. The cigarette sailed out and landed on the carpet. Justin clawed at the noose cinched tight around his neck. His legs kicked at nothing.

Radical Action

* * * *

"How are we going to work in this weather?" the driver of the crew-cab pickup asked as rain pelted the windshield. "The excavation's going to be a mud hole."

"That doesn't matter to the superintendent." The man in the passenger seat issued his own complaint. "He gets a big bonus if this job finishes ahead of schedule."

The driver snorted. "And we'll be lucky to get paid on time."

Colt slumped in the backseat, wrapped in the warmth of a stolen sweatshirt, while the two men in the front grumbled. He was sure his problems were far more serious. Thoughts of the lost cassette tape, the key to his future, were maddening. But hitch-hiking back to Aspen was unsettling. It was certain that the thugs from E-Force were hunting him.

The drone of the diesel engine lulled Colt into lethargy. His energy reserves were drained. The voices of the contractors became background noise, and his eyelids grew heavier. Chatter on the radio was a subtle intrusion upon his state of near-slumber. The last light of cognizance was receding when Colt heard the utterance of his name. Icy fear trickled through his veins.

"According to the FBI, Colt Kelley shot and killed Howard Anderson and another man early this morning." The newsreader related a shocking version of Colt's story. "The name of the second victim is being withheld pending notification of family members. Authorities stated that Kelley is linked with the vigilante group, E-Force. He's considered armed and dangerous. Anyone, with information should contact FBI Special Agent Travis Price."

Colt kept his breathing even as his description and a phone number were provided over the radio. In numb dismay, he comprehended his divergence from the realm of reality. The insidious E-Force tentacles were spread much wider and farther than he had ever fathomed. With panic setting in, Colt realized he was sinking into an abyss from which he would never emerge.

Colt's gaze darted toward the front of the truck. The construction workers had stopped talking. Via the rearview mirror, his gaze locked with that of the driver. He detected the man's suspicion and alarm.

"You're the one they're talking about," the driver said. The guy in the passenger seat whipped around, his expression betraying anxiety.

The vehicle was forced to decelerate. The surrounding pack of traffic ground to a halt at a red light. Colt bolted from the cab before the wheels stopped rolling.

"He's a killer!" The men in the truck issued warnings to nearby motorists. "The cops are looking for him!"

Colt ignored the bewildered faces and sprinted across the road. He vaulted a guardrail and disappeared over the embankment.

* * * *

"Damn this traffic!" Max Reichner brought his fist down hard on the steering wheel.

Vehicles choked the interstate. The rearview mirror displayed traffic backed up far behind the black Porsche 911 Turbo. A mudslide was the culprit for the predicament. The radio announcements provided no word on when the debris would be cleared.

Time was one thing Reichner hated to kill. Staring at the back of a truck, he asserted that the delay didn't matter. Luke Parson was still destined for a harder death than Justin Yeung. That would be worth the wait.

An SUV maneuvered out of the left lane ahead. Reichner watched with interest as it ventured toward a cable strung between steel posts. At one section, the pilings were grotesquely twisted; probably because of some previous wreck. A few were missing all together. The driver of the sport utility charged through the breach in the median barrier and crossed to the eastbound lanes of the highway. Once the tires were on the pavement, the vehicle fled down the mountain.

Other motorists followed the first escapee. Reichner's eyes narrowed when an older model sedan lurched off the blacktop. It fishtailed and rooster tails of mud sprayed from the rear wheels. The driver of the battered car persisted until his bid for freedom was a success.

Convinced his Porsche could provide the same reprieve, Reichner cranked the steering wheel hard. He felt the tires drop off the edge of the road when he charged toward the gap in the median barrier. The tires lost traction in the mud. His 911 faltered. Reichner jammed the gas pedal to the floor, and the sports car writhed.

The turbocharged engine labored to push the speedster to solid asphalt that beckoned from beyond the strip of saturated soil and grass. A violent jolt shook the car. The Porsche careened sideways and slammed into a post with a loud crunch of metal.

Swearing profusely, Reichner redlined the tachometer, but the car was locked in a grip of steel. The assassin opened the window and thrust his head out into the rain. He was dismayed at the heavy damage to the left side of the car. The tires and axles were mostly buried in the muck.

"Damn it!" Reichner slammed his fist on the gearshift. He could feel the eyes of countless motorists gawking at him with amusement.

The eruption of anger cooled. A highway patrol cruiser appeared in the eastbound lanes of the interstate. The flashers activated, and the state police car stopped forty feet from the disabled 911. Reichner was dead calm when the trooper emerged.

* * * *

The Landcruiser was gone. It didn't matter because Colt had no intention of driving the vehicle. That would be like waving a neon-orange flag for the whole world to see. The place where he had been accosted was simply the origin of his search. The end of the line was the EcoFriends office.

Colt was facing an implausible dilemma. It seemed logical to turn himself in to the police and explain he had nothing to do with the brutal murders. But maybe it was an E-Force ploy to get him to go to the cops. Colt didn't want to place the hangman's noose around his own neck. On the other hand, maybe the murder accusations were intended to scare him away from the authorities. *It's a maddening puzzle.* The deck was stacked against him. One of two fates appeared inevitable; a murder conviction or disposal at the hands of E-Force.

I've got to find that tape. Colt plodded along his escape route. His probing eyes played across the ground.

When Colt rounded a corner, his heart skipped a beat. A chattering conglomeration of people, including a few children, gawked at an area cordoned off by crime scene tape. Police officers and investigators surrounded chalk marks near the curb. It was the outline of a human body. In an instant, Colt realized that his second alleged victim was the man with the dog.

The wary gaze of one of the cops fell upon Colt. The framed fugitive was a cockroach exposed on a kitchen floor when the lights were suddenly turned on. Utilizing all the composure he could muster, Colt averted his eyes and commanded his legs not to run. The ball cap he had snagged with the sweatshirt was a thin disguise.

Trying to remain nonchalant, Colt sauntered forward with his shoulders hunched and head down. When he chanced a glance, the officer was reprimanding a kid tugging at the crime scene tape. Moving past the spectacle, he heard a spectator's opinion about what had happened last night. Colt smothered the burning desire to bellow the truth.

Like steel filings to a magnet, Colt's eyes were drawn to a child rooting around at the base of a hedge. His spirits leapt when he spied a cassette tape in the boy's hand. The tape had been lost in the collision with the unfortunate dog-walker.

"Hey, you found my tape," Colt said quietly as he advanced toward the little boy. "Can I have it back?"

"I found it," the preschooler asserted. "It's mine."

"That tape belongs to me. Please give it to me."

"No!" the boy said. "It's mine. You're a stranger!"

"What's going on?" a woman's voice demanded. "What are you doing to my son?"

In alarm, Colt whirled to see the boy's mother rushing forward. Behind her, a black man in a suit turned his attention toward the clamor.

"He has my tape." Colt positioned himself between mother and child.

"Get away from him!" The woman slowed her pace.

"That's Colt Kelley," Special Agent Marvin Hill declared. "He's the killer!"

The woman was wide-eyed with terror. "Tommie, get over here!"

The boy bolted, but he wasn't fast enough. Colt grabbed him by the arm. The woman went into hysterics and charged with flailing arms. Colt was careful not to hurt the child when he wrenched the tape from his grasp. People screamed as he fled. The mother snatched up her howling son.

"Don't let him get away!" Hill drew his gun and chased after Colt.

Colt sprinted down the street with the speed of an Olympian. At an intersection, he turned and headed for Main Street. When he reached the busy thoroughfare, a police cruiser veered from the traffic and screeched to a halt.

A cop burst from the vehicle. "Stop where you are!"

A bellhop was knocked over as Colt careened into a hotel. The revolving door spun.

Colt rumbled down a stairway to the basement level and

barreled past hotel staffers pushing laundry carts. At the end of a hallway, he slammed against a metal door. It banged open to a small parking garage.

"Don't move!" Two men raced toward him. "You're under arrest."

Colt darted back inside scrambling for cover. Hill was at the bottom of the stairs, blocking the path of escape.

Hill raised his Glock. "There's nowhere to go."

In desperation, Colt bolted down a side corridor. He ducked into a service elevator and hit the button. The heavy doors closed as Hill rounded the corner and aimed his gun. "He's in the damned elevator." The rogue agent shouted to his comrades.

Colt bolted onto an upper floor and pounded down the hallway. Every door he checked was locked. Desperate for some means of protection, Colt snatched up a room service tray. The contents spilled and splattered on the carpet. With labored breath, he continued on, looking for some means of escape. A window was at the end of the corridor. The steel railing of a fire escape was beyond the glass.

Hill stepped out in front of Colt, panting and pointing his pistol. "End of the line, asshole. Drop the tray."

It was a point blank shot. Colt had no choice but to comply. His throat tightened when Hill pulled a Ruger SR40 from under his suit coat. The dirty federal cop tossed the gun that had killed Howard Anders on the floor at Colt's feet.

"Pick it up, or I'll blow a hole in your chest right now," Hill commanded in a low voice.

It was a setup...a way for Hill to justify a kill shot. Colt's hammering pulse filled his ears as he bent to retrieve the gun. Maybe it was loaded. Maybe he could squeeze off a quick shot.

Hill was taken by surprise when the door next to him opened. A woman screamed at the site of his brandished firearm. Colt snatched the tray and hurled it at Hill. It sliced through the air and caught Hill on the side off the head.

Knocked senseless, the man fell against the terrified woman.

Feet pounded up a staircase as Colt snatched up the Ruger pistol at his feet. He scrambled out onto the metal deck of the fire escape. Colt slid down the ladder, descending two levels. Deliverance arrived in the form of a rumbling dump truck in the alley below. Taking an instant to time his leap, Colt dropped into the bed of the hauler and slid down the mound of dirt.

* * * *

The last patient of the day was gone. Carrie sat with her head in her hands. Her emotions swirled down the drain of despair. Overnight, she had plummeted from soaring heights of happiness to the depths of scorned dejection. Awash in bitter cynicism, Carrie felt as if her heart was shattered. Everything in life seemed wasted.

Devoid of energy, Carrie ambled toward the front of the clinic with Bandit at her side. She stopped at an open door. Inside the tiny office, a therapist was filing a report on a computer.

"Thanks for filling in for me tomorrow, Paulette." Carrie leaned against the opening.

Paulette smiled. "No worries. Are you okay?"

"I'm going through a tough time." Carrie shrugged and looked away.

"Is it that guy you've been dating?"

"It's not worth getting into right now," Carrie replied without conviction.

Her coworker's face hardened. "There's another woman."

"He's not the person I thought he was." The lump in Carrie's throat was too big to swallow. "I trusted him, and he made me look like a fool."

"Only an idiot would cheat on you." Paulette stood up in a huff.

"It doesn't matter." Carrie smothered pain with bitter indignation. "He lied about everything."

"You'll bounce back." Paulette stepped forward with a hug. "You don't need that dirt bag."

A moment later, Carrie popped her head in the window of the reception and billing office. The face of the bleach-blond receptionist contorted with exasperation. Papers were stacked and strewn on her desk.

"If women were in charge, insurance wouldn't be so darn complicated." The receptionist flung a claim form in disgust.

"I feel your pain. I'll be back on Monday."

"You take care, honey. Everything will be here when you get back."

Carrie retreated to her vehicle with Bandit at her heels. She tossed her purse next to the packed suitcase on the backseat. The dog claimed his customary place riding shotgun.

* * * *

A silver sedan rolled into a medical office parking lot in Grand Junction. Gordon Trovato pulled his sport coat over his broad shoulders and sauntered into the building. Joey Morris followed, tugging at the crooked knot of his tie. It felt as constricting as a hangman's noose.

The bleach-blond raised an eyebrow. "Can I help you gentlemen?"

Trovato peered through the sliding window. "We're here to see Carrie Forde."

"And who might you be?"

"We're detectives." Trovato offered a badge. Morris followed suit.

"She's gone. Y'all just missed her."

"Where did she go?" Morris was annoyed. He was tired of problems.

"I don't know." The receptionist frowned. "How 'bout y'all tell me what's going on?"

"Have you ever seen this man?" Trovato held up a photograph of Colt Kelley.

* * * *

Clouds of steam billowed from below the hood of Justin's clunker. Luke coaxed the rattling contraption to the front of an auto repair shop in the town of Parachute. The building looked ready to collapse.

A mechanic in a grease-covered shirt swaggered out and eyed the hissing engine. "The radiator's shot. You should have called for a tow instead of driving."

Luke pretended not to hear the condescending comment. "Can you fix it?"

"I'll have to get some parts delivered." The mechanic stuffed his hands in his pockets.

Luke spent the next three hours pacing around the dirty waiting room and thumbing through outdated magazines. It was a maddening waste of time. Finally, the mechanic walked in from the garage area. The pungent odor of cigarette smoke wafted from his clothes.

"The radiator for your car just showed up," the mechanic said.

"You just got it?" Luke was incredulous. "I thought you'd be done by now."

"It came from Grand Junction." The man shrugged. "There's a delivery fee."

Luke counted the bills in his wallet. "Just hold off with the repairs. I need to make a phone call."

"We shut down at 6 o'clock, buddy. It's thirty bucks to leave the car here overnight if we don't start work."

Luke stormed out of the shop in disgust. Several minutes later he stood in front of a restaurant with a pay phone pressed to his ear. A voicemail message activated. *Where the hell are you, Justin?* Luke jammed the phone back on the hook.

In despair, he slumped to the ground with his back against the brick wall. All Luke's plans and dreams were shattered. There would be no chance to meet a girl like Sarah Farmington and fall in love.

Drowning in self-pity, he considered surrendering to the authorities and imploring them to look into his allegations about the United Media Network. It would never work. An innocent custodian was already dead. The murderers would stop at nothing to eliminate anyone who posed a threat to the UMN's dark criminal secret. Perhaps there was a slew of victims that had stumbled upon some part of the truth.

"I could be the only obstacle left." Luke mumbled, lifting his head from his hands. "If I fail, Marchotti wins…everything."

The epiphany reminded Luke that his battle wasn't just about his future. There were friends and family to protect. With renewed determination, he stood up and spat in the direction of the mechanic shop.

Luke bristled and trudged toward the interstate. "Keep that piece of crap car, you crook."

* * * *

Delilah lunged for the phone in her Glenwood Springs motel room.

"It's Colt. What the hell is going on?"

She exhaled. "Colt, your voice sounds so good."

"You've dragged me into a mess," Colt said without warmth.

"I'm sorry but you're the only one who can help me," Delilah stammered.

"Yeah? Well, I'm having trouble helping myself right now."

"Please tell me you're okay." The blood vessels in her

neck tightened.

"I don't know what okay means anymore." Colt was angry. "I just know you're part of E-Force. Now everybody thinks I've got some freaking connection too. Did the cops let you go or something?"

"I bolted from the hospital." Delilah huddled as if trying to stay warm in a winter gale. "I'm afraid of Zed Cain. I told this FBI guy Price all about E-Force and the plans for the Developers' Forum on Friday."

"E-Force is going to pull something on Friday? Wait a minute. Did you say the FBI agent is named Price?"

"Yeah, he wanted me to cut a deal." Delilah's explanation gushed out.

"Delilah, you can't trust anyone." Colt's concern was pronounced. "I think Price is the guy Deb Olson talked to. You remember Deb? Well, she ended up dead."

"My God. I'm so scared. Please help me, Colt. You've always been there for me and I love you so much for it."

"You've got to get out of that motel. Anybody who's listened to my answering machine knows where to find you."

"I was at your house," Delilah said. "Your key is still hidden in the same place."

"That was stupid, Delilah." Colt didn't hide his displeasure. "You're a fugitive. By showing up at my place, you implicated me in this shitstorm."

"I needed food and a place to sleep," Delilah whined. "While I was there, some men showed up and came inside. I hid under your bed until they left."

"Were they cops? Did you see their faces?"

"No, but they talked like New York mafia guys or something," Delilah replied. "Their footsteps were heavy. I think they were big."

"It must have been the two gorillas who waylaid me. That's how they knew about the phone messages. Listen, I want you out of that motel."

"Where should I go?" Delilah was scared and confused. "I don't have a car or any money."

There was a moment of silence, and then Colt said, "Go over to the hostel on Grand Avenue. I'll get in touch with you there. Right now, I've got to make sure Carrie is safe."

"Who's Carrie?"

"My girlfriend." There was no hesitation by Colt. "Now do what I told you."

Delilah pulled on the clothes she had taken from Colt's wardrobe after abandoning her own wet garments in his bathroom. After popping a couple more pain relievers, she limped to the front of the room. Her knees nearly buckled in fright when she yanked the door open. A man in coveralls and a ball cap was on the walkway. It was Special Agent Price!

In panic, Delilah tried to slam the door shut, but Price was too fast. He sprang forward and stuffed his body into the opening. She tried to pin him against the doorframe, but the struggle was futile. The corrupt cop reached out and grabbed her fleece pullover. Delilah tore away from the clawing grasp and fled toward the telephone next to the bed. Price was on her the moment she ripped it from the cradle.

Delilah fought as hard as a lioness, but the man was too strong. Finally pinned face-down on the bed, she tried to squeal for help. The bed covers muffled her cries. Price jammed a gloved thumb into a pressure point on her neck. Delilah whimpered and writhed in pain.

"Shut up, or I'll kill you. I swear I'll do it now."

Delilah submitted, and her body went limp. The brutal prodding stopped. Price tore the phone from her grasp as if he were pulling a weed from a garden.

Price stepped back. "Get up and keep your mouth shut."

Turning her frightened eyes to Price, Delilah saw the gun in his hand. It had the effect of a coiled snake. She ignored the agony induced by the injuries from the wreck and scrambled to her feet.

"We had an agreement, Ms. Francelli." Price replaced the phone on the nightstand. "You didn't hold up your end of the bargain."

"I was afraid of E-Force," Delilah said, shaking.

"Don't give me that bullshit. Where's Colt Kelley?"

"I don't know. I haven't seen him."

Price thrust the gun to her head. "You've been in contact with him. I want to know all the details of your conversations."

"We only talked on the phone for a few minutes." Delilah felt her legs trembling. "I swear I didn't tell him about our deal."

"Did you mention my name?" Price asked.

"Colt said you were dangerous."

"Tell me where he is!" The rogue federal agent shook Delilah by the shoulder.

"I don't know." She sobbed. "Colt told me to go to the hostel. He said he had to check on somebody named Carrie. That's all I know. I swear it is."

"You betrayed my trust and caused me a lot of trouble." Price lowered the gun and moved backward.

"I won't do it again." Delilah cried.

"Damn right you won't. Take your clothes off."

At first Delilah resisted, but Price was insistent. Under the muzzle of his Glock 23 she had no choice. After striping, Delilah stood shivering with her arms folded across her breasts. Her eyes were cast down at the floor in shame.

"Turn around and march your ass into the shower"

"Please don't hurt me." Delilah begged as she shuffled into the bathroom. "I wasn't trying to--"

Delilah was cut off in mid-sentence when Price clubbed her. Her naked body pitched forward. The metal bathtub reverberated at the impact of her head. A trickle of blood flowed from under her crumpled form and dribbled down the drain.

"It's bath time, young lady." Price turned the handle on

the faucet.

* * * *

The home of Phillip Barrett was tucked away in the spruce trees of Evergreen, Colorado. It was a beautiful setting for a magnificent house. In the living room, the early evening sun streamed through the expansive windows, bathing the comfortable leather furniture in warmth. Phillip Barrett and John Harris had chosen seats near the giant stone hearth to sip their drinks. While their spouses engaged in conversation outside, Barrett summarized the precarious situation of AmeResort Corporation.

"The situation sounds grim." Senator Harris shook his head with concern.

"E-Force has pushed AmeResort to the brink of financial collapse," Barrett replied with uncharacteristic glumness. "The physical damage is minor, but people are scared. Our sales and stock are down. Investors are pulling out. Business deals are coming apart."

"Do you have any support in the local communities?" Harris set his glass down and crossed his arms.

Barrett finished off his beverage. "It's fading fast. We're fighting a losing public relations campaign. The media reports this stuff as if E-Force weren't responsible for criminal actions. They make it look like AmeResort deserves to be ruined and punished."

The Senator clenched his jaw. "What's your plan to counter the assault?"

"The Developers' Forum I mentioned earlier." Barrett refilled his glass of scotch. "We'll have speakers and exhibitors from the industry and associated professions. I hope we can form a coalition with the power to thwart the media and get the truth out to the public. We're not just interested in profits. AmeResort is a committed leader when it comes to preservation of habitat and historical sites. And we provide a lot of people with good jobs."

"You're building a team." Harris nodded approval. "That's a good strategy."

"Besides changing our public image, we need to push for legislation that favors responsible development," Barrett said. "You have leadership skills and political experience. We all need your help, John. I need it more than anyone. It's not easy for a bull-headed old man like me to admit that."

"I understand," John Harris said. "You're talking about advancing core principles and ideas. The environmentalists have advanced their agenda at every level of politics for decades. Unfortunately, many of them seem more anti-American than pro-environment. I want that type of radical stopped as much as you do."

"I know you're a strong ally, John. You can garner support for a united campaign of opposition. We need immediate effective action. The FBI can't seem to catch those E-Force scumbags. But even if they're stopped tomorrow, our overall predicament won't magically improve."

John nodded in agreement. "You're right. The public is the key to ultimate victory over environmental terrorists. It's vital to educate Americans about the differences between the core values of AmeResort and the manifestos of extremists. When the radicals are exposed and the stakes for America are clear, people will clamor for the eradication of E-Force and every other terrorist group."

"The countermeasures start tomorrow." Barrett thumped his palm on the arm of his chair. "Your talk is first on the agenda."

"I'm looking forward to it." Senator Harris smiled.

Barrett clasped a hand on his friend's shoulder. "I'm deeply indebted to you, John."

"That's ridiculous." Harris waved dismissively. "I still owe you. Let's go see what our wives are plotting."

* * * *

The ranch occupied an obscure patch of the desolate rolling plains of eastern Colorado. A skirmish line of weathered pines bent against the perpetual assault of prevailing winds. There was a battered house among a cluster of deteriorating outbuildings. The place was a junkyard of broken-down vehicles and farm equipment. Wind-borne dust shimmered gold in the light of the retreating sun.

Fourteen members of E-Force, the entire clandestine clan, were gathered in the old barn. Facing his comrades, barrel-chested Lamont Williams was nearing the end of a fiery speech aimed at subduing fear and uncertainty. His job was to make Howard Anderson's death the catalyst to spark anger in the timid team members, cementing their resolve to continue the fight.

"We can't allow what we've built to wither and fade." Williams' rich bass voice boomed. "Remember what we're fighting for. Howard Anderson made you believe E-Force could change the world. Tomorrow, we can make history!"

Heads nodded, and some within the congregation voiced solidarity. Standing amongst the flock, Trigger Ruddock discerned that Williams had nearly accomplished his assignment. The ruse to cast Anderson as a fallen hero was working.

"Howard Anderson possessed unparalleled dedication and conviction." Williams continued to advance the contrived image. "When Colt Kelley betrayed us, Howard fabricated a plan to stymie investigators. He became a martyr when the gutless traitor gunned him down. Now we're faced with two choices. We can allow the actions of a coward to destroy all we've worked for, assuring that Howard died in vain. Or we can draw on his undying spirit and courage and fuel our wavering souls to continue the war against capitalist criminals. Stand with me and tomorrow we will avenge the death of a leader and strike another blow against the forces of hell!"

The group erupted in passionate cries. Led by Ruddock, they chanted and pumped their fists with raw unbridled emotion. Anger boiled over in a rabid primal urge to attack and destroy. While the frenzy played out, Ruddock glanced at Zed Cain. The tall dark assassin stood silently at the side of the room, clearly unimpressed by the fury.

"Everybody, take it down a few notches!" Ruddock was revolted by the task of elevating Anderson to the lofty heights of a deity. That's the way it had to be.

The team quieted down, and a sober silence replaced the din. Ruddock transitioned from his role as rabble-rouser. All the hype in the world wouldn't salvage an ill-planned or poorly-executed mission.

"The mission tomorrow depends on each of you." Ruddock's voice cracked with venom. "If any one of you fails, the entire operation will be compromised. We're going to go over the plan one last time."

The E-Force mission would be a coup de grace; a mortal blow to AmeResort. It would be delivered at the company's new Gateway to the Rockies Conference Center in Boulder. That was where the Developers' Forum was scheduled to begin at 8:00 am.

Months earlier, E-Force had enlisted the aid of Stephen Chandler. The turncoat AmeResort executive had helped Trigger Ruddock, Lamont Williams, and Jarvis Landy infiltrate the security staff at the conference center. All three men were scheduled for duty in the morning. The rest of the strike team would arrive with the forum attendees.

"Marla Wells will have her television camera rolling when the forum gets started," Ruddock predicted as he surveyed the faces in the barn. "She's easy to manipulate. Each time we contact her, she's eager to advance our cause. She'll do anything for media glory."

"Live television coverage is critical for our success,"

Cain said.

"The other pawn is that actor, Drew Harmon." Ruddock sneered. "He thinks Stephen Chandler is a financier of environmental movements. Harmon swallowed Chandler's claim that tomorrow's forum can be the foundation for a charismatic activist leader to build a legacy. Chandler offered a fleet of buses if Harmon could recruit protestors to stage a surprise assault on the conference center. When Harmon found out a television crew would be on the scene, he tied his tongue in knots with promises to rally an army of demonstrators. He's been given specific instructions on how to proceed with his protest. The dumbass has no idea that he's a decoy for our operation."

Ruddock paced in front of his charges. "Harmon's little army should arrive at the start of the forum. In the control room, the surveillance camera network will give me a godlike view of everything. When the protestors get close to the facility, I'll lock all exterior doors. I'll also activate the jamming transmitter to block cell phone service inside the building. What happens before the lockdown?"

"All team members posing as attendees covertly proceed to the designated caches outside the auditorium," one of the men said.

"What do you do, then?" Ruddock's eyes swept the room.

"Retrieve the weapons and enable the radio earpieces," somebody else said.

"And put the masks on." Carla, the only woman in the group spoke up.

"Each of you will remain hidden until my mark." Ruddock glared at his subordinates. "I'll order all AmeResort security personnel except Williams and Landy to secure the lobbies. Our two guys will move inside the forum auditorium. All forum organizers, exhibitors, and attendees will be directed into the auditorium as a supposed security precaution. Nobody else moves until I tell you."

There were nods of understanding from the hooligans facing Ruddock. They reminded him of a pack of dogs waiting for instructions from a handler. "My signal will be relayed while the protestors are pounding on the doors. That's when we crash the party. Lobby team leader, what do you do?"

"We use the tranquilizer darts to neutralize the four AmeResort guards within thirty seconds of the signal," a tall man with a big nose said. "Carla and I take the north lobby. The other two handle the south side."

"Stage team leader, when do you move?" Ruddock barked his question.

"We breach the auditorium doors only after the guards are taken out," a muscular team member said. "Three of us move from the north and three from the south. We commandeer the forum within one minute without firing a shot."

"Anybody who pulls a damned trigger answers to me." Ruddock glared at the group. "While the stage team hijacks the forum, Williams and Landy will detain that bastard Barrett at the podium."

Ruddock turned and pointed a finger at Williams. "We'll have a captive audience and a rolling television camera. That's when you get to be MC."

"I take care of the introduction." The big African-American man nodded. "Then I give Marla Wells the written questions for an impromptu interview of Barrett."

Barrett would be forced to explain why profits and power for AmeResort justified a sentence of environmental destruction for future generations. The volatile arrogant CEO was expected to explode into a rabid tirade against E-Force, who had been tormenting him for months. The strike team had been assured that the spectacle would seal the fate of AmeResort in the court of public opinion.

"Outside, the protesters will be straining against the doors." Ruddock clasped his hands together. "At the right moment, I'll deactivate the locks. The angry horde will pour into the auditorium. It'll be chaos. All you have to do is melt into the mob and disappear in the fray."

When Ruddock finished the review, there was silence in the barn. The magnitude of the mission was inescapable. Zed Cain stepped in front of the group. He was a man they all feared.

"You all know your responsibilities." Cain's eyes were devoid of emotion. "E-Force is about to slay a giant. The course of a nation will change and the world will follow."

* * * *

Carrie Forde faced a beautifully-crafted door. Chimes of the doorbell echoed inside the house and she admired the stained glass panes set in the wood. Bandit sniffed around the porch until the door opened. A bright smile adorned the face of the Hispanic woman in the doorway.

"Ah, you must be Carrie." The housekeeper reached out and clasped Carrie's hand. "Your mother and father are with Mr. and Mrs. Barrett. I will take you to them."

Nervous, Carrie hesitated, but Bandit was eager to follow the kindly escort. Taking a deep breath to steel her resolve, Carrie ventured into the magnificent house.

Lori Harris said when her daughter trudged onto the back deck, "Carrie, it's so good to see you! You've been away for so long."

The arms of her mother were at once familiar and comforting. Time and distance had changed nothing. It was as if the past difficulties had never occurred. Carrie felt an upwelling of emotion.

"I should have come back a long time ago." Carrie refused to let a tear escape her eyes.

"I'm just thankful you're here now," Lori replied quietly.

"Thank you for coming, Carrie," Senator Harris said

when it was his turn to embrace his only daughter. "I've missed you."

"Same here, Dad." Carrie's voice was choked. "It's a shame how things turned out."

"Father doesn't always know best," Harris said with regret.

"It's wonderful to see you," Caroline Barrett said after a hug. "How's my goddaughter?"

"Life's had its challenges," Carrie replied with a feeble smile. "It was a lot simpler when we used to spend time together when I was a little girl."

"You're as pretty as ever." Phillip Barrett embraced her in a bear hug. "I don't think you've changed since high school."

While Bandit explored his new surroundings, Carrie fidgeted with discomfort. She felt undeserving of attention and adoration from people she had shut out of her life for years.

"Let's all sit down." Barrett motioned toward the inviting deck chairs. "We have a few minutes before dinner is served."

To Carrie's dismay, she was the topic of conversation. Her mother and father had questions about the happenings in her life. Caroline and Phillip Barrett expressed genuine interest too. Carrie provided polite, yet brief responses. Her bids to change the topic of discussion were unsuccessful.

"So Colt couldn't make it?" Lori Harris broached the dreaded subject.

"We had a falling out." Carrie struggled to not betray her pain. "It's just one of those things."

"I'm sorry to hear that." Lori Harris didn't seem to be fooled. "I had the impression he was someone special."

"Everybody's special." Carrie shrugged and feigned indifference. "Or maybe nobody is."

"Hang in there, honey." Caroline Barrett leaned forward with a gentle smile. "The right man is out there somewhere."

Barrett wagged a finger. "You just let me interview him first. I want to make sure he's got the right stuff."

"I'm sure you've got your own truth detector," Senator Harris said with a bit of uncertainty.

"You bet, Dad." Carrie looked down at the deck and remembered another man who had trampled on her heart. "I know how to pick 'em."

A reprieve from the painful charade was granted when the housekeeper appeared and announced that dinner was ready. Carrie excused herself and hurried for the bathroom. She didn't want to let anyone see her cry.

* * * *

The doors opened to an upper floor of an upscale hotel on the outskirts of Boulder, Colorado. Chris Morgan stepped out of the elevator, irked that Marla had requested him for her escapade.

She thinks she's a damned queen or something. It's no big deal for us to wait in the lobby for twenty minutes.

Chris could hear muffled voices and televisions emanating from behind many of the doors he passed in the hallway. It was proof that the hotel's rates weren't reflective of the construction. When he arrived at Marla's room, the cameraman lifted his hand to knock. A cell phone ringtone inside halted his knuckles an inch from the wood.

Morgan heard Marla's declaration when he cocked his head to listen. "There's an Echo of the Foxtrot from Oscar, Romeo and Charlie."

Perplexed, Morgan moved his ear closer to the door. A realization hit him: Most of the words in Marla's phrase were used by military and law enforcement to represent letters of the alphabet.

She spelled out, E-F-O-R-C. Morgan's jaw dropped. *Marla's talking to E-Force.*

A shiver traveled up his spine. If Marla discovered him

290

eavesdropping, he would be in deep trouble. E-Force was a dangerous group.

"I understand." Marla's voice filtered through the door. Chris estimated that Marla had listened to about a minute of dialogue from the E-Force caller. Whether it was plans or instructions, he could only guess. *What if E-Force is planning something at the Developers' Forum?* Morgan's silent thoughts were racing. *That means Marla knows it's going to happen. She's part of a plot.*

There was movement inside Marla's room. Chris made a quick decision. Holding his breath, he took several steps backward. After faking a cough, Morgan strode forward with no attempt at stealth. When he knocked, footsteps charged the door. It jerked open, and Marla faced him with suspicious eyes.

Morgan greeted Marla with his best poker face. "Everybody's here for the meeting. You weren't answering your phone."

"I was in the shower." Marla's intensity abated a little. "Tell the team I'll be down in a few minutes."

"So we're going to provide your viewers with a new perspective tomorrow?" Morgan asked, noting her hair was dry.

Marla's eyes flashed fire. "This forum will have a lasting effect on people."

Icy fingers clawed at Morgan's backbone again. A hint of sinister and foreboding truth had escaped from Marla.

"I'm not sure I understand." Morgan fumbled, even as his conscious screamed at him, demanding that he figure out what was going on...and find a way to stop it.

"That's why I'm in front of the camera. Go tell everybody I'll be down in five minutes," Marla said. She closed the door in Morgan's face.

* * * *

291

A curtain of black smothered the Redlands neighborhood on the southwest side of Grand Junction. The feeble glimmer of streetlights was no match for the cloak that blotted out the moon and stars. Colt stumbled along unfamiliar streets. At last, he found Carrie's house. All the windows were dark. During the sojourn from Aspen, Colt was terrified that something terrible had befallen Carrie. Deb's death proved that E-Force would not hesitate to kill a woman if it suited their needs.

For a few seconds, Colt hesitated on the front porch. If Carrie was inside, he didn't want to scare her by sneaking in. A few soft raps on the door elicited no sign of life.

Colt stepped off the porch and felt his way along the side of the house. In the back, he groped blindly until he found the spare key that Carrie kept hidden. With some fumbling, he unlocked the door that led into the garage. The next door led inside the house.

"Carrie, it's Colt." He called out softly several times. There was no response.

He remembered that Carrie kept a flashlight under the kitchen sink. After knocking over everything inside the cabinet, Colt's hand finally settled on the cylindrical handle. The batteries were weak. It would have to do. He was afraid to turn on the lights.

Colt shined the dim beam out into the garage. Carrie's Cherokee was gone. A quick search confirmed that she wasn't in the house. *Where could she be?* Colt fretted. There was no sign of foul play, but his anxiety was soaring.

Feeling defeated, Colt collapsed on the living room couch and switched off the flashlight. He prayed for Carrie's safety. *Please, God. I know I've strayed. Just give me the strength and insight to solve the problems I've created.*

Sinking deeper into the couch, Colt's ability to string together coherent thoughts disintegrated. He was no more functional than a surgery patient recovering from anesthesia.

His exhausted mind went into hibernation, pulling the plug on his beleaguered body. A deep sleep descended.

It was several hours later when Colt's eyes fluttered open. In a state of confusion, he detected subliminal fear quickening his pulse. A scuffing noise outside the house catapulted him from the couch. Colt hardly dared to breathe as he stood with his ears tuned for any noise. The sound came again, closer to the backyard.

Somebody's sneaking to the back of the house! Colt's thoughts were panicked. *The E-Force bastards tracked me down...or maybe they're looking for Carrie.*

Colt brandished the Ruger Hill had tossed on the floor of the Aspen hotel. His jaw was clenched as he crept toward the kitchen. With no bullets in the chamber or magazine, Colt knew he was a sitting duck.

* * * *

The small jet, buffeted by turbulence, neared Denver an hour later than anticipated. A severe lightning storm had delayed takeoff from Garfield County Airport. Onboard the plane, Special Agent Price was under the crushing pressure of a crisis manager. He had sold his soul for the payoff promised by Darius Marchotti. At one time, it had seemed like a huge sum of money, but Price's perspective had changed. He was afraid he had thrown everything away for something of little worth.

"You're supposed to be a professional!" Marchotti yelled over a cell phone connection. "I see no evidence of that."

"I found Delilah Francelli," Price said, dismayed that Marchotti had elected to discuss the operation on a cell phone. It didn't matter that the tycoon owned the cell service provider.

Marchotti refused to be pacified. "The liability to this operation still exists."

"It's about to be eliminated," Price said in reference to Colt Kelley. "We had to overcome some complications."

"I don't want excuses. I want results. Barrett has got people breathing down my neck with this damned lawsuit."

"I'm confident we'll succeed," Price said, but a pit opened in his stomach.

"I have no tolerance for failure. My plans can't be modified. Do you understand?"

"It's crystal clear." The blood vessels in Price's head threatened to burst.

There was a click, and Marchotti was gone. The conversation was over.

How in the hell did I get into this situation? Price pounded the armrest on his seat. "No amount of money is worth this!"

Colt Kelley was still alive, and the investigation was beginning to boil over. Information could only be repressed for so long. And the false leads Price had conjured up would soon evaporate. *If everything doesn't stay glued together for the next twelve hours, there'll be hell to pay.*

Chapter Eighteen
Thursday, June 14 (night)

Everybody in the room shouted in a chaotic free-for-all. Drew Harmon was no longer in control of the dialogue. More than twenty radicals, all outspoken leaders, were gathered in his Denver hotel suite. They were accustomed to running the show and convincing people to listen.

"We need to get back to business!" Harmon attempted to reign in the rowdy group. "This bickering is pointless."

A piercing whistle echoed off the walls. Pixie Butterfly shouted. "Everybody needs to pipe down and listen to Drew!"

Pixie was the president of StayGreen. Several days earlier, Harmon had provided her with the information from Stephen Chandler. After some checking, she confirmed an unpublicized Developers' Forum was planned in Boulder. It was a prime opportunity for activists to expose the scheming capitalist scum. The assortment of organizations gathering for the One World Festival provided an ideal recruiting ground. While the groups didn't all agree on goals or methods to advance agendas, they all considered corporate America an enemy.

Pixie had taken it upon herself to determine who would join StayGreen's campaign. With some research, she ascertained how to contact the leaders of each candidate group. Since Harmon was a celebrity, his task had been to invite each person on her list to an exclusive party in his hotel suite. After a little socializing, Pixie hoped everybody would band together for a common cause.

"Please continue, Drew." Pixie looked to the incapable actor after she brought order to the fray.

Harmon wished he had written down more of what Pixie told him to say. The opportunity to demonstrate his leadership skill was slipping away. People crammed onto the furniture amongst a littering of paper plates, cups, and bottles did share one thing...expressions of disinterest. A few stood up, apparently on the verge of heading for the door.

"It's clear we have philosophical differences." Harmon steadied his voice. "But we all want to protect this planet."

A young man with a hand-rolled cigarette challenged the premise of solidarity. "We're not going to magically agree on how to do that just because we can party together."

"Let's focus on what bonds us together," Harmon said. "We all know corporate developers are destroying everything we care about. Tomorrow, there's a chance to expose their criminal behavior."

"What about security, man?" somebody asked. "My people don't dig getting arrested."

"Security will be almost non-existent," Harmon said. "No one knows about this thing. The cops have other problems."

A woman asked, "How do you know your informant's telling the truth?"

"Because he provided the money for the charter buses," Harmon retorted haughtily.

One bedraggled fellow voiced hesitation. "We should have had more time to consider this."

Muttering agreement from the others in the room annoyed Harmon. "Those corporate bastards tried to keep this secret. I just found out about it a couple of days ago. But now we have a chance to screw up their plans."

"So you want us to come in on buses?" a man with dreadlocks and spectacles asked.

"That's right," Harmon replied. "There're ten buses. Maybe we can cram eighty people onto each one. When we show up at the conference center, we'll head for the building as a group. I know which entrance we can use to get inside and breakup their powwow. The developers will be freaking out while we wreck their forum. We'll outnumber them four to one. The television crew will get it all on tape."

"What happens after all that?" another activist asked.

"We get back on the buses and head to Red Rocks," Harmon said. "Activists around the world would jump at this chance. But it's our opportunity. Who's going to seize it with StayGreen?"

There was a murmur of discussion about the ramifications of what Harmon was proposing. The radicals shared a hatred of developers, especially AmeResort. Damaging corporate America without an extraordinary amount of risk was an enticing prospect. While the decibel level of the conversation heightened, people nodded in agreement.

"Count my group in!"

Others voiced their support while intensifying applause signaled that an aura of solidarity had begun to cement the disparate radicals. They were ready to hear the rest of the plan and deliver a stinging blow to their common foe.

* * * *

Standing in the darkness, Luke Parson put his head close to the door and listened. Hearing nothing, he moved his hand to the doorknob. To his surprise, it turned. The door was unlocked.

With his resolve steeled, Luke pushed the door inward. He winced at the tortured squeak of the hinges. After slipping through the opening, Luke slipped into darkness befitting a subterranean labyrinth. His breathing echoed like a steam boiler in the deathly silence.

Luke's shin cracked against something hard that fell over and made a racket. *Crap that hurt!*

A bright light illuminated without warning. Luke detected movement behind him. He whirled to face the threat. An impact slammed him into a set of metal shelves. As Luke and his attacker crashed into some shelving and thudded to the floor, stored items jarred loose and rained down on the combatants. Something heavy struck Luke on the temple. The bright light faded, and he slipped into unconsciousness.

* * * *

The parking lot on the outskirts of Denver was eerily devoid of human life. Special Agent Travis Price hurried past the rows of empty vehicles. Reaching an undistinguished sedan, he unlocked the door and got in. He started the engine and left the desolate place in the darkness. Merging into a smattering of traffic, Price pushed down on the accelerator. A glance into the rearview mirror revealed a shadow of movement.

"Son-of-a-bitch!" Price panicked when the phantom in the backseat lurched forward.

The car veered left as Price twisted, flailing for the gun in the shoulder holster under his coat. Horns blared when his car careened into the path of oncoming traffic. Headlights were bearing down. Price cursed and yanked the wheel back to the right. Tires screeched, and the vehicles avoided a head-on collision.

"Settle down, Price," the apparition said. "You'll kill us both."

"Cain! What the hell are you doing here?"

"Just keep driving."

"There's a plan for communication!" Price snapped as he regained his composure. "This bullshit is unacceptable."

"The problems for this operation are compounding." Cain showed no emotion.

"Yeah, no shit." Price turned the car onto a quiet street. "Are you trying to screw it up even more?"

"The elimination of Kelley should take priority," Cain said.

"It is. You need to stick to the game plan."

"What about Parson? He should be taken out before we proceed."

"He's not our responsibility." Price was awash in stress and impatience. "Marchotti's got people on that. We're not altering the plan."

"It's foolish to be inflexible."

"Nothing has changed." Price glared into the mirror. "Do you understand that, Cain?"

Cain's hard eyes pierced through the dark, but Price wasn't intimidated. The payoff was all that mattered, and it hinged on the successful implementation of Marchotti's plan. Cain had to be kept in check, and Price was the puppet master, pulling the strings to make people dance and fulfill the godfather's directives.

"This is almost over. We'll do what it takes to protect ourselves. E-Force is an expendable asset. Anderson was the only one of them smart enough to figure that out."

"They can't be depended upon." Cain shrugged.

"It doesn't matter," Price said coldly. "As soon as Ruddock fires the first gunshot, all hell will break loose. When I return fire, the E-Force fools will be tin cans on a fence. It'll give you the chance to put a bullet in Harris' brain. His death will be blamed on a bunch of idiot, narcissistic radicals who bit off more than they could chew. The television footage will show their operation degenerate into mayhem and death."

Cain tested Price's dedication to the cause. "You still believe we can succeed?"

"Absolutely," Price replied with renewed confidence. "You and Ruddock will skip out while I finish off the radicals. We collect our payments and disappear."

"Kelley or Parson could be a wildcard." Cain's tone was ominous.

"Their chapters end tonight." Price stopped the car. "And this is where you get out."

James D. Kellogg

* * * *

When Luke Parson's eyes reluctantly fluttered open, his head was thundering. His temple felt swollen and bleeding. Attempting to assess the injury, Luke discovered his hands were bound...his ankles too. As his mind churned, he became cognizant that he was on a concrete floor with his back propped against a wall. Light emanated from an open door. The luminance cleared the mental fog and Luke recalled the blinding light and the sneak attack from behind. He could only guess how long he had been unconscious.

The scuff of a shoe set off alarm claxons. Luke craned his neck in fear. His heart palpitated when the silhouette of a man filled the doorway. It advanced toward him. Luke couldn't utter a sound when the man stood over him. With the dim light behind him, his features were as indiscernible as an executioner. A glint of light betrayed the blade in his hand. With his hands tied behind his back, Luke was helpless. The man grabbed his leg and dragged him away from the wall. Luke saw the flash of the slashing knife. He screamed in horror and closed his eyes.

Luke never felt the pain of being skewered. Instead the sharpened steel severed the rope binding his legs. He was pulled to his feet and hustled into the house with his arms still restrained. When he was shoved down onto a kitchen chair, Luke looked up to see a black pistol aimed at his face.

"You're a long way from Lakewood, Mr. Parson," Luke's captor said. "You made the trip for nothing."

Luke's state of alarm soared into the stratosphere. His discoveries at *Issue Insight* were about to be erased forever.

The gun was thrust closer. "What the hell did you people do to Carrie Forde?"

"What do you mean?" Luke asked, scared. "I don't know anyone named Carrie Forde."

"Don't give me that bullshit." The man cuffed him on the head. "You were breaking into the house. You were either hunting for her or me."

With his mind racing, Luke struggled to conjure up a bluff. He thought about claiming to have transferred his information about the UMN conspiracy to somebody else.

"You made a big mistake by showing up here tonight." The man placed the muzzle of the gun against Luke's forehead.

Luke swallowed hard and looked past the weapon. Like a safe clicking open, his memory unlocked. *It's Colt Kelley. He's the guy who killed Howard Anderson!* The realization had the effect of a strong wind on a house of cards.

"You can't keep killing people." Luke's voice cracked. "Eventually somebody will stop you."

"Shut up, you whining piece of crap. You and the rest of Marchotti's people are the murderers. Now my life is ruined."

Though he was trembling with fear, Luke was confused by the reference to Marchotti. Squinting, he noticed that Colt's clothes were filthy. His exhaustion and stress were obvious. "I don't understand what you're talking about. Darius Marchotti didn't send me."

Colt pressed the pistol harder against Luke's head. "Lies aren't going to save you. You sons-of-bitches killed Howard Anderson and framed me for it. Now I can't find Carrie. If anything happened to her, you'll all pay...all the way up to Marchotti."

"Marchotti wants me dead!" Luke exclaimed while he tried to make sense of the situation with his captor.

"Probably because you're the most inept clown working for him," Colt retorted.

"You don't understand." Luke decided to take a chance. "I don't work for Marchotti. I'm a threat to his organization."

"Of course you are," Colt's reply was drenched in sarcasm.

"It's true. I've got information that implicates Darius

Marchotti in a criminal conspiracy. They'll kill me to keep the lid on it."

Colt Kelley took a couple steps backward, but kept the gun raised. The expression on his face betrayed bewilderment and hesitation. "You're telling me you're a victim like me?"

Luke nodded and swallowed hard. "I'm just a regular guy who made an earth-shattering discovery. And I've got a feeling that you didn't kill Howard Anderson. You're probably innocent."

"Of course, I'm innocent." Colt was indignant. "I've got proof that I was framed. E-Force is hunting me down to get it."

"I believe you," Luke said. The reference to E-Force set off a shock wave of excitement. "I've been blamed for a murder I didn't commit too. It's all tied to Howard Anderson."

Colt slowly lowered his weapon. "Why did you come here?"

"Because Howard Anderson was an imposter." Luke's answer was blunt. "His real name was Jonathan Forde. I came here to talk to his ex-wife...Carrie Forde."

Colt scoffed. "I don't believe it. You're telling me Carrie Forde was married to Howard Anderson."

"The marriage ended when he was still Jonathan Forde." Luke explained eagerly. "She may not know about his identity change. I came here to get more information about that. Why are you here?"

"Carrie's my girlfriend." Colt stared down at the floor with dejection. "At least, she was my girlfriend. And Howard Anderson was my boss. This is all insane."

"We've got to find out what Carrie knows about her ex-husband's activities," Luke said. "She may have information that could help clear both of us. Where is she?"

"I don't know." Colt turned and walked away with his head hanging low.

"We need to find her. She could be in danger."

"No kidding." Colt bristled with pent-up anger. "Listen, I understand the threat. E-Force and a bunch of corrupt FBI agents have been trying to knock me off for the past forty-eight hours!"

"This goes way beyond E-Force," Luke said. "We've uncovered part of huge a conspiracy. I think Marchotti is pulling all the strings."

Colt's ire cooled, and he pulled a cassette tape from his pocket. "The evidence of that might be on this."

"What's on that?" Luke couldn't tear his eyes away from the outdated recording medium.

"I was in the building when they killed Anderson. Before the murder, there was talk about Marchotti."

"We have to turn that tape over to the authorities." Luke strained at his bonds. "Why haven't you done that already?"

"It's not that simple." Colt spoke with annoyance. "Who knows which cops and what agencies are part of this thing. I've been preoccupied with staying alive."

Luke slumped back in the wooden chair. "I know what you mean. I've had my own trials."

"Maybe we can help each other." Colt raised an eyebrow. "If we put our heads together, there's a chance we can figure a way out of this mess."

"It's worth a try." Luke nodded affirmation. "Besides, you've got the gun."

Colt held up the Ruger SR40 and shrugged. "There aren't any bullets in it. It's a long story."

"I don't know whether to laugh or cry." Luke felt a bit foolish. "How about untying my hands now?"

"That sounds like a reasonable request." Colt grabbed the kitchen knife from the counter.

"There's something I don't understand," Luke said as he struggled to rise from the chair. "How did you know my name and address?"

"They're printed on your driver's license." Colt tossed

Luke his wallet.

* * * *

The boulevards in historic south Denver had been home to the city's wealthy and elite for a century. Huge trees sheltered mansions that were testaments to classic architecture and expert craftsmanship. Stephen Chandler's home was among the most striking. Much of the gray granite exterior was covered with English ivy. Ornate ironwork accented the crests of steep rooflines.

"Are you sure all your people understand the buses can't wait for them?" Chandler paced around the den of his coveted home. "Timing is absolutely critical."

"I conveyed that message to all the group leaders," Harmon replied over the phone.

"When your radicals are off the buses, you've got to make sure they all advance to the entrance I specified. There's not going to be time for a damned pep rally in the parking lot."

"Don't worry. I'm a natural leader."

Chandler was annoyed by Harmon's arrogance. "You better be right. I'm spending a lot of money on this, and there won't be another chance."

When the phone call was over, Chandler slumped onto a couch. Several years prior, he had been a protégé to Phillip Barrett. During his meteoric rise in AmeResort Corporation, he became sexually involved with a female supervisor. When Barrett discovered the affair, Chandler and the woman were subjected to a formal review and disciplinary action by the operating board.

Though the humiliating incident remained confidential, rumors and gossip abounded throughout the company. Chandler stayed with AmeResort to temper suspicion from his wife. With hard work and diligence, he eventually regained his status with AmeResort Corporation. But the scars never healed.

It had been about a year since Trigger Ruddock first contacted Chandler. The founders of E-Force had wanted an operative inside AmeResort Corporation. Harboring a burning desire for revenge, Chandler accepted the offer to become a well-compensated spy. He sold his soul, and there was no buying it back.

The AmeResort board member smothered his intentions while ensuring that Ruddock, Lamont Williams, and Jarvis Landy were added to the security staff at the Gateway to the Rockies Conference Center. At first, Chandler could only speculate about the motivation for such tactics by the E-Force radicals. But when E-Force ordered him to organize a low-profile meeting of developers at the conference center, the ugly truth oozed out. They wanted Barrett and his collaborators set up like bowling pins.

After Chandler assembled the components of his forum, Ruddock issued a new directive on behalf of E-Force. At the eleventh hour, he was forced to convince Phillip Barrett to solicit the participation of Senator John Harris. Pushing aside any misgivings, Chandler worked hard to persuade Barrett to enlist the help of his old friend. Finally, the old man had decided the future of AmeResort was more important than his personal pride.

As the date of the Developers' Forum approached, Chandler laid more groundwork for E-Force. The executive contacted Marla Wells with a manufactured request from AmeResort, a plea for more even-handed media coverage. As expected, the television hussy had jumped at the opportunity to meet at the event. But Chandler couldn't repress a disturbing fear that Marla might know something he did not. He had enabled E-Force to carry out a plot that he didn't fully understand.

"Like a damned fool, I did what you bastards wanted," Chandler mumbled as he folded his trembling hands under his chin. "You better not stick a hatchet in my back."

* * * *

For twenty minutes, Colt and Luke discussed their experiences from the past few days. Their stories could have been from a far-fetched spy novel. But truth was stranger than fiction. Luke began his tale with the disturbing findings of his search for a link between Darius Marchotti's business empire and radical environmentalists like E-Force. He told Colt about Jonathan Forde's turbulent days as a Harvard graduate student and his subsequent disappearance at sea after being indicted on felony charges.

"Forde disappeared while free on bond, and the cops weren't suspicious," Colt mused, shaking his head with disbelief. "That doesn't pass the smell test. Maybe he killed that girl on the boat to make his death seem more apparent."

Luke winced at the suggestion. "You could be right. Jonathan Forde was just a footnote in my research until I found out he worked for *Issue Insight Magazine*."

"That's when you decided to hack into the United Media Network files?" Colt leaned back in his chair and crossed his arms.

"I had to find out more." Luke tapped the flashdrive lying on the kitchen table. "It turns out Forde was from a wealthy family. He married Carrie Harris when she was a college student, before her father was a Senator. When he supposedly drowned ten years ago, they were separated but not divorced. Carrie was probably the rightful heiress to Forde's estate, but everything went to Marchotti's humanitarian organization."

"How did you figure out that Forde became Anderson?" Colt asked, flinching at the thought of Carrie and his boss, as if an arrow had pierced his heart.

"I'd never heard of Howard Anderson until he voiced support for E-Force on television," Luke replied. "I decided to hire a private investigator to dig into his past."

"That television stuff was the beginning of the end."

"The P.I. came back and told me he suspected that Howard Anderson was an imposter." Luke leaned forward with excitement. "It took a while before I realized I'd already stumbled upon his true identity…Jonathan Forde."

Colt frowned in contemplation. "Maybe Darius Marchotti gave Forde his new identity."

"I think you're right." Luke nodded. "Marchotti used the Common Cause for Humanity organization to funnel Forde's donation back to him. A big chunk of it was the seed money for EcoFriends. Marchotti's minions will do anything to protect that secret. They killed a janitor and blamed it on me to keep me from going to the police."

A flash of anger ignited inside Colt. "You came here to see if Carrie could help you out of this mess. Didn't you worry that might put her in danger?"

"Finding Carrie Forde seemed like my only hope." Luke swallowed deeply. "I didn't want to hurt her, but I needed something to blow the lid off the conspiracy and save my life."

Colt relented, knowing he had imperiled Carrie more than Luke had. His emotions were getting the best of him. The fact that Carrie was married to the former incarnation of his boss was a hard pill to swallow.

"It's hard to believe that she knows about her ex-husband's transformation into Anderson." Colt argued against the tendrils of doubt creeping into his soul. "And there's no way she's aware of his involvement with E-Force. Carrie hates those bastards."

Luke shook his head with sympathy. "The truth doesn't seem real anymore."

Colt had a horrible fleeting vision of Carrie conspiring with Anderson and the rest of the E-Force criminals. Feeling betrayed, turbulent thoughts swirled through his head. While everything had fallen apart around him, Carrie had been his rock.

307

Sitting at Carrie's table and mired in despair, Colt understood he had put his faith in the wrong things for a long time. *I've neglected God, the one true source of constant strength.* With faith in God, a person can find the power and guidance to overcome anything he or she is faced with. Colt remembered being taught about the love of God in Sunday school as a kid. That love was founded in forgiveness. Colt realized that with faith and forgiveness, he could weather any storm.

"I haven't heard Carrie's side of the story yet," Colt admitted. "The truth is shattered in a thousand tiny shards. It's up to us to piece them together."

Luke agreed with a nod. "It's time to finish swapping stories."

When Colt described his transgressions with EcoFriends and the startling discoveries that Deb made, Luke listened quietly. Revulsion contorted his face when Colt asserted her knowledge amounted to a death sentence. Colt related how his plan to avenge Deb's murder and bring E-Force down had resulted in an inadvertent recording of the murder at the EcoFriends office.

"I can't believe you made a cassette tape?" Luke replied wryly. "I didn't know anybody used those anymore."

"CIA surveillance technology isn't my specialty."

"How good is the quality of the recording?"

Colt rolled his eyes and stood up. "I haven't had access to many cassette players lately. Maybe there's one around here somewhere."

The two men rummaged around Carrie's house until they found an old boom-box in a closet. At the kitchen table, Colt inserted the tape and they listened with bated breath. The soundtrack to the drama from Anderson's office was clear. The two men heard the names Price, Cain, and Marchotti stated repeatedly. It was indisputable damning evidence against Darius Marchotti.

"This proves Marchotti is the head of a huge

conspiracy!" Luke said.

"The puzzle is starting to come together." Colt nodded his head thoughtfully. "They mentioned a big event that E-Force has planned for tomorrow. It has to be the Developers' Forum Delilah started to tell me about."

"Who's Delilah?" There was a blank look on Luke's face.

"She's my ex-fiancé." Colt shrugged and walked away. "I just found out she was part of E-Force."

Luke raised an eyebrow. "Holy crap! You need to communicate more with the women in your life."

"Save it, Dr. Phil. You don't come across as a romantic authority."

"I'm not," Luke said glumly.

"Delilah got busted when that E-Force operation in Mt. Crested Butte went bad." Colt retrieved Carrie's phone.

"She's in jail?" Luke was obviously confused.

"She's in hiding." Colt elaborated while he searched for a phone book. "I told her to go to the hostel in Glenwood. I've got to make sure she's okay, and then I can get more details about this forum."

The man at the hostel responded to Colt's inquiry a moment later. "A young lady named Delilah? Yeah, she's here with us."

"Let me talk to her," Colt demanded.

"That's not possible right now. Are you Colt Kelley?"

"That doesn't matter. Just get her on the phone."

"Maybe you should come in and--"

Colt hung up the phone, cutting the man off.

"What's wrong?" Luke was unable to hide his impatience.

Colt's mouth was dry as cotton in a desert. "I think cops are staking out the hostel. Somehow, they found out we were going to meet there."

"Did they catch Delilah?"

"I don't know." Colt had a terrible premonition. "I need

to check the motel."

Luke gulped and nodded as Colt lifted the phone again.

"I'm calling for Delilah Francelli," Colt said when the front desk attendant answered. "She's a guest at your motel."

"Are you a friend or family member?" the man asked.

Colt's stomach dropped. "I'm a friend."

"I'm sorry to inform you that Ms. Francelli had an accident," the attendant explained. "She drowned in the bathtub. It appears she fell and hit her head."

Colt hung the phone up without saying another word. A brewing emotional storm caused him to clench his fists. At the center of his internal tempest, swirling feelings condensed into hatred.

"What did they tell you?" Luke asked. "Where's Delilah?"

"She's dead, drowned in a bathtub. It's a lie. They killed her."

"I'm sorry. I don't know what to say."

"E-Force is killing everybody around me...people I care about." Colt's throat was tight and his eyes were moist. "Carrie's been ripped away. There's nothing left to lose. I'm going to Boulder to end this. I'll take my own radical action. I'll stop E-Force or die trying."

"I'm going with you. You can't do it by yourself."

"More people may get killed." Colt was skeptical when he stared at Luke. "That means us."

Luke refused to back down. "I understand what we're facing. I'm tired of being on defense."

"Okay." Colt nodded slowly. "Let's stop these scumbags."

Colt and Luke took a few minutes to gather some food and bottles of water. It all went into a couple of grocery bags that Colt found in a cabinet. Boulder was a long way from Grand Junction, and time was short. Finding some means of transportation was critical.

The beam of Colt's flashlight stabbed through the

darkness when he yanked the garage door open. In startled surprise, he skidded to a stop. Luke thudded into his back. Special Agent Malcolm Hill knocked the light from Colt's hand and shoved him backward. His feet tangled with Luke's, and they both fell to the kitchen floor. Colt rolled and tried to scramble up

"Don't move, asshole." Hill pointed his Glock pistol. "It would make my day to pull the trigger."

* * * *

Memories abounded as Carrie sat on the bed in her old bedroom. When she was an innocent young girl, problems and pains had been fixed with a kiss and a hug from mom or dad. The recollections of childhood melded with those of tumultuous teenage years and the complications of life that carved a chasm between Carrie and her parents. New people, places, and pastimes had whetted her appetite for self-discovery, spurring her to make the foolish decisions and choices of youth. The difficult transformation into womanhood was exacerbated by her parents' increasing commitment to political campaigns and the duties of public office. Dwindling family time became a forum for mutual criticism. Feeling resentful, Carrie had pushed her parents and siblings farther away.

After high school, Carrie headed to Princeton on a track and field scholarship. Free of the reigns of supervision, she fell in with radical students whose agendas where on the opposite end of the political spectrum from her father's beliefs. It was an act of defiant rebellion...fulfilling and liberating. Academics and athletics suffered as she was drawn deeper into the self-destructive behavior of some of her newfound friends. Near the beginning of the downward slide, Carrie had met Jonathan Forde when he came from Boston to speak at a campus protest. He was a natural leader with charisma and magnetism. Carrie was a stunning young beauty looking to set a new course in her failing life. Two months after their first encounter, the couple was married.

During the months that followed, Carrie careened away from everything she had known. And with ravenous hunger for political relevance, Jonathan Forde instigated and led increasingly violent demonstrations against anything that exemplified capitalism or authority. Carrie was pulled into a vortex of drugs and alcohol, passed freely among many of her radical acquaintances. Plans for a college degree were discarded in the ash heap of indifference, the athletic scholarship squandered. The last strand of the tether to her family was severed, and Carrie plummeted toward certain destruction. There was nobody to arrest her fall. Forde provided no intervention or support. Instead he was romanticizing with other women. Carrie's pain and humiliation were crushing. Her marriage was a crumbling cornerstone below a life that was already on the brink of total collapse.

During Carrie's darkest hour, when the will to live ebbed, she was beckoned by an ember of truth that refused to be extinguished. Since birth, Carrie's life had been built upon a foundation of religious faith. It was something she had blindly accepted as a child, questioned as an adolescent, and rejected as a young adult. Nonetheless, that unyielding footing had remained buried below the surface of her conscience. At that desperate time, Carrie rediscovered the steady platform provided by God and prayed for direction and the strength to persevere. It worked.

Feeling new resolve to surmount the obstacles in her life, Carrie left Jonathan Forde and limped back to Colorado. It still hurt a little when Jonathan disappeared at sea. The divorce hadn't been final, but she rejected any claim to his estate. Carrie wanted nothing relevant to her past. Such a mindset helped her start anew, but also assured continued estrangement from her family. For years, Carrie was afraid to chip away at the daunting wall she had built.

The experience of being home again was bittersweet. Carrie was ashamed of the things she had done and the way she had treated her parents. But it was undeniable that being in the familiar house felt good. It was the place where the deepest fibers of her roots were planted.

As Carrie reflected, a tear rolled down her cheek. Bandit looked up at her in a manner that suggested affection melded with concern. A warm feeling of gratitude pervaded her.

"You're steadfast and loyal." Carrie reached down and petted the dog. "You're everything Colt wasn't. I'll never play the part of the fool again."

Lori Harris appeared in the doorway. "Is everything okay, Carrie?"

"Everything's fine, Mom." Carrie's tone conveyed little conviction.

"Time and distance haven't changed my love for you." Her mom's affirmation was warm and inviting. "I'm always here if you need me."

With a quivering lip, Carrie could not hold back the tears that welled up in her eyes. A day ago, she had felt separated from her mother by a wide and deep chasm. In the swirling storm of grief, the canyon walls crumbled and filled the gap.

"My heart is broken. It's just not fair."

"I'm so sorry, honey." Lori Harris sat down and embraced her daughter. "It hurts me to know you're in such pain."

"It seemed so right." Carrie whimpered through the tears. "I put myself out there for Colt. I loved him. He said he loved me."

Her mother leaned back after the long hug. "And then he hurt you."

"He lied to me!" Carrie snapped in a flash of anger. "He was still in love with another woman."

"It's not fair when people take advantage of you." Lori shook her head and bit her lip. "The pain of betrayal is agonizing, but you have to face it. After you let all your emotions out, the healing process will start."

"I know I have to deal with the pain, Mom." Carrie sighed and wiped her face with a sleeve.

"You're a strong young woman, Carrie. I know you can make it through anything."

Senator Harris arrived in the hallway. "I came to say goodnight…am I interrupting something?"

Carrie shrugged. "I've been dealing with a personal problem. It's not worth wasting more time."

Knowing he wasn't getting the whole story, the Senator's brow was furrowed with concern. He was hesitant to press for more information. Hoping for direction, he looked to his wife. Lori Harris acknowledged with a subtle nod.

"I was hoping we could spend some time getting reacquainted, Carrie." Harris' venture was cautious. "It might be good for both of us."

"Do you really have the time?" Carrie asked with a hint of skepticism.

"I'll make time," Harris said as his wife looked on. "How about tomorrow?"

"Maybe we could go for a walk," Carrie suggested, surprised at her eagerness. "It would be kind of like we used to do."

"That's a good idea. Let's do it in the afternoon after I'm done at the Developers' Forum ?"

Carrie frowned. "What's that?"

"It's a strategy session to help developers improve their ability to deal with the current political and social climates," Harris answered. "Environmentalists have vilified the industry and E-Force has beaten up AmeResort. Phillip Barrett asked me to participate in the forum and provide guidance from a political perspective."

Carrie's eyes narrowed. "So they're looking for ways to defeat E-Force and other extremists."

"That's part of it," Harris said, "but we really want to

promote responsible development practices and improve the image of the industry."

"Will they let me into the forum?"

"You can go if you want to." Harris couldn't hide his surprise. "It won't be real exciting."

"That doesn't matter," Carrie said. "I just want to join the fight against those wackos."

John and Lori Harris exchanged perplexed glances before bidding their daughter goodnight. Carrie didn't tell them that she had settled upon a way to vanquish her pain with strength and resolve. She was ready to take an active role in the battle against radical environmental terrorists. It didn't matter if the foe was E-Force, EcoFriends, or Colt Kelley. They all deserved the same fate.

After one last scratch behind Bandit's ears, Carrie turned out the light and retreated below the bedcovers.

* * * *

When the phone on the desk rang, Special Agent Price was reluctant to answer. Every call conveyed problems and bad news. But he had no choice.

"Kelley's in custody," Hill reported.

Price exhaled. "Thank God. Did he have the evidence?"

"It's in my possession." Hill confirmed that he had confiscated the tape Colt made at the EcoFriends office.

"Excellent." Price felt a wave of relief. "Now we can finish this operation."

"There's something else."

"What's that?" Price felt his blood pressure rise again.

"That reporter, Luke Parson, was with Kelley."

"I thought somebody was taking care of him?" Price was concerned to learn that Marchotti's people hadn't eliminated Luke. "How did he end up there?"

"I don't know," Hill answered frankly. "What do you want me to do?"

"I need a directive." Price was hesitant to act without consulting Marchotti. "Get them to a secured location."

After replacing the phone on the cradle, Price was worried. Marchotti's people had failed. It was disturbing that Kelley and Parson had both ended up at Carrie Forde's house. If they had collaborated to initiate some sort of scheme, the repercussions could be disastrous.

"You better have some answers, Marchotti. I'm not taking a pay cut."

* * * *

The soft thuds of Trigger Ruddock's shoes echoed through the empty corridor in the Gateway to the Rockies Conference Center. Weapons and radio earpieces were in place at the designated locations. As Ruddock approached a steel door, Jarvis Landy was waiting for him.

"Is everything ready?" Landy asked.

"As long as those E-Force halfwits don't screw up, this operation will be a success."

"They still don't have a clue?" Landy seemed hesitant to believe that the radicals had been so thoroughly manipulated.

"Are you kidding?" Ruddock scoffed. "Those ignorant fools have all got blinders on. They're all committed to their ignorant E-Force bullshit."

"That doesn't mean they won't run like rabbits when the shit hits the fan tomorrow."

"We've been over this a hundred times," Ruddock said. "I'll be the glue that holds everything together until the shooting starts. After that, it won't matter what those idiots do." *You don't know the whole truth either.*

Jarvis Landy griped and pushed open the heavy door. "That's why we get paid the big bucks."

The two AmeResort infiltrators stepped into the rear service bay. Ruddock punched a code into the keypad on the concrete wall. The alarm system was activated, preventing would-be intruders from gaining entry to the empty conference center. Tomorrow, that same system would help transform the facility into a prison gone mad.

* * * *

Colt and Luke lay face down in Carrie's kitchen. The sound of footsteps predicated the shadow that fell across the floor in front of their heads. They could both see the silhouette of the pistol pointed down at them. Feeling a burst of frustration, Colt struggled with the handcuffs that restrained his wrists behind his back.

"Are you trying to be a superhero?" Hill put his foot on Colt's back and jammed the barrel of his gun against his head.

"You don't scare me," Colt rasped through the pain. "I'm not afraid to die."

Hill taunted Colt. "Soon you're going to wish I'd shoot you."

Colt clenched his fists in fury. Beyond the point of fear, he was looking for a chance to fight back, and the rogue FBI agent could sense it.

"The rest of your short lives are going to be filled with unbearable pain." Hill took a step backward from his detainees. "Both of you get up. We're moving out."

While Luke scrambled to his feet, Colt made a point of delaying. Aggravated, Hill grabbed Colt's bound arms and hauled him up.

"Don't screw around with me, asshole," Hill said as Colt grimaced with pain and rage. "You like things slow? I'll make sure you can take your time dying."

Hill shoved his prisoners forward. Before they reached the door to the garage, the light in the kitchen went out. Everything was quiet, except the rain outside the house. A flash of lightning chased away the darkness for an instant. Hill switched on a halogen light before his prisoners could take advantage of the power outage.

"What are you going to do now?" Colt jeered when Hill's beam hit him in the face. "Is this part of your plan?"

"Shut up. A damned blackout won't save you." Hill focused his flashlight on Luke. "We're going to take a walk."

"Should I just wait here?" Colt continued his disrespect for the corrupt agent.

"You can get your ass in the closet." Hill violently pushed Colt. "I'll be back after your buddy's stowed away."

Colt cursed when his head struck one of the shelves in the pantry. The door slammed shut, leaving just enough room to stand. The door was solid and the lock could only be manipulated from outside. In the confined space, it was impossible to gain the leverage to kick the door down. Colt pressed one hip against the door and doubled over. Stretching to the max, he worked his cuffed hands across his buttocks en route to his hamstrings.

* * * *

Luke's pulse pounded as he moved along the garage. Crashing thunder pursued bolts of strobing lightning in the soggy pitch black. He shuffled his feet in an effort to avoid stumbling and falling. *At least I'm not handcuffed like Colt.* The cold steel of Hill's Glock 23 jabbed the back of his neck.

"Keep moving," Hill ordered, soaked and impatient.

Staggering forward, Luke finally reached the front corner of the garage. The driveway was just ahead. The glow of a streetlamp formed a meager alliance with the dim radiance from exterior lights on a few nearby residences. It was clear that the power outage was limited to Carrie Forde's house. Feeling an unwelcome stab of trepidation, Luke's senses were attuned. Hill forced Luke against the wall and moved alongside his detainee. The FBI agent craned his neck to look around to the front of the house.

A sound like a watermelon hitting concrete coincided with a startled grunt. Something warm splattered on Luke. He heard the heavy thud of a body collapsing onto the ground. Luke hyperventilated with revulsion and terror. *He just got shot!*

Booming thunder blended with the sound of Luke's thumping heart. Too frightened to move, he crouched on the saturated ground.

This can't be happening. Each discharge of atmospheric electricity confirmed that Hill was dead, shot through the head. *This is insane!*

While Luke cowered in terror, the invisible assassin was still out there…waiting. Numb with cold and fear, Luke was desperate for some means of protection. *Where the hell is his gun?*

Luke groped on his hands and knees. Another sizzling bolt of electricity betrayed the elusive pistol. It was still in the dead man's hand. When Luke's hand touched the corpse, he recoiled in horror. He repressed his revulsion and wrenched the weapon from Hill's lifeless grip.

With the Glock in hand, Luke felt no less vulnerable. *I don't know how to shoot this damned thing.* His hands trembled. *Maybe you just pull the trigger.*

Fear coursed through Luke's veins. He scurried along the siding. *I've got to get back inside. I've got to free Colt.*

Before he could round the corner to the back of the house, warm steel pressed against the back of his head.

A German-accented voice rasped. "Leaving the party so soon, Mr. Parson?"

Luke nearly fainted with fright. He stood impotent, while Hill's pistol was ripped from his grasp. The gun against his skull didn't waver.

"You will catch cold out in this rain." The accent slithered across Luke's nerves.

A moment later, Luke was prodded back through the

garage and into Carrie's kitchen. In the pitch black, he tripped and nearly fell. With his night vision goggles, Reichner never faltered.

"Where is your friend?" Reichner demanded coldly.

"He's locked in the pantry." Luke was dismayed by his admission.

A rough shove propelled Luke in the direction of the pantry closet. When Luke was five feet from the pantry door, Reichner pushed him aside. In rapid succession, six bullets thumped from the assassin's gun. Luke gasped in startled terror at the slugs splintering through wood. Brass casings clinked on the floor. Something heavy thudded to the floor inside the closet.

A metallic spring announced the ejection of the magazine. Luke heard the click of a new one loaded into the weapon.

"Open the door," Reichner said.

Luke shuffled forward and placed his hand on the knob. "I can't do it."

The slide on the Walther PPQ chambered a round. "I told you to open it!"

Given no alternative, Luke disengaged the lock and pulled the wooden shroud away from the vertical coffin.

* * * *

Reichner shoved Luke aside. There was no devastated body. His night vision goggles revealed a hole in the closet floor. It was a trapdoor to a crawl space.

"There are easy ways to kill vermin." The tone was indifferent, that of a cold-blooded exterminator.

Reichner produced a small canister, twisted the top, and dropped it into the forbidding opening. The distinct hiss of gas escaping the metal container was muffled when he kicked the trapdoor shut. After slamming the pantry door, Reichner engaged the lock.

320

"Move." Reichner shoved Luke toward the exit.

As soon as they were outside, Reichner took a few seconds to bind Luke's wrists with a plastic zip-tie. A moment later, he marched his prisoner to a stolen delivery truck parked on the street. A hinge groaned when the doors swung open. Reichner muscled Luke toward the gaping entrance of the tomb on wheels.

"I'm not getting in there." Luke dug in his heels and struggled. "Somebody help me!"

Reichner chopped his captive's legs with a vicious kick. Luke fell on his face. The German psychopath ripped the night vision gear from his head. He dragged Luke up and wrenched him around. His hand gripped Luke's throat.

Reichner pressed his face close to his next victim. "You will die a much slower death than Justin Yeung."

"You maniacs killed him," Luke wailed. His body went flaccid and wilted toward the ground. "Justin, I'm sorry."

"Get up, you schwein." Reichner struggled to keep Luke pinned against the rear of the van. The temptation to deliver swift death soared. But flashing images of agonizing torture depicted a more fulfilling reprisal. Seething with anger, Reichner punched and heaved until his unfortunate detainee was loaded. Gasping for breath, he slammed one of the doors shut.

A blur of movement exploded from the side of the truck. Caught off guard, the assassin's arm shot up in instinctive defense. The swinging steel bar sheared his radius and ulna upon impact. The Walther and suppressor jolted from his grasp and clattered across the wet pavement. A second strike slashed the air an inch above Reichner's head as he ducked. Metal clanged off the cargo door. Before the German could regain his balance a crushing blow across the back sent him reeling to the street. Like a writhing serpent, the killer twisted to one side. The steel bar bit into the asphalt at the spot he vacated.

* * * *

The impact of the tire-iron against the pavement sent a stinging shockwave through Colt's arm. He recoiled at the resonating pain. It was an instant of vulnerability. Reichner swept his leg and caught Colt across the back of the knees. He went down hard on his back, the impact expelling air from his lungs. A large knife materialized in the assassin's hand. Colt retreated from the first lunging assault, but the blade still sliced through his flesh. Hardly feeling the pain, he lashed out with the tire-iron. The makeshift weapon connected with Reichner's shoulder, sending him spinning back to the ground.

Reichner was a deadly opponent. But he had sustained serious injury. That gave Colt a chance in the life and death battle. No trained fighter, he utilized his considerable strength and quick reflexes.

From his knees, Colt grunted and swung the length of steel at the reeling killer's head. He whiffed. The momentum of the erroneous swing exposed his torso. Reichner delivered a mule kick to Colt's chest. He thumped onto his back again. The assassin sprang, plunging the knife downward. Colt caught Reichner's arm with both hands and stopped the tip of the wicked blade inches from his heart.

Hampered by his shattered arm, Reichner grimaced and pressed down. The knife blade didn't budge. The hired killer tried to knee Colt in the groin. The blow was off-target. Reichner gave up on impaling his victim and threw an elbow. The pain in Colt's mouth was seasoned with the taste of blood. He responded with a ferocious head-butt. Blood gushed from a cut that opened above Reichner's eye.

Colt struck again, and the executioner's body shuddered. Writhing with the violence of a man possessed, he worked his leg under Reichner's torso. Colt kicked upward with all his might, launching the assassin backward. Amazingly, Reichner bounded to his feet. Colt clambered up, desperate to fend off the next blitz.

"Stop right there!" A sharp command pierced the night. "Don't move!"

The combatants snapped their heads around. Luke stood in the downpour with Reichner's Walther in his bound hands. The gun was aimed at the assassin's chest. It was a point blank shot.

With the blinding speed of a striking cobra, Reichner hurled his knife. Luke flinched and pulled the trigger. The bullet slammed into the German's chest an instant before the knife embedded in Luke's shoulder. The killer lurched backward. A tortured cry escaped Luke's lips. He dropped the gun and sank to his knees.

Unbelievably, Reichner regained his footing and didn't fall. He rushed toward the gun lying on the rain-soaked street. Colt slammed the killer into the back of the van. Reichner's head cracked against the unforgiving metal. Both men ended up on the pavement a few feet from where Luke moaned in agony.

Colt started to scramble for the gun. Reichner clawed for something below his jacket. His hand reappeared with a small round object. Colt gasped. *A grenade!* The killer was about to pull the pin with his teeth.

Fueled by a rush of adrenaline, Colt jerked the knife from Luke's shoulder. Luke screamed in pain as Colt turned and thrust the blade. Reichner shuddered when the knife skewered his neck. The assassin emitted a short gurgle and his arm fell limp. The grenade clunked to the pavement and rolled under the van. The pin was still in the deadly device.

Exhaustion descended upon Colt. His lungs burned for want of oxygen. *The Man upstairs was with me again.* Luke sat clenching his teeth and gripping his wounded shoulder. Neither man spoke for a while. The blood from their wounds was diluted by rivulets of rain. Finally, Colt stepped back to the lifeless killer. Without a shred of remorse, he yanked the knife from the sinewy flesh.

"I thought you were dead," Luke said weakly while Colt used the blade to cut the plastic restraint on his wrists. "That crawl space was full of poison gas."

"There's another way out." Colt didn't provide further details.

"How'd you get out of the handcuffs?" Luke asked with bewilderment as Colt moved away.

"Magic. Can you stand up?"

Luke winced. "Yeah, but this stab wound needs medical attention."

Colt rummaged through the cab of the delivery truck. "I found a first-aid kit. We can stop your bleeding and apply a field dressing. Let's get this son-of-a-bitch loaded and out of sight first."

Colt helped Luke get to his feet. Together they dragged Reichner's body. It left a crimson trail.

"I can't believe that bullet didn't drop him." Luke grimaced.

"He's got a Kevlar vest." Colt rapped his knuckles on the body armor under Reichner's shirt. "Lift on three." They hoisted the corpse and shoved it toward the back doors.

* * * *

The headlights on Kevin Pinkard's BMW stabbed through the night as he sped toward the Redlands from downtown Grand Junction. A ZZ Top song drowned out the rain. After a late night at the office, the young attorney had abandoned the mountain of research material on his desk.

Pinkard's car rounded the corner with the agility of a formula racer. The headlights pierced the thunderstorm and exposed a horrifying sight. His foot jammed the brake pedal to the floor. The sports car ground to a stop a dozen yards from Colt and Luke who were loading the bloody corpse into the delivery truck. It was a scene from a horror movie.

Holy shit! Feeling an upwelling of panic, Pinkard jammed the transmission of his car into reverse. The tires spun on the wet road as he accelerated backward and whipped the car around. Images of his wife, at home alone, flashed through his mind. As he sped away from the scene, Pinkard groped for his cell phone. His quivering fingers fumbled to dial the police.

Chapter Nineteen
Friday, June 15 (morning)

A limousine rolled into a service bay in the rear of the Gateway to the Rockies Conference Center. Fluorescent lights reflected off the polished black paint.

"Look who's here." Trigger Ruddock snickered in the security control room. A surveillance monitor provided him with a front row seat to witness the arrival. The chauffeur opened a rear door. A passenger with a cane emerged. It was Phillip Barrett. "Welcome to the show, you arrogant ass."

Carrie Forde stepped out onto the concrete. Ruddock whistled under his breath. The last person out of the vehicle was John Harris. *Couldn't have an assassination without you, Senator.* A smile creased Ruddock's face.

The start time for the Developers' Forum was drawing near. Ruddock switched to the view from a different security camera. Over two hundred attendees had arrived. Many had migrated into the main auditorium. Others conglomerated around the food and beverage counters in the lobbies. *They're like cattle in a feedlot.* Ruddock smiled.

Using the controls in front of him, Ruddock checked out the scene in the auditorium. A television cameraman waited near the stage. Standing nearby, Marla Wells touched up her makeup with a compact.

"You're not part of the story anymore, honey." Ruddock snorted with contempt. "We played you like a Stradivarius."

* * * *

An ambulance rattled up a meandering dirt lane in rural Routt County, Colorado. Progress was slow and the strobe flashers were inactive. A few sheriff's deputies moved aside to let the emergency vehicle pass when it entered a grove of aspen trees. It stopped next to the delivery truck containing

Max Reichner's corpse.

"The dead guy's in the back," Sheriff Cox said to the paramedics.

The sheriff ambled back to his Ford Explorer and a weathered rancher. "So you just discovered this an hour ago?" Cox asked.

"That's right." The man removed his hat and scratched his head. "Any idea who it is?"

"I don't have a clue," Cox answered honestly. "An attorney from Grand Junction saw a couple men loading a bloody corpse into that truck last night. That's all I know."

"Why do you think they stripped the body almost naked?"

"Who knows?" Cox shrugged. "I'm more concerned about the whereabouts of the killers. They couldn't have gotten far without a vehicle."

The rancher suddenly looked queasy. "They might kill to get another."

Cox nodded in agreement. "I need all my deputies back on the road."

One of his men sauntered up. His weary expression was evidence of a duty shift spanning sundown to sunrise. "We just got a call from dispatch. Bill Taber claims somebody stole his new pickup truck. It's a red Dodge three-quarter ton."

"Taber's place is only a couple of miles away," Cox mused. "Put out an APB on that truck. It's got to be our fugitives."

* * * *

Squeaking brakes announced a charter bus stopping one hundred yards from the Gateway to the Rockies Conference Center. Drew Harmon was the first to clamber out of the metal behemoth. Others spilled out behind him, forming an undulating conglomeration. Nine more transports from the convoy rumbled in to the parking lot. Pungent diesel fumes wafted above the asphalt. Similar to some sort of biological process, people poured out the folding doors, inexorably drawn together. They congealed into a rowdy crowd of more than eight hundred.

"The corporate scum are in the south wing of the complex." Harmon screeched through a megaphone and pointed the way.

"Let's rip that place apart!" a protestor said.

"Down with the greedy!" another cried. Bottles smashed against the ground for emphasis. Like a Mongol horde, the radicals surged toward their objective.

Harmon scurried to claim a place at the front of the rag-tag charge. He imagined it was the factory where his drunken old man had worked.

The extremists filtered through an increasing density of parked vehicles. One ruffian used a baseball bat to smash a window in a shiny red Dodge three-quarter ton pickup. More glass shattered and tinkled to the pavement. The escalating rage of the dissidents jabbed the actor.

"We're an AmeResort nightmare." Harmon pumped his fist. "Let's give those bastards a day to remember!"

* * * *

"We've got an army of vagrants headed our way." A worried security guard's voice crackled over the radio.

Ruddock jeered at the storming beatniks displayed on one of his security monitors. "It looks like 'Night of the Living Dead.' I'm initiating emergency lockdown procedures."

Ruddock activated the remote locks on the outer doors. He watched Harmon strutting in front of the mob.

Keep your head on straight, dumbass. You've got a job to do.

* * * *

Yuri Zharikov reclined on the couch in Darius Marchotti's office and ran a hand through his thick red hair. Battling boredom, his thoughts strayed to stimulating memories of the computer systems administrator at his downtown loft. Sale had pleaded like a woman. Such begging only provoked Zharikov to pound the man's soft flesh with more violence. When Sale was unconscious and on the verge of death, the Russian brute dragged him onto the balcony. His limbs twisted and fluttered on the long plunge to oblivion. It was another exhilarating day on the job for Zharikov. He was the punisher...the purveyor of Marchotti's retributions.

"Years of planning and preparation are about to come to fruition." Marchotti stabbed an index finger at his television screen. "Do you understand the magnitude of what is about to take place?"

"The most powerful politician who opposes your ideology is about to be eliminated." Zharikov scratched his chin in thought. He knew E-Force had been created for one sole purpose. It had nothing to do with the ideals of the radicals recruited by Howard Anderson. E-Force was a tool to lure Senator John Harris into the hands of death.

"It's bigger than that," Marchotti said. "I'm about to become the most powerful force in American politics."

"I don't fully understand." Zharikov's admission was accompanied by a frown.

"With Senator Harris gone, opposition to the campaign finance reform bill will disintegrate." The pitch of Marchotti's voice elevated. "The bill will pass, and the President will sign it. After the new campaign laws are in effect, the media will control political campaigns. I'm the media!"

"The law will put the media in charge of politics?" Zharikov asked uncertainly.

"Of course it will." Marchotti bolted from his chair. "The media is going to have control of every candidate's television and radio advertising."

Zharikov shrugged. "I don't see how that makes the media powerful."

"The media is the wildcard. There are so many forums to affect public perception of politicians and policies. Political talk shows, news reports, magazine articles, editorial columns...the list goes on. We already have the power and influence to make or break almost anybody. But when the new legislation becomes law, politicians will be completely at our mercy. Nobody will have the money or means to promote anything different than what is conveyed by the media. The entire political landscape in America will be under my control. I'll shape this country from this day forward."

"You'll be a czar," the Russian concluded.

"That's just the beginning." The media tyrant clenched his fist. "My empire will extend far beyond the borders of this nation. My humanitarian centers will ensure huge populations dependent on my benevolence. Politicians indebted to me will make sure the money keeps flowing. The world won't feel my grasp until it's too late."

"Your plan is thorough." Zharikov nodded and pursed his lips.

"There are no loose ends. That's why I ordered Valdez to eliminate that FBI turncoat, Hill."

"I thought I'd be responsible for that task." Zharikov sulked.

"It was cleaner to use that psychopathic German. Travis Price will be added to the hit list after my foe is vanquished." The monster lurked in Marchotti's fiery gaze.

* * * *

Protesters squashed against thick glass panes that

comprised the outer wall of the lobby. Fists and heavy objects pounded on the transparent barrier. Translucent doors rattled and strained against the crushing load.

"Are you sure all those doors will hold?" The supervising guard asked Ruddock. Like his colleagues, the guard was inexperienced.

Ruddock's reply was transmitted back. "That reinforced glass would stop a bullet. But I want everyone in that auditorium as a security precaution. And don't worry. I called the cops."

"Everybody head into the forum!" the security guard said to the straggling attendees who gawked at the drama unfolding outside. "We need to clear the lobby."

A gaggle of business people were herded toward the inner sets of doors. A female security guard stepped in front of two grubby and unkempt men. "You gentlemen don't have your ID badges. You can't enter without them."

"They're at our seats," Luke Parson said.

"Your badge should be displayed at all times." The supervising guard provided backup.

The woman scrutinized the two would-be intruders. "I need identification that I can check against the attendee list."

"That mob out there is the security concern," Colt said with a wave of his arm. "You've got a riot to deal with."

The supervisor shot an uncomfortable glance at his subordinate. If the mob breached the outer barrier, the security staff wouldn't have a chance. They would be as helpless as sailors inside a torpedoed U-boat.

"Take these men to the control room," the supervisor told his female subordinate. "I'll notify Ruddock."

"This is ridiculous!" Luke blurted out. "You can't treat us this way."

Colt exploded in outrage. "I'm an associate of Phillip Barrett. Take me to Mr. Barrett, and we'll straighten this out."

The commotion attracted the attention of a burly man in

a sport coat. "How'd that son-of-a-bitch get in here?" Gordon Trovato growled and rushed toward Colt.

Colt bolted, knocking the woman guard off her feet. Trovato bellowed for Joey Morris and took up pursuit. Disoriented, the supervisor tottered after them.

After a few steps, the guard regained his senses and radioed the control room. "A couple of those rioters made it into the building."

"How the hell did that happen?" Ruddock's voice blared across the radio. "Detain them!"

"One already took off. Two attendees are chasing him."

"Damn it!" Ruddock seethed. "Send one man after the bastard. And get those other two clowns back to the auditorium. I want everyone else to maintain perimeter positions."

"Klum, track that dirtbag down!" The supervising guard sent a junior man on the chase. Klum departed with the stiff stride of a rusty tin man.

When the supervisor turned around, the woman guard was sitting on the floor. One hand massaged a goose egg on her forehead. Luke was gone. "Where'd the other guy go?" he asked, fuming.

Her face flushed red with humiliation. "I don't know."

* * * *

Stephen Chandler's opening remarks broke off with the abruptness of a broken pencil. His hands clamped onto the sides of the podium. Several dozen people piled in from the lobbies, prodded by sharp commands from the security guards. *The apocalypse is starting.* The color drained from his face. The muffled din of the protestors suddenly sounded more like the war cries of ten thousand barbarian warriors. The unexpected pandemonium sent a shock wave of fright rippling through the audience. An anxious murmur escalated into an uproar. Attendees leapt to their feet and jostled toward the aisles.

"Ladies and gentlemen, there's no cause for alarm!" Chandler called out, desperate to prevent the forum from disintegrating. "Please return to your seats."

An aura of danger pervaded the massive room. Chandler's pleas for calm and order were ignored. Lamont Williams and Jarvis Landy loped down to the front of the auditorium. The two pseudo-guards took positions at either end of the stage. Their presence didn't placate the mounting panic. Travis Price trotted across the stage. Hope welled up within Chandler. The traitorous AmeResort executive stepped aside and relinquished the microphone to the FBI agent.

"I'm FBI Special Agent Price. I'm here to assist with security. Let me assure you, there's no cause for concern. Please return to you seats."

The roar of the masses receded. Nervous chatter accompanied the migration back to the rows of seating. Chandler exhaled with relief. A crisis was averted. He glanced at the television cameraman capturing everything on film. Marla Wells stood nearby, providing hushed rapid-fire commentary.

"A group of dissidents has gathered outside." Price provided an explanation while the aisles cleared. "The conference center has been locked-down to prevent any unauthorized entry into the facility. As a precaution, the security staff has cleared the lobbies and exhibition hall."

Someone said, "Somebody needs to call the police!" Chandler observed people extracting cell phones from purses and pockets.

Price reacted to the same sight. "Your phones won't work. The security system blocks all cell phone signals. That will prevent insurgents from communicating with an operative inside this facility. The conference center's chief of security has alerted the police. When they arrive, they will deal with the riot."

Chandler reclaimed his place behind the podium. "Who says land development isn't exciting?" His weak attempt at humor garnered no laughter.

"Let's get this show back on the road." Chandler felt the lonely uncertainty of a soldier about to storm a beach. "It's time to get the important people up here."

* * * *

Chris Morgan lowered his camera and whispered. "We should get some footage of the riot outside."

"Stay here!" Marla was indignant. "Security won't let you out in the lobby."

"We should give it a shot. All the excitement is out there."

"I'll make the decisions. The real action will be in here."

Chris was taken aback by Marla's slip, an admittance that she knew something was about to happen. His intuition had been right.

"Keep the camera rolling," Marla demanded.

* * * *

The hallway terminated in a plywood barrier. It was the end of the line for Colt. Maybe not. He backed up a half dozen steps and charged forward. The ferocious impact of his shoulder garnered splintering results. The makeshift plywood wall gave way and crashed down under Colt's body. The racket echoed down the empty hall of an uncompleted wing of the Gateway to the Rockies Conference Center. The final stages of construction had ground to an abrupt halt; a testament to the dire financial straits of AmeResort Corporation.

Colt picked himself up and raced along the bare concrete floor of a dark corridor. The spackled seams of unpainted drywall flashed by on both sides.

When Colt glanced over his shoulder, there was nobody in sight. Part of him wanted to find a place to hide and rest. It wasn't an option. E-Force had to be stopped. But their plan was still impossible to dissect.

I've got to get to Barrett. That's the only way to stop it.

Turning into another hallway, Colt was met by the heavy odor of new building materials. He sprinted past doors that were hung only weeks earlier. The hardware and locks were installed. There was no place to escape.

The heavy bang of a fire door reverberated through the empty space. Pounding footsteps behind him pushed Colt onward. He was determined to punish the lungs and legs of his pursuers. *Come get me, you bastards.* Colt rounded a corner and found Joey Morris blocking his path. The winded man was staggering.

"Stop right there, you son-of-a-bitch!" Morris waved his gun and lumbered forward.

Colt turned and retreated. His breathing mimicked a steam engine climbing a mountain pass. Nearly boxed in, he ripped at the doorknobs he rushed past. One of them turned. It was unlocked! Colt shoved the door open and lurched inside.

* * * *

Trovato huffed around a corner just in time to see a door slam shut. His partner rushed from the opposite direction and reached the escape portal first.

Morris panted and tried the knob. "It's locked."

"We've got him cornered." Trovato's chest heaved. He doubled, palms pressed against his lower thighs.

"Maybe there's another way out." Morris took a step backward. "I'm going to break the door down."

A security guard appeared at the end of the hall. "Hold up, Joey. Barney Fife just showed up."

The guard scurried to the scene. His utility belt looked

like it might drop down around his legs. "Who are you guys?"

"We're AmeResort Special Security." Trovato displayed an identification card. Klum peered as if he were examining a rare stamp. Finally, he backed up and nodded.

"Do you have the key for this door?" Trovato asked. "Your terrorist is holed up in there."

"Yeah, I've got a key."

"Klum, I need an update." The supervisor's worried voice crackled over the radio.

"We isolated the intruder in a mechanical room on Level 3 of the new north wing," Klum reported.

"What are you doing in that area?" Ruddock had heard the transmission. "Do not engage. I repeat. Do not engage!"

"But I've got back-up with me," Klum said.

"What are you talking about?" Ruddock demanded. "Who's with you? All security personnel are supposed to be positioned in the lobbies."

Klum stammered in confusion. "I've got some AmeResort guys with me."

"Get everyone out of there!" Ruddock snapped angrily. "Do you copy?"

Trovato snatched the radio out of the guard's hand. "This conversation is over. We're not letting that son-of-a-bitch escape."

A smug smile creased Morris' face when Trovato switched off the radio. The gray-haired tough motioned the guard to the door. He gulped and stepped forward with his key in hand.

* * * *

A round of applause went up at the introduction of the host of the Developers' Forum. Phillip Barrett nodded and hobbled to the podium with his walking stick. Lamont Williams watched Stephen Chandler shake his boss's hand

and scurry away. *Chandler is nervous. So am I. What the hell is an FBI agent doing here?*

Through the earpiece, Ruddock ordered the team not to deviate from the plan. Ten strike-team members were huddled in storage rooms and closets, hiding like scorpions under rocks.

In just moments, all hell would break loose. Williams glanced at Jarvis Landy at the other end of the stage. His comrade appeared calm and collected. The husky E-Force operative tried to draw on the display of confidence.

Time seemed to slow such that seconds became minutes. Phillip Barrett's words sounded sluggish, as if a digital soundtrack was malfunctioning. The dialogue was almost incomprehensible to Williams.

"It's with great pleasure that I introduce my good friend, Senator John Harris." An ovation erupted at the end of Barrett's introduction of the forum's special guest.

A Senator was never mentioned in operation planning. Williams' eyes snapped to a lanky man in a suit who rose from the front row of seating. His gaze was hijacked by Carrie Forde seated next to the vacated chair. *She's gorgeous.* When Williams tore his attention from the mesmerizing siren, Harris was striding toward Barrett with confidence and poise.

At that instant, the radio signal squawked in Williams' ear. He jolted as if he had grabbed a high voltage line. Harris and Barrett clasped hands next to the podium. Williams barely breathed, counting down the seconds. Before he made it to forty-five, the doors to the auditorium banged open in quick succession. Masked men brandishing assault rifles charged into the room.

Barrett's bodyguard rushed to protect his client. Williams saw Landy's arm come up with a tranquilizer pistol. The dart dropped the burly guardian. Williams unsheathed his weapon and charged toward Barrett and Harris. Before anyone could react, he and Landy held the pair of patriarchs at gunpoint.

In the aisles, the masked terrorists screamed obscenities and swept their weapons across the stunned people. Shock and disbelief dissipated into fear and screams of panic.

"Everybody sit down and shut up!" Williams shouted his command when attendees leapt up and pushed toward the aisles. "Get your asses back in the chairs!"

Williams barked orders while the terrorists bellowed insults and jabbed their rifles at the gathered mob. The hostages recoiled from the armed assailants and pressed together in the inner areas of seating. Terrified cries echoed throughout the cavernous room. Within a minute of the hijacking, the fearful captives quivered in quiet subjugation.

"Bring that television camera closer," Williams demanded. "We have a message for the world."

"Get up there." Marla shoved Morgan forward.

Williams pointed at her. "Come up on the stage with your microphone."

Everyone in the auditorium watched the television anchor scurry up the stairs. At the podium, she was dwarfed by Williams' bulky frame.

"Are you here to take more cheap shots?" Barrett glared at the woman.

"Shut up!" Williams threatened the developer with his Colt pistol. "You'll speak only when directed."

Ignoring Barrett's outburst, Marla appeared on the verge of smiling. For some reason, it irked Williams. It seemed that she was trying to upstage him.

"We are E-Force," Williams declared to his captive audience. "Our mission is to defend this planet from those who destroy it in pursuit of corporate profits."

Williams knew that by now, Ruddock had isolated the signal from Chris Morgan's television camera. The digital feed from the camera was transmitting out of the conference center, directly to the Channel 4 studio in Denver. It would be broadcast across the whole network.

"All who stand against us will be defeated." Williams delivered his memorized assertion. "The world now understands that we can reach anyone. Even Phillip Barrett, head of AmeResort Corporation, can no longer engage in criminal behavior with impunity."

Barrett was red-faced with rage and humiliation. Williams turned toward his nemesis. "Marla Wells is an acclaimed television journalist. We're going to commandeer her talents."

The auditorium was quiet while Williams thrust a sheet of paper toward the smug journalist. The detainees had no idea that she had crafted the questions written on it. "Time is short, Ms. Wells. Begin the interview."

There was fire in Barrett's glaring eyes. Senator Harris stood silently. Williams continued to ignore the politician. He didn't know what else to do.

"Mr. Barrett, do you consider AmeResort to be a leader in the development industry?" Marla asked before thrusting her microphone toward him.

"How dare you participate in this criminal act? Don't start with your condescending garbage!"

"Answer the question, Mr. Barrett," Williams snapped. "You're making a poor impression on the viewers."

Barrett clenched his fists. It was a delight to watch him struggle to remain under control.

"Do you believe AmeResort is a leader in the industry?" Marla repeated. "Is AmeResort in a position to shape trends in development?"

"Yes." Barrett refused to provide further explanation.

"I see." Marla raised her eyebrows. "Last year the money AmeResort Corporation spent to lobby against environmental regulations was ten times the amount the company spent on programs to protect the environment. Since you confirm AmeResort is an industry leader, the public should expect this trend to expand across the industry."

"That's absolutely false!" Barrett's ire was rising. "Every one of our projects is designed to minimize environmental impact."

"Corporate financial records show your lobbying expenses greatly exceeded donations to conservation, preservation, and humanitarian causes."

"You're talking about radical agendas," Barrett said hotly. "We support organizations that don't aim to restrict freedom with unconstitutional laws and regulations."

"But it's undeniable that you've established close relationships with influential politicians," Marla argued. "It seems your goal is legislation that's favorable to AmeResort and other developers."

"You're twisting the facts." Barrett was losing his temper. "We're not anti-environment. And I'm not going to apologize for exercising the rights granted by the U.S. Constitution."

Marla countered with a fake smile. "The corporations and industries with the most money can dictate how the Constitution is interpreted. Those who want to protect the planet don't have that advantage."

"The anti-development people have been afforded every opportunity." Barrett seethed, pointing an accusing finger. "AmeResort follows the rules. Criminals like E-Force want to change the game and strip freedom from American citizens."

"Your assertion doesn't stand up to scrutiny, Mr. Barrett." Marla looked to Senator Harris. "You play by a different set of rules than everybody else. Why else would all of you meet with Senator John Harris in a forum that was kept secret from the public?"

Williams stepped closer when there was no response from Barrett. "Answer the question, Mr. Barrett. The world is waiting."

* * * *

Trovato and Morris readied their weapons while Klum unlocked the door to the mechanical room.

"We shouldn't be doing this." The guard protested the act of insubordination. "I'm going to get fired."

"Quit whining and open the door," Trovato said.

The guard inhaled a deep breath and threw the door open. Trovato and Morris charged inside with firearms at the ready.

Shiny HVAC equipment hummed in the mechanical room. A maze of ductwork and plumbing surrounded machines and men. All three pairs of eyes fell upon a stepladder. It stood under an open access panel in one of the large air ducts.

Trovato cursed. "He went up there. Where's all this ductwork go?"

"I don't know...maybe to the auditorium where they're holding the forum," Klum replied. "I think it's on the other side of that back wall."

Morris examined the ducts above his head. "We've got to flush him out."

Trovato glanced at Klum's utility belt. "You've got a flashlight. Climb up there and take a look."

Hesitant to comply, the Barney Fife double moved to the base of the stepladder. He shined his light at the dark void. There was no sound other than the soft whoosh of air. "I can't see anything. We should cease and desist as Ruddock ordered."

Trovato didn't relent. "Go up the damned ladder and look inside there."

"He's not armed," Morris said. "A weapon wouldn't get through the scanners at the doors."

Klum stepped onto the ladder and climbed up a few rungs. Under duress from the other two men, he went higher until his head was at the opening in the sheet metal. With great caution, Klum thrust the flashlight and his head through the portal.

Standing below, Trovato and Morris heard Klum's muffled cry of surprise. A dull thumping sound coincided with a violent shudder of the guard's body. Klum and the ladder crashed to the floor, blood spilling everywhere. The man was shot through the head.

"He's got a gun!" Trovato darted away from the overhead opening.

Taking a different tact, Morris jerked his Berretta M9 upward and pulled the trigger. His gun boomed. The slugs tore jagged holes in the conduit. In violent response, bullets ripped down through the sheet metal in a hail of death. The impacts sent Morris staggering until he crumpled in a heap.

Searing lead slammed into Trovato's leg, halting his flight for life. The burly man clawed his way across the floor, desperate to escape the deadly barrage. The HVAC system offered cover. Trovato left smears of blood along his path of retreat. Something banged overhead.

Trovato rolled in defense. An assailant swung down from the access panel and landed lithely. The burly bounty hunter frantically fired, but missed. Slugs from his Sig Sauer P220 blasted through the wall and into the upper reaches of the auditorium. Trovato's adversary tumbled across the floor. The thumping of his suppressed, semi-automatic pistol contrasted the thunder of the big man's weapon.

One of the bullets hit Trovato in his left shoulder. He grunted in pain. The killer darted to the side in a flanking maneuver. In a final act of defense, Trovato struggled to wrench his body around. Two more slugs slammed into his torso. He had failed his client, Phillip Barrett. *Colt Kelley and E-Force beat me.* Hollering in agonized rage, Trovato emptied his magazine in the general direction of the attacker. A bullet punched through his forehead. In an instant, life withdrew from Trovato's body.

* * * *

Zed Cain stood over Trovato holding a Heckler & Koch MK 23 pistol. His stare was as cold as the dead man's. Cain glanced at his other victims. *Two confirmed kills.* It was hollow retribution. He had been seconds from dropping Senator Harris with a 6.8mm bullet to the head.

The air vent led to the auditorium and provided a vantage point with an unobstructed line-of-site to the stage. It was a simple matter of timing. When Ruddock allowed the protestors to surge into the forum, Price was supposed to initiate the shooting. At the outset of the ensuing carnage, Cain's task was to assassinate the senator. His weapon was a Barrett REC7 assault rifle like those carried by the E-Force terrorists.

"You assholes set off the powder keg early." Cain kicked the nearest corpse. He could hear hell breaking loose in the auditorium. The entire mission was on the brink of failure. The rifle was still at the vent. *Maybe there's still a chance to pick off Harris.* Cain loped to the toppled ladder.

* * * *

Panic erupted in the commandeered forum when booming gunshots sent bullets shredding through the air above the hostages. Travis Price cringed at the screams of terror. It was worse than fingernails on a chalkboard. Refugees from the flying lead sought cover, pressing into the aisles and clambering over rows of seats. The half dozen masked gunmen were unable to halt a stampede of several hundred detainees toward the exits.

Price watched several men assault an E-Force terrorist. As he was overwhelmed, the muzzle of his rifle belched. A woman in a business suit was cut down.

The E-Force gunfire had the effect of dousing a fire with gasoline. Doors burst outward under the crushing pressure of bodies. But there was no salvation beyond the barriers.

Instead, the escapees were met by a screaming horde of rioters. The outnumbered developers were driven back. The tsunami was relentless, pushing everyone into the vortex of chaos. Fueled by fear and rage, people with vastly different ideologies collided and melded. The common trait of human violence ignited. A brutal melee spread with the speed of a wind-driven wildfire in dry chaparral.

Price struggled against the mass of humanity. He hollered in his radio, baffled by the shooting that had triggered the stampede. "Ruddock, what the hell happened?"

"Cain's position was compromised." Trigger Ruddock responded from the security control room. "There was a security breach."

"You opened the doors early!" Price pushed toward the stage. "The damned mob is in control down here."

"There's a freaking army of cops arriving outside." Ruddock's voice sizzled over the radio. "Somebody got the word out. The mission's aborted."

"Like hell it is!"

Price had almost fought his way to the stage when gunfire escalated like a string of firecrackers on the Fourth of July. The would-be hostage-takers were besieged by both attendees and rioters. The noise was deafening. With E-Force terrorists firing their weapons with abandon, some protestors unveiled their own weapons. Everyone was blasting away with the ferocity of rival drug gangs in a turf war.

Spurts of blood marked each impact of bullets with human flesh. The armed and unarmed were targeted without discretion. Mad scrambles ensued for possession of weapons dropped by the fallen. The auditorium was a war zone with no reprieve.

* * * *

"This is insane!" Luke cried out near the top of one of

the sloping aisles. He was thrashed around by the mob. His feet stumbled on bodies and slipped on blood. Luke held on to anything he could reach; a seat, somebody's shirttail...it didn't matter. To fall meant death. He would be crushed under the stampede.

A haggard woman with tangled dreadlocks pressed against Luke. For a moment, body stench overpowered the acrid odor of gunpowder. A splatter of blood hit Luke's cheek. The female dissident shuddered and collapsed. A convulsion racked Luke's body. The deadly projectile had missed him by inches. Survival seemed dependent only on luck.

A man in a black uniform was forcing his way into the auditorium. *Thank God. The police!* A trickle of hope boosted Luke's drive to survive. The seep of optimism was flushed down the toilet of despair when an E-Force terrorist swung his gun around. A chunk of the wall exploded next to the cop's head when the gunman pulled the trigger.

* * * *

Climbing onto the stage, Price brandished his Glock 23. With brutal indifference he blasted a terrified E-Force member who was trying to load a new magazine in his REC7 rifle. The man crumpled. Price whirled toward the podium. Barrett was sprawled on the floor. Williams loomed over him. A couple yards away, Landy and Harris were engaged in a grappling match.

Price aimed his pistol and pulled the trigger. Crimson drops of blood were flung on Barrett's shirt. Williams released his grip and staggered backwards. His face was a contorted mask of shock. Both hands clasped the wound on his chest. Another slug from Price's gun sent the stocky black man reeling against the other pseudo-guard. Williams grabbed at Landy's clothes as he sank to the stage.

Jarvis Landy released his grip on Barrett. He recoiled

and shoved Williams down as if he were a dog humping his leg. Blood contaminated his hands.

Like a puma, Senator Harris sprang at Landy, delivering a judo chop to the man's neck. As Landy doubled over, Harris grabbed the terrorist by the arm that held the gun. A hard punch to the nose drew a stream of blood. The Senator twisted and used a judo throw to slam the terrorist to the floor.

Price swore and started forward. Flying bullets sent him scrambling to the floor. He glanced at the splintered holes in the nearby wall. The air was thick with screams and the pungent smell of bodily fluids. *I'm going to finish this freaking thing.*

Price scrambled back to his feet. Carrie Forde broke out of the mob. She pounced onto the stage. The young beauty was bent on reaching her father. The rogue FBI agent spied Chris Morgan. Marla's cameraman captured all the drama on the stage. Price knew he was on live television and saw the inevitable hurtling toward him.

* * * *

Colt Kelley waited in the shadows of the utility room, watching Zed Cain. *Damn it, I wish I had that gun.* He had been forced to leave Reichner's Walther PPQ in the stolen Dodge pickup truck. It would have set off the metal detectors at the doors.

With fluid movements, Zed Cain snatched the toppled stepladder and set it upright. With the agility of a leopard, the cold-blooded killer ascended. He reached up to clamber into the air duct.

I will fear no evil. Colt bolted from his hiding spot and tackled Cain with a ferocity that sent the ladder crashing over. Cain went down hard. The extreme force of the impact jarred the MK 23 from his grasp. It clattered and skidded across the floor.

Colt leapt upon his enemy and pummeled without mercy. He was driven to destroy Cain with his bare hands. The E-Force assassin was the demon that had killed his friends...the devil that had ripped Carrie away.

Utilizing the strength and savagery of a man pushed to the edge, Colt pulverized his opponent. The E-Force assassin twisted, flailed, and kicked. His strikes glanced off as if Colt were a hunk of iron. In desperation, Cain tried to gouge the young man's eye. Colt deflected Cain's arm with one hand and grabbed his throat with the other. A vise of steel clamped the killer's airway closed.

Unable to breathe, Cain tore his arm from Colt's grasp. Wrenching his body violently, the tall man reached for one foot. Colt glimpsed gray metal emerge from his adversary's boot. *A knife!* He flinched when Cain thrust the weapon upward. The cold steel hit something hard and failed to penetrate the flesh of Colt's torso. Cain pulled the knife back to strike again.

Colt released his strangle hold and arrested the knife-wielding arm with both of his hands. The defensive move came at a price. Cain took advantage of the change in body position. He splayed one leg off to one side and thrust down. In one quick heaving twist, Cain rolled. Locked in the two-handed struggle of death, Colt was thrown to his back. In alarm, he managed to cock his legs under the assassin. Tapping every fiber of muscle, he drove his legs upward. Cain was hurled away as if launched from a catapult.

In a flash, the combatants were on their feet. Cain slashed with the knife. Colt dodged the attack and retreated. Cain struck again. The blade swung toward Colt's throat. He parried to avoid being skewered. Capitalizing on the decoy, Cain swiped out with a sweeping kick. Colt's legs were cut from beneath him, and he landed hard on his back. Stunned by the impact, he was defenseless.

Cain pounced to butcher Colt, but slipped on blood from the murdered men that had formed a pool as slick as an ice-covered pond. He thudded to the floor.

Colt flailed and tried to rise. His fingers fell upon Cain's suppressed MK 23. Covered in blood, Cain leapt up and lunged for the kill.

Still on his back, Colt reeled in the pistol and took aim. A hint of rage burned in Cain's eyes. He slowed and reared his arm backward. Colt prayed there was still a bullet in the magazine and squeezed the trigger. Thump! A .45 caliber slug hit the assassin as he hurled his weapon. The knife careened off the concrete, inches from Colt's side. Cain staggered and collapsed. Colt pulled the trigger again. A metallic click declared the ammunition clip empty.

Climbing cautiously to his feet, Colt stared at the assassin's motionless body, expecting a sudden attack. It didn't come. The blood draining from the prone form added to the carnage in the room.

"Paybacks are hell."

The muffled sounds of gunfire emanating from beyond the wall suddenly seemed louder. Without wasting another second, Colt rushed over and yanked the 10mm Delta Elite from Klum's holster. His white knuckles tightened around the handgrip. He turned and sprinted into the hallway.

* * * *

The mass of humanity inside the auditorium was caught up in a violent tempest. Those carried by the unstoppable tsunami had little control over their fate. One could only flail at the surface of the fray and avoid death below hundreds of crushing feet. The din of shouts and screams was punctuated by thundering firearms. Hot lead ripped through the writhing swarm. Both guilty and innocent were ravaged.

Near the center of the clash, Drew Harmon hyperventilated with terror. "I can't breathe." He was pressed from all sides. His shell-shocked nerves were overloaded. This wasn't a movie set...the violence was real.

Harmon's quest for glory died. Rasping for breath, he flailed his fists with wild abandon.

"Get away from me!" Harmon bloodied a woman's nose. "Let me out of here!"

* * * *

The spectacle of Harmon's meltdown was broadcast on live television. From his vantage point on the stage, Chris Morgan's camera lens happened upon the actor while he panned across the bedlam. Recognizing the star, Chris zoomed in on the shocking sight. Flinching at the flying bullets, he filmed while Harmon screamed, punched, and clawed.

"He's lost his mind." Morgan was disgusted by the behavior so different from that of the rock-steady characters Harmon portrayed on the silver screen.

In disbelief, Morgan watched the Hollywood hero grab a woman by the hair and yank her down. She disappeared below the melee. The actor clambered over the fallen obstacle and continued his unhinged quest for self-preservation. A man in the crowd intervened. Chris Morgan's camera recorded Luke Parson's clobbering blow to Harmon's jaw. Satisfaction filled Chris when the actor spun around and sunk below the swirling stampede.

With Harmon dispatched, Morgan panned across the chaos. *Where the hell is Marla?* She had fled at the first gunshot. His camera swung back to the stage just as Senator Harris dispatched one of the E-Force terrorists in a security guard uniform. Special Agent Price rushed toward the victorious politician and restrained a young woman. Carrie Forde yelled and fought with the FBI agent.

A mob of people poured onto the stage. Morgan's position was overrun. Terrified people slammed into him, and he labored to stay afoot. The camera bumped and jerked while Morgan was swept away by the tidal surge. He nearly tripped over the body of an E-Force terrorist. His lens briefly fell on the motionless gunman who had been beaten to a pulp by his hostages.

The unstoppable current pushed Morgan toward an auditorium exit. The doors were nearly torn from their hinges as people squeezed through the bottleneck. Morgan was among the lucky individuals expelled through the gateway to life. The less fortunate were pressed up against the wall with no chance of escape.

* * * *

Carrie Forde spied her father again when the stampede dissipated. After nearly being trampled, he was rising to his feet. Blood streamed from his temple. Phillip Barrett was on the floor. Looking stunned, Carrie's dad turned and strived to pull his friend up.

"Get off me." Carrie wrenched her arm free from Price. "Dad, I'm coming!"

The Senator's head snapped up. "Carrie, get down! He's going to shoot."

Carrie was in full stride when the gun blasted. Her step faltered, but she didn't fall. The bullet had passed by her. In shock, Carrie witnessed a man kneeling behind her father jerk as the bullet from Price's gun tore through his chest. Seemingly in slow motion, Jarvis Landy thudded face-first onto the floor. The weapon in his outstretched hand boomed at the impact.

Harris cringed and whirled around. He stared at the dead man in shock.

"Dad, are you okay?" Carrie threw her arms around her father. "I think that terrorist was about to kill you!"

"I'm fine, honey," Harris said, embracing his daughter and kissing her on the head. The emotions of father and daughter poured out with intensity.

"I'm Special Agent Price." The corrupt federal agent

flashed his badge. "I need to get you to a secure location, Senator."

"I'm thankful for your marksmanship, Price." Harris nodded with gratitude. "My daughter's coming with me."

"There's a car in the service bay." Price's eyes darted about warily. "Please come with me."

* * * *

Chris Morgan charged back into the auditorium. A dozen cops were securing the facility. *Why couldn't they have gotten here before this tragedy?*

It was Morgan who had alerted police to the likelihood of an E-Force attack at the Developers' Forum. With nothing more than a hunch brought on by Marla's suspicious behavior, Chris had worked hard to persuade them that the threat was imminent. In the end, their arrival was too late to save many lives.

The television camera relayed the terrible aftermath of a battlefield. Bodies covered the floor haphazardly. The stench of feces and urine wafted in the smoke-filled air. Pitiful cries of the wounded and injured beckoned to a few compassionate souls who scurried to aid the fallen. A horrifying number of victims were dead and beyond help.

A man huddled on the floor caught Morgan's attention. Clasping his hands over his ears, Drew Harmon was sobbing. The actor's true character had been revealed to the world. *Harmon is a fraud.*

With disdain, Morgan turned his lens from the pathetic display to the stage. His pulse surged. The FBI agent prodded Senator Harris and the woman toward a backstage door. Price's pistol was still drawn

"Drop the weapon!" Police officers advanced with guns trained on Price.

* * * *

"FBI." Price displayed his badge. "I'm on your side." The cops hesitated.

"It's okay." Harris provided reassurance. "Price saved my life." The cops lowered their weapons.

Landy, was aiming at me, idiot. I would have let him kill you and this would be over! "I've got to get Senator Harris and his daughter to safety," Price said. He gestured toward Phillip Barrett, who was still sitting on the stage floor. "That man needs help."

Two police officers moved to assist the AmeResort CEO. Price's heart raced. The blood rushing through his veins and arteries thundered in his ears. He placed a hand on Carrie's shoulder and coaxed her toward the back door. "We need to keep moving." Price prodded the pair. "This area's not secure."

"Carrie!" a voice called out from the back of the auditorium. "You're in danger!"

Everybody turned to see a haggard figure rushing down an aisle. His movements conveyed the desperation of a man leaping to grab hold of the last helicopter leaving a fallen Saigon. There was a pistol in his hand.

"Stop where you are!" The cops converged on the threatening newcomer.

Alarmed, Price's overriding goal was to get Harris to his car. Warped logic told him the politician could still be dispatched like Marchotti wanted. It was the only way to get the payoff...to save some semblance of a future.

"Colt, what are you doing here?" Carrie gasped and shoved the FBI rogue away.

"I came to stop all this." Colt Kelley kept advancing. "Marchotti's people are trying to kill me. It's all because of E-Force."

Price's mind was on the verge of a meltdown. *Hill captured Colt Kelley along with Luke Parson.* In the phone call last night, Marchotti had been clear. His people were sent to snuff out their lives. *How did Kelley materialize in the smoldering ruins of this operation?* Something snapped inside Price's quivering brain.

"That's Colt Kelley." Price raised his Glock. "He's one of the terrorists."

* * * *

"No! Don't shoot him!" Carrie grabbed Price's arm before he could squeeze the trigger.

"Your damned goons failed," Colt didn't back down.

"Get off." Price tried to wrench his firearm from Carrie's grasp.

Colt felt a surge of anger. Deb and Delilah flashed through his mind again. Unwilling to stand by and let the woman he loved get hurt, he advanced ignoring the commands of the police.

"Back off." Price raised a hand to strike Carrie. "That man's a killer!"

Harris moved to rescue his daughter. "Stand down, Price. If you hit her, your career is over."

Colt stiffened when he heard the name of the rogue FBI agent. Suddenly, he recognized the voice of the man who had helped kill Anderson, Deb, and Delilah. "Let her go, you murdering bastard." He trained Klum's Colt Delta Elite on Price.

The cops shouted. "Drop your weapon now!"

"Keep moving." Price dragged Carrie backward. "Let's go, Senator."

"Price is the real killer," Colt cried out. "He's working with Darius Marchotti and E-Force."

"Sergeant, stop him." Harris looked for help from the police.

The cops in the room had encircled the standoff. With weapons drawn, half a dozen officers accosted Colt and confiscated the pistol.

"You set me up, you piece of shit." Colt fought to stay on his feet. "You and E-Force are murderers. You're all Darius Marchotti's puppets!"

"Drop your weapon." The police sergeant's order was directed at Price.

"Put that terrorist in handcuffs." Price's eyes were those of a man clinging to the edge of a cliff.

* * * *

Chris Morgan was breathless as the drama unfolded in front of his camera. Colt bellowed and resisted the cops wrenching his arms to fasten handcuffs.

"So many people are indebted to Mr. Marchotti." The statement boomed from the sound system. It was the voice of Special Agent Price. "Surely, you didn't suspect my first loyalty was to the FBI?"

A collective hush descended in the ravaged auditorium as the damning dialogue from the EcoFriends office emanated from the huge speakers. Entrusted with Colt's cassette, Luke had managed to fight his way to the sound booth. The soundtrack of a murder was sent out on live television. Wearing a horrified expression, Price stood petrified.

The recording went on. "Mr. Marchotti will be disheartened. He gave you a chance to escape the consequences of your past crimes. We had such big plans for you, Howard. Now, E-Force will make history without you."

* * * *

"How the hell is this happening?" Marchotti stalked in front of the television. "The whole damned operation is a failure. Harris is still standing!"

Zharikov was shiftless. A quarter of an hour earlier, his benefactor was on the verge of incalculable power. Now the